David Suttner

Law Dogs

The Guns of Ivory Thompson

AUSTIN MACAULEY PUBLISHERS™

LONDON • CAMBRIDGE • NEW YORK • SHARJAH

Ordering Information
Quantity sales: Special discounts are available on quantity purchases by corporations, associations, and others. For details, contact the publisher at the address below.

Publisher's Cataloging-in-Publication data
Suttner, David
Law Dogs

ISBN 9798889105435 (Paperback)
ISBN 9798889105367 (ePub-e-book)

Library of Congress Control Number: 2023918569

www.austinmacauley.com/us

First Published 2024
Austin Macauley Publishers LLC
40 Wall Street, 33rd Floor, Suite 3302
New York, NY 10005
USA

mail-usa@austinmacauley.com
+1 (646) 5125767

Chapter 1
Encounter at the Wire

The western cattle range of the 1880s was ever-expanding after the thundering herds of buffalo were replaced. Ranches pushed across the prairies and over the hills into the green valleys of the blue Colorado Mountains rising in the distance.

The cattle represented gold on the hoof. Along with the cattle came the railroads, telegraph, cattle barons, cowboys, cattlemen, miners, farmers, stores, saloons, gamblers, gunmen, desperadoes, highwaymen, and fancy ladies, all flowing westward, following the ranchers and the prospectors, the strikes and failures, the booms and the busts, always seeking. Following in their wake came other hard men watching and seeking plunder and easy money.

Three riders coming down from the high country heard hammering before they saw the lone cowboy bent over at work next to a wobbly fence post. He paid little or no attention to his surroundings, except occasionally mopping his face with a red bandana. The day was hot, and it was only mid-morning.

His Morgan-bay mare, trail-worn and un-curried, stood nearby with reins tied to a fence post. Slowly, she chomped and tugged at the dry grass at the base of the fence. Across its saddle draped the cowboy's coat and vest, with his bedroll cinched behind it.

The cowboy removed an iron staple from his mouth with his left hand and carefully positioned it with his thumb and index finger. He tapped it to hold, then used his right hand to hammer the staple over a strand of barbwire into the post. He then proceeded to hammer another staple onto another strand. The hammer blows rang out over the quiet afternoon—almost like a church bell calling folks to prayer.

The cowboy straightened up. He was a large man, over six foot in height, dressed in faded jeans with both suspenders and a wide black leather belt with a military buckle inscribed with the letters U.S.A., cinched tightly around his waist. He was conspicuous for not having a gun holstered on it.

He stood solid, with his feet spread shoulder-width, intent on his work. He was shod in worn, dusty, square-toed work boots. A sweat-stained blue checkered shirt covered his broad shoulders and thick chest. The skin around his blue eyes was puffy and swollen from lack of sleep and too much exposure to the glaring sun. His hair, the color of late autumn hay, was collar length and escaped around a broad-brimmed high-crowned hat with its stampede strap loose at his chin. He was unshaven, dirty in appearance, and looked worn out.

Glancing toward a small rise to the East, the cowboy witnessed first the heads and then the mounted bodies of the trio of men ride up to the top of the rise, pause, and survey the range. The lead man had a large, square-jawed, unshaven face. He was a big man, unkempt in appearance, with hard gray eyes.

He rode with a rifle in his saddle boot at the ready and carried two ivory-handled six-guns strapped to his waist. He wore a leather vest over a faded blue shirt. He looked relaxed and confident as he carefully studied the man at the fence. Pulling his hat brim down to shade his eyes, he slowly walked the horse forward a few paces.

Following close behind, on either side, road two of the hardest-looking men the cowboy had ever seen. One, a mid-sized Mexican, was wearing a black flat-topped hat with fancy embroidering. Across his chest, he wore crossed bandoleers filled to capacity with stubby-heavy cartridges. He was mounted on a beautiful black horse with full-blooded Spanish ancestry and sat high on a fancy California saddle with silver inlays and covered stirrups.

The cowboy noticed his black-handled six-shooter, probably a Colt, in a black tie-down holster. He looked fast. He also carried a Winchester rifle in his right hand with its butt resting casually on the saddle in front of his leg. The cowboy studied the weapon and, from the hex-barrel it looked like an 1873 model Winchester, might be a .38-40. A black mustache drooped on either side of the Mexican's hard mouth. Then, flashing beautiful white teeth, the Mexican smiled and said something to the leader, who nodded.

The other man, an Indian, or perhaps a half-breed, dressed in leather britches, rode shirtless. A large, wicked-looking knife, known as an Arkansas toothpick, was strapped to his side. A leather bag tied with a cord dangled from his neck. He wore no sidearm. He was lean with hard muscles exposed to the sun. His black braids hung down on either side of his clean face. He carried a big bore Sharp's rifle in his right hand, held at the ready with its butt resting lightly on his saddle. His finger was on its trigger, and his thumb on its hammer. His eyes scanned the terrain while lightly holding the reins in his left hand.

The trio paused again to survey the range. The Indian sat still on his pony and then suddenly stood up high in the stirrups of an old army saddle and twisted around to scan the back trail as if expecting something. After a moment, he nodded assent, and the three, with Square-Jaw in front, rode slowly and eased down toward the cowboy.

Removing the last staples from his mouth, the cowboy walked to his horse and dropped his hammer and the staples into his saddlebag. He slowly removed a large red bandana from his hip pocket and his battered Stetson high-crowned hat from his head. He wiped its band and then his face, careful to make sure he had no sweat in his eyes and awaited their approach.

"Afternoon," the cowboy said in greeting, "mighty hot weather we're having. Something I can help you'uns with?"

The big, square-jawed man walked his horse a few feet in front of his two companions, a position of leadership. Rising from the saddle, he flexed his body, rolled his large shoulders, and stated, "You live around here?"

"Yes sir, we got a small ranch over the next rise—run a few head of cattle and put in some fodder crops." His voice trailed off.

The square-jawed man nodded toward the rise behind the cowboy's back and asked: "over yonder?"

"Yes sir, just me and the family…"

"Family, you say?"

"Yes, sir, just the missus and our youngin'. She's thirteen and going on thirty…a real handful living out here. It's pretty lonely for a kid. We don't have much, but I'm sure the missus can rustle up some grub for you 'uns."

The square-jawed man studied the fence, rising in his saddle to follow its line. He said, "I hate barbed wire. I don't like hemming critters or people in. It ain't natural."

"Well, sir," replied the cowboy, "I ain't parcel to it myself, but the agreement I have with the big ranch to the north is that I keep it mended…you know…it's in writing."

"Fernando…Lobo… either you like barbwire?" The Mexican shook his head in the negative while the Indian continued scanning the horizons as if in anticipation of trouble.

"Well, sir," said the cowboy, again slowly removing the red bandana from his hip pocket, mopped his face, and then returned it. "Sure, is a hot one today. I got a pump at the house and can sure give you some sweet cold water and refill your canteens."

"How do you know our canteens need filling?" The square-jawed man demanded.

"I was just guessing by the looks of your mounts. They've been ridden hard, and it's a dry country." The cowboy responded and added, "Didn't mean nothing by it."

"He didn't mean nothing by it," Square-Jaw mocked. Either you boys hear such a thing? He didn't mean nothing by it?" Fernando flashed an evil grin as Lobo's black eyes continued to dart around the range.

Square-Jaw smiled and said, "Now tell me about that farm of yours and your nice little family."

"Like I said, mister, it's a small ranch. Me, the missus, and our youngin work it. The wife likes to put out a garden, and me…"

"Now tell me about your missus. Fernando here would like to meet her and Lobo there now; granted, he ain't much to look at, but he sure does like to play with little boys and girls, don't you, Lobo?" The Indian nodded with no change in his facial expression.

"Now dirt-farmer," Square-Jaw addressed the cowboy with the ultimate insult, "I understand that your youngster is thirteen…hmm," he thought, "maybe a little old for Lobo, but I guess he'll have to make do. Now tell me about that missus of yours?"

The cowboy stood in place, gathering his thoughts, then responded, "Please, mister, we're peaceable folks, Christians. I'm unarmed 'cepting for that old single-shot rifle there," he nodded toward his horse, "I use it to bring down an occasional elk. We don't want no trouble."

"Well now," Square-Jaw sadly shook his head. Fernando, did you hear that? He doesn't want any trouble. Do you think we should ride away because he's so Christian and white?"

"No, Señor. I think it might be fun to play a little game with this hombre. I rope him and pull him home to his little Christian family. Give him a free ride behind…it'll make him nice and, how do you say, tender. Then I'd like to meet his wife, after you, of course, Señor."

Square-Jaw rubbed the stubble on his chin as if thinking, saying, "Sounds like a good plan, Fernando. You rope him, and then we'll all visit his little Christian family." Fernando smoothly placed his rifle in its saddle boot and leaned forward for his lariat. He had the free end of the rope dallied around his saddle horn while he began to loop the other end.

At that moment, the cowboy reached back again for his red bandana for what appeared to be a final wipe of the sweat from his face.

Instead, the trio watched the bandana fall to the ground at his feet, their eyes fixed on it as the cowboy's right hand came up fast from behind his back with a short-barreled .45 Colt, and his left hand went to work fanning its hammer. The explosions of multiple .45 rounds hammering into flesh and bone rang Square-Jaw's ears.

The ear-splitting explosions spewed a cloud of acrid smoke and spit lightning flashes of lead from its muzzle. His aim was unerring as if guided by intuition. His movements were rapid, smooth, thoughtless, and automatic.

The first two rounds hit Fernando in the throat, almost severing his head and blowing bits of his bloody pulp and spinal matter out in a spray. The rounds pitched him backward, off his horse, and out of the fight. Without a pause, the flames spit lead into the Indian's side, and then his shoulder, but he still lived and gamely went for his rifle, and instinct finally sent a fatal thumb-sized hunk of lead into his chest tearing a huge tunnel into his heart.

The Indian had vainly tried to move his horse out of the line of fire and was still kicking its side as his body died. Dropping his rifle, he tumbled to the ground. Now, two were out of the fight. The Indian's pony reared in fright, pivoted, and broke into a gallop, disappearing over the rise in the direction from which they had come.

Chapter 2
High Stakes Game

The thunderous report of the Colt revolver, which in truth sounded like one mighty elongated roar, faded away. The gray stinking cloud of black-powder smoke curled around the scene and slowly dissipated as the cowboy leveled his pistol toward the chest of the square-jawed man who sat frozen in surprise. It was cocked and aimed at the center of his chest.

"Now it's your turn, you son of a bitch. Go for it." The cowboy's words were hard as flint.

The square-jawed man hesitated. He had never seen such fancy gun work. The gunman had accurately fanned the shots into his two men, killing both. Who was this man? He had heard of this fancy shooting, but where?

"Wait!" He cleared his thoughts and raised his hands a little with palms out in supplication. "Look here, we were only funning you. We weren't actually going to do anything--just having a little joke." Now Square-Jaw's face perspired, and his eyes began to sting from the beads of sweat that were playing havoc with his vision. He didn't move a muscle and sat frozen in his saddle.

"Funning, was it?" answered the cowboy. "A joke, my ass. You were playing with me the way a cat plays with a mouse. I'll tell you what, mister; I'm going to have a little fun with you."

"You know what I told you about having a family and a ranch over the next rise, well, that was just bullshit. I ride for the Little R brand and work for Mr. Kincaid. He's the biggest cattleman in these parts and the law in these parts. We've got no sheriff or marshal hereabouts. He's the law unto himself. Now listen and listen well, because your life depends on your answer, and I don't have time to jaw with you. Mr. Kincaid is one of those men who runs his ranch like a king of old England. He's a hard man, but a fair one. He believes in what he calls rehabilitation. Do you know what that word means?"

The square-jawed man was confused but nodded that he had heard the term. His breathing began to relax a little, and his eyes shifted around from the bodies of his companions sprawled out with their blood soaking into the thirsty ground.

He looked at the muzzle of the short-barreled .45 leveled at this chest. Squinting hard, he saw it was a six-round model with the five visible chambers empty. He thought he had fired five shots, but the one under the cocked hammer was covered by the barrel, and he couldn't tell. Had he fired five or six shots? It all happened so fast. Glancing down, he saw Fernando's head almost shot off, and Lobo had what looked like three wounds. He could have fired five or six.

Should he pull leather first, or run him down? No, it's best to keep him talking and wait for his chance. "Yeah, I know what it means?"

"Good," continued the cowboy, "because Mr. Kincaid believes that there is something good in each man and, if given the opportunity to see the errors of his way, he can change. Take me for instance. I was caught relieving Mr. Kincaid of a few heads of cattle—almost five years ago. They caught us fair and square, and after our partners, Lefty and McAllen, got shot to pieces, I surrendered. The old man Kincaid gave me a choice. Stand trial before him as the lawgiver, like in the Old Testament, or be hung on the spot." The square-jawed man began to listen with interest.

"Well, you can see I'm still here, but I had to admit every mean and ornery thing I'd ever done during that trial. When it was over, and I had said my piece and begged for mercy, Mr. Kincaid pronounced the sentence. I was given a one-year sentence of hard labor on the ranch—just like a convict or a slave." The cowboy seemed to smile in memory.

"At the end of that year, I was given another choice. I could have my horse, saddle, gun, and the clothes on my back and ride away as a free man, or I could swear an oath of loyalty to Mr. Kincaid as a hired hand and get $100 a month and found.”

The square-jawed man leaned forward with real interest and said, “A hundred a month, why that’s more ’en twice the going wage.”

“True, said the cowboy, but you see, I have special talents. I’m fast, as you saw yourself, and I don’t miss. I said I get a hundred dollars each month, and I’m worth every cent of it to Mr. Kincaid. I’m what you call one of his enforcers.”

A hundred dollars a month thought Square-Jaw when all was said and done, he didn’t make that much in rustling, robbing, and killing, but still, there were other side benefits to his line of work that money couldn’t buy.

“Now you have a choice, mister. Either go for your irons or unbuckle your holsters and drop ’em. Either way makes no difference to me. I’m just following orders. What’ll it be?” The cowboy extended his arm a little and lined up his shot, dead-center, but it really wasn’t much of a shot at that distance.

“Hold on a second,” uttered Square-Jaw. With all his attention, he focused on the big bore, which was palmed firmly in the cowboy’s right hand. It was cocked. A single action Colt waited for a slight squeeze of the trigger finger. Had he fired five or six shots? With all his squinting, he couldn’t tell what was under that reworked hammer. Was it a live or a spent round?

He said, “I think you fired all six rounds when you fast-fanned on my compadres. I think you are holding a losing hand.” Square-Jaw studied the cowboy’s face, looking for some tell, some reaction, and a hint at his bluff. He saw no change; only a brief smile played about the cowboy’s lips.

“You willing to call my hand? I fired five rounds and have one waiting for you. I’ve counted my shots since I was knee-high to a grasshopper. Any man who doesn’t is a fool, and I can’t abide a fool. Try me. Mr. Kincaid said we can kill in self-defense, and we can kill anybody resisting arrest. We just can’t kill an unarmed man. You’ve got your pistols hanging on your hip. You're not an unarmed man. So, let's get on with it. Supper will soon be waiting."

"You going to give me a chance ain't you? At least put your gun at your side." Square-Jaw sweated out his decision. He might take him in a fair fight.

The cowboy's pistol remained firmly aimed at his chest's center, and a .45 makes a big hole at that range. How did he palm it so fast? He must have had it hidden in the back, near the red bandana that was still lying on the ground. A back belt holster explained how he got it out so fast. But why hadn't he seen him going for it? I thought he was going to mop the sweat on his face again. I thought he was scared. That's why. He almost had it all figured out.

Now Square-Jaw was sweating with the sun beating down on him, and his mount was uneasy. His eyes smarted, and he was unable to blink away the sting. He tried to knuckle the sweat from his eyes and pondered his position.

Square-Jaw played enough poker to know when a man showed fear or excitement. Every man had his tells, his little signs. You learned to read 'em so you know when it's a bluff, so you can raise the stakes. You need to know when to call a bet and when to fold and throw in your hand.

"What'll it be? I can't just stand here all day. But I can only kill you if you draw on me or resist arrest. So, I'm arresting you on the count of three. Drop your gun belt, or I'll kill you," he paused, and then loudly said, "One."

Drops of sweat hung on Square-Jaw's eyelids, and his eyes smarted as he tried to blink the drops away. He tried to swallow, but his parched throat cried out for some of that cold water he'd heard about. He moved his fingers in anticipation. The cowboy stood stock still with his pistol pointing directly at Square-Jaw's heart and calmly said, "Two."

"All right, you win!" He had one last play, and it should work. Square-Jaw raised his hands in surrender, then lowering his right hand, he loosened his tie-downs and unbuckled his gun belt. He hesitated for a last glance at the .45 pointed straight at his heart. With a nod of his head in acceptance, as if surrendering, he let the belt with his holstered guns drop to the ground at the cowboy's feet. He expected the cowboy's eyes to follow the gun rig to the ground. All he needed was a split second, and he started to make his move to his vest pocket but froze. The cowboy's eyes never left his target.

"Now, off your horse. Easy, and don't move your hand. I'll kill ya if you do."

The cowboy stooped to pick up the rig with its two ivory-handled pistols in his left hand and thumbed the hammer tab free without ever taking his eyes off his target. Moving back a pace, he waited for him to dismount.

He removed one of Square-Jaw's big .44 Remington with his left hand and allowed the rig to fall to earth. He twirled it a few times to feel its balance; it felt good, and he smiled. Though he was a Colt man himself, he liked it. He checked the .44's cylinders and, unlike his weapon, found it contained all six rounds. He listened to its music as he rolled the cylinder along his right sleeve. It was a long barrel with a factory hammer, not made for fanning, but it had a nice weight, good balance, and could be reworked.

"You carry all six rounds, one even under the hammer." The cowboy commented aloud. "Now give me your hold-out you were going for in your vest pocket. Now!" he commanded.

"I ain't got no hold-out."

"You want to die here and now by your own gun? Sure, you do, and if you don't drop it now, I'll put one between your eyes with your own pistol." The cowboy swung the left hand up to Square-Jaw's head and cocked the hammer.

Square-Jaw's shoulders sagged. He heaved a sigh, slowly removed a small two-round derringer from a vest pocket, and let it fall to the ground.

"Got any more weapons I need to know about? Cause if you do and lie to me when I find out, and I will, I'll blow your wick out."

"No, I got nothing else on me."

The Remington .44's mechanism was as smooth as silk, and the cowboy enjoyed cocking and releasing the hammer with his thumb. The cowboy motioned for Square-Jaw to move back against the barbed wire fence where he could easily cover him. "Now turn around. If you move or try anything, I'll kill you." Square-Jaw slowly complied, his hands still in the air.

The cowboy then removed the side arm and rifles belonging to Square-Jaw's deceased companions out of easy reach. "Don't worry," the cowboy said, "I'm not going to shoot you in the back the way you boys do." Square-Jaw heard what sounded like five empty cartilages being punched out. So, he confirmed that the cowboy had only fired five rounds and was glad he hadn't pulled on him. Then he heard what sounded like the cowboy rolling over and searching each body by pulling up clothing and patting for extra weapons.

All the cowboy found was a 20-dollar double eagle gold piece and three silver dollars on the Mexican. He slipped them into his jeans pocket and mused how little crime paid. He walked over to his horse and dropped the hand weapons into his saddlebag. He emptied the Winchesters, carefully collecting the rounds, and replaced the rifles in their boots. Then he opened the breach Sharp's rifle and levered out the heavy round. Examining it, he thought about how this would do the trick from a long, safe distance. He placed the round in his saddlebag and leaned the rifle against the fence.

"Can I put my arms down now?"

"Sure. Turn around. Go over there, nice and slow, and put your two friends over the mounts. Tie 'em down underneath, nice and tight. Be careful with the Mex. Take his bedroll and tie it around his chest and head. I don't want his head to fall off."

"Hell," blurted Square-Jaw, "You put both rounds through his neck. Some shooting! Where did you learn to shoot like that?"

The cowboy didn't answer, loaded his Colt with five rounds, checked to ensure an empty chamber was under its hammer, and slipped it into his back holster. He then buckled on Square-Jaw's gun belt. Seeing him doing this caused Square-Jaw to grimace with pain and mutter curses under his breath. The son of a bitch only carries five rounds, he thought. I could have taken him.

"What will I ride if I tie Lobo across my saddle?"

Pulling the right holstered pistol, he spun it, feeling its balance, and said, "Just do it! I bet they both got hair triggers."

Square-Jaw grunted an assent as he checked to make sure the knots holding Fernando and Lobo were tight and asked, "At the end of the year or so, do they give you back your own guns?"

"Can't say," answered the cowboy, leaving Square-Jaw a bit puzzled.

"Well, did they give you back your own guns?"

"Said, I can't say." The cowboy snatched and replaced the Remington several times from the left holster, then did the same with the weapon on his right hip. The right-handed gun was faster. His movements were so fast that they seemed a blur. He was having fun with the weapons.

After finishing his task with much grunting and sweating, Square-Jaw asked, "Can I get a drink from the canteen there?"

"Sure," the cowboy tossed him the canteen and said, "A condemned man gets a final request."

"Huh." Square-Jaw looked confused. "What do you mean condemned man? I did everything you asked. Now take me to Mr. Kincaid for my trial."

"Well, you see," answered the cowboy, "what I'm aiming to tell you is that there ain't no Mr. Kincaid, and there ain't going to be a trial. There is no spread over the rise. You got any last words?"

"You can't just kill me. You said that…" his voice trailed off as it finally registered that he had been cleaned out in the highest stake game of his life. He had been bluffed and holding the winning hand he had folded. He had been set up. His mount was too worn to have come from a nearby ranch. He saw it in his mind's eye.

"Your gun was empty, wasn't it?"

The cowboy just nodded and smiled. "I only carry five rounds in the cylinder, and, unfortunately, I had to use three on your Indian friend there. I misjudged. My mistake, but all's well that ends well."

"You don't work for no ranch either. Then who are you? A bounty hunter?"

The cowboy nodded again and said, "You and your partners are worth a lot of money, dead or alive. Where were you boys headed? Seems like you had a destination."

"North of Durango, to the town of Silverton. You plan on taking me in alone, do you?" Square-Jaw was angry at himself that he had been bluffed. He had three chances to put this bounty hunter down and had failed to take them. He could have killed him right off. Then, after he killed his partners, he could have gunned him down, and the third time, if he had just pulled his hold-out gun. It was a long way to the nearest town. Maybe he'd get another chance on the trail.

"I have been thinking about that and just decided that I can't afford to take a chance on taking you back alive. I'll admit you boys wore me out. I'm too tired. No, you're like a wild, crazed animal. Too dangerous to capture, but your hide is worth real money. No, I'm not taking you back alive." Square-Jaw's mind spun in disbelief.

"I've trailed you three across two states from the Indian Territories. It was simple enough. I just followed your trail of robberies, burned cabins, and butchered bodies. I rode wide around your camp last night after I was sure you were headed this way. I picked the hammer and staples up from the last cabin you burned. The farmer didn't need them anymore. I knew you'd follow the hammering sound right to me." Square Jaw's eyes were filled with hatred, waiting for the slightest chance to act.

"At that cabin, someone had blown a big hole through the farmer with probably a Sharps rifle at a long distance." He glanced at the rifle leaning against the fence. "I also found the body of a Pinkerton man trailing you with his chest blown open just like that farmer. I respect your skills too much and can't afford to take you back alive, but I won't make you suffer the way you made that farmer's wife spend her last hours on earth. Do you need time to ask forgiveness before you meet your Maker?"

Square-Jaw shook his head in disbelief from side to side and said, "No. You can't…"

"Fine by me." The cowboy's right hand, quick as a pit viper's strike, pulled the right-hand pistol from its leather and shot Square-Jaw twice in the center of his chest. The .44 drove deep into its target, shoving the man back into the barbed wire where it snagged and held him, slumping in death. The motion caused the Sharp's rifle to fall to the ground.

The cowboy punched out one of the empty cartridges and exchanged it for a live round from the left-handed revolver. He spun the revolvers to ensure the empty rounds were safely under the hammers, leaving the reeking gray smoke to drift over the range. The cowboy never kept one under the hammer.

After finding Lobo's horse pulling at some grass over the rise, he lifted and pulled Square-Jaw off the wire, quickly searched his body, removed a tooled leather wallet, extracted all but $15.00 in cash, and replaced it. That should be enough to plant 'em. Crime seemed to have paid better for Square-Jaw than his partners. He thought as he slid the stack of greenbacks into his wallet and placed it in his own pocket. He'd count them later.

He had to get under Square-Jaw to heave him up and across the pony's saddle. His death had come quickly, and there wasn't a lot of blood, but he was sure he got some of it on the back of his shirt. Then he tied the corpse's wrists and feet securely under the mount, picked up the Sharp, and slid it into the pony's rifle boot.

He attached Lobo's pony to Fernando's black and then to Square-Jaw's mount, which was carrying Lobo. Oh, hell, it didn't matter which horse carried whom. He formed a nice little pack train.

Before mounting his mare, the cowboy cleared all the misgivings and thoughts about killing an unarmed man from his mind as he retrieved a stack of wanted posters from his saddlebag and smiled as he mentally added up the amounts. Old Square-Jaw's name was Ivory Thompson, and he had a half-dozen wanted posters out on him. Returning them to his saddlebag, he mounted, with the lead rope in hand, and moseyed his little pack train toward the nearest town with a telegraph, a train, a sheriff, a saloon, and a bath. He was sick of his life and, for the first time, would have a chance to change it along with his name. The cowboy gave a few quiet clucks and clicks with his tongue, smacked his lips with a kissing sound, and moved out.

Chapter 3
Arrival

The cowboy stopped in a valley a mile or so from the place of the killing to tighten the ropes holding the three dead men draped over the saddles with wrists tied under the horses' bellies to their ankles. The Mexican's head seemed to be holding. The grass was green, and a small stream meandered down from the high country. He let the horses drink, relieve themselves, and chomp on the grass for a spell. He needed rest but was afraid to lay down in the shade for fear that he would fall into a deep sleep. Leaning against his mare, he wondered if he had the energy or will to remount.

The mounts were jittery and started snorting and blowing. The one packing Square-Jaw tossed his head and whinnied his disapproval. Taking his time, the cowboy petted and gently talked to each mount, giving each a lump of sugar from his pack.

Steeling his nerves, he clumsily remounted, bone tired. The procession of death moved out. He had checked the maps, and by his reckoning, there was a distant town with maybe a hotel and a hot bath, a saloon with cool beer, a railroad, a telegraph office, and most importantly, a sheriff's office. He was feeling pretty good.

The afternoon grew hotter as the cowboy clucked his parade along the trail. The flies buzzed loudly around the load, planting eggs into the decaying flesh and feasting on the raw nutrients surrounding the wounds. The blanket covering the Mexican's swaying head swarmed with insects. Nature gives instinctive commands to the buzzing flies, hoping they will soon produce maggots and a new generation. The horses' tails were busy swishing the bothersome flies away as they plodded along.

For the rest of the afternoon, the cowboy walked his line of burdened horses from the rolling prairie land into the hill country and onto a rutted stagecoach and telegraph road that ran parallel to a train track toward the mining town of Durango.

Entering the town from the east, he saw that the telegraph poles and train tracks continued into the distance away from the berg. It looked like they met at some point toward the sun setting behind the pinkish-red mountains in the distance. He thought, funny how that works. He knew the tracks did not meet. How could they? Yet his eyes told him they did. You can't even trust your sight some of the time, he thought. He pondered what, if anything, he could trust.

His entrance into the town, down its one main street, was causing quite a bit of interest among the locals. He only paused once to inquire about the location of the sheriff's office. Several men, who looked like bar flies and town loafers, followed until he stopped his line laterally in front of the sheriff's office and jail, a two-story brick building facing the south side of the street.

"You men, be careful there. Don't get too close. The horses spook easily." He cautioned the gawkers. "They've been known to kick and bite. Better stay clear." They backed up a few feet, still gawking and commenting to each other about the gruesome sight. The cowboy swung off his horse and, a bit stiff-legged, mounted the stairs to the door with a sign marked "Sheriff's Office – Jail."

Knocking first but not waiting for a response, he entered the office area. Four men were playing poker on a small table pressed up against the bars of a cell, with one man sitting on the edge of the cell's bunk and playing his cards through the food slot. They looked up.

"Evening, gentlemen." The cowboy stepped in, closed the door, removed his trail gloves, and approached, saying, "Would one of you be the sheriff for this county?"

Their game stopped while the four men in the office still held their cards while seriously appraising the stranger. He was no longer young but not yet old either. Tall, an inch or so above six feet in height, and well-built with a stubble of growth on his face and his dirty hair hung below his high-crowned hat. He wore a two-gun set of black tooled holsters with loops filled with extra rounds while the ivory-handled guns hung low within easy grabbing distance. His eyes were cold blue, blinking, and tired.

One of the men at the table tossed his cards down and stood. "I'm Sheriff Pat Williams, and who might you be?"

"Sorry to interrupt your game, gents. I'm Thorn Hagman, er, ah," he hesitated, "Hagerman is my name, a Pinkerton agent. I've been on the trail of an outlaw named Ivory Thompson and his two compadres, a Mex, and a half-breed. I don't rightly know their names, but they probably have papers out on 'em. All three were bad desperadoes. I've got a wanted poster in my saddlebag on Thompson. He's wanted dead or alive for murder, arson, rape, train robbery, and other high crimes and misdemeanors. Also in the saddlebag are my credentials from the Pinkerton Detective Agency and a letter assigning me to this case. Their bodies, weapons, and mounts are outside."

Sheriff Williams, of average height, was a stocky middle-aged hombre with a graying mustache. He also wore his gun low on his hip. The sheriff was a no-nonsense man with dark, suspicious eyes who did not suffer fools.

"Yes," the sheriff slowly said, "I've seen bulletins on all three, Thompson and his pals. They are or were a bad lot. Do you have all three outside dead? All three? You looking for the rewards?" The stranger at the door didn't bother to answer.

"Billy and Teddy, get out there and check on 'em. Billy, you know what to look for. Then, take the corpses over to the funeral parlor. Tell Mr. Dobbs I'll talk to him after a while. Take their mounts, saddles, and such over to the livery. I'll check on 'em later. Also, bring me their weapons and saddlebags."

"Sure thing, boss," Billy answered while the two men tossed down their cards as chairs were scuffed across the rough plank floor.

The fourth man leaned back, studied his hand for a second, and, in disgust, tossed his cards down on the table. "Damn it all! My first good hand and the game ends," he muttered to no one in particular. Reaching through the food slot, he quickly examined each of the hands in turn, grabbed the cell bars, and stood up to watch. "Damn it all to hell!" he exclaimed, "I did have the winning hand." The prisoner felt like something mighty big was happening and didn't want to miss out.

The sheriff studied the stranger with particular attention on the two ivory-handled pistols and said, "Why don't you take that gun belt off and make yourself comfortable? Hang 'em up on that hook and have a seat." It may have sounded like a polite request, but it was a command. The man calling himself Thorn didn't like to be ordered about, especially about giving up his guns. It made him feel naked as a jaybird.

The room was silent, and for the first time, both men facing each other became aware of the ticking of the big-faced railroad clock hanging behind the rolltop desk. The ticking grew louder with each second.

The man calling himself Thorn Hagerman wondered what the sheriff was up to. Was he planning on getting rid of him and claiming the rewards?

Inhaling deeply, he unbuckled his gun belt and, turning to the row of pegs on the wall, hung the gun rig up. He'd take a chance that the sheriff was up and up, but just in case, he still had his back gun and the little two-shot derringer tucked into a vest pocket, the same weapon he had also appropriated from Ivory. It was chambered for .45-long Colt rounds--a mighty big round for such a little gun.

"I understand Ivory got his name by carrying ivory-handled pistols. Is that true?" The sheriff approached the gun belt and, turning to the stranger, asked. "Mind if I take a closer look at 'em?"

Without waiting for an answer, he withdrew the right-handed Remington .44 pistol and felt its weight and balance. He checked to ensure it was loaded, then twirled it around his trigger finger a few times. Satisfied, he slid it back into its holster and palmed the second one.

"Not identical to the one you carry in your…" he stopped mid-sentence and looked carefully at the gun belt, "in your right holster. This one has a factory 7 ½ inch barrel, and it shoots straight at over fifty yards. Interesting, the right-handed gun has had its barrel length cut to what?"

He holstered the left pistol and laid the right hand one on the desk, retrieved a wooden ruler from the rolltop desk, and measured. He said, "It's a hair over five inches with no front site to drag on the leather. Other than that, they are as pretty a matched set of single-action Model 1875 as I've ever seen. They are both chambered for centerfire metallic .44 cartridges. They are both finished in that new blue-black heat treatment. It's supposed to protect the gun from rust, but you must keep 'em well-oiled. As for me, I prefer a Colt .45, Peacemaker, but these are quality pistols."

They both stood above the pistol, admiring its lines. The sheriff picked up the second pistol and spun the cylinder, listening to the clicking music. The five rounds spun around in the heavy frame with one empty chamber. After twirling it a few times, he cocked and released the hammer, glanced to make sure its hammer was above the empty chamber, returned the gun to its holster, and eased the hammer tab in place.

The man calling himself Thorn had developed a new respect for the sheriff in the past few minutes. He knew his business and wore his gun in a low quick-draw holster without a safety tab holding the hammer in place. He probably carried six rounds, at least in town.

The man calling himself Thorn slowly answered the earlier question, "I don't know how the hombre got his name, but yes, they were his ivory-handled pistols. He lost 'em to me in a high-stakes game."

"Hmmm," the sheriff acknowledged. "I'm not saying you didn't win 'em from the deceased. Just curious about his name, that's all. Was it a poker game you two were playing?"

"No, not as such. I told him to drop his gun belt or get to usin' them. He made the wrong choice."

"Was this before or after you took care of the other two?"

"After. They were so used to killing sodbusters, store clerks, raping and killing women, and the like, that they forgot how to deal with a Pinkerton."

"Hmmm," the sheriff nodded. But his curiosity about his name raised red flags about the man calling himself Thorn Hagman or Hagerman.

Thorn liked his new first name, and he thought about his own many aliases. Thorn Hagerman, the name he was currently trying on, had indeed belonged to a military vetern turned Pinkerton agent. He had come across his body a few weeks ago on the trail. He knew the Pinkerton man was tracking three men. He was the fifth rider and hung back a mile. He heard the shot thunder rumble across the hills at dusk.

In what was called a cold harbor, he camped that night cold and weary, with no fire, no coffee, and little sleep.

The next morning, he had come onto a grove of trees near a stream. On the ground lay a body on its back. The round had blown him off the back of his horse and left a big hole in his chest. His bay horse, a handsome reddish body with a black tail and mane, was unhurt and was chomping on grass nearby.

Searching the saddlebags, he found a bill of sale for the animal from a rancher in Colorado. He would sell the horse and saddle in a town along the way. From the other papers and warrants he found in the dead man's saddlebags, it looked like he had also been after the same trio that he was trailing.

He was probably hanging back to sneak up on them early in the morning while they slept, but he didn't count on an ambush. It was just the luck of the draw that the Pinkerton had been a little closer.

He had been hit dead center of his chest by a large-bore rifle, probably a breech-loading Sharps rifle good for up to a thousand yards or more in the right hands. He had found out later that the same type of rifle had been carried by the half-breed who had most likely ambushed a half dozen or more along the trail.

Ivory had probably had the half-breed do a little back trailing to find himself the perfect spot to lay up for an ambush. Strange, the breed didn't even go back to confirm his kill or collect the weapons or the horse. Did he know he was farther back and also following? The outlaws must have been in a hurry to get someplace, and he had been very confident of his shot.

At that moment, back in the grove, two thoughts crystallized into decisions. First, he decided to become Thorn T. Hagerman. He really didn't care much for the last name; it sounded too Dutch. It's funny how when he rode with the Missouri Guerrillas in the war, he was afraid others would find out he was really born a German, or as they preferred, a Dutchman, and kill him as a spy.

The Germans came to Missouri in swarms after their failed revolution of 1848. Daniel Boone opened the state to farmers and didn't care who settled along the great Missouri River and its fertile valleys as long as they were good folks.

However, the Germans were hated by the southern settlers who were moving in from Tennessee and Kentucky and farther south for their pro-union sentiment and anti-slavery attitudes and because they were foreigners and had their own language and religions. So many Germans had enlisted in Mr. Lincoln's army that they spoiled the governor's plans to take Missouri out of the Union and capture the federal arsenal in St. Louis, thus depriving the Confederates of needed arms and ammunition.

Later, he had been just as afraid that someone in the German farming towns he knew along the bend of the Missouri River would find out that he had ridden with Bill Quantrill and was on a scouting mission for Confederate General Sterling Price and hang him as a rebel spy. That was lifetimes ago, or at least four lifetimes if you counted each identity as one.

But he now had a letter and credentials made out to a real, deceased Pinkerton agent. If anyone checked, he would stand pat on his bluff. He had buried the real Thorn T. Hagerman with most of his personal belongings, except the dark duster and his personal papers, in the soft, moist earth near a grove of cottonwood trees with no cross or any way of identifying the body if it was ever discovered.

He had taken time to study the corpse. He was about 5'10" or so, a little shorter, but he could buy some lower-heeled boots to make up the difference. His hair had been light brown and close-cropped around the ears and collar. His next haircut would be high and tight, as it was called. Easy enough to fix, and his eyes were also blue. He had worn western range clothes with a blue checkered shirt and a leather vest. His duster had been long and dark, and he wore black pointed-toed boots and braces to hold up his pants. An old tintype picture of the deceased and a pretty little woman showed him in a black broadcloth suit wearing a starched white shirt with a string tie. He thought that would be easy enough to duplicate.

He was now Thorn and would answer only to it. That night, he sat thinking as he played with the two sets of iron handcuffs he had found in the saddlebags with the date 1871 stamped on their frames. He sat thinking as he locked, unlocked, opened, and closed them. The only problem was he didn't know what the middle initial stood for. None of his papers gave his full name. He would have to be very careful, and he might even be able to collect the salary or reward from the Pinkertons. In the letters he read and reread, some from his wife, dated years before, he learned dates and facts, such as a daughter in a school in St. Louis.

His second decision back under the cottonwood trees was to circle wide around the trio and not give them a chance to ambush him. It would take time, but it was worth it, and they were moving in a northwesterly direction. He would ride all night, circle them, and set them up for tomorrow. They would have to come to him on the ground he had chosen. This he had also done.

The sheriff motioned toward the pot-bellied stove, bringing him back to the present, "I said, do you want some coffee? Coffee's on, and there's an extra cup. Help yourself."

"Sorry, Sheriff, just plain tired, I guess. Haven't had much sleep the past few months."

Feeling the sheriff's eyes on him, Thorn walked over, touched the pot to judge its heat, poured himself a cup of tar-black liquid, then motioned toward the sheriff, who nodded and held out his cup to receive a warm-up.

Thorn thought the coffee was strong enough to wake the dead, hot and strong, just the way he liked it. "This is mighty fine coffee, strong enough to wake up my dead granddad too," he said. Both men smiled.

"Is it all right to give your friend there a cup?" Thorn motioned toward the prisoner standing behind the bars.

"Sure, give him some. Hold out your cup if you want some." This was quickly done.

The sheriff chuckled to himself and said, "Have a seat. Take a load off. You're right. It is mighty good coffee. I developed a taste for it in Dodge City during the cattle drives as a kid. It's Arbuckles' Ariosa blend."

Both Smitty and Thorn nodded in agreement.

"Yep," continued the sheriff, "a pinch of salt and some eggshells does the trick and cuts the bitter taste."

"Salt and eggshells, you don't say." Thorn was learning something new every day.

"Yep, the eggshells help settle the grounds to the bottom." The sheriff reached over, rolled up the desktop, and returned with a bottle of Old Overholt Rye Whiskey.

"Sweeten it up a little," he splashed a good shot in his own cup and, with a nod of assent, splashed an equal amount into Thorn's cup.

Thorn smacked his lips in satisfaction. "Now this is real whiskey," he studied the bottle, "my goodness, it comes all the way from Pennsylvania."

Smitty held out his cup but was disappointed when the sheriff recorked the bottle and returned it to his desk.

"Sorry Smitty, but that's what got you in trouble in the first place as town drunk," the sheriff said in explanation.

Just then, the door opened, and the two deputies came in carrying an armload of rifles, pistols, and saddlebags.

Chapter 4
Law Business

The two deputies carried their loads across the floor as the sheriff quickly gathered the cards. The two men dumped the arms and bags on the table. "All right, Billy, tell us what you learned." The sheriff's right hand was poised above his holster, carefully watching Thorn.

"Just like he said," Billy answered, "all three are deader than hell."

"Yep," the other deputy chimed in, "deader than doornails."

"How were they shot? Any in the back?"

The room was silent, and the prisoner stood in his cell and leaned forward to hear the answer. Everyone in town knew how the sheriff felt about a bounty hunter bringing in a dead man shot by a rifle at a long distance, or up-close shot in the back, or worse yet, ambushed with a scattergun, even if the poster said "Wanted Dead or Alive" the sheriff would have no part of it.

The sheriff considered them plain assassins. Just pure and simple murderers, and he would do his damnedest not to pay out a cent and hold an inquest with the hope of returning an indictment of manslaughter. He would use the funds to give to the widows and orphans, if any, or to other good causes like improvements to the jail and salaries of peace officers.

"No sir," Billy said, "No holes punched in any of their backs. All were in the front of the neck, chest, shoulder, and side. Seven holes in all—nothing in any of their backs." Some mighty good shooting, the sheriff thought.

There was a noticeable relaxation of tension in the office.

The sheriff turned to the stranger and said, "Fine, Mr. Hagman, er, I mean, Hagerman, show me your credentials, and we'll talk," he watched carefully for a reaction and, finding none, assumed that his confusion over his name was just due to tiredness and lack of sleep. Hell, he'd been there back in the war.

That went well, thought the man who had become Thorn T. Hagerman at that moment. He asked the sheriff if his deputies would be able to take the corpses over to the undertaker and arrange for pictures the next morning. The sheriff nodded in agreement. "Can they take the mounts to the stable for grain feeding and brushing?" He handed the sheriff three silver dollars for handling this task.

"By the way, sheriff, would you mind asking one of the deputies to stay with the undertaker and watch as he inventories their personal effects? I'm hopeful they'll have enough to pay for planting 'em."

The sheriff smiled and nodded. "Billy, you heard the man. You stay with the undertaker while Teddy takes the horses to the stable. We've got some work to do." The sheriff handed both men a coin, and the deputies left on their errands with smiles. He dropped the third coin into an old coffee can on his desk, holding some copper coins. "Thanks, that'll go into the coffee fund."

Turning to his desk, the sheriff said, "Let me go through my stack of papers while you get me yours. I need to do some paperwork and get some wires off if you ever hope to see that reward money."

Thorn reached into his saddlebag and retrieved the wanted poster on Ivory Thompson and two general description posters for the other two, which had belonged to the late real Mr. Hagerman, now deceased and hopefully forgotten.

"By the way, feel free to strap on your pistols," Sheriff Williams nodded toward the black gun rig hanging on the wall. "You best hurry over to the barber across the street, before he closes. Have him order you a hot bath and a shave. He'll stay open if you tell him I asked."

The new Thorn Hagerman nodded, retrieving his gun belt and buckling it on. Then he tossed his saddlebags, which contained spare clothing and the bundle of the dead man's letters, over his shoulder and left, saying, "Much obliged." He wasn't about to leave them here for the sheriff's perusal.

Sheriff Williams acknowledged the value of saving the county money. In a few minutes, he found five additional posters and two Western Union telegrams dealing with Ivory Thompson and his gang. The rest of the posters and warrants dealt with folks wanted back east. Williams quickly did some math at his desk and broke his pencil's lead while totaling the rewards.

He sharpened it with his pocket knife and began composing a telegram on a Western Union pad. Reading it aloud, he crossed out a word, made another change, thought better, and rewrote a new telegram.

Amazing, he thought, in a few minutes, his new message would be transmitted to Denver, the U.S. Marshals Service in Washington D.C., and not to forget the public, a copy to the Rocky Mountain News, also located in Denver. A special request in an additional telegram would go to Chicago, Illinois, for information on their agent, Thorn Hagerman. It will be sent to the Headquarters of the Pinkerton Detective Agency.

Looking at the preliminary reward money totals, he whistled and rocked back in his chair. He had never seen so many zeros before. It looked like the Pinkerton agent was going to be a rich man.

Finally, after an hour's work, the sheriff unlocked the cell door and said, "Smitty, I'll be back soon. Keep an eye on the place and sweep up, empty the trash, and, for God's sake, dump your slop bucket in the privy and wash it out. It smells to high heaven in here, and don't go near my desk or touch any guns, or I'll skin you alive. Understand?"

"Yes, sir, sheriff. You can count on me."

With his messages in hand, the sheriff hurried to the telegraph office, which was situated in the train depot. Turning the corner, he almost bumped into Mike Todd, who was hurriedly exiting the Belle Saloon on Main Street.

"Evening Mike, didn't see you coming down the steps," said the sheriff. "What's your hurry?"

"Oh, it's you, sheriff. Good evening. It was my fault that I wasn't paying attention. I was hurrying home so as not to be too late for supper. I told the missus I'd have only one beer after cashing in the weight in gold placer and flakes I panned out during the last few months. Truth be told, Sheriff, I only got enough hard currency from it to pay our credit account at the general mercantile, pick up some notions for the missus, and buy two beers. I'd better get going."

Mike Todd hurried to his big-eared mule, Rufus, tied to a cast iron hitching pole on Main Street. Standing on the sidewalk above the mule, he swung on the animal's bareback. He spent several moments encouraging the animal with oaths, heel kicks, and body movements as to the importance of his errand. The mule finally walked up the street, ignoring his rider's antics. The sheriff smiled as he watched its ambling regardless of Mike's insistence.

Mike was a good citizen, the sheriff thought as he hurried toward the depot. Mike had married Sissy Monroe and settled on a claim and acreage up the draw. He built a nice snug cabin, farmed some, raised a few head of cattle, and in his free time played at being a gold miner. Mike was one of the nicest men in town. Wished we had more like him, he thought. The town was full of rowdies, drunks, loafers, plus a fair number of really bad hombres. Men like Mike never carried a sidearm and depended on the law to protect them. Everybody liked him and his pretty little wife.

The sheriff walked briskly to the telegraph office and signed the voucher to process the telegrams. The bill totaled $3.40, but he didn't mind. It was billed to the county. He knew that, at best, it would take several weeks for any of the smaller rewards to flow in, and the county's expenses would first be deducted from the payments.

Next, he needed to visit the funeral director, Mr. Dobbs, to check on his deputies and determine if any hard currency was available for the burials. If not, he could hold their weapons pending sale to pay the charges. He could get a writ to sell the horses if they didn't have enough, but he doubted that would be necessary.

Again, his thoughts wandered to the fancy holsters and .44 pistols Hagerman claimed he had won from Ivory. Strange indeed! Did Hagerman mispronounce his own name due to tiredness? Trailing for weeks, much less months, will do that to you. He put those thoughts on the back burner.

The "closed" sign hung in the funeral parlor's window. Ignoring it, the sheriff pounded three times (knock, knock, pause, knock) on the locked door, his signal, and soon, a gaunt man in a rubber apron and long rubber gloves unlocked the door. He was a thin, balding man of indeterminate age nervously chewing on an unlit cigar.

"Sheriff, your boys have gone to the stable to see about the horses. I'm working on the bodies now. Do you want to view the 'ceased?" The sheriff followed him through an open door into a large back room with four tables upon which the three bodies were laid out face down. The strong chemical smell made his eyes smart, and his nose began to run. The fourth table remained empty, but the night was still young.

"You'll be pleased to know the Indian was carrying a leather pouch containing some silver jewelry and half a dozen gold teeth with some gold denture wire. It must be worth something. I gave it to Billy. He'll take it to the Assay Office in the morning to see what it's worth."

"Don't that beat all?" mused the sheriff, "They even stole their teeth after killing them."

"Let's hope they were dead," came a reply that left the sheriff uneasy and concerned about the depth of human depravity, but thankful the trio was brought in a deceased state. Had they been alive, it would have become his responsibility to feed and guard them up through their trial and hanging. It would give them plenty of chances to escape and put everyone in danger, including himself and his deputies. He would have done it because it was his job, but he would have worried about his deputies and the town folk. He thought, thank goodness I don't have that problem.

"No. It's you I want to talk to. Billy and Teddy looked at 'em and told me that none were shot in the back. Do you agree?"

"Yes, Sheriff, you can see for yourself. All shot from the front or, in the case of the Indian, the side, probably while turning or twisting. They were all good clean shots."

"Fine, fine. Any cash on 'em?"

"Yes. Fifteen dollars in greenbacks."

"Good. That should plant 'em." The sheriff glanced at the bodies, "But I want you to extract all the rounds and put them in separate containers, washed and cleaned up, and labeled with time, date, the body extracted from, and, if you can, the type and caliber of bullet. Can you do that?"

"Come on, Sheriff, that'll take hours. We just rolled 'em over for you to look at. Besides, the Mexican was shot in the neck, and the bullets passed through, lost."

"Don't cry about that. Just do as I say and have good notes and penmanship. There will be an inquest, and I want everything just right. You will be on county business, so you can bill at a reasonable rate and give the bill to me." With that assurance, the undertaker's mood dramatically improved, and he began to hum an aria from the Opera Carmen as his cigar bounced in time with the tune. The sheriff gave a goodbye nod and next headed to the Belle Saloon.

Stepping through the swinging batwing doors, the sheriff paused to look around, made his way to the end of the long oak bar, and planted his right boot on the brass rail bolted to the bottom of the bar running its length. It was one of the few improvements shipped in from the East that really did make Western life more comfortable, and the fancy gilt mirror behind the bar gave him eyes in the back of his head.

Half a dozen trail hands, miners, city folks, clerks, and such stood at the bar talking, sipping beer, or drinking shots for some or both. The Belle was the newest and finest saloon in town. It housed gaming tables and tables for poker and ladies pushing drinks in low-cut dresses showing plenty of décolletages, with bare shoulders and ample cleavage. Also, a piano player with a pet monkey riding on his shoulder played a spirited jig and reel of "Turkey in the Straw."

"What'll it be, Sheriff?" A short, portly man in a dirty apron toweled the bar before the sheriff and waited for his answer.

"Give me a shot of Old Overholt rye and a beer. Put it on my tab, Charlie." The bartender nodded and made a small mark on a pad under the bar.

Soon, there was a tall shot glass with two fingers of amber liquid, his usual double, and a foaming beer stein on the bar before him. Taking the shot glass in his left hand, he saluted the painting on the wall above the bar of a nude lady affectionately named Belle. She was of heroic proportions lounging, *au naturel*, on a sofa, with one arm casually placed beneath her head and not quite showing all her wares. The sheriff tossed off the fiery liquid. The nude painting was the toast of the town, and everyone, including the sheriff, saluted her and then shot his drink in one quick gulp. He felt the glowing warmth of good liquor flow through his body. Things were going to work out just fine.

"All right boys, listen up." The sheriff's booming voice cut through the conversation like a hot knife through butter, and the room fell to a murmur as folks turned to look. The roulette wheel's ball made a final revolution and dropped with a clatter. The barmaids and standing gents turned toward the sheriff as he leaned back on his elbows against the bar facing the crowd. The acapella singers stood silent, waiting their turn to sing the choirs. The singers standing near the piano swallowed the final words of their song as the last piano note hung briefly in the air, and all fell silent. The monkey chattered twice and sat watching on his master's shoulder.

"Sorry to interrupt your festivities, but a Pinkerton agent just rode into town with the bodies of three of the worst highwaymen and murdering wasters ever to terrorize Colorado. Their depredations are well known to some of you." Several men muttered about not knowing that word and scratched their beards in thought. The sheriff continued, "Their leader went by Ivory Thompson, but I'm sure he had other aliases, monikers, and handles."

The sheriff paused again to make sure this crowd understood him and continued. "The three deceased will be propped up in front of the funeral parlor tomorrow morning at 9:00 a.m. for viewing. We can't leave them out too long because of the heat. Take a good look at them. Those of you that knew 'em, make your mark or sign the book and be willing to swear under oath as to your statement as such. Some of you may have to testify at the inquest, for which you'll receive the usual county fee. That's it, gents, back to your merriment." The sheriff finished his beer and left.

Two rough-looking drifters at the far end of the bar had listened with interest to the sheriff's announcement without turning toward him, then hunched their shoulders and leaned over their beers in anonymity. They had been in deep whispered discussions after observing a prospector having a whiskey and two beers at the bar, bragging about his rich claim and buying his pals on either side a drink.

The taller man, clearly the leader, did most of the talking while the smaller man nodded in agreement and grinned, licking his thick lips a time or two. The taller man caught the eye of the bartender, ordered and paid for two more drinks, and asked about the prospector who had just left.

He was informed that it was Mike Todd, a nice guy, married to one of the cutest little girls in the county. They lived up the trail behind the saloon a few miles up the grade. Nice folks."

"Where does that trail take you?"

"Oh," the bartender answered, "it winds around for ways and eventually takes you to the mining settlement of Silverton, but there is the narrow-gauge railroad you can take, so nobody uses it much."

The bartender left to wait on other customers. The two men finished their drinks and quietly left the saloon.

Chapter 5
Hardy Breakfast

The patrons of the Belle Saloon, who were still sober, discussed the need for positive eyewitness identification before the state and towns would pay out the offered rewards. The banks, stage lines, railroads, and such would only pay out after the state paid, and then only if there was no other way to dodge the payout, such as lack of positive identification. Such identifications resulted in silver dollars changing hands.

Several cowboys decided to make it an early night so as to be at the funeral parlor in the morning. Some drifters and old timers approaching fifty years of age, knew of Ivory Thompson from past exploits and tall tales. Most had only heard stories about him, and a few had ridden with him or with one of his gang members at some point. Some only knew of him through his likenesses from a sketch on a wanted poster. But it was money for the taking, and many decisions were made to call it a night.

But like the old saw about the three frogs sitting in a pond on the lily pad when two decided to jump in. How many were left? The answer would be three. Just because a frog or a cowboy decides to do something with the best intentions doesn't mean he does it.

The miners and city folks who had to be at work in the morning drifted away early, leaving ranch hands, drifters, gamblers, and the ladies of the night to continue the party. Unfortunately, the folks who were in the best position to name the dead outlaws would themselves be dead to the world the next morning.

Thorn began to regain consciousness. After his hot bath in a tin watering trough with fresh water, for which he paid an extra two bits, followed by a shave and haircut, he vaguely remembered registering for a night's lodging at a nearby hotel. He had been so exhausted that he didn't remember signing in or going to his room, but he must have because he was waking up in a bed. He had better check to ensure he signed in under his new name. No more mistakes, he promised himself. He had been without sleep for the past two days, and his body was trying to play catch up.

It was late, after dawn, when he finally opened his eyes. For a moment, he didn't know where he was or, worse yet, who he was. His head spun as he stumbled across the unfamiliar room to pour water from a pitcher into a bowl. He splashed the chilled water over his face and hair. Taking a coarse towel from the rack, he briskly dried off and looked in the mirror. He combed his shorn hair and studied the clean-shaven face. Who was the stranger looking back at him?

"Thorn," he muttered aloud, "I'm Thorn Hagerman, Pinkerton agent. That's who I am." He quickly changed into his other shirt and pants over his spare red union longjohns.

He remembered leaving the clothes he wore into town to be laundered, mended, or discarded, as in the case of his other union suit and only pair of socks, which were worn thin beyond hope.

Now firmly in character, Thorn adjusted his braces and strapped on the double gun belt with the heavy Remington pistols. Then he slid his cut-down Colt into his back holster and patted to ensure the little hold-out derringer pistol was still in place in his vest. Turning, he saw his vest covering his back, hiding his Colt, yet loose enough for a quick draw.

Then pausing, he removed and carefully checked each of the four weapons before replacing them and putting on his high crown hat, which now felt too large. Funny, his spare shirt and trousers felt dirty and stiff after his bath, and after his shave and haircut, his hat felt misshapen and loose on his head. He pulled it lower in front, stomped his bare feet into his worn boots, hefted his saddlebags over his left shoulder, kept his right hand free, locked the door, and exited the room.

Coming down the stairs to the lobby, Thorn noticed that the night clerk who had checked him in was off duty. In his place was a young boy, still in his teens, cleaning the lobby area. Upon seeing the stranger with two ivory-handled pistols tied down standing before him, he was startled. "Oh, you must be Mr. Hagman, room seven? Good morning, Sir. I'm Jimmy, the day clerk and porter. Hope you had a restful night's sleep."

"Yes, I had a fine night's sleep, but the name's Hagerman, not Hagman. It's Thorn Hagerman. I was pretty tired last night. Let me see the register and make sure you can read my chicken scratching."

"No problem. I was having a little trouble reading it, but the sheriff looked at it on the way to breakfast and gave me the correct spelling."

"Good man, the sheriff. Tell me, Jimmy, where is a good place for breakfast, and where can I get some new duds and boots?"

"Sir, that's easy. There's a dining room through those doors there in the hotel, and several others are on Main Street. They're all good. The mercantile store is further up the street, but it won't open till 9:00 a.m., so you got plenty of time for a good breakfast and a look-see."

Now feeling more comfortable with his new name, Thorn decided to eat in the hotel. Noticing the sign pointing to the privy, he first went out back and, after its use, had another hand washing at the community sink, this time with a chunk of lye soap.

The dining room was already busy with a waiter and a waitress coming and going with platters of food and pots of coffee. He was looking forward to a big breakfast with lots of coffee, maybe reading a paper, and smoking a cigar.

The clatter of the tableware and clinking of items on tables mixed with the buzz of conversation came to an abrupt stop as he strolled through the doors and looked for an empty table. The customers froze in conversation with forks paused in mid-air, and many hastily swallowed their food with audible gulps. All eyes were on the stranger wearing the two tied-down ivory-handled pistols. The word sure gets around early in Durango.

"Over here," the sheriff's voice boomed across the room. He raised his hand and motioned. Thorn had no choice but to approach. The noise of eating resumed. "Billy, you scooch over some and make room for the Pinkerton man." Billy moved his coffee cup and saucer over and shoved his dirty plate and tableware aside so as to give Thorn ample elbow room. The sheriff and Billy occupied positions with their backs to the corner walls while Thorn was forced to sit with his back open to the world.

"Did you have a good night's sleep?"

"Fine. Just fine." What was it with everyone wanting to know how well he slept?

"Sally," the sheriff motioned to the waitress, "give this man a cup of your coffee, and I'm sure he'll want to order breakfast." Turning to Thorn, the sheriff asked, "How do you take it? Cream and sugar?"

"No, sheriff, I like it black."

Soon, a cup of steaming black coffee was placed before him, and a young woman asked what he wanted for breakfast.

"Thick steak fried medium, with potatoes, coffee, and, do you have apple pie?"

"Sure do." She smiled.

"Bring it on."

"I've got some business to take care of. Billy, after you finish your coffee, I want to see you at the office at about 9:00 a.m." Billy nodded assent as the sheriff retrieved his hat from a wall hook and left. Thorn's eyes followed him out, and he noticed most of the men eating were bareheaded. A few cowboys wore theirs, but all the town men had removed theirs and hung them while the women kept their bonnets or hats on.

Thorn turned back to study the mug of steaming coffee that had appeared on the table. Getting up, he said, "You mind?" Hearing no response, he occupied the sheriff's seat and settled in. He then turned his attention to his coffee and felt Billy's eyes on him. "You got something on your mind? Spit it out."

With elbows on the table, Billy leaned forward and, in a low voice, asked, "If it ain't too personal, how'd you get into your line of work detecting and going after killers and all?"

"I had a hard life, son. My folks both died when I was a kid and I had no real family to help me. Life is hard, and if you live, you'll soon find out what you are good at. I'm good at this sort of work, tracking and shooting. What's your relationship with the sheriff, if you don't mind my asking?"

Billy was hesitant in his reply but decided to open up. "He's my uncle on my mother's side. I finished school at fifteen and first went to work at the dry goods store. A cousin runs it, but I wasn't cut out for working indoors as a shopkeeper. This job opened, and Uncle William, sorry, I'm not supposed to call him that, but everyone hereabouts knows that he's my uncle, gave me the job. It's got its advantages, but it don't pay much."

"So, it doesn't pay much," Thorn acknowledged. Are you looking for a bigger paycheck, maybe, and a little adventure?"

At that moment, the food and more coffee arrived, and conversation ceased as Thorn got down to the business of eating his fill. When he finished a second generous slice of apple pie and his fourth cup of coffee, he sat back and stretched and said, "Mighty good breakfast, but I couldn't do it every day. Tell me Billy, what's the best store for new clothes and boots? I also need some ammunition, Remington .44 and .45 Long Colt."

"The mercantile store will have about everything you need, but check out the boots at the cobbler's place up the street. He has a sign of a boot out front and has some good pairs. It's a bit pricy, though. We also have a gun shop further up. It's almost nine o'clock," Billy said as he studied the clock on the wall. "I'd better get going. Nice meeting you, Mr. er…"

"Hagerman, Thorn Hagerman is the name. Nice to meet you too, Billy."

Thorn watched the young man weave around the tables, greeting, shaking hands, and speaking briefly with a dozen locals.

Thorn's life had been very different from Billy's when he was his age. Remembering back to the fall of 1863, he had just turned fourteen and had been ordered on a scouting mission and had missed the Lawrence, Kansas raid, or as it was now more popularly known, the Lawrence Massacre of September 1863, where they burned the town and killed over 180 men and boys.

General Sterling Price was planning a raid up into Missouri, a slave state, in the fall of 1864 to take St. Louis, a strategic spot on the confluence of the Missouri and Mississippi Rivers. Thorn remembered how he had been told his detachment would gather information about union fixed positions, defenses, supplies, stock, and arms and report back to Quantrill.

Later, following the infamous attack on Lawrence, the Confederate government withdrew its support of Quantrill's irregular forces. Regular Confederates considered them no better than outlaws and bandits. After an incident that he didn't care to remember, he decided to go his own way. When the group split up, he had gone south rather than back to Quantrill's camp to fight under him until his final raid into Kentucky in May of 1865, where Quantrill met his death on June 6th near Louisville. He was only 27 years of age.

Changing his name once again, this time to Mitch Michael, he left behind his devil-may-care gregarious youth along with his prior name in Missouri's autumn mist and mud and rode south, through Arkansas, and into dry, hot Texas. At the age of 14, he was becoming a proficient killer with a rifle, pistol, and Bowie knife. With no family or friends to tie him down, he had no plans or purpose for his life, taking each day as it came. With nerves of steel, he craved adventure and danger, the more, the better, and kept few of his old notions about morality.

Chance brought him into contact with the Texas Rangers, desperate for hard-riding gunmen. Though too young to join, he lied about his age and, with his new name, volunteered to chase Apache, Kiowas, Comanches, and outlaws on punitive raids. He was learning the art of ambuscade and tracking. This was a dangerous time to be in West Texas, with most of the men-folk and rangers fighting the final losing battles of the Civil War. He stayed with them until the war ended, and his unit disbanded.

Later, a year after the war, he fell in with two Yankee Pinkerton agents on the trail of a gang of highwaymen who had robbed a stagecoach carrying a Federal Army payroll protected by their company. In the incident, the highwaymen robbed and killed a passenger reluctant to part with a ring of sentimental value.

They followed the gang's trail for three days, staying back and waiting until the dark of a moonless night when Mitch was tasked to scout out their camp. He cautiously approached, found a little rise with a good vantage point, and with the field glasses he had borrowed from one of the Pinkertons, lay prone carefully studying their campfire, picket line for horses, and lay of the land. They did not post a night guard, and he counted four figures silhouetted against the flames moving about, eating, drinking, and smoking. Occasionally, he heard snatches of conversation with the word Monterrey clearly audible, followed by laughter. After taking a leak and rolling out their blankets, the men settled into sleep near the fire.

An hour later, back at the Pinkerton's cold harbor, Mitch explained in detail the clearing layout, horses, fire-pit, sleeping arrangements, and cover. They agreed to use only shotguns and pistols, leaving the rifles behind for fear of hitting one another in the dark. They chose the wee hours of the morning to approach the camp on foot from three sides, with Mitch, being the smallest, crawling his way behind any cover another 10 yards toward the sleeping camp. At that point, after making sure all was clear, he was to take aim and fire the blast that was to commence the action.

"Do I first order them to surrender?" Mitch honestly queried.

The Pinkertons laughed at his naivety. "Boy, this is a military operation, not Sunday school. We are dealing with murderers and outlaws who would as soon kill you as give you the time of day. You can't arrest their kind. They'll try to kill you along the way. Do your duty and blow 'em to hell where they belong. Do you understand?"

Mitch, a big, tough boy for his age, had misgivings. He had faced similar orders before, and the thought brought back bitter memories of another time and place, but with a similar order. Here, there was one difference: they were trailing a gang of killers and outlaws, not innocent soldier boys who had surrendered. "Yes, sir, I understand."

Crawling silently to a place of cover behind a bush, he waited a few extra minutes to ensure the other two had time to get into position. He was only a stone's throw from the fire, still glowing red and outlining three sleeping figures. The fourth man must be on the other side of the fire.

He raised himself up and took careful aim at the middle sleeping figure with the double-barrel 10-gauge Greener, which he had never shot before. In his excitement (or, is a better word, anxiety, he thought), he accidentally jerked both triggers. The recoil from the blast of the barrels almost disjointed his shoulder and knocked him back on his butt. The heavy load of buckshot blew the man and his blanket to tatters, scattering bits of him and his gear into the fire. Mitch lay stunned on his backside, still holding the smoking weapon. He was dazed, his ears rang, and he couldn't hear any sound outside his head. For several minutes, he was out of the fight.

The others started firing first one barrel of their scatterguns, then next the second, and finally pistols at point-blank range into the other sleeping outlaws. Mitch saw flashes and the silhouettes of bedrolls jerk around as men tried to get up and go for weapons but were cut down in their attempts. When Mitch picked himself up and staggered to the fire, it was all over, and he could still hear nothing but ringing. He noticed some of his hearing had returned by the next morning as they surveyed the killing ground. It was a disgusting mess in the daylight.

Without much help from Mitch due to his sore arm, they buried the outlaw's remains in a shallow common grave, took inventory, and returned to Austin in triumph with what seemed a parade of the outlaws' horses, weapons, and the stolen strong box strapped atop a saddle with its contents intact.

Mitch was teased good-naturedly and congratulated by handshaking politicians. He was embarrassed as all get out when forced to show the governor the ugly purple bruise still remaining a week later on his shoulder. From then on, he was known as the Shotgun Kid, who had been kicked on his behind by a mule of a gun but, he had hung on to it and killed an outlaw.

"More coffee?" The pretty waitress held a steaming pot of coffee toward his cup.

Thorn had been brought out of his reveries and back to reality. For a moment, he heard the persistent low ringing in his ears. Normally, he could dismiss it, but thinking about his past brought it to mind.

"No thanks, but a mighty good meal, Mrs. ah…"

Her face lit up with a smile as she began to collect and pile the dirty dishes on a tray with a clatter. "It's Sally, Miss Sally, come back and see us again."

"I'll do that, Miss Sally," Thorn thought she was a mighty pretty gal when she smiled. He retrieved his hat from the wall peg, planting it squarely on his head, and left the establishment with over a dozen pairs of eyes scrutinizing him.

Chapter 6
One Life Ends, Begin Another

Thorn's first errand after breakfast was to find the mercantile store on Main Street. No problem. It was just a block up the street. After examining the merchandise, he picked out several pants, shirts, and coats and, in a small back dressing room, made his decision as close to the style and materials he saw in the marriage photo and study of the corpse of the late Thorn T. Hagerman. He settled on two gray cotton shirts, a string tie, braces buttoned to trousers made of black broadcloth, and a black two-button matching coat with long tails made of the same material.

Next, after trying on a half-dozen hats, he chose a black Stetson flat-top hat with a furled brim that favored the one worn by the deceased. Checking the inside band label, he noted that it had come all the way from Philadelphia, Pennsylvania. Surprisingly, he had always thought that Stetsons were made in Texas. Texans or want-to-bees usually wore them. A lot of good things came out of Pennsylvania. He thought he might like to visit there after this business was over.

Looking at himself in the full-length mirror in the back of the store, he decided to wear his new duds and gave the clerk an extra four bits to have his old clothes washed, mended, and returned to his hotel.

His next stop was the cobbler's shop, which he easily found with its boot sign creaking in the breeze. It didn't take long to try on several pairs of low-heeled black stovepipe boots with leather-tooled inlaid patterns before he found the pair that fit him to a T. Say, what was his middle name, he wondered again?

He stuffed his pants legs into the boots and looked at his new image in a full-sized mirror set to show off his boots. For the first time in his life, he thought about his appearance and its effect on other folks. He liked what he saw. He would have to think about what he would do with the rest of his life and his newfound wealth.

His third stop was at the gun-smith where, after introductions and a proper amount of small talk, he questioned the proprietor about the possibility of having the hammer on the shorter Remington reworked and flattened out some and smoothed so it could be used as in fanning pistol. They discussed how, in the old days, some gun hands would have their triggers removed. The gun was fired when it was cocked. Unfortunately, the gun hand had little accuracy and often didn't live to assess the technique.

From one professional to another, they discussed the trigger pull of a Remington single-action pistol, and the force necessary to fan or cock it while the trigger was held down. It could be done, he was told, but the mainspring would have to be replaced, and the hammer reworked. It would cost about ten dollars and take about a week before he could have it back.

When asked if he was in a hurry, Thorn had to stop and admit that he had nothing planned for the next few weeks while waiting for the reward money to pour in, so he gave up his right-handed pistol. He ordered two boxes of Remington .44 ammunition at five cents a round. He was informed that not many people carried them because they were so high. The army had not adopted it for the cavalry. It would take about a week to get a hundred rounds of .44 delivered on the next order by train from Denver. Seems like most things in Durango take a week. He bought plenty of .45 long Colt ammunition at two cents a round.

After picking up some cleaning brushes, rods, gun oil, and a small roll of linen cloth, he asked for his purchases to be delivered to the sheriff's office for safekeeping. He might as well get his name spread around town. Thorn inquired about the directions to the bank.

In a few minutes, he stood at the counter filling out a deposit card for the stack of greenbacks he handed to the clerk for re-counting. He looked around while the sorting and counting took place and noticed the eyes of every customer in the lobby focused on him in open curiosity but with no hostility.

With his brace of holsters hidden under his open coat and his other two weapons hidden out of sight, folks seemed to view him as less sinister and frightening. He smiled, touched his hand to his new hat, and nodded to two ladies at the next teller's station. The younger one smiled and dipped a little curtsy while the older one nodded and appraised him with open interest.

"Good day, ladies," he said, returning to his task. He could get used to being somebody of importance, not just a saddle tramp and a bounty hunter, now that he had a sizable deposit from the cash he had found on Ivory.

When the counting was done and agreed upon, he signed a statement showing two thousand three hundred dollars in deposit, a small fortune. He slid the receipt into his large leather wallet, already crammed with dollar greenbacks, five-dollar silver certificates, beginning to be called fins, and a score of saw-bucks. This would provide enough cash to meet his needs during the next few weeks. He then decided to walk around a bit and get to know the town before he visited with the sheriff. That might be a good place to clean his weapons and learn about the telegrams sent about the rewards for the deceased.

Crossing the street, he walked back down Main Street, passing several saloons, diners, and shops that might be nice to check out later. Winding up at the depot station, he found a comfortable spot on a bench out of the sun and wind and settled in for a good long think.

Most of his life had been filled with actions and reactions. He'd never had much time to map out his life. Sitting there in the filtered sunlight, he pulled his brim over his eyes and closed them. First, he saw a red shimmering dot in a field of wavy green, and then darkness rolled in as his eyes adjusted to the shade. Taking a deep breath, he relaxed and let his mind drift back to the war years, to '63, on that afternoon with his best friend when his life had changed again.

The heavy Missouri air was thick with humidity and the sound of buzzing insects as he and his best friend, Pete Wilson, lay stretched out and drowsy after rough-housing and skinny-dipping in the river's bend. The water ran fast and clear over a sand bar, the perfect spot for two teenage boys to lie side by side on the gravel atop their clothes with fingers laced under their heads, eyes closed as the sun's strong rays dried and warmed their bodies.

"Come on, Karl," the red-headed boy implored. We can meet at the old mill. It's their meeting place of sorts. They said we'd each get a new gray Kepi Hat, a rifle, powder, and shot when we take the oath."

"Look here Pete, I've told you already, our families are on opposite sides of this debate. Why, I'm a Dutchman, as you called my people. My father and mother were both born in the old country of Bavaria, and…" His voice trailed off in sad memory. He really missed his parents, especially his mother.

"But they are both dead." Pete interrupted, "Besides, who took you in and gave you a home after your folks passed on that winter? We did. The Wilson family is who. We are your family now. You are no longer a square-headed Dutchman. You are one of us, and you pretty much speak nearly as good as any Missourian. No one could tell you started out as a Dutchman."

"I'm grateful as all get out. It's just that my family came over from the old country to get away from…lords, kings, and such," muttered Karl.

"From what?" Pete rolled on his side toward Karl and, raising his head, propped an elbow under it for support. He needed to look his friend directly into his eyes. "We ain't got no kings or lords and such here. We're Missourians. My family came from Kentucky after Daniel Boone opened up this area for settlement. This is our home now, and Abolitionists are threatening it and, and…ah…Radical Republicans. Every good and loyal son owes it to his home state to shoulder arms against northern aggression." Pete tried to repeat the recruiter's words he had recently heard at the clandestine meeting where new recruits were being sought for the irregular forces of the Confederate Army.

"Look, Pete, my family didn't believe in slavery, and Missouri is a slave state. Every man has a right to his own life and the fruits of his labor." Karl repeated the words he had often heard his father say at a meeting of the Wide-Awake Society that formed as the war broke out and German men joined the Union cause. But that was before the epidemic swept through the village and laid both his parents low. It took its time killing them that winter. They called it pneumonia.

"But they knowed Missouri was a slave state when they moved here. It's like the fellow who builds his cabin next to his neighbor's pigsty and then complains to the town council about the smell. No, we were here first, and your kin came to our land. We welcomed you, but now you want to change our way of life with foreign ideas and such."

"What foreign ideas and beliefs are you talking about?" Karl snapped.

Pete said, "Why most of you around here are papists, and if that ain't bad enough, there's a parcel of blockheaded Lutherans, and some of those foreign folks in St. Louis don't even believe in our Lord and Savior. They call themselves freethinkers, and such. They are evil to the core, says our pastor. What do you say to that?"

"Sure, my father's family came from a Catholic region of Deutschland. We've been Catholic for hundreds of years even before the fighting ended in that really long war, the Thirty Years War."

Pete whistled saying, "Thirty Years War! My goodness, what took 'em so long?"

Karl said, "The Lutherans from up north in Sweden fought us folks in southern regions. They thought they were better than us. They had a warrior king named Gustavus Adolphus, who had the devil's strength and courage, but he got himself killed in battle. He had no son to take over, only a daughter, Princess Christina, who had been trained in arms and rode horseback to the sounds of cannon fire. But she switched sides, became Catholic, and signed the treaty to end the long war."

"You don't say. Just like that, she changed sides and went against her daddy and his family. My, oh my! I bet there was hell to pay for that," said Pete, "Say, Karl, the Yankees up north think they are better than us and can tell us what to think and how to live, so you think that devil Lincoln could get killed like that king?"

"It's a different setup here." Karl continued. "We have a republic where the president is elected and doesn't lead his army into battle. We have generals for that. If Mr. Lincoln were to die, they'd bring up another politician to replace him, and then war would go on. As for the freethinkers, in this country, I guess every man got a right to believe what he wants, even if he is a damn fool believer, so long as he doesn't hurt anybody else."

"There you have it, Karl. You said what I've been thinking," said Pete triumphantly. "In their land, they can believe any such nonsense they like, but they are coming down here with their army and navy and invading us. Killing us and taking our property. Ain't that what you're talking about?"

Pausing, Pete looked right into his friend's eyes and said, "In Missouri, each man, each white man that is, can decide for himself how to live and to have slaves or not if he can afford 'em. My family don't have any and don't want them. My old man says it makes a white man lazy to have them doing all the hard work." Karl silently absorbed the argument.

"But we have that Yankee Baboon, Mr. Lincoln, with his army and calvary invading our territory…aided by those damned blockheaded Dutchmen. Karl, you and me are nearly brothers, and we should be looking out for each other. We should be joining up before all the fighting is over. It ain't like in the old country where they take thirty years to finish a war; here, we get it done quick. We're practically family, and the way I see it, you owe us."

Karl closed his eyes tightly and experienced the red glow and flashes of starlight under his eyelids, "All right, you've made your point. Let me think it over. Are you joining up tomorrow, no matter what I decide?"

Pete nodded his assent and added, "We Wilsons are of English Scotch stock, my daddy says, and once we make up our mind, there ain't no way to stop us short of planting us six feet under."

Karl murmured, "I'll let you know tomorrow after I sleep on it. Let's get dressed and get back home. We've got some chores to do."

Chapter 7
Gunplay

An unfamiliar rattling and rolling noise interrupted Thorn's thoughts. Raising his head with a jerk, his right hand instinctively palmed the empty leather holster on his right hip. Then he saw a porter in a red railroad cap pushing a squeaking handcart filled with boxes and packages along the platform toward a boxcar on a siding probably destined for Denver.

Thorn watched the porter mop his face with a red bandana and do an old man's shuffling walk back to the depot office. Reaching behind his back, he brought out his trusty Colt .45, checked to ensure the hammer rested on an empty chamber, and slid it into the empty right-hand holster.

It didn't fit exactly right, but it would have to do. He could always go back to his old gun belt, now at the bottom of his saddlebag in the hotel. Its holster had been handcrafted for his Colt Single Action revolver known as the "Peacemaker" because of its effective use in the hands of lawmen. He had once thought of becoming a law dog, but the pay was meager, and the risks no different.

His Colt had served him well over the years, but there was just something special about that brace of Remington .44s he had taken from a notorious gunman. He wondered how many men those pistols had killed. Its centerfire bullets were designed to be the same size as the internal diameter of the barrel, with a little step at the rear to allow the bullet to fit into its case. The rounds were pre-lubricated for better gun maintenance in the field. They were quality weapons firing quality ammunition. There was no sloppiness in their construction, unlike his first pistol, a worn .36 1851 Navy Colt that had been taken off a dead Yankee sergeant killed by Pete and passed on to Carl when he acquired a better brand-new version from a dead Yankee officer, also killed by Pete.

Carl's old weapon had a lot of play in its parts, and the rifling in the barrel was worn smooth. It spits lead out of its barrel and from the side gap where the parts were loose and worn. After pouring a heavy powder charge into a cylinder and using the ram to force the lead ball down below the frame so it wouldn't hang up, Carl would try to brush or blow off the residue of black powder. This often didn't work. So, he'd spread whatever was available, including spit, on the top of the cylinder to keep the weapon from igniting the loose powder around the other cylinders and blowing off a hand and maybe one's head.

Normally, even with a new gun, you get a small amount of lead spitting out the side when a ball was shaved a bit while being blown out of the cylinder into the barrel, but what a sight when you fired the cap and ball gun, fully charged at night. With the cylinder top well lubricated with grease, lard, or butter, it was like the fireworks display on the 4th of July. The grease on the end of the cylinder would also ignite and spew out of the gun, lighting up the night. A night battle was indeed a sight to behold.

Things had sure changed a lot since the days of the old ball and cap pistols. Thorn's thoughts returned to his boyhood when he first changed his identity. He and Pete had left the next evening with blanket rolls slung around their chests, the way they had seen soldiers march by on their way to battle. Thus far, there have been two major battles to control Missouri. The Rebs had won the first, The Battle of Wilson's Creek, in August of 1861, and the Yankees the second, The Battle of Pea Ridge, fought in Northwestern Arkansas in March of 1863. The Yankees were left in control of the state.

The boys made their way quietly out of the house, carefully closing the back door and racing across the yard to the rutted road leading to the rebel's hideout. The moon was bright, almost full, and the sky was dazzling with stars, but the boys were too excited to be away from the farm to bother looking up at the heavens.

Karl was quietly walking behind Pete, thinking about his parents' support for Mr. Lincoln, but Pete was right. He was like a brother to him, and they had taken him in after his folks died. He had made his choice to support his friend and brother. Nothing else mattered.

"Now listen up, Karl. Some of these old boys don't like the Dutch much, understand? They blame 'em for keeping Missouri in the Union even though the Stars and Bars of our glorious battle flag has one star in it for Missouri. So, we are going to change your name. You can no longer spell your name with a 'K'; from now on, you spell it with a 'C,' like other folks."

Karl, now Carl, nodded. It wasn't much of a change. He could live with it.

"As for your last name, I've been thinking, hell, I can't even pronounce it right…"

"It's Himmelberg. It means heaven's hill in German."

"What kind of a name is that? We can't go around calling you Mr. Heaven Hill. It sounds too foreign. No. Not no more. It ain't your name. You got to have a good American name like mine." Pete thought for a minute, then snapped his fingers and said, "That's it. As of now, you are Carl Wilson, my brother."

"But we don't look anything alike Pete. You are redheaded with green eyes. I'm blue-eyed and not a redhead. I have light brown hair."

"Good point. We can't be brothers by blood, but my folks could have adopted you after your folks died. That's almost the truth, ain't it? That's the best kind of lie 'cause you don't have to remember it."

Carl nodded in agreement.

"No more foreign talk. Understand? Not any. We are brothers by adoption. If anyone bothers to ask, let me do the talking. Now, say it ten times. I am Carl Wilson. Say it!" Carl said his new name ten times and began to like the sound of it. He also liked having his best friend as his brother.

"Besides," Pete explained, "The Battle of Wilson's Creek is the same as our family name. It's a good sign, ain't it?"

"Yes, Pete, It's a good omen and a good name. I'll be proud to be your brother."

Their lives were turned upside down that evening at the old mill. After eating cornpone fried in bacon drippings (the older men had gotten there first and feasted on the bacon), they were sworn in with an oath to the Confederacy and their leader William Quantrill.

They were each given a wool butternut forage cap, an old, well-worn 1853 Enfield muzzle-loading rifle, a horn of black powder, a box of caps, and a pouch of lead .577 Minie balls. They spent the rest of the evening learning to clean, load, unload, and reload their weapons again, salute, and tell their right foot from their left foot.

Because of the possibility of someone reporting them to federal authorities who controlled the area, they were not allowed to fire fully loaded guns. Still, their sergeant named Winters did let them fire three or four caps on empty rifles to get the feel of them. They were told that they would be capturing their sidearms in battle. Most of the old timers carried two pistols on them and another two on their mounts into battle. It would mean more, they were told, if they took the pistol, powder flask, and belt with pouches for caps and balls off a dead Yankee they had personally killed rather than if they were just given to them.

During the next few weeks, they learned the night signals, mainly bird calls, necessary in stealing horses and supplies for Quantrill's Raiders, who were turning Missouri and Kansas into a wasteland.

The recruits learned to ride with the reins in their teeth and a loaded Colt pistol in each hand. They practiced charging hell-bent on leather, pretending to pour a terrific amount of lead into the enemy. When camping in an isolated area, they practiced firing six pistol rounds at a target, first on foot, then on horseback, first walking, trotting, then at a fast lope, and finally at an all-out gallop at breakneck speed. They would then bring their mount to a stop and reload their pistols with fresh cylinders without dropping the little locking pin or the cylinder. That was a real trick.

When you dropped anything, and most of the recruits often did, they had to dismount and get down on their hands and knees to find the lost item, with no exceptions. It was easy to find a cylinder, but that little locking pen was a bear to find, and several were permanently lost, rendering the weapon useless. When you dropped anything, you were the butt of jokes and horseplay until someone else made a dumber mistake. It took weeks of practice before the recruits could change out cylinders without a mishap at a lope.

They were becoming a formidable fighting force with men carrying four pistols, and a shotgun or a rifle. Thus far, the recruits had not engaged the enemy, but soon, they would be going out on dangerous missions and raids.

They gathered with others one spring evening west of Jeff City on the bluffs above the Missouri River. Jeff City was what the locals called Jefferson City, Missouri's state and Confederate capitol before the Union army composed of Dutchmen and Yankees from across the river in Illinois, home of that Ape Lincoln, and Iowa had defeated the Confederates at the Battle of Pea Ridge. Groups of recruits now had to travel at night and hide from Union patrols. Men arrived in small groups and pairs to serve under the famous guerilla leader William Quantrill.

Once settled into the camp, there wasn't much to do until the big man arrived. Several of the boys and younger men practiced quick drawing and spinning revolvers and discussed the best methods to carry and draw. The older men got into it with quickdraws and shooting contests, and aided by a jug of John Barleycorn, everyone had a good-o' time until one old buckskin-clad recruit, who was a bit in his cups, tried to show off in front of the young recruits. Folks watching roared with laughter and made rude comments when he fumbled his draw, tried to catch it in the air, and dropped his pistol.

It hit the ground hard and discharged with a thundering roar and a cloud of smoke. The laughter stopped when a new young recruit, no older than Carl, screamed. The lead ball hit the boy square in his stomach, ripping his guts apart. He flopped to the ground and curled into a ball, screaming and crying out his mother's name.

There was nothing to do for the rest of the evening but listen to him die and complain about how old men shouldn't be allowed to have strong drinks and play with guns. The old doc tried to give the boy some whiskey, but it just made the boy sicker, and he screamed even louder. It was a miserable evening for most of the recruits.

When the sergeant was asked why they didn't put the lad out of his misery, he replied that they had better get used to the screams of the dying.

The boy's death didn't seem to interest one young recruit named Jessie, who was particularly skilled and deadly accurate with a pistol. He and his older brother, Frank, had a personal hatred for the federal officers and yearned for revenge. Frank just watched his young brother practice his quickdraws and show off in front of a group of admirers. Frank sipped his coffee and discussed plans and plights with the sergeant and some of the older raiders he knew from the Bloody Kansas days. Following Jessie's example, Carl and Pete cut off the flaps of their holsters, and from that day forward, they kept the pistol's hammer over an empty chamber.

Carl and Pete practiced drawing and shooting at bottles and targets, but if truth be told, Pete's shots were more accurate, and his draws were faster. But Carl had mastered the skill of hitting an object thrown in the air. He could follow the object's upward curve and fire at that split second before it began its downward descent. He wasn't able to explain it. He just did it.

Later that night, William Quantrill and two dozen hard cases rode into camp and retired to their tents. Much later that night, Pete was awakened and told to go to the big man's tent for a meeting. It was an honor not bestowed on Carl.

The next morning, they buried the recruit after a reading from the Good Book by William Quantrill, resplendent in his gray officer's uniform. Carl never even knew the boy's name. He had just arrived in camp a few minutes before being shot. It was an unfortunate accident, and as far as Carl knew, nothing happened to the old coot who was responsible for the shooting.

The next morning, camp broke up into parties. Most of the men road west with Quantrill on a big raid into Kansas at a place called Lawrence. There would be plenty of booty and spoils of war to be had there. Those men were excited because it had been a Union stronghold in the bloody days before the war, and John Brown, the hated abolitionist, had operated in the area with his sons. He had been hung before the outbreak of the war for his attack on an arsenal at Harper's Ferry, Virginia. Other groups were given different orders, and they rode separate ways.

Carl and Pete were assigned under Sergeant Winters and two other boys, Brent and Jenkins, to head back east on a raid along the great bend in the Missouri River to steal cattle, horses, and supplies. There were a lot of fat old Dutchmen and their wives and children living on little isolated farms and small villages while the men folks were fighting back east for the Union cause. It should be easy picking.

Chapter 8
Drink Your Coffee Black

Within three days of leaving the encampment, Carl and Pete found themselves lying in the early morning dew on a slight tree-lined ridge above a fertile valley with golden fields ready for harvesting, fenced-in gardens overflowing with bounty, barns, and outbuildings with cattle, and a white two-story farmhouse with gray smoke streaming from its kitchen chimney. Sergeant Winters hunkered down, came to the top of the rise, and peeped over, "What you boys see? Any cattle?"

"Yes, Sir." Pete turned so his whispered voice would reach the sergeant's ears. We see four or five cows in the fenced-in area behind the barn. I haven't seen anybody coming or going from the house, the barn, or the privy. Wait, here comes someone now, a woman, old by her looks, going to what looks like the hen house for eggs. I guess she is getting ready to fix up a big breakfast."

"A big home-cooked breakfast sounds good about now. Any men folk or soldiers?"

"Not so far as we have seen," answered Pete, who had taken up the field glasses.

"Keep looking, and don't do anything until I get back. You both stay put right here. We're going to scout out the next valley, and we'll be back in an hour or so. Just stay put and keep your eyes open."

"Yes sir," they both whispered.

The sergeant turned, still bending low, and slowly worked his way down the ridge to the horses and the two other men. Straightening up, he said, "They'll wait here and keep an eye on things while we have a look-see at the next valley over yonder. I know there's a Yankee horse company somewhere around here. You can't hide a hundred or so men in these hills without somebody finding out."

The three men mounted and slowly walked their horses down a game trail toward the next valley. Climbing an incline, still covered in a wooded area, they saw from the tree line the smoke and dull glow from dozens of campfires. They had stumbled onto a large union camp. Scores of horses were picketed on two long lines, with rifles stacked in front of tents, all neatly lined up in the early morning mist. A supply wagon and an ambulance were parked further on, with more tents and picket lines in the misty distance.

"If only I had a dozen good men, we could take that entire company. They ain't had reveille yet. Must not be 6:00 a.m. We got to hurry before it gets light."

Some fifty yards away, they saw two figures in Yankee capes hunched near a smoldering fire, trying to keep warm and heat their morning coffee. The men were pickets and should have been spread apart, not brewing coffee. The smoke from the early morning fire mingled with the mist, causing poor visibility on their part.

The sergeant dismounted, brought out his field glasses, and studied the two Union soldiers and the lay of the land. "Jenkins, take the horses back about a hundred yards, nice and easy, and you stay with 'em and keep 'em quiet. Brent, come with me. You still got that cowbell you found the other day and was fixing to give to your maw on the farm?"

"Yes Sarge, I got it in my bundle on my mount."

"Get it, don't make any noise, and come with me." The two men slowly moved to the forest's edge bordering a freshly mowed field and knelt.

"Now Brent," he whispered, "get behind the bole of that oak tree over there," he pointed with his pistol, "and when I give you the signal, rattle that cowbell just like Ol' Betsie was moving her head chewing cud."

Brent nodded his understanding and gave his rifle to the sergeant. Then he quietly crossed the ground and, removing his pistol from its holster, listened for the signal.

A Morning Dove quietly cooed to its mate, followed by the distinctive dull sound of a cowbell floating across the field.

"Did you hear that?" Both Union soldiers looked up across the field to the woods. "Come on, let us get Milch for our Kaffee." The boys still had their thick German accents.

Leaving their rifles by the fire, they each picked up a tin cup and approached the huge oak tree behind which they heard the cowbell. "She must be behind that tree," said one of the boys as he ducked beneath a lower branch and came around the massive trunk, fully expecting to see a cow.

What the boy saw caused his eyes to pop open in surprise, and he dropped his cup. Instead of a cow, he saw a man wearing an enemy butternut field cap holding out a cowbell in one hand and a cocked pistol aimed at his heart in the other. He had a big grin on his face. He rang the bell again and let it fall to his chest. A cord around his neck secured it. He then placed his index finger to his lips in the universal sign for silence and motioned his hands up with his pistol. The young soldier at once complied with hands held high.

Within seconds, there was a trashing of weeds and grunts as the second Union soldier came around the tree with his arms high, followed by the sergeant holding Brent's rifle.

"It's true what they say about Dutch farm boys being blockheads," The sergeant's comment gave both Confederates a chuckle at the Union soldier's plight.

"Brent," the sergeant ordered, "go get Jenkins and get over there, put out their fire, get their packs and rifles, and don't forget their coffee." He again laughed, "You boys should learn to drink your coffee black."

The two Union soldiers were gagged with their bandanas and ordered to put on their packs and sling their un-capped rifles over a shoulder with their barrels down before having their hands securely tied in front of them. Short ropes were then tied to the saddle horns of Jenkin's and Brent's mounts with ends tied to the bound hands of the two humiliated men and led back to where Pete and Carl watched the early morning activities of the farm.

"Well, looky here at what the cat dragged in." Pete rolled over, slid a few yards down the slope, and stood to get a good look at the prisoners.

"How many men over there at the farm," the sergeant inquired. In the meantime, Carl scuttled down the slope before standing. "No men folk about, except for one old man I saw walk out to the privy with the help of a cane. Two women, one old and another younger, and two little children are all we've seen about."

"All right, first things first. Brent, one at a time, free 'em up and get 'em out of those uniforms."

"Come on," Brent ordered. "You heard the sergeant. Get them duds off and pronto."

Soon, the two Union boys sat with gags pulled down and their hands and ankles securely bound, dressed only in their red long-handled underwear, barefooted and depressed. One boy was sniffling, unable to wipe his nose. He began to whimper and sob. The other boy began to pray in German, a prayer Carl knew well, the "Our Father."

"Vater unser, der du bist in Himmel…" he earnestly prayed.

Brent and Jenkins were judged by the sergeant to be about the right size and quickly dressed in blue uniforms. They marched up to the farmhouse door, pounded, and demanded admittance. Within half an hour, they were back with three heifers tethered to a rope and a gunnysack filled with bacon, flour, and coffee.

"Right," the sergeant smiled, "change out of them uniforms and pack 'em up tight. Bill wants 'em for something special. Unfortunately, Bill said these boys can't be turned loose and spoil his party." The sergeant unsnapped the flap on his holster, removed his pistol, and spun the cylinder to examine the firing caps fitted to the nipples. It spun freely with no hang-ups.

"No wait," Carl said as he stepped in front of the prisoners, "You can't kill them. They are prisoners of war. They surrendered and are unarmed. We can take them back with us and exchange them for two of our boys."

"Those are the orders, Carl. You took an oath to The Cause. I always knowed you was a crybaby. Move aside, or you'll get the same. Those are the orders right from Colonel Bill Quantrill himself." But Carl stood his ground, facing the sergeant. He folded his arms across his chest.

"Damn it to hell and horseshit," the sergeant said in exasperation and lowered his pistol away from the two men. "All right, Carl, you win." Carl breathed a sigh of relief, dropped his arms, and stepped forward when suddenly the sergeant sidestepped him while swinging his pistol and taking aim. He fired two quick shots dead center into their chests. They died with disbelief and confused looks on their faces, as the black holes in their long john's uppers issued streams of blood. Both boys' heads drooped, but not before the praying soldier said a final "Amen."

"What's done is done," the sergeant roared. The French have a word for it, called fait accompli. It's over. There is nothing to do but accept it. There is nothing to do now but get rid of those corpses. We got to get moving before it gets light." The sergeant holstered his sidearm but didn't snap the flap closed and turned his back to Carl as he examined the cinch on his mount's saddle.

"No, it's not over," said Carl. "You murdered those two boys. That ain't right."

The sergeant spun toward Carl with his pistol grip already in hand and was clearing leather when a shot rang out from Pete's gun, punching a hole dead center in the sergeant's chest. The sergeant had a puzzled expression as he staggered a step or two as his fingers lost their grip. His pistol slipped from his hand and fell back into his holster. The sergeant's lips, unable to speak, formed the word "Why?" He then pitched face forward before Carl's feet.

Carl stood looking down at the figure before him. His right hand had not even gone for his gun.

"Why?" Pete repeated and answered, "You're more of a blockhead than them Dutchmen because he's my brother, that's why." Turning to face Brent and Jenkins, who were awkwardly standing half out of the Yankee uniforms, Pete spun his pistol and neatly dropped it back in his holster, and facing the men, he asked, "Do we have a problem here boys?"

"I got no problem, Pete," said Brent.

"Me either," said Jenkins.

"Right, now get out of them uniforms before you get 'em dirty. Tote all three way back in the brush and pile a lot of limbs and such on 'em. It's a damn shame about the sergeant getting himself killed in a shoot-out with them two Yankee boys. The good news for his family and The Cause is he got 'em both before he died…a real hero."

After a moment of silence, he said, "Carl we need to talk." They walked together out of earshot of Brent and Jenkins, who were already busy hauling the corpses deep into the brush and bramble.

"Carl, you best be on your way, seeing how you feel about this."

"Why did you shoot the sarge?"

"That's the same dumb question the sergeant asked. I told him we were brothers and bound to look out for each other. Oh, I know how you felt about those two boys, being Dutchmen and all. The sergeant would gun you down and tell me it was that fait accomplish a thing. That's bullshit. I heard the orders from Colonel Quantrill in the tent when we were introduced. He needed them uniforms. What was that word he used? He called it a ruse of war, a trick of sorts. Military deception, he called 'em. He also used that fait term, saying that you do the dirty deed, and folks have no choice but to accept it. Quantrill is sure one smart soldier. He knows all about the French wars. You see, the sergeant was following orders, but he didn't have to do the deed in front of you. He could have waited behind or ordered me to. You didn't need to be involved."

"You would have done that…killed those boys?"

"Carl, this is war. It's not a game, even though we sometimes make it out to be. People, good people, innocent people get killed every day, hell, every hour and minute of the day. Remember that kid who got gut shot the last night in camp? He didn't deserve to die like that before he had ever been in a fight. It was just his fate, his turn. Yes, I believe in The Cause. I follow orders, but I know you can't or won't follow some orders. I can't have you ride with us."

Carl took a deep breath and turned away from Pete. He leaned against a tree, head in hand. Pete stepped up behind him, grabbed his shoulder, and spun him around.

"Snap out of it. Where are you off to? You know you can't ride with us!"

"Not sure, but away from the killing. Maybe the southwest."

"As long as I never see you again in Missouri, go where you please. Carl, you are going to have to change names again. They got your name on the rolls as Carl Wilson, my brother. As far as we are concerned, Carl Wilson died today defending our gallant sergeant in a gun battle against some Yankees. He was buried out here in the brush with their bodies never to be found. That's how the report will read when I turn it in. By and by, I'll let Ma and Paw and little sis know that you died in a gun battle out here. You also died a hero. Is there anyone else back home you want me to tell?"

"No. No one else."

"I don't want you popping back up out of the grave. It could prove embarrassing, to say the least. Understand?"

"Yes Pete, I understand. By the way, I won't be needing this butternut cap anymore. It's yours, seeing how you lost yours a while back, and as long as you are still fighting in this War of Northern Aggression, you'll need a cap." Carl took off his forage cap and handed it to Pete, who, in turn, removed the black floppy-brimmed hat that he had picked up along the way, placed it on Carl's head, and snugged it down.

Studying the Confederate markings on the top of the forage cap, Pete said, "I'll keep and honor this Kepi forever, and every time I see it, I'll think of you, my dead brother." He then swept back his long red hair and firmly placed it on his head.

"Take care, brother."

"You too."

The man formerly known as Carl Wilson pondered how his life had been turned inside out. He mounted and turned south toward the Arkansas-Texas line and parts unknown.

Chapter 9
Telegrams

A distant train whistle jolted Thorn out of his reveries. Looking down at the track, he saw the Denver and Rio Grande Western Railroad's huge steam engine rumble and clank as it hissed on its arrival. Folks began to drift out of the waiting room onto the platform.

Some had come to welcome arriving passengers, while others were outbound. Durango was a transfer point from Denver, Colorado, to Santa Fe, New Mexico. Prospectors and miners transferred at Durango to a narrow-gauge line that ran through the high wild mountain wilderness and the rich mining region of the San Juan peaks, a range of the Rocky Mountains, to the secluded town of Silverton. They could have just as easily named it Goldton because both riches were pulled from the range.

Thorn stood up and stretched his legs. He ambled over to lean against the wall in an out-of-the-way spot to watch the train pull in.

There was something fascinating about watching the giant locomotives that pulled the ore cars up and down the mountains to the smelters in Denver. From his first sight of a train years ago in the war, he loved them and detested anyone who damaged them or held up their passengers or mail cars.

America was becoming a very rich nation. No wonder folks were calling this its Gilded Age. Soon, he would be an important man with a place in society, a position, and a name. Could he pull this new identity off? He had read and reread all of the late Thorn T. Hagerman's letters and telegrams for clues about his identity and personal facts. He was beginning to feel that he really was Thorn. But the thought kept coming back: what did that middle initial stand for?

The train pulled in with screeching brakes and billowing clouds of steam. Thorn believed in sleeping light, with one eye open as the saying goes, and while awake, always kept his head and eyes constantly moving about, looking for unusual happenings or threats.

From habit, he scanned the area and the crowd waiting for the train's arrival. His peripheral vision noticed the figure of a man he recognized. Directing his attention, he saw Billy, the deputy sheriff, emerge from the telegraph office with a bundle of yellow Western Union telegrams bound with string in his left hand. Billy quickly made his way across the platform and disappeared back in the direction of the sheriff's office and jail. Strange, he hadn't bothered to glad-hand or speak with anyone during his exit. What would be so important to cause him to break his habits?

The only thing Thorn could think of was that Billy had collected the telegrams about the rewards for Ivory Thompson and his partners. That interested him, so he began walking in the same direction.

Soon, Thorn stood on the plank sidewalk and rapped on the sheriff's door before entering. He interrupted Billy, standing looking over the sheriff's shoulder, saying something about a telegram open on the desk.

"Hello, Sheriff. Deputy. Thought I'd stop by and see if you had any luck about the rewards."

"It's good of you to stop by. Yes, we have some preliminary inquiries from banks, railroads, stage lines, all victims of the deceased, all wanting pictures of the deceased and proof as to their identities, sworn to under oath at a court inquest. We're working on those things right away. We should have the pictures this afternoon and have found a few who knew them by sight. So far, there is nothing from the capital except an acknowledgment of receipt of my telegram. These things take time."

"Oh, that's no problem, Sheriff. I like this town and am considering settling in the area when all is said and done. I've been on this bunch's trail for months, and I'm whipped. At the least, I'm going to take a nice long rest."

He chuckled and said, "You deserve it, Thorn. It's a tough job you did. Taking on three desperadoes and bringing them all back dead is amazing. I've ridden on many a posse and scouted for the army for a few years. That was after I was a Deputy Marshal in a Kansas cow town. I had my share of thrills and saw the elephant in the war. You may have been a little young for that unpleasantness. Did you serve in the late war?"

Thorn almost answered honestly from his memory but checked himself and thought of how the late Thorn T. Hagerman would answer. "Yes, I volunteered in the 24th Michigan regiment, part of the famous Iron Brigade. I was mustered out after I caught a rebel ball at the battle of… but it doesn't matter." Thorn's mind raced, trying to remember which battle had been Thorn's last. He had come across it in his honorable discharge paper, but damn if he could remember the specific battle. Rather than give a wrong answer that could be found out, he said, "That was a long time ago, and the memories are not that pleasant. I'd as soon forget that part of my life."

Billy looked at Thorn with open skepticism. In his opinion, a man should be proud to talk about his war exploits. Hell, if he had any, he surely would be.

The sheriff nodded, glancing at a long telegram in front of him. "By the way, what did they nickname you boys…of the Iron Brigade?"

"Why, we were known by friend and foe alike by our black hats that had the Maltese Cross as our regiment's design. Yep, we were the Black Hat Brigade, a part of the Iron Brigade. Our boys reinforced the Iron Brigade after the battle of Antietam in the early fall of sixty-two. We fought the Rebs in every major battle in the eastern theater of war and, got shot to pieces in more than one battle. What about you, sheriff? Where did you serve?"

"Yeah, I served, but like you said, that was long ago. Why bring up unpleasant memories? But I need to get some information about you that is requested in this here telegram from the Pinkerton Agency and the Federal Marshal's Service."

"Sure, go ahead," Thorn edged closer, trying to get a look at the telegrams in question.

The sheriff took out his pencil and, after sharpening a new point on it, set up his papers so he could read the questions and take the answers. "First, full name and birthday?"

Horse hockey, Thorn thought. Not only did he not know his middle name, he couldn't remember his birthday. "My name is Thorn T. Hagerman… and…ah…"

There was a sudden pounding on the office door as it was swung in with force by a frantic man in worn, dirty overalls with a felt cap pulled down low over his head. He had to stop to catch his breath and inhaled several deep lungs full of air before continuing, "Sheriff Pat Williams? Which 'ne of you is he?"

"I'm Sheriff Williams, and who might you be?"

"I'm Holly Beams, my wife Madge and I are neighbors to Mike and Sissy Todd. They are in the last cabin up the draw. Sheriff, Mike Todd was murdered, and Sissy, his pretty little wife, violated and beaten pretty badly. Come quick!"

"First, sit down here, Mr. Beams. Take your time and tell me what happened. Billy, get him a cup of coffee." The sheriff motioned for him to take a seat. The telegrams were forgotten for the time being.

After gulping the hot brew, he continued, "We come from Ohio and bought the claim and moved into old man Baker's cabin in June. I don't get into town much, so we never met. My missus and Mike's wife became pretty good friends during the past few months. My wife, Madge is her name, told me after breakfast this morning that she was going over to Todd's place to borrow a cup of sugar and have a chat. About half an hour later, she came running back home. I hadn't gone off to the sluice yet, and she told me that someone had murdered Mike Todd, tore up their cabin, and done had his way with his wife. Beat her up pretty bad. Madge found Mike's body outside the cabin door, and his wife was on the bed. Her private clothes had been torn off her, and she was, well, you know, violated."

"Is she alive?"

"Yes, at least she was when Madge left her to come and get me. I came straight here to get help. She went back with a rifle so she could be of help when she comes to."

"What time did this happen?"

"Sheriff, it just took place just this morning. I don't have no watch, but not long ago."

"You did real good Mr. Beams." Turning to his deputy, he ordered, "Billy, go get doc and a buckboard and get up to Mike's cabin, the one after old man Baker's place. You know it?"

"Sure do. I've been up there half a dozen times hunting and fooling around panning for gold."

"All right, get on it, and Billy, keep your eyes open. We got a murdering rapist in these hills." Billy nodded.

"Mr. Beams, catch your breath, finish your coffee, and then return to your cabin with Billy and the doc. He'll drop you off at your place, so wait for me there. I'll see you after I've checked out the Todd place. We'll drop your wife back at your place on our return trip with… our return to town. I'm heading to saddle my horse and then going straight up to Mike's place. I'll see you on my way back to town."

"Can I go and do some work, or do I have to stay at the cabin?"

"Sure, you can work as long as you are nearby, within hailing distance, but be careful and keep your eyes open. I'll get your statement later. You know, on second thought, it might be better if you and your wife held up at your cabin till I get there. You got an extra gun?" Mr. Beams nodded in the affirmative.

The sheriff turned to close his roll-top desk with the telegrams inside when Thorn touched his shoulder and said, "Do you want me to take those questions with me and fill 'em out for you?"

The sheriff hesitated and handed the top telegram to Thorn, who carefully folded the paper and placed it in his wallet.

"Yeah, that'll save me some time. I'm obliged," said the sheriff. "By the way, I also served in the Union Army, and we may have fought alongside each other in some of the same battles, but we'll talk about that later."

"I'm happy to help out Pat. Can I call you Pat?"

"Sure thing, Mr. Hagerman."

"Just call me Thorn. It's to my advantage, too. Maybe I can speed up the process a bit. By the way, could you use some company on your outing? I have nothing planned today except to clean and oil my guns, and I can do that anytime. I bought some cleaning materials and ammunition and asked them to deliver them here. Is that okay?"

"Sure, and I would be obliged for the company. Now, let's get our horses saddled."

"Smitty," the sheriff called out to the prisoner reclining on his bunk as he took two Winchesters from the gun rack and pocketed a handful of cartridges. "The cell door is open. Clean this place good and tell Teddy to get on up to Mike's cabin when he returns from delivering that summons for the magistrate. Let him know what's going on, but don't talk to nobody else, and warn Teddy to keep his mouth shut about what you heard!"

"Sure thing, boss." Smitty swung his legs off the bunk, opened the cell door to look for his mop and bucket, and muttered about how a prisoner's work was never done.

"Also, accept Mr. Hagerman's gun supplies being sent over and put 'em up so they don't get mixed up with our supplies."

"Yes boss, got it."

The sheriff and Thorn walked quickly to the stables. The sheriff went to the stall holding his Mustang mare, and Thorn opened the stall door to his Morgan. Both animals snorted and snuffed their riders in anticipation. The men hurriedly fitted the harnesses and placed the bits in their horses' mouths. They then threw saddle blankets and saddles over their horse's backs, tightened cinches, and checked tack. After loading the Winchesters, they slid the rifles into the saddle boots. In a few minutes, they headed out of the stable doors at a trot up the trail into the miner's region.

"Funny thing," said Sheriff Williams. "I just about ran into Mike Todd last night. He was flying out of the saloon and almost ran into me. Said he was hurrying on home to his supper. He said he had cashed in some gold placer, paid his account at a store, and bought some items for his wife. He also said he had a drink or two at the saloon and was hurrying home on his mule. It must have happened after that. He was a nice man and didn't even carry a gun."

Thorn wondered what kind of fool would cash in gold, where everyone knows everybody else's business—it seems everybody knows about something before it happens. Have drinks at a public saloon, then ride home to his young wife, and not even carry a gun—what was he thinking?

They rode along the rutted trail shaded in coolness, with the sheriff in the lead, followed closely by Thorn. Both were alert and silent. Their horses' iron shoes thudded on the rocky ground and occasionally slipped in the loose gravel. Thorn noticed that a time or two, the sheriff's horse sent a spark flying off some flinty stone. Thorn wondered if a horse's iron shoes had ever caused a forest fire.

Chapter 10
Depredation

Teddy met up with Sheriff Williams at the turnoff to the Beams' cabin and was sent over to stay with Holly. Ten minutes later, while still some distance from Mike's cabin, Sheriff Williams and Thorn pulled up and carefully looked around. All was reasonably quiet, with the normal background noises of birds, the wind rustling through the aspen trees, small animals scampering, and such. Thorn nodded his okay, and the sheriff rose up from the saddle and shouted, "Hello cabin! This is Sheriff Williams. Hello, cabin!" The body of a man lay face down, spread-eagle a yard or so from the cabin door, which was closed.

The sheriff's horse gave a nervous whicker, unsure of a place with the smell of blood. Thorn's Morgan mare softly breathed a whinny and gave a quiet neigh for good measure. "Good girl," Thorn said as he looked around, leaned forward to smooth the fur on his horse's wither, and patted her.

A second later, the cabin door opened, and a rifle barrel poked out. "Sheriff! Is that you?"

"Yes. Are you Mrs. Beams?" No response from the cabin. "I spoke to your husband, Holly. Told him to go back to his cabin and wait for our return. I've sent for a doctor and a wagon, and they should be here soon. But first, put down your rifle. We're coming in, and I need to speak with you and check on Mrs. Todd."

"All right, sheriff, come on in."

The cabin door suddenly closed, increasing the sheriff's apprehension of a woman in a cabin with a rifle probably pointed at the door he had to enter. He should have asked Holly if his wife was the nervous type.

"Thorn, you wait out here. I'll wave if all is on the up and up." Thorn nodded in agreement and continued looking around.

The sheriff rode to the front, stopped for a few seconds observing Mike's body, swung his leg over the horse's rump, and slid his foot out of the left stirrup coming down, careful to keep his mount between him and the cabin door.

After patting his horse's withers to calm it down, he wrapped the reins around a porch post and said, "I'm coming in. Don't shoot! Mrs. Beams, aim that rifle at the floor, will you please." Carefully staying to the left of the door, keeping the heavy frame between him and the woman inside holding a rifle, he slowly pushed the door open and called out, "Mrs. Beams, is that you there? Is everything all right for me to enter?"

"Yes, but how do I know you are the sheriff?"

"Fair enough. Since we've never met, how about I toss my badge in for you to see?"

"Do it," she said. Sheriff unpinned the tin star and tossed it in. It made a faint metallic ring as it hit the floor and bounced.

After a moment, she said, "Good enough. Come on in sheriff."

The sheriff motioned for Thorn to come forward and called for him to check out the rear yard, which held a pig pen and a chicken coop, and look around the yard. Then, with his hands up, free of weapons, he entered framing himself in the doorway. If she wanted to kill him, this would be the perfect place to do it, but at some point, you have to trust your instinct and take a chance.

He found Mrs. Todd just beginning to stir in the bunk. She was disheveled and had several bruises showing on a bare shoulder where the quilt had slipped down.

The sheriff turned to the woman calmly sitting in a rocking chair with the rifle across her lap with the barrel pointed toward the floor. He asked, "So, you must be Mrs. Beams. What time did you arrive here this morning?"

"At about the second hour, it was light enough to read by."

"All right, did you see anybody hanging around?"

"Can't swear to it sheriff," she answered as she handed him back his badge. "But I think I heard men's voices laughing and cursing way up the trail. Laughing and talking about how one of them was leaving a string of little bastards all across the country. After that, I only heard some distant swearing about not having found any gold, and then they were out of earshot."

"Thank you, Mrs. Beams. You are a very brave woman to come in here with a dead neighbor at the doorstep and help her," he nodded toward the bunk, "and then to come back again and render aid."

"It's my Christian duty sheriff." She then quietly asked the sheriff to wait outside while she finished bathing Mrs. Todd's private parts and got her into a decent dress that wasn't all ripped apart. The sheriff understood and was a bit embarrassed to be in the cabin under these circumstances.

Where were Billy and the doc, he wondered. He went outside to consult with Thorn.

Thorn said, "There were two of them and a pack animal that looks like a mule from the shoe size." Next, he motioned to some horse apples and a fresh set of tracks leading north along the trail.

"I know Mike rode a long-eared, cantankerous mule, and I don't see it about." The sheriff surveyed the yard and the outbuildings. "That agrees with what Mrs. Beams had to say. She heard two of 'em laughing and talking about one of 'em leaving a 'string of little bastards across the country and how it was too bad about his not finding any gold. We should be able to question Mrs. Todd shortly. Let's look at the body."

Thorn dismounted and tied the reins around a limb near some grass. Both men approached the body. It didn't take much examination to see that he had been shot in the back. They didn't need to roll him over to know he was dead. The deceased wore work pants with suspenders over his union suit. He was wearing one of his moccasins. The other was lying in the dust where he had pivoted as he tried to return to the cabin. Thorn speculated aloud that the deceased had probably arrived home, removed his work boots, which sat on the edge of the porch, taken off his work shirt, and entered the cabin. Something or someone caused him to come back outside, then he turned back, and ran toward his door before being gunned down.

"How do you figure that?"

"Look at his steps. He turned there," Thorn pointed to the scuff marks in the loose soil near where his moccasin lay. "He was moving and running fast for the door when he was shot. See the length of his steps and see when he was shot. He skidded in the dirt. That was his motion and weight propelling him forward on the ground. He was shot in the back, could have been a .45, and came to rest here."

The sheriff studied the body from several angles and nodded in agreement. Mrs. Beams stepped to the door and called the sheriff, "You can come in now."

"She's sitting up and can talk to you. I've put some coffee on. Would you want some?" She turned to the man standing behind the sheriff in the doorway and asked, "Is this your deputy?"

"No, Mrs. Beams. Let me introduce you to Mr. Thorn Hagerman. He's a lawman of sorts, a Pinkerton agent, sent out here to help clean up a nest of hornets."

"It's nice to meet you, sir." She gave a quick curtsy, turned to the coffee pot on the stove, and got the cups.

Turning to the woman sitting on the edge of the bunk, the sheriff said, "Mrs. Todd, I know this is a bad time, but I've got to ask you to help me catch the men who did this to Mr. Todd and…and to you. Can you answer a few questions?"

"I think so, Pat. I'll do my best, and please call me Sissy. That's what everybody calls me. I heard you say that this man is a Pinkerton. Is he going to help bring those killers to justice?" For several seconds, no one answered.

Thorn said, "I'll offer my services to the sheriff if he can use me."

The sheriff gravely nodded and said, "Now tell us what happened."

"Mike was late as always when he went to town and had a drink or two. He is a very sociable person. So, when he rode in late for dinner, I started to give him what for, but he handed me a pound of coffee and a pretty ribbon for my hair. You can't stay mad at him for long." She paused, took a deep breath, and gazed at nothing for a few moments. Both men waited impatiently for her to get to the killing of her husband and the assault.

"We had just sat down to supper, had chicken and dumplings, Mike's favorite, when we heard someone call from outside, real polite like. We went to the door, and I saw two strangers standing in the evening shadows beside their horses. The bigger one said they were lost and asked their way into town. Mike went out to see if he could help. I stayed inside and waited. I heard some words but couldn't make out what they were saying. Then I heard Mike call out my name, and he came running back to the cabin yelling for me to get ready to bar the door. Then there was a gunshot, and Mike screamed and fell right in front of me. I just stood there in disbelief. Then I tried to get the door closed, but it was too late. I couldn't get the bar on it in time. It swung in hard, knocking me back, and they were inside and on me in a flash."

"Can you describe them, Sissy?" The sheriff took out his pencil and pad and started to jot down some rough notes. He hated doing reports and was glad Thorn was here to verify the facts.

"One was tall and big, over six feet. A strong-looking man, rough, but could have been good-looking, except for a scar on his cheek." Remembering for a second, she touched her right cheek and said, "The lantern was on, the scar was on his left side as he faced me. The other was a little peep squeak of a man with a rat's face," she shuddered at his memory. "He was about six or seven inches shorter, and thinner, with drooping shoulders. The little one started to do things to me. He grabbed my breasts and twisted, hurting me, and he grabbed me in my private place. He tried to kiss me when the bigger one pulled him off and shoved him aside."

"What happened next?"

"I started to scream and cry, and the little man came back to me and told me to hush up, or he would give me what for. Then he began to laugh. The big one told him he could look and play with me, but not to touch my privates again or hit me."

Mrs. Beams handed out cups of hot black coffee. When she gave Sissy her coffee, she patted Sissy's hand and said, "You're doing good. You have to be strong." This gave Sissy a chance to collect herself and continue.

"The big man was busy tearing up the place looking for gold. He said he knew my husband had a poke of gold hidden here, and he wanted to know where it was. I screamed that Mike had taken the little bit he had panned the past few months into town to cash it in and pay our bill at the store. The big man began to slap and punch me, saying that I was lying and that I had better tell him the truth. The little runt jumped around like a monkey, slamming his fist in his other hand and laughing like a madman." She stopped, wiped a tear from her face, and continued.

"The big man began tearing at my clothes, and I think I fainted or passed out, for the next thing I remember, he was atop of me grunting and, you know sheriff, he was forcing himself in me. He finished and got off me and, he had, well, I'd rather not say anymore, but he hurt me, and I was bleeding down there. I closed my eyes again, and I guess I passed out for the next thing I knew Mrs. Beams, there, was gently washing my face and…and helping me."

At that moment, a jangling wagon was heard coming up the trail. The sheriff thanked Sissy for her narrative and told her that the doctor had arrived.

She buried her face in the quilt and cried. The sheriff went out to talk to Billy and the doc.

Sissy stopped crying and stood up awkwardly, supporting herself with a bedpost, and asked Thorn, "Are you going after them?"

He thought momentarily and said it would be up to the sheriff and the town council.

"I have no jurisdiction here; without a warrant or a wanted poster, there is nothing I can do now."

Sissy was confused, "How so, the town council?"

"Well, to put it bluntly, the question is, will they post a reward for this depredation and appoint me a special deputy?" he answered truthfully.

"You mean you only go after a criminal with a bounty on his head?"

"You see," he answered slowly, "I need to know that I'm operating within the bounds of the law, and if it's a bounty and wanted dead or alive, then no one complains much about how I bring him in."

"I see. Do you do this for a living Mr. Hagerman? Is it your profession, being a manhunter? Do you kill only for money? Those two vermin murdered the best man I've ever known. He never hurt a living soul, and what they did to me, a real man would go after them and horsewhip 'em before hanging 'em both to the nearest tree." Sissy was breathing hard, and her eyes flashed a hatred Thorn had not often seen in a sane person.

The doctor, black bag in hand, entered giving Thorn an excuse to vacate. Madge stayed rocking in her chair with rifle firmly in hand. After a fifteen-minute examination, the doctor was satisfied that no bones were broken. He congratulated Madge on her excellent job cleaning up the cuts on her face and left an ointment for her scratches and bite marks.

Bringing a small bottle from his bag, he handed it to Mrs. Todd, saying, "This here is laudanum. It's a powerful painkiller and will help you sleep. You only need a spoonful. It should help get you through the next few days. Time will heal you, Mrs. Todd. Wish I could help you more, but I have other patients to see and need to get going." With that, the doctor snapped his bag shut and departed.

Madge said, "Sissy, I have to go soon, but I'll try to come back tomorrow." A call from outside brought Madge to her feet with the rifle still in her hand, and she headed out to the wagon. After carefully placing her rifle in the back, she hurried up to a seat next to the doctor. They had placed Mike's body in the back and covered it with a canvas sheet. Billy sat behind the seat holding on to the bench and wearily keeping an eye on the form.

The sheriff stepped back to the open door. "Sissy, do you want to stay over at the Beams' place or go on into town to the hotel? I can send a deputy back to close up this place."

"I'll just stay here sheriff. I have a lot to think on," she said dryly. Sissy was numb, cold, and scared. She had not even had a chance to say goodbye to Mike. How had he gone so soon?

"I can't keep you from staying here, but I think it would be better for you to be around people. You'll be safe enough with Madge and Holly. Mr. Hagerman lives at the hotel in town, and you'd be plenty safe there."

"It's not my safety I'm thinking about. It's what do I do next. I'll be in town when I have it figured out. I'll be reading the Good Book and praying on what to do. I'll see you tomorrow afternoon. Maybe by then, you and your town council will decide how much my husband's life is worth, to say nothing of my virtue." She stepped back into the cabin, barred the door with a thud, and thought about Mike and their session of lovemaking before supper.

"What do you think Pat?" Thorn asked. "Should we go after them? They can't be more than five hours ahead and don't seem to be covering their tracks." Thorn felt the old excitement of the chase and was eager to start.

"No Thorn. We don't have the supplies and such. Besides, I've got to get the town council's permission before I go gallivanting around the county chasing after desperadoes who may soon be out of my jurisdiction. We have to take this one step at a time. Let's stop by the Beams, check on 'em, and pick up Billy. Tomorrow, we'll see what's what."

Before heading back down the road to Durango, Thorn stopped, looked back in the direction the owl hoots had taken, sighed audibly, and followed the sheriff.

Chapter 11
Stampede

Thorn and the sheriff caught up with the wagon after it delivered Madge Beams back to her cabin. Holly and the deputy waited inside with the door locked and the windows shuttered closed. They picked up Teddy and formed a solemn and miserable party as they rode back to town.

"Teddy, you take the doc home first and then the deceased to the funeral home. Tell Dobbs I want to have the lead removed from Mike. I'll talk to him later. Billy, you head over to the office and check on Smitty. I'll be at the saloon, then back to the office if you need me. Now get!"

Thorn leaned over to gently pat his mare and asked, "Could you use some company? I could use a drink."

"Sure, I've also got some business to take care of, but it won't take long." The two tied their bridle reins to the hitching rail out front of the Belle, walked up the steps to the boardwalk, and entered through the bat wings. The place was unusually quiet.

The sheriff and Thorn bellied up to the corner of the long bar as the bartender spotted them and approached, "What'll it be sheriff, and your friend, ah Mr. Hagerman?"

"A shot of rye for each and a beer chaser, Charlie. We got some trail dust to cut." They each assumed the normal position of a booted foot on the bottom brass rail and leaned into the bar. Within seconds, Charlie brought them two mugs of foaming beer followed by two double shots of the top-shelf whiskey, not the usual red eye and rot gut served to the locals.

"Here's to you," said Thorn as he raised his shot glass, but the sheriff turned his glass to the nude framed painting of the lady named Belle, as was his custom. Thorn waited for him to salute her so he could clear out the dust in his throat, but instead of toasting her, he turned back to Thorn and said, "Back at you." Both men knocked their drinks back, followed by quickly downing their beers.

The bartender stood patiently waiting to see if there was a second order of drinks, but the sheriff leaned forward and said, "Charlie, do you remember Mike Todd in here having a drink or two last night?" Charlie nodded that he did.

"Do you remember him talking to two strangers before he left to go home for dinner?"

"No sheriff, but I did see Mike talking to some of the regulars about his claim and how he's panned some placer gold, enough to pay his tab at the mercantile store. He had a shot and a few beers, but I didn't see him talking to any stranger. Come to think about it," Charlie flipped his bar towel over his shoulder and leaned in close, "there were two strangers just down the bar from him, and, now that I think about it, they asked some questions about Mike after he left."

"What did they ask?"

"Oh, just the usual. Who was he, and where did he live?" Charlie fell silent, realizing that he had overstepped his bounds. He became agitated and glanced around to make sure no one was listening.

"You heard what happened to Mike and his missus?" asked the sheriff.

"Yes sheriff, the doc was in just a minute ago and spread the word that we have a murdering killer in the area, and he told, in general terms, that Mrs. Todd had been violated and beaten up some. That's probably the reason most of the miners have left early." The sheriff nodded.

"What did the two look like?" the sheriff asked. Charlie thought for a minute and said, "The talkative one was a big man, as big as your friend here," nodding toward Thorn. The other was a little weasel-faced guy. He was shorter, slimmer, and hunched over. He did a lot of smiling, lip-smacking, and laughing when the big man talked."

"Did you notice the face of the bigger man? Anything special?"

"Ah, let me think. He may have had a scar on his face, but I can't be sure. They didn't stay long."

"Did you hear what they said?"

"No, they paid up and left soon after Mike. Do you think that they…" Charlie let his question trail off.

"I would think they fit the bill to a T, and Charlie, if I were you, in the future, I'd be more careful about what you tell strangers about your customers. Understand?"

Nodding stupidly, Charlie, now thoroughly chastised and feeling guilty for his part in the affair, was happy to fill the order from a trio of rambunctious cowboys at the other end of the bar. The three were hooting and hollering and ready for some action.

The piano player, with the monkey as his companion, began plinking out a tune loved by all, the Stephen Foster classic known as "Camptown Races." Everyone in the bar, able to sing or not, joined in after the piano player belted out the verses about camptown ladies, horseraces, gambling, and railroads. With each refrain, the men would sing, "Doo dah, doo dah day…I'll bet my money on the bobtail nag, somebody bet on the bay."

"What do you think Pat?"

"Sounds like they are our boys. I must get to the mayor's house before he goes to bed. Stop by in the morning, and we can have breakfast at the hotel dining room, or you can come by the office later for coffee. We need to talk, but I've got to go now." The sheriff turned and quickly made his way out of the bat wings.

One of the cowboys garbed in range wear had a big sombrero pushed back off his head, which was held with a leather stampede cord. His eyes were bright with drink and showed a good nature. He, laughing with his friends, called the bartender over and, in a voice bold enough for all to hear, said, "Charlie, what did the bartender say to the horse when he entered the bar?"

"Hmmm, not sure, Chris; what did he say?"

"Why the long face? Get it? Why the long face?" He and his friends burst out laughing and back-slapping each other like schoolboys, which they were young enough to be if they lived in different circumstances.

Charlie guffawed as if he had heard the old saw for the first time. "That sure is a good one, Chris."

Walking back toward Mr. Hagerman, he muttered, "Never gets old, does it?"

Thorn smiled and said, "Charlie, bring me another beer and have one yourself, and don't look so glum, just remember what the sheriff told you, and give those three cowboys at the end of the bar each a beer." Thorn slapped a two-bit coin on the bar and said, "What is it, Charlie, heads or tails? Either way, I pay."

"Well, since you're buying, either way, I say heads."

"In that case, I pay," and he shoved the coin toward the bartender who, looking down, realized it was tails. On the way out, Thorn noticed the three cowboys trying to find out who had bought them beers, but Charlie said, "I don't know the name of the stranger and that he had already left." Maybe there was hope for this town.

That night, when Thorn stopped by the hotel desk to ask if there were any messages, he received a sealed envelope with his name written on the front in a woman's fine cursive hand. In a time and land where most men couldn't read or write more than their names, he received a note from an unknown woman. Pocketing it, he went up the steps to his room and listened at the door momentarily before unlocking and stepping in.

Seeing nothing out of place and hearing no unusual sounds, he went to the window of the darkened room and moved back the curtain to gaze out on Main Street. He saw a six-mule hitch wagon with its driver flicking its reins going down the street, and two horsemen were trotting the other way. A tired-looking woman leaned against a pole under a gas lamp on the corner. Unfortunately for her, a city cop walked up and moved her back down the street to the cribs and brothels where she belonged. Everything in its place and a place for everything had been one of his German father's favorite sayings.

Closing the curtain, he lit the coal oil lamp from a small box of "strike anywhere" matches and adjusted the wick for better light. This reduced the acrid petroleum smell to a tolerable degree. He checked to make sure the bed pot had been emptied and the ceramic pitcher resting in a matching bowl on the marble-topped washstand was full of fresh water. All was in order.

Hanging his gun belt on the bedpost within easy reach, he removed his hideaway .45 from its holster and placed it on a small table next to the bed along with the little two-shot derringer.

He noticed a strange iron device on the floor beside the bed shaped like a longhorn steer. With a smile, he realized it was used to pull off boots. Placing the toes of his left boot firmly on the back of the device and wedging the boot heel of the other firmly between the steer's horns, he easily pulled his right boot off, then the left. "What won't they think of next?" He could sure get used to living in this town hotel. Normally, by now, he'd curl up in a thin blanket with his head on his saddle and be lucky to have a little banked fire of ember to try to stay warm. He removed his new duds and hung them up in an armoire closet that smelled of rich, clean cedar.

Pulling the letter from his coat pocket, he sat on the edge of the bed near the lamp and tore open the envelope. It was undated and read, "Mr. Hagerman, I've decided to come into town for the night. I would like to see you for breakfast at our hotel. I have news you may find of interest." It was signed by "Mrs. Sissy Todd."

He stretched out on the bed dressed only in his long red johns and listened to its iron springs squeak as he tried to find a comfortable position. Interesting, he thought. She changed her mind and came into town and was here in this hotel. He wondered what her news might be, then dismissed her from his thoughts.

Ah yes, he realized he could have this life. It was within his reach. What was he doing getting mixed up with this two-bit case? He'd tell Pat tomorrow that he had to move on, maybe to Denver, and would be in touch regarding the rewards. He had opened an account at the bank, and they could be deposited there. Besides, hanging around here will only increase his risks of being found out before he could cash in on those rewards.

The two who snuffed out the miner's wick won't get posted much of a reward, if any. Now there was the fact of the wife, Mrs. Sissy Todd, being raped and beaten. Nothing got Western folks riled up as much as raping and beating up a woman, that is unless it was by the woman's husband. In this case, they might post a modest reward, but it probably wouldn't be worth his while.

Finally drifting off to sleep for a few hours, he awoke with an urge to empty his bladder. Pulling the pot from under his bed, he carefully leaned over and let go but got some splatter back. How in the hell was a man supposed to take a leak without splattering himself? After another try, this time aimed at the side of the pot, and controlling the stream improved the situation. Finished, he went to the table holding the water pitcher, splashed some into the bowl, and washed his hands and face.

Finding a small clean wash rag on the stand, he dipped it into the water, squeezed it out, washed his feet, and mopped the floor near the pot. He balled up the rag, tossed it into a corner, and lay down again. He would have to figure these things out during the day when he could see better what he was doing.

He lay on his back with his fingers laced under his head, but soon turned to try one side, then the other with the springs squeaking in protest. Finally sliding his right hand under the pillow, he tried sleeping on his stomach, but soon gave it up and went on his back again. This was his natural position. There was plenty to think about and remember.

He had first learned to sleep on his back in Texas, after the war with the Texas Rangers. He was young, age-wise, but old in experience. He remembered changing his name to Mitch Michael and bragged that he had been a scout for General Sterling Price. That went a long way because almost all the men had served under General Hood in the late war or had been too young to go traipsing over to Georgia, Tennessee, and Virginia with Lee, and had to stay with the women folk and tend the ranches and farms during the unpleasantness.

It was during this period when there were Indian raids and bands of outlaws from both sides of the border who raided and stole cattle and horses. Both are hanging offenses in Texas.

Mitch never mentioned being involved with Quantrill Raiders. It seemed like neither side respected them. One evening in what was it, '66 or '67, Mitch was riding with a no-nonsense group of rangers on the trail of cattle rustlers. They had killed a ranger in a running gun battle earlier that week, and he was out front of a group of hardcore men tracking the killers of their brother-in-arms.

With the aid of his old field binoculars, Mitch spotted the herd and riders moving down a draw on their way to Old Mexico and out of the jurisdiction of the Texas Rangers. It was near dusk, and all agreed to pull back and rest for a few hours, letting them bed down for the night. With the Comanche Moon soon to be up, bright, and full, they planned to surround their camp and call for their surrender. It was agreed that if they fought back, even one shot, they all would die, surrender, or not.

Mitch lay on his back, boots on, fully dressed when the order came to quietly check gear to ensure nothing banged or rattled. The moon was so bright you could have read a newspaper by it. They walked their mounts a mile or so to a rise above a grassy valley where some of the herd was lolling around, and the majority had bedded down.

Mitch was ordered to crawl up a slight rise and reconnoiter. The outlaws' campfire was banked and almost gave no glow. These old boys, thought Mitch, knew how to set up a camp. Horses were saddled and hobbled, ready to ride. They had maybe five or six-night hawks out keeping watch on the herd. They were within a day's ride of the Rio Grande River and freedom. He wondered why they hadn't just gone through the night. The outfit reminded Mitch of a

Quantrill raiding party, but they weren't fighting Yankees this time. They had underestimated their enemy.

Mitch slipped down the rise and trotted back to the Rangers. He approached his captain and whispered, "Sir, they are down there only a quarter mile away, but they are in a good defensive position. They've got about a half dozen night guards prowling about keeping an eye on things."

"What do you suggest, corporal?"

"Sir, if we go in guns blazing, I have a feeling a lot of our men are going to get shot to pieces. They look like they've got military experience and are heavily armed. Their horses are saddled for an early start."

"So, do you have a plan?"

"Yes sir. If we were to send, say, six men down riding real slow and cautious through the herd, later, say when the moon sets, they'd blend in and could get around the herd on the other side of the guards. No one would be expecting us. I think we could put the night hawks out of action when we give an alarm. Once hell breaks loose, we stampede the herd back toward their camp. You and your men get into the trees over there," Mitch pointed toward the grove. "You'll be safe enough there. Once the herd passes your point, you and the boys swoop in and finish the job. Come up here and look at the layout, Sir."

The captain also belly-crawled to the top of the little rise and studied the situation with his field glasses. Satisfied with the plan, they slid back down and called a war council. Six men, including Mitch, would go around the camp and slowly walk through the herd to the far side. The captain found the grove, a good flanking location where he could hide his remaining troops while waiting for the stampede. Hopefully, the herd would stomp out most of the rustlers in their camp. They waited for the full moon to set.

Mitch was ordered to be the first to leave, and only after the rest of his men had filtered through under cover of darkness would he signal to start the herd stampeding toward the rustler's camp. Each ranger had a minimum of two pistols and a shotgun or a carbine rifle. They could sure make a lot of noise. Mitch studied the full moon. It would set near sunrise. He felt the excitement building. Once again, he would be in the lead, giving the signal to charge.

Chapter 12
Hangings

Things had settled down, and the moon had set, leaving the pre-dawn dark and quiet as Mitch led his men cautiously around and through the herd. Spotting the form of a distant cowboy, Mitch waived and continued slowly moving forward, leaving it up to his men to pick their best way around. Finally passing the bulk of the herd, with only a few strays beyond, Mitch raised his body up in his saddle for a better view and hoped his men were all in position. He decided to wait a few more anxious minutes and pulled a revolver from his right holster, cocked it, and pointed it in the air. He waited another minute and then pulled the trigger with a rebel yell. With the blast and flame from the pistol, he started running his mount at the herd. Other shots and yells followed.

The cattle spooked, jumped up, and twisted one way and the other. Dark figures were screaming and firing guns in the air in front of the herd. The cattle pivoted away from the gunshots, turned back in a panic, and stampeded right toward the rustlers' camp.

All was chaos and confusion, with steers bawling and crying as they thundered up the draw. Several rustlers tried to get to their mounts, but many hobbled horses, already on the ground, twisted in the ropes, kicking and floundering in fear before the panicked herd stampeded over them.

A few of the rustlers bravely stood their ground, waiving blankets and firing their weapons in an attempt to turn the maddened herd away from their camp, but it was a fool's errand. The cattle, pushed forward by those in the rear, stomped blankets and men into the earth, jumped over fires, and rushed away from the dangers behind. Several mounted rustlers were smashed off their ponies and went to the ground under the thundering cloven hoofs of a thousand animals.

A few men near the front of the herd were left alive and engaged in some gunplay with the rangers. One man bolted south but only made it a few dozen yards when his mount was shot out from under him by a ranger's carbine. The horse went down in a heap and flipped head over heels, slamming its rider to the ground and coming to rest half on top of the unconscious form.

The captain shouted "Charge," and his men broke free, hell-bent for leather, dodging the few remaining cattle straggling or limping along after the main body of the herd. Mitch caught up with the captain and galloped past him with a rebel yell screaming from his mouth.

The action was a total success. The captain pulled up his mount and waited for Mitch to return. Reaching over, he shook Mitch's gloved hand and said, "As good a job as I've ever seen. You were right. There were some game men among the rustlers. I'm glad I listened to you. Mitch, I'm putting you in for a citation and a promotion. If we had had more men like you, we'd won that recent war."

Mitch smiled in the glow of the compliment. The next hour was spent rebuilding the campfires, boiling coffee, collecting bodies for burial, and gathering up the few still alive for hanging. None of the rangers had been wounded or injured. It was a small scrimmage by conventional standards, but a complete victory.

"Let the herd go, men. We'll collect them on the way back," said the captain. "Let's get this next dirty business over with and then get the burial detail started."

Turning to Mitch, he ordered, "Corporal, begin collecting the injured rustlers and bring them up."

"Yes sir."

They had found four men still living, two with broken arms, one with broken legs, and enough internal injuries that they would have to hurry to hang him while still alive. He was already drifting into unconsciousness. And then there was the man who tried to get away. The one whose horse had been shot out from under him while trying to escape was still unconscious, and it was against the rules to hang an unconscious man.

"Throw some water on this one and wake him up," Mitch ordered. "Can't hang a man and send him to hell without giving him a chance to make his peace with his Maker."

A ranger splashed a bucket of water on the face of the man lying prone on the ground. Sputtering and shaking his head, he tried to raise himself but was only able to open one eye, the other was swollen shut, and said, "Guess I didn't make it."

"No, you surely didn't," said Mitch. Studying his bearded face, he thought he recognized him. "You got any last words before your sentence is carried out?"

The man looked up in surprise, "Sentence?"

"Yes, you and the others had your trial when you killed the ranger last week. You got anything to say before it's carried out on you and your men?"

The two men with broken arms grimaced in pain but kept their silence. "Corporal, you want me to tie their hands behind their backs."

"No, I don't think they are in any condition to do anything. Well men, got anything to say before the sentence is carried out?" Neither spoke.

"All right by me. Get 'em on their feet and march these two first to that cottonwood tree. You," Mitch pointed at the newest ranger recruit, a boy of not more than seventeen, about Mitch's age, but compared to him a callow youth on his first outing, "have Cookie bring his wagon over here."

The cook was busy putting on a kettle of beans, and pork and pots of coffee over the coals of the fire and told the young messenger in no uncertain terms that he was busy and could take the blankety-blank wagon over himself. The cook busied himself around the fire, swearing and cursing everyone and everything in sight. He had no interest in being anywhere near another hanging.

The young recruit hopped up on the wagon seat, released the brake, and clucked the team around and under the limb of the cottonwoods. Stopping the wagon, he pulled up on the hand brake and jumped down to drop the tailgate. "This will make a dandy platform to hang 'em from," he said, smiling at the two injured men who looked over, and one snarled. "Can one of you get my chew from my pocket? It hurts like hell when I try to move my arm."

"Sure thing," said Mitch. Nodding to the kid to go over and pull his chew out of his pocket, the other said, "Can I get one of you boys to build me a smoke unless you are in a hurry?"

"Someone got paper and tobacco?" asked Mitch. Several rangers moved forward, anxious to do a final good deed for a fellow human being, hoping that someone would do the same for them under similar circumstances.

An older ranger, probably in his thirties, already had his paper expertly rolled out in his left hand and was tapping a small cloth pouch with an open tie string with the index finger of his right hand. He poured the right amount of tobacco, carefully licked the paper, and rolled the ends. He poked it into the mouth of the prisoner, fishing out a Lucifer from his vest pocket, snapped it to life with his thumbnail, and gave the man a light. As one prisoner inhaled the smoke deeply in his lungs, the other chewed his plug with rapid jaw movement, trying to work it and get the most flavor before it was too late.

"About ready corporal?" asked the captain as he and a dozen rangers approached the tree to witness the justice due to these miscreants.

"Almost Sir. They are having a last smoke and chew. Won't be but another minute."

"Well, get on with it."

The prisoner then spat out the smoldering stub of his cigarette as it burned near his lips.

"Get this one up on the wagon. When I give the word…who's driving?"

"I am Sir," said the young recruit. All he had to do was drive forward on command, and he didn't have to watch the actual hanging.

"Fine son, get up there on the seat and listen for the command."

The first prisoner was lifted to a sitting position on the tailgate as two rangers came up on either side to help him stand. "Damn, that hurts. Can't you be more careful, you clumsy ox?"

"Sorry, didn't mean to hurt you."

"Don't worry," said the other ranger, "what we have here will take care of all your pains and ailments." The other ranger fashioned a noose with the rope's end, threw it over the thick limb coming out from the tree, and pulled down hard, testing the rope and limb. "A perfect hanging tree," he mumbled. He tossed the other end back and told a ranger standing next to the tree, "Tie it good and tight." This was done, and the noose was placed around the prisoner's neck.

The captain asked, "What's your name, and do you want anyone notified about your demise?" The rustler was game and didn't say a word.

"Right, do it," said the captain, but the young man driving the wagon had forgotten to release the handbrake. When he shook the reins and said, "Gitty up," the pair of farm horses lurched forward and stopped with a jerk as the brake held.

The prisoner on the tailgate lost balance, but the rope kept him from falling off the wagon. The two rangers in the wagon bed were ready for the movement and quickly stood and tried to ease the choking rope on the prisoner's neck when the young driver suddenly released the brake and drove forward, causing the two rangers to fall, tumbling to the ground. One grabbed the legs of the prisoner, and all heard an audible "crack" as the prisoner remained suspended in the air. The ranger released the legs and climbed back aboard the wagon.

"Damn, have you ever driven a farm wagon before," barked the captain. "All right son, bring it around, and let's do it again."

"Sorry, Captain, it won't happen again." He drove the wagon around in a wide loop as the two rangers climbed back on board for the ride.

The captain looked around for his corporal and found him behind the tree. He said, "Mitch, bring the other two prisoners over." Mitch nodded and trotted back toward the campfire.

The second prisoner, still chomping on his chew, was brought over and asked for his name, "Jenkins, William Jenkins, late of the CSA, and that poor soul you just hung was named Brent, never knew his first name. No captain, there ain't nobody to notify." He then spit a long stream of tobacco brown juice toward the captain. It hit just short of his feet, splashing on his boots. "Didn't have no proper spit, dry mouth captain."

The captain moved back a yard or two as the second rope was tied to the tree with its noose tossed over the limb and fitted around Jenkins' neck. The command was given, and the wagon smoothly pulled away on its circuit, leaving the second man twitching and jerking at the rope's end.

Mitch returned with one prisoner whose hands were tied behind his back, and except for an eye swollen closed, he didn't look too worse for the rough handling. He had been lucky to take that spill and come out of it without any broken bones.

Mitch approached the captain and reported, "Sir, the prisoner who was stomped up pretty bad just passed on. We only have this one left."

The prisoner stood looking up at the two bodies gently swaying from the squeaking limb and shook his head in disgust. "Damn," he said.

As the wagon rattled back into its place, the young driver had to avoid the legs hanging down under the limb as the two rangers ducked down.

"Get him up there," ordered the captain.

The prisoner was led over to the tailgate and ordered up, but he had trouble climbing up with hands tied behind him. He was hauled up by the two guards, and a third rope fashioned with a noose, tied to the tree, was tossed over the limb; the noose slid over his neck and tightened. They had this hanging thing down to a fine art.

"Hope you boys ain't got too much weight on that limb. Sure, hate to have it break and spoil your party."

"Those two men had a chance for a smoke and a jaw. You want anything?"

"Oh, you mean like the last request? Sure, how 'bout a snort of some good spirits?" The rangers smiled and chuckled about the wisdom of his request.

"Corporal, please go over there and retrieve a bottle from my saddle bag."

Mitch nodded and hurried over to the captain's mount, which stood a few yards off grazing. He was soon back with the requested bottle of red-eye.

"Well, untie the man's hands so he can have a good drink; be quick about it," he ordered.

This was done, and as Mitch handed the bottle up to the condemned prisoner, he began to recognize the voice and the features, even swollen, of someone he had met a long time ago.

"You want to give us your name, and if you got any kin, you want to know about your demise?"

"Sure, my name is Pete Wilson. Some call me Red, but I'd just as soon as nobody knew how I met my end."

Mitch gasped and stood back to gaze at the prisoner as he took a second swig, which drained the bottle, and handed it to one of the guards.

"You got any last words to say?"

"Yeah, you boys are pretty good about shooting horses, but you need to practice your skills at hitting man-sized objects. Let's get this done with."

Before the captain could give the command, Mitch yelled, "Halt. Sir, I know this man. He saved my life during the war. He was a loyal Southern soldier. Don't hang him, Sir."

"Sorry corporal, but those are the orders. Stand aside, or you'll be complicit in an attempted escape and guilty of disobeying a direct order. Both are hanging offenses. This will end your career."

"Sir, I can't. He's my brother. I haven't seen him since the war."

"Oh, hell Carl, let it go," said Pete. "I knew it was you the minute I laid my good eye on you. Let 'em get on with it."

"You two are really brothers?" asked the captain. "You don't look alike." Both men nodded, and Pete said, "My family adopted him as a kid when his folks died. We were raised together as brothers, and we even went off to fight for the glorious cause together."

"Hells bells," but as soon as the captain spoke, the kid snapped the reins and moved forward. The two guards were taken by surprise and held onto the sideboards as the wagon lurched forward, leaving Pete swinging from the rope. Mitch grabbed his legs and wrapped his arms around him, lifting him to keep him from choking on the rope.

"Damn it all to hell, let that man go, that's an order."

"No Captain, I can't. I owe him my life," cried Mitch.

The squad of rangers stood watching the strange scene play out. "How long could one man hold another one up to keep him from hanging?" one of the rangers murmured.

"Damn you both to hell. You are disobeying a direct order." The captain yelled, "Oh hell with you both," looking toward the ranger standing by the tree, "Cut him down. Hurry up before he chokes!"

"Corporal Michaels, you are under arrest for …hell, arrest them both and tie 'em to that tree."

Thorn smiled as he remembered the captain's blue fit when he came over later that evening with a plate of beans and two cups of coffee. "Cut 'em loose and go get some supper," he ordered the ranger standing guard.

"Mitch or Carl, or whatever the hell your name is, you are officially struck from the rolls of the Texas Rangers, all past wages are forfeited, and if you ever set foot again in Texas, you will be hunted down like the cur you are and shot dead. Are we clear?"

"Yes Captain," said the former corporal.

"As for you, Red," nodding toward Pete, who was busy shoveling down the plate of beans and drinking his coffee, "what am I going to do with you?"

"Corporal, take that miserable cow thief brother with you and skedaddle before I change my mind. I've brought your horse and an extra mount for you, Red. And neither of you is ever to set foot in Texas again under the pain of death. Is that understood? Do I have your words of honor that you'll never set foot in Texas again?"

"Sure, thing captain sir," said Red. "And much obliged for the beans and coffee."

"Yes, Captain, and thank you," Mitch awkwardly stood waiting for perhaps a handshake or a farewell gesture of some sort, but the captain pivoted and marched back to the campfire and his men.

"Carl," Pete said while chewing a final mouthful of beans. Do you want your cup of coffee?"

They rode out of Texas to the town of Les Cruces in the New Mexico Territory, where they parted. "We're now even," said Mitch, still angry that he was now wanted in two states under different aliases. He had a good career with the Rangers, had a position of authority, and was looking forward to the citation and promotion. Now, he was on his own again with nothing. Well, not exactly nothing, the captain had packed enough grub for two and two canteens filled with water. He had placed a Henry rifle in Mitch's boot with fifty rounds of extra ammunition but no pistol and nothing for Pete.

"You going to be all right without a gun?"

"Sure, but how about some of that grub and half a box of cartridges?" What he could do with twenty-five rounds of .44 caliber ammunition and no rifle, Mitch couldn't figure out. He handed the items over, and they rode in different directions.

Pete pulled up a short distance away, turned in his saddle to salute Carl, and then rode away.

Chapter 13
Breakfast Meeting

The next morning, Thorn awoke to a bullwhacker's cracking whip and cursing at his team as they slowly proceeded up Main Street. Going to the window, he watched the conveyance trudging away. Washing his head, face, and hands, he dried and combed his hair. Taking a small pouch of salt and baking soda from his saddlebag, he poured some into his hand, and using the corner of the drying cloth, he dampened the white substance and began to scrub his teeth with the cloth. This was one of the few remaining habits from childhood. He licked the rest of the powder from his hand, took a mouthful of water from the pitcher, swirled it around, and spit it into the basin. Washing his hands again, he quickly dressed in the clothes he had worn yesterday.

He might get three or four days of wear out of his new dress shirt but not the months of wear he was used to. He would have to buy another shirt or two and talk to the barber about laundering his shirts, long johns, and socks. Running his hand across his cheeks, he could feel the stubble beginning to grow out. He could get another shave or grow a beard. The business of getting a shave with hot towels and mounds of barber's foam was immensely pleasing. This whole civilization thing was nice, but it is getting complicated and costly in terms of time and money.

Putting on his gun belt, he slipped the two pistols in place, his old cut-down Colt on the right side and the long-barreled Remington on the left. Then he slipped the little derringer into his vest pocket. Placing his new hat squarely on his head, he looked in the mirror at a well-dressed western gentleman and tilted the hat slightly in a rakish fashion. He liked the appearance.

Going down the stairs, he stopped at the front desk, said good morning to Jimmy, and asked if he had any messages. Checking his room number's box, Jimmy said, "No," and wished Mr. Hagerman a good day.

On the way into the dining room, he stepped aside for a granny and a young girl, probably her granddaughter. He pinched his hat brim, gave a slight nod and a smile, "Good Morning ladies." The granny smiled and nodded as they entered the busy dining room serving breakfast.

Entering behind the pair, he spotted Sheriff Williams and Billy at the same table they had occupied yesterday. It was probably their regular spot in a corner where they could see the door, kitchen area, and the diners. Once again, Thorn was forced to sit with his back to the room. It felt uncomfortable, as if folks were watching him, which they were.

The Morning Gazette, with bold headlines: MURDER OF MINER AND WIFE OUTRAGED, was open on the table. Looking around, he saw several copies being read and some quoting to companions. All were discussing it.

"Not really fit reading for folks having breakfast," the sheriff murmured as Thorn picked up the paper and began scanning the article. The sheriff noticed two interesting things about Thorn. First, unlike most folks who could read, he didn't move his lips; and second, how quickly he read the article, turned to the follow-up page, and finished it in seconds. He then folded the paper and put it on the table.

"At least it's accurately reported, as far as we know. Who spilled the beans?"

The sheriff tapped the paper with his forefinger and said, "After Doc spread the word, it could have been anyone. It doesn't matter; it's probably best to keep folks alert."

The town was excited, and several men unknown to wear guns had them planted in plain site on their belts. Unlike yesterday's normal boisterous chatter and clatter, the conversations had a strange low hum.

"Coffee," more of a statement than a question as the waitress poured refills and set a mug of steaming black brew in front of Thorn.

"Thanks, Sally, and the usual breakfast." She repaid Thorn with a dimpled smile and went back into the kitchen. Thorn noticed for the first time that her eyes were deep blue with the brightness and sparkle of polished lapis lazuli, the stone of wisdom.

"A real sweet lady," he noted to no one in particular, and the sheriff and Billy gave no response. To them, she was just Sally, an old maid in her 30s, too picky to marry and settle down, just the waitress, a fixture in the restaurant.

"What did the mayor and the town council say about the reward for Todd's killers and all?" Thorn posed the question without mention of his earlier request for the special status of a lawman.

The sheriff took another long sip of coffee and cleared his throat, "We have a bit of an impasse. Seems as if Todd's claim is outside the town boundaries. They were not registered to vote and didn't pay any township taxes. They are as outraged as anyone, but I don't see them posting a bounty."

Billy looked up from his steak and eggs and asked, "He bought the claim, didn't he? Had to pay some taxes on it for filing."

The sheriff nodded and replied, "True, but that was to the county property office, not the town. Like us, we work for the county. Though in truth, I was actually voted into office by a majority of town folks here who are registered to vote in town, county, state, and federal elections. The Town Marshal heads the town's police, who are paid with town's taxes."

Thorn whistled and leaned back to ponder the complexities of modern life. He had never voted in any election anywhere under any previous name. He wondered if he should register under his current name. "Did we learn anything from the undertaker?" Thorn inquired.

"No, just as we suspected. One round was fired in his back at fairly close range. It shattered his spine. I have it here." The sheriff plucked a glass bottle from a pocket and placed it on the table. It had a tin screw-on lid. Inside was a smashed, deformed hunk of lead from a .45 pistol, based on its weight. Inside, on a small piece of paper, was written the date of death and the victim's name, signed by the undertaker. Thorn looked at it before handing it over to Billy. None unscrewed the lid to examine the kill shot.

"So where does that leave us, sheriff? Last night, I received a message at the hotel that Mrs. Todd had come into town and wanted to talk with me this morning. I believe that's her coming through the door now."

The sheriff looked up and motioned for her to come to his table before Thorn could excuse himself to meet with her alone. Sally was carrying a platter of food toward their table.

The three men stood as she approached, dressed in a simple black dress down to her ankles and buttoned to her neck, where a bruise was still visible above its collar. She wore a small clam-like hat on her head with her bruised and puffy face hidden under a black veil. She wore no jewelry, not even a wedding band. Her eyes were red from what? Probably from crying, thought Thorn.

"Sissy, please join us," The sheriff stood and motioned toward the empty chair, and all seated themselves. Thorn busied himself by tucking a napkin under his chin and cutting his steak into bite-sized pieces. Billy resumed his breakfast. The sheriff asked, "Coffee, or is it still tea?"

"Coffee is fine this morning, Pat." The sheriff caught Sally's attention and motioned for an extra cup of coffee for his new arrival.

"Would you care for some breakfast, dear," Sally asked as she filled her cup.

"No, just, coffee," she replied still standing and looking at the table of men. Her husband had been murdered, she had been viciously assaulted, and nobody gave a damn. It was tough sitting there eating breakfast as if nothing had happened. Sissy silently promised herself she would be tougher.

All eyes in the dining room were on the back of Mrs. Todd, the lady who was violated and her husband murdered just yesterday at about this time. A neighboring woman whispered to her lady friend that she didn't look too bad for the wear. Some thought it was improper for her to be in public during a period of mourning, sort of like when a woman was with child and nearing her labor. Some things should be just kept private. Besides, if a real man had ravaged her, she might even now be pregnant, it was whispered. Hadn't Sheriff Williams courted her a year ago, even taken her to the annual church box supper? He had been sweet on her before she decided to wed the much younger Todd. The tongues wagged. Sissy turned slightly, holding each whisperer's eyes with a hard cold look. She was young, but she let them know she would make Mike proud. She gathered her strength as the people shuttered their eyes and looked down at their plates.

"I was going to ride out and see you this morning Sissy. Glad you came into town. I've got some news, but it's not all that good. The town council is balking about a city reward. Some minors who frequent the Bell have gotten a subscription and raised fifty dollars toward the reward. He was well-liked by all, a very affable man."

Billy stopped eating and exclaimed, "Fifty dollars! Is that all?"

"Go back to your breakfast, Billy. This doesn't concern you," said the sheriff.

But it did concern him. He had admired Sissy from afar for years, and when his uncle was courting her, he wanted to cry out, "You're too old for her." But she had married a good-looking, jovial young fellow that no one could complain about. Billy had wished them well at their wedding. Funny, Billy thought, his uncle had been out of town on official business at the time and had not attended the wedding or the festivities. But now, Sissy was a free woman, and Billy wanted to claim the honor and bragging rights by killing the men who had done this to her, reward or not. He returned his attention to his plate.

"Sorry Sissy, but that's the hand we drew. The town council is also reluctant to give Mr. Hagerman here any special police powers because he's a stranger and not a citizen here." Thorn briefly looked to Mrs. Todd to gauge her reaction, but nothing registered.

The sheriff reached over and patted her hand, "Don't worry Sissy, we've wired out a description and a warrant for their arrest. It's been sent on to Silverton and points south and west. It won't be long before somebody gets them."

She removed her hand from under the sheriff's and said, "You are the county sheriff, why don't you go after them yourself, Pat?" The question stung him and hung in the air between them.

"Sissy, the law isn't that simple. Unlike Mr. Hagerman here, Billy and I have duties and obligations to a parcel of folks and can't just take off after every desperado."

She didn't respond to him, but turned toward Thorn and directly addressed him. "Mr. Hagerman, you are a bounty hunter are you not?"

Thorn nodded.

"If so," she continued, "I have here the deed to our property and claim and a signed affidavit before a notary public offering it as a reward to anyone who brings in the killer or killers of my husband, dead or alive." She removed the papers from her purse and laid them on the table.

"I'm not sure this is strictly legal Sissy," commented the sheriff as he perused the documents. "Not just anyone can post a reward, and it has to be in legal currency," he returned the documents to her. She placed them back in her purse and snapped it shut.

"Then make it legal Pat." She pushed back her chair forcefully and abruptly. Before the men could stand, she had departed with every eye in the room following her, including a tall wrangler at the next table. His tan sombrero pushed back off his head, held by a stampede strap.

"Well," said the sheriff. "Are you going after them?" The question was asked directly to Thorn.

"Pat, for a fifty-dollar reward and a played-out claim? I don't think so. I've got some business to attend to in Denver and need to take care of it. When is the inquest?"

"Oh yes, I meant to tell you. It's the day after tomorrow, Friday. What day of the month is that? Let's see. This is the…" Walking by with orders of apple pie, Sally said, "This Friday is the 13th, don't you know."

"Very well Pat, I'd like to leave on Monday, 16th, for Denver by train. I'll leave my mare and saddle at the stables paid up through the end of the month. I'll keep my things at the hotel also. Do you think you'll know about the reward money by then?"

"We have lined up five eyewitnesses who will testify to the identities of the three deceased. We need to get this taken care of and get them planted. Dobbs says they are getting gamey. As to the rewards, I should be hearing about some of them by the end of the month, once I send out word as to the findings of the inquest. So many different papers were out on those boys from Idaho through Wyoming and Colorado. You are going to be a mighty rich man. No, I don't blame you for not going after those two-bit murderers…"

"You forgot rapists," said Thorn.

"True, but still only worth fifty dollars for the two of 'em."

"I'll do it." Said Billy, pushing his plate of half-eaten steak, eggs, and fried potatoes aside.

Thorn and the sheriff looked at Billy as if they didn't know him. "What are you saying, Billy? You can't go after two killers," the sheriff said.

"And why not? I don't see anybody else doing it."

"Billy, I'll not give you that assignment," The sheriff said.

"Don't matter sheriff, I'll resign and go after 'em on my own."

Thorn put his coffee cup down with a clatter and looked straight into Billy's eyes, "Have you ever killed a man? No, wrong question. Have you ever faced a man who meant to kill you? Here, we have two killers, a team, and they work together. You'll have to kill or bring in two men who would just as soon kill you as look at you. Pat is saying, and I'm agreeing, that you don't have the experience. You'll just get yourself killed."

The chair at the next table scratched back on the plank floor as a tall, good-looking wrangler stood and faced the three men at the next table. "Excuse me, I'm Chris Walling, and I've killed before in fair fights. I couldn't help but overhear your conversation. I wasn't eavesdropping. I'll go with you, kid. Just say the word. I'm between outfits and thinking of returning to Texas for a spell. I'd be honored to tag along with you."

Thorn noted the young gunfighter's easygoing manner. He wore his two pistols in cross-draw fashion high at his waist. He looked like he knew how to use them. He was the same jovial young cowboy he had bought a beer for the previous night.

"Where are your two friends from last night at the Bell?" Thorn inquired.

"Oh, they headed back to the ranch, but I'm free, white, over twenty-one, and ready for adventure. I'm footloose and fancy-free, you might say. I was hired as much as a gun hand as a wrangler, but the threat of rustlers never materialized, so I'm heading on to greener pastures."

Billy stood and shook hands with Chris, then introduced the two men still seated, "This is Thorn Hagerman, a Pinkerton agent, and Sheriff Pat Williams."

"Pleased to make your acquaintance," Chris said, as handshakes were offered all around. Chris was offered a seat and a half hour later they agreed to meet back at the sheriff's office after they had a chance to think things over and talk in a more private place.

Chapter 14
Practice Makes Perfect

An hour later, Thorn and Chris sat listening to the sheriff as he argued with Billy about the wisdom of going after the two miscreants, with or without Chris' company. Chris sat patiently, seeming to take no offense from the remarks. The sheriff, now in the role of uncle, was genuinely concerned for his nephew's safety. Billy, in turn, was just as strong in his position as it was his duty.

"All right, be bullheaded. Just don't expect me to be the one who tells my sister, your mother when you get your fool-self killed," Sheriff Pat Williams sat sour-faced and crossed his arms as a final gesture.

"Chris," Thorn asked, "what's your experience with gunfighting? You were too young for the war, weren't you?"

"I'm from Texas," he answered as if that was all anyone needed to know. I've been in a fair number of scrapes and a range war or two. I get top dollar as a gun hand."

"You got any paper out on you?" the sheriff sat up and asked.

"Not one, sheriff. I'm clean as a hound's tooth. All my gunfights were stand-up, fair fights. They were ruled self-defense."

The sheriff nodded and said, "If you are set on going on this fool's errand, so be it. I can't keep either of you here, but I don't like it."

"Tell you what, Pat." Thorn smiled. "Tomorrow, let's all ride out of town to a secluded spot and have some target practice. I'll let you know if they are ready."

Pat nodded in agreement. He knew the results of Thorn's gunplay by taking down three notorious gunmen. "How does that sound to you boys?"

"I'm always up for practice," said Chris, "Maybe I can learn something from the famous Pinkerton agent, and a lawman, but maybe they'll learn something from me. Problem is I've only got half a dozen rounds to my name, and I'm tapped out of coin. I got cleaned out last night at a card game at the Belle. I only had enough coin for breakfast."

"No problem, the sheriff and I can provide all the ammunition we need, right Pat?"

"Sure, as much as we need. What time do we want to leave? In the morning, after breakfast. I can leave Teddy in charge of the jail and office while we're gone, and Smitty can keep him company."

The next morning, after breakfast at the hotel dining room, Thorn picked up the table's tab, and the four men saddled up. The sheriff had a gunny sack full of empty cans and bottles for targets. Thorn, dressed in his old range clothes and boots, looked like a different man, rough and dangerous. He carried 400 rounds of .45 ammo, both Colt and Schofield, in his saddle bags.

They rode up the trail past the Beams cabin, where no smoke was coming out of the chimney, and no one seemed to be working the sluice. They continued farther back a mile or two beyond the Todd place to the entrance of a pretty little valley with a good stream running through. They dismounted, loosened the cinches, and let their horses graze.

The sheriff walked about twenty yards to a fallen tree trunk, lined it with an assortment of bottles and cans, and said, "Okay, boys, have at it."

"No way sheriff," said Chris as he loaded all the cylinders on his Schofield and Colt pistols from two boxes of ammunition, "You two got to show us your stuff first."

Thorn said, "I noticed yesterday that you carry two pistols, the Schofield and the Colt Peacemaker. They use different ammunition, but did you ever notice that you can fire the Schofield S&W ammo in the Colt, but not the other way around?" Billy listened with interest. He did not know that.

"Sure," said the sheriff, "'cause the Peacemaker rounds are a little longer and won't fit in the Schofield, but the Schofield rounds are shorter, and they'll fire in the Colt."

"I didn't know that," said Chris. "I thought I had to carry two different types."

"That's why you are here, boys." The sheriff pulled out his long-barrel Colt Peacemaker, carefully aimed, and sent a tin can flying. Next, he hit a bottle, sending a shower of flying glass around the target. "It's not the man who shoots first who always walks away, but often it's the man who shoots true."

"Well said," said Thorn, and snatched his shortened Colt from his right holster. With the palm of his left hand, he fanned five quick rounds into a can, making it hop and dance along the ground. Twirling his Colt in his right hand, he dropped it back in its holster, then with his left hand, pulled the .44 Remington long barrel and fired five rounds in quick succession, making four cans fly off the log and smashing the fifth bottle. "But I'd rather be the man who is both fast and accurate at the same time." Thorn reloaded his weapons—this time every cylinder and dropped them back home.

Chris whistled in admiration, "So that's the quick draw and fanning I've been hearing about. I hear that you are having some custom work done on your cutdown Remington over at the gun shop." Are there no secrets in this town? Thorn thought. "Both of you boys, do you count your shots?" asked Thorn.

"Mostly," admitted Chris. "More than once, I got too excited and lost count and let the hammer fall on an empty chamber."

How about you, Billy?"

"Mighty fine shooting, both of you," said Billy, not wanting to admit he'd never learned to count his shots, nor had he ever had a reason to. But he would begin today, and he thought he might get him a second pistol. "I see four more cans standing. I'll take the two on the right, Chris, you take the two on the left. Let's show 'em how we do it. Sheriff, say when."

Both stood facing the target with their right hands poised above their pistols. "Now," called the Sheriff.

Both drew and fired, with Chris' can dancing away a split second before Billy fired, hitting his first target. Chris' second shot knocked a can high into the air, and before Billy could aim and fire his second shot, Chris fired a third round, knocking the final target skyward. Billy lowered the cocked hammer when suddenly Thorn, not to be outdone, pulled out both pistols and began firing at the air-born can, making it dance and jump as it disappeared into the distance.

"Holy smoke," gasped Chris. "Remind me never to have a gunfight with you."

Another two hours were spent practicing long-distance shots at fifty and seventy-five yards. They practiced different stances, quick draw, shooting contests, the duck and dive moves, and quick-fire practices without aiming. It was like a kid pointing his index finger and saying, "Bang." Soon, they fired all their spare ammunition. The sheriff had acted more as a referee than a participant. All that moving, ducking, going to the ground, and rolling around was for younger men.

By mid-afternoon, they had built a fire by the fallen tree. After examining the punctured cans, they ate the sandwiches Pat had packed and finished a pot of range coffee, also compliments from Pat.

"This is as pretty a valley as I've ever seen," said Thorn to Pat. "Who owns it?"

"I think it's still part of the Todd holding, back up to that ridge in the distance over there," he pointed.

"You could sure raise a herd of fine beef up here," mused Chris. Billy nodded in agreement.

Riding back to town, they stopped at the Todd cabin, which was still empty, and rode by. They next studied the sluice where Mike spent time panning. Billy had panned for gold a few times and found enough placer gold to buy two beers at the saloon. They found no one around. "Sissy must still be in town," said Pat.

At the Beams cabin, they hailed, but it was also empty and locked up. Pat thought they must also be in town until this thing blows over. "Folks are scared."

Once back in town, they stopped first by the stable to put up their horses. "Give my mare and Billy's horse a good feed and a rub-down with a burlap gunny sack or such," said the sheriff to the stable hand. The county owned the sheriff's and Billy's animals, and the stable contracted for their care.

Chris sat on his roping pony, wondering where he and his pony would sleep tonight. Looking over toward Chris, Thorn said, "Let's unsaddle. Your pony's room and board are on me."

Chris and Thorn unsaddled their mounts and slung the blankets and saddles over rails at the same time. Chris grabbed an old gunny sack from a peg, began wiping down his pony, and then began on Thorn's beautiful Morgan mare. He took notice of her stockings and muzzle, which were dark brown against the black coat, and commented to Thorn, who grunted an acknowledgment. Thorn made himself busy, found a pitchfork leaning against the wall, and tossed some sweet-smelling hay into the two long manger boxes in the empty stalls. The hay was good and clean, and it had been reaped and gathered before the grain seeds had been shaken from the stalks. Bits of dust particles hung in the air, caught in a shaft of sunlight. Their mounts would eat well tonight.

"Much obliged," said Chris. He had never been given much in life and learned not to expect anything. He was quickly developing friendships and loyalty with these men.

"No problem," said Thorn. It looks like you're part of the crew. Let's head over to the sheriff's office. I left my gun cleaning kit there. After the workout, all our guns could use a good cleaning and oiling."

Arriving at his office, the sheriff sent Teddy to see if any telegrams had arrived. He returned shortly with a handful bound in string, placed them on the sheriff's desk, and left for the evening. The sheriff slowly looked them over. More promises of payment of big rewards if the inquest provided evidence of the bandit's demise. Thorn pulled out his wallet and handed the sheriff the telegram with all the answers inked in. Thorn had spent the evening going through Hagerman's papers to find the answers.

Smitty was rousted out of bed and told to get the extra blankets. They had another guest for the second bunk in Smitty's cell. Chris again smiled and nodded his thanks.

"By the way, Chris," the sheriff motioned him over to his desk. The other men stopped and looked over, "I don't have the money in the budget for another full-time deputy, but I can bring you on part-time, and under the circumstances, I could use another gun hand. That is if you want it?"

"I am sure obliged, sheriff."

"Raise your right hand, and Smitty, bring me that Bible over there," Smitty uncovered it under a pile of old dog-eared copies of the National Police Gazette magazines. The one on top, which he took a second to admire, had a cover picture of a sweet and demure young woman who had been the victim of a vicious crime. Smitty uncovered the Good Book and held it for Chris to place his left hand on and raise his right.

"Repeat after me, I …give your full name, do solemnly swear…"

"I, Christopher B. Walling, do solemnly swear…"

"To uphold the Constitution of these United States and the State of Colorado…"

"To uphold the Constitution of the United States of America and the State of Colorado…"

"And to obey the orders of my superior and enforce the ordinances and rules of this county, so help me God."

"And obey the laws and rules and such, so help me God."

"Welcome aboard Chris. You are officially a deputy of La Planta, Colorado."

"La Planta…I'll be. I always thought this was Durango County." The other men, including Smitty, who also thought they were in Durango County, had a good laugh and congratulated Chris. They settled into disassembling the weapons and cleaning each part, oiling where it was needed, and reassembling under Pat's watchful eyes. By the time they finished, they had bonded as a unit.

Next, the sheriff sent Smitty out for a plate of sandwiches and a pail of beer, which they all shared. Finally, after a long day, Thorn returned to his hotel, Billy went home to his mother's house, and Chris settled into his new bunk. The sheriff went to his desk to reread the telegrams.

On arriving at the hotel, Thorn checked to see if he had any messages, but still none. Upon opening the door to his room, he immediately noticed a new smell…a woman's smell of lavender mixed with perfume. "Don't be alarmed, Mr. Hagerman. It's just me. The maid let me in. I told her I'd forgotten my key. I've been waiting for you most of the afternoon."

Thorn stepped in and stood with his back to the wall, keeping the door wide open. He checked out every part of the room where another could hide. They were alone. "What can I do for you, Mrs. Todd?" He did not move from his spot. Being alone with another man's wife in a hotel room, even a dead man's widow, could get a man killed, even a careful man.

"Have you thought of my offer?"

"It was a topic of discussion this afternoon, Mrs. Todd. It seems you have two gallants who want to slay your dragons, Billy and a wrangler named Chris."

"But not you Thorn? Why don't you call me Sissy, everyone does."

"Thank you for coming by, Mrs. Todd, but we don't know each other well enough to be on a first-name basis. To answer your question, I'm not going after the two, but those two I mentioned probably will. You need to be talking to them. You'll find them over at the sheriff's office tomorrow morning before the inquest, which is set for 10:00 a.m. The sheriff swore in the wrangler this afternoon as a part-time deputy. Tell me, Mrs. Todd, what's the score between you and Pat? Every time he's around you, he goes cow-eyed."

"We're old friends, that's all. He courted me for a while before Mike and I married."

"Another thing, more personal, if I may?" She nodded.

"I noticed this morning you didn't wear your gold marriage band. Why?"

"You're observant Mr. Hagerman. I sold it and Mike's, which I picked up from the undertaker when I went over to say my goodbyes. I had to get some ready cash to pay for the copy of the deed, the affidavit, burial, food, and the hotel room. I have enough funds for another week. I want you to know Mr. Hagerman, confidentially, Mike found a rich vein of gold near the cabin. It'll have to be mined, but it'll be worth a fortune."

"Then why are you giving everything to go after a fool's reward? Pat and the law dogs will eventually get those two skunks, or somebody else will kill them. If you know what I mean, life has a way of coming full circle around?"

"What comes around goes around, as the old saying goes. Is that what you mean?"

"Sure, so why give it up? You've got a handsome spread of land."

"Because Mr. Hagerman, I like you…very much… and under the right circumstances, I could even love you. But, if you'll excuse me, I'll go to my room now. Good night."

Thorn watched her walk down the hall, enter her room at the end, and slowly closed the door without looking back.

He entered his room, locked the door, and, for good measure, braced a chair's back tight under the doorknob. Stranger and stranger, he thought. She was beautiful or would be again when her bruises settled down, but what was her game? She had both Pat and Billy going goo-goo over her, and now Chris was in the picture. She did have a nice figure when viewed from behind.

Chapter 15
Inquest

The wood-framed courtroom was already filled to overflow and was warm and close, smelling of packed spectators when Thorn entered wearing a new shirt, black string tie, broadcloth vest, suit, and freshly polished boots. He walked up the courtroom aisle with every eye centered on him, the heroic Pinkerton agent.

He removed his hat and sat it on the table before him as he sat facing the judge's desk. He sat next to Sheriff Pat Williams, who, in turn, was seated next to Mrs. Sissy Todd. She was dressed in mourning black, with a veil demurely shading her face. From her dark hair tied back in a bun tucked under her little hat to her laced-up stylish black shoes, she looked every bit the grieving widow.

It was difficult to see her face, but it looked like much of the swelling had gone down, and the bruises were fading. She sat ramrod straight with knees pressed tightly together. Her hands folded in front, rested on the table, holding a white lace handkerchief. She wore no jewelry, brooches, or even the small ladies' watch pinned to the bodice, which had gained popularity then. She was the epitome of stoic Western womanhood and was admired for her dress and deportment.

A bench along one side wall contained the other witnesses to be called, and six wooden chairs lined up on the other side awaiting the jury.

"All rise for the Honorable Thomas X. Clark, Magistrate of Durango, Colorado," called the bailiff. The spectators arose together as His Honor entered from a rear door. "You men take off your hats and put out those cigars. It's offending the ladies."

"Seat the jury." Six tried and true men entered the same door and seated themselves in the vacant chairs reserved for them along the wall.

Seeing that all his orders were complied with, His Honor seated himself. He read aloud the statement as to "the legal purpose of the inquest, which is to determine the truth as to the death of three individuals brought before this body, and to ascertain if their deaths were justified, accidental, or criminal. In addition, this inquest also had the task of determining the cause of the recent death of Mr. Michael Todd and the, ah, violation of his wife," the magistrate paused as everyone stirred and murmured at the term used, then explained, "were these criminal acts committed by a known or unknown person, or persons?"

"Call the first witness in the matter of Ivory Thompson and companions."

The bailiff called the sheriff, who, after being sworn in, gave his name, date of birth, and position held. He went on to produce several wanted posters with poorly illustrated likenesses of Ivory Thompson and two telegrams alerting him to be on the lookout for Ivory Thompson, a known outlaw, and two members of his gang traveling together, one a Mexican national, the other an Indian, or half-breed, of an unknown tribe, names unknown.

Thorn remembered their names but thought it wiser to let sleeping dogs go undisturbed and get this show underway.

"Do you know if the trio was apprehended?"

"Yes, your honor. On September 9th of this year, the Pinkerton agent," nodding toward Thorn, "rode into town with the three outlaws over the backs of their mounts."

"Were they alive or deceased?"

"All dead as doornails, your honor." The spectators snickered and laughed.

The magistrate ignored the interruption and asked, "Did you ascertain if fair or foul means had been used in bringing them to justice?"

The sheriff then explained in detail the puncture wounds sustained by each. The status of the Mexican's neck wounds caused several men and women to gasp, with one lady fainting dramatically in the arms of her companions, resulting in a five-minute recess. She was treated with an aromatic spirit of ammonia by one of her lady friends, who, as luck would have it, just happened to have such a vial of the reviver in her handbag.

With the stinging odor of the aromatic still in the air, the magistrate resumed examination by asking the jury members if any had questions. Half a dozen questions followed regarding weapons and the caliber of slugs used to detach the Mexican's head. The sheriff fielded the questions with answers that were satisfactory to the court. No further questions were asked, and the sheriff was dismissed.

The undertaker Dobbs was called next. To everyone's surprise, they learned that he had a first name, Maurice, and he was only 29 years old. Everyone thought he was decades older, but with his bald head uncovered for the first time in anyone's memory, it was agreed that he looked much older.

Undertaker Dobbs reiterated the nature and types of wounds found on each of the three deceased. When asked if he could identify the type of rounds used in their death, he produced two small glass jars containing smashed slugs and slips of paper for the magistrate and the jury to look at. He stated that he had retrieved the lead, at the request of the sheriff, from the bodies of two of the deceased, and had washed them and placed each in the appropriate jar with its identifying slip of paper. Everyone smiled and nodded at the efficient method of handling the request, with only a few off citizens grumbling about the wrongness of relieving a body of the weight that killed 'em, that it might have been necessary for the final judgment. The magistrate rapped his gavel and asked, "Why only two jars?"

The undertaker, Maurice Dobbs, smartly answered that it was because the two rounds that killed the Mexican and almost severed his head had passed through and were lost. This explanation seemed to satisfy the jurymen. The lady who fainted earlier began to swoon a little but, after looking around, sat up straight.

"Any more questions for this witness?"

Hearing none, the magistrate told the witness, "You are excused."

His testimony was followed in quick secession by the first of five eyewitnesses swearing to the known identity of Ivory Thompson. After the swearing-in and each giving name, date of birth, and occupation, the cowboy, wrangler, loafer, and two stove-up old horsemen were each asked if they personally saw the deceased Ivory Thompson at the funeral home with his companions, and, based on the witnesses' prior personal knowledge of him, would swear to his identity. Each, in turn, answered in the affirmative.

The jury questioned each as to his whereabouts and the circumstances of his knowledge. Not satisfied with the answers, one juror began to gesture by pounding his fist into his hand and calling a certain witness a known liar and teller of tall tales. Chairs were pushed aside, and the two issued personal challenges to combat. As a matter of law, the magistrate ruled that eyewitnesses confirmed Ivory Thompson's identity and that his two companions' identities were unknown and not in issue. The identity of a Mexican and an Indian did not warrant the court's attention.

A lunch break was called with the court to resume at 1:30 p.m., enough time for the men to retire to one of the four saloons for beer and a free lunch laid out. The lady who had fainted and retinue retired to the hotel dining room for lunch and a review of the case thus far. The sheriff went into the magistrate's chamber. At the same time, Thorn remained seated at the table, reading some old newspapers he had found in the sheriff's office and reviewing some documents he retrieved from an inner coat pocket.

Mrs. Todd looked around for her friend and a quiet place to go during the period, but Madge and Holly had left. She was approached by Billy and Chris, who escorted her to a nearby restaurant for a light lunch paid for by Billy. Everyone was back in their seats by 1:20 p.m. The magistrate returned to his desk promptly at 1:30 p.m. with everyone standing and all the men bareheaded.

"We'll now wrap up the Thompson inquest. You folks can be seated." Everyone sat in unison, and the afternoon session began with, "Mr. Thorn Hagerman is called as the next witness."

"Yes, your honor," Thorn stood before the magistrate and was sworn in by the bailiff.

"What is your name, birth date, and occupation?"

"I'm Thorn T. Hagerman, born November 9, 1841, in the newly admitted State of Michigan." The few who could, did the math, and hurried whispers passed around the room about how young he looked for a 44-year-old man. Good stock and clean living seemed to be the general consensus.

The magistrate gaveled for silence and asked the court reporter, "Did you get that Mr. Secretary?

"Yes."

"Fine, we'll continue. Everyone settle down." The magistrate ordered.

"What is your occupation, Mr. Hagerman? Oh, by the way, for the record, is that your full name?"

"Your honor, my full name is Thorn T. Hagerman, and I was a Pinkerton agent but recently resigned. I've done enough killing. I want to settle down." The whispers flowed around the room as this tidbit of news was digested.

"Really? Resigned? Well, but for the record, what does the 'T' stand for?"

"In truth, your honor, I don't rightly know. I lost both of my folks when I was young, and I'm not sure what it stood for. If I ever knew, I'd forgotten."

"Not to worry Mr. Hagerman, it's just a formality. Now, back to the case at hand, said the magistrate. Please describe your pursuit and final encounter with the trio of outlaws who are wanted in Colorado, two other states, and the Oklahoma Territory for murder, arson, armed robbery, destruction of public property, and assorted charges of rape and sodomy, to name only a few listed in the warrants."

The minister, a man calling himself Brother Michael, leaned near his deacon and whispered, "It's from the Bible… Sodom and Gomorrah were two cities destroyed by God for their wickedness and unnatural acts."

"Quiet in the court," bellowed the bailiff. The chastised red-faced minister lowered his head and prayed for strength.

For the next three-quarters of an hour, Thorn provided a carefully scripted and rehearsed narrative of his orders to capture the gang, the many-month chase, and finally the encounter with the trio of outlaws. He provided documents to the court at appropriate times regarding his honorable discharge from the Grand Army of the Republic and his subsequent hiring by the Pinkerton Detective Agency of Chicago.

He skipped rather quickly over the actual killing of Ivory Thompson and his men, painting it in only with the broadest strokes. Everyone thought he must be a God-fearing, modest man not to brag about such an epic showdown, but the magistrate let it pass and ruled the three died in a gunfight with a Pinkerton agent in the pursuit of his duties. The killings were justified.

The magistrate then called a ten-minute recess.

Upon re-entering the courtroom, the magistrate again motioned for the room to be seated and began the Case of the Killing of Michael Todd and Other Ancillary Matters. The spectators again murmured and scratched heads as to the new word replacing the known term "rape" of the star witness. Most had come to hear about her ordeal. The killing of a miner was sad, but a rather common occurrence. However, the rape and beating of a well-built young wife was a rare occurrence worth attending to.

The first witness was again Sheriff Williams, who was already under oath. He briefly outlined the facts leading him to the Todd cabin, who had accompanied him to his cabin, and what was found. No questions followed.

Maurice Dobbs' appearance was even briefer. In response to a question, he answered, "Yes, Mr. Todd was shot in the back by what looked like a .45 slug." He then presented a familiar glass jar to the magistrate for the jury. One jury member rattled the misshapen lump of lead around the glass jar until the magistrate gave a piercing look of annoyance. The jar in question was then returned to the judge for safekeeping.

Next came Mr. Holly Beams, who gave a brief statement, followed by his wife Madge, who described in detail what she heard and saw as she arrived at Todd's cabin. She provided a graphic picture of the cabin's disarray, the state of Mrs. Todd's dress, and her physical condition. Things were getting interesting, and the jury and spectators hung on to her every word when the magistrate thanked and excused her. Again, there were no follow-up questions.

Thorn was called and described how he happened to be in the sheriff's office when Mr. Beams had come in to give the news. Next, he explained what he learned from examining the footprints, horses, and a stolen mule's tracks at the cabin. As to the number of culprits, he stated two, one large man and a smaller companion, based on their boot prints. There being no additional questions, he was excused.

Next came Doc Howard, who, after being sworn in, described himself only as Doctor Howard, which the court accepted. He described in excruciating detail the call to render help, the bumpy wagon ride, the assistance he gave to Mrs. Todd, and her emotional and physical state of being.

One of the jurymen asked him directly if she had been raped. The room was silent as the good doctor thought about how to delicately answer such a question, especially with the lady seated nearby.

"I think you should direct that question to the next witness, Mrs. Todd." The jury and spectators sat back in their seats, obviously unhappy with his answer. "No other questions. This witness is excused."

"Next, call Mrs. Sissy Todd."

As she rose to be sworn in, the whispering increased as old stories and gossip about her courtship with the sheriff were repeated. After identifying herself and giving her birthday, she was still only twenty. She was asked to tell what had occurred on the date in question.

She picked up the narrative with Mike's trip to town with his small bag of gold placers to exchange for cash. His trip to town included going to the store to pay their account and buying a few items before going to the saloon for drinks with his friends. She knew this because her husband had told her before he had been murdered, but no one bothered to question the hearsay statements. He had hurried home for dinner and was late.

Next, she told how he had given her a bag of freshly ground coffee and a new ribbon for her hair. At this, she, along with most of the women intently listening and some of the men, began to tear up, and she paused to lift her veil and wipe away the tears. Regaining her composure, she adjusted her veil and continued the narrative.

The room was silent, with heads leaning forward to hear her words. She told of his cleaning up and their sitting down for dinner, of Mike saying grace and beginning to eat when they heard someone from the yard calling out, saying they were lost and could we give directions to town. She told of Mike going out into the yard and how he yelled for her to get ready to bar the door, his running steps, and the shot, followed by her unsuccessful attempt to close the door. She tried to close and bar the door, but the door was kicked back in, knocking her down on their bed. Finally, they came in and how the big man, after a while, pushed the smaller rat-faced one away from her. Then as the big man had his way with her, the little one watched and danced around the cabin.

The court listened in stunned silence as the magistrate cleared his throat and asked, "Mrs. Todd, I know that this is difficult, but can you tell the jury if you were raped by one of the men and if you had ever seen either of them before? And can you describe the big man and his companion?"

The first question she answered with a single word, "Yes. He raped and beat me; and no, I never saw either man before," and with surprising clarity, she gave the approximate height, weight of her attacker, his scar, and that of his miserable smaller companion. There were no further questions, and Mrs. Todd was excused.

"There being no further witnesses, do you want to retire to my chambers? How do you say?"

The men leaned in together and quietly discussed the case. Several men nodded in agreement, and after further discussion, one man rose and said, "Your honor, it's pretty clear that the deceased, Michael Todd, was the victim of foul play by one or both strangers. We don't know which one of the two killed him, but we do know that one, described as the "bigger man," did assault and rape Mrs. Todd in violation of the laws of Colorado and human decency."

A man on the jury said, "Their descriptions should be sent out far and wide, and further, an additional $50.00 should be added by the township of Durango to the miners' subscription as a reward totaling $100.00 for their return dead or alive for their crimes."

The courtroom exploded in applause, stomping, whistling, and clapping hands in approval. The Honorable Thomas X. Clark nodded his approval and said, "All right, folks." As the magistrate regained control of the courtroom, he said, "Sheriff, you heard the jury."

The bailiff commanded, "All rise while His Honor leaves the court. This session is closed." All stood for a few minutes, and the crowd began to disperse and express their feelings that the Honorable Thomas X. Clark did a good job.

Chapter 16
Happy Trails

Leaning against the wall near the courtroom exit, Chris glanced at his partner, Billy. Chris was as happy as the cat who ate the canary. He had a warm place to ride out the winter, plenty of good chuck to eat, and a stall with sweet hay for his pony. He wore a new set of duds, well, new to him, even though they were the cast-offs Thorn was going to dispose of. On his worn leather vest was pinned a shiny new deputy badge.

Across from him on the other side of the door sat Billy, both nodding as they spotted the young man fitting the description supplied by Smitty last evening. The young man rose from his seat and fitted his hat atop his head and, after looking around, began to follow Thorn down the aisle toward the main exit. He looked determined and up to no good.

Smitty had come in last evening with the pail of beer and sandwiches from the Belle for their dinner and approached Billy with a nod and a whisper that he had something to say.

"Well, what is it Smitty? Cat got your tongue?"

Smitty looked knowingly over toward Chris, who had emptied his cup of beer and was chowing down on a meat and cheese sandwich.

"He's all right Smitty. He's one of us. Say what you got to say before he eats and drinks our share."

"All right then. I was over at the Belle, and Charlie spotted me a free beer on the house, seeing that I'm now the unofficial turnkey. So, I took the beer to my favorite corner and began sipping on it, out of the way, don't you know."

"Get on with it," said Billy as he watched Chris pour himself a second cup of beer and began eyeing the dwindling stack of sandwiches.

"I couldn't help but listen in on the conversation around the corner of the bar. This young slick with long black hair and a tie-down quick draw holster on his right hip was telling the men at the bar how he had come up from El Paso after a fair stand-up fight with a notorious gunslinger that none of us had rightly ever heard of. Hold on boys, I need to wet my whistle." Smitty poured himself a cup of beer, took a deep swallow, and continued. "He told the fellows that he had heard about a damned Pinkerton skunk who had bushwacked three good men, and he was going to cut him down to size after the court hearing. He's dressed in fancy duds, wearing colorful braces and a dark blue shirt. He carries a black-handled Colt on his right hip and looks fast. That's about all I know. Let's eat."

Billy and Chris discussed the situation and agreed not to tell the sheriff or Thorn. Rather, they would take care of the problem themselves and prove they were ready for dangerous law work and could be trusted to go after criminals.

The next morning, they attended the inquest, lounged around the front doors, and kept an eye on the young man seated in the middle of the gallery. After most of the folks had exited, Billy nodded toward Chris and rose to allow Thorn to pass out of the court. Then suddenly, sticking his left leg out, he tripped up the young man, causing him to stumble and almost fall. Both deputies swung around and latched onto the youth's arms to support him, with his arms unable to go after his iron.

"Oh, so sorry about that," said Billy.

"Say, what gives! Let me go."

"Excuse us," said Chris. "Let us help you out of the door. We sure don't want anyone to get hurt exiting a public building we are responsible for guarding."

With that, Chris barked, "Stop." As they halted, he was inspired to reach down toward the floor and deftly removed the young man's Colt from its holster. He had already observed no trigger tab holding it in place. He pretended to pick it up from the floor.

"Why, looky here! You dropped your shooting iron. Let me put it back for ya." With that, he dropped the pistol into the youth's holster backward and pushed down on its grip, firmly locking it in place. "We sure don't want you to lose your nice shooting piece."

They walked the youth roughly down the stairs in what saloon bouncers call the "bum's rush." With the youth's feet flying and unable to gain traction, they quickly descended the stairs and around the building to an alley whose entrance was secluded by an empty one-horse carriage parked at its opening.

"What gives? You can't get away with this. Let me go."

With that, the deputies released their holds and left him to support himself on his unsteady feet. Backing up a few yards, they faced the young man, who was now all business.

"We know who you are and what you've come for," said Billy. "We are here to stop you."

"What do you mean? I just came into town to watch the circus a little. Good entertainment, that's all."

"Not a chance," said Chris. "You were shooting off your mouth last night at the Belle in front of a half dozen friends of ours who said you were bragging about you being a gun hand and how you put down a dangerous man that no one hereabouts had ever heard of. Also, we know you aim to take down the Pinkerton agent who brought in your three friends. Don't deny it. We know it all."

The youth, his greasy hair mussed with his hat pushed to one side, and his shirt pulled out from under his pants, one of his braces had popped its button and dangled. He looked even smaller and more foolish, standing with feet apart, poised to fast draw with his right hand poised nervously above a pistol shoved in backward. During his confusion, he had not bothered to look down, rather he knew it was holstered by its weight.

"First, what do we call you?"

"They call me Hell on Wheels. I'm instant death."

A big smile spread across Chris' mouth, and his eyes crinkled with laugh lines. "My oh my, that's a good one. I think you've been reading too many dime novels. What do we call you?"

"You don't need to know 'cause you and your friend ain't going to be around long enough to call anybody anything."

"Brave words, I'll give you that. Kid, you're game, that's for sure." Chris snapped his fingers and said, "I've got it. We'll call you Kid. What do you think Billy? Will that be good for his tombstone?"

Billy nodded hard eyes with no smile and said, "At least it's short."

"All right, let's do this if that's what you want. For you see, we are here to see that you or no one else guns down Thorn, and if by some chance you do get by me, which you won't, Billy here is a deadeye shot and will put one right into your ticker. Savvy?"

"What is this Thorn fellow to you boys?"

Billy stepped a pace forward and answered, "He's one of the finest men we've ever met. He takes us out to practice our shooting skills and helps us any way he can."

The kid didn't understand. He had never had any man to care about him, except to go and fetch his drink, chop his wood, boss, and slap him and his mom around the farm. He asked, "What's he getting out of it? Is he forming a gang?"

"Maybe," continued Billy, "but not the kind you are thinking about, but a gang of lawmen. We're sick of the robbers, killers, and rapists terrorizing the common folks. We, and our kind, with the help and training from men like Thorn, are going to put an end to it."

"There's even more. It's bigger than that," said Chris. Billy looked at his friend in surprise, not knowing what he would say next. "We've got this plan to form a real band of law dogs, as hard, if not harder, than the ones we are going after. Big rewards are floating around on men like Ivory Thompson and his friends. You wouldn't believe how much Thorn is getting paid for bringing them in, dead or alive. He'll soon be the richest man in the county."

The kid was impressed with the plan and whistled in admiration.

"So," said Chris, "you have a choice. Either go for it and die knowing that you'll have a Christian burial and a marker, or promise us you'll ride out of town and never come back gunning for Thorn. But I'll tell you, if you are ever looking for a fair fight, I'm here to accommodate you, but it wouldn't be fair for you today. You see, I pulled a trick on you…"

At that moment, the side door to the courthouse opened, and their attention was drawn to the Honorable Thomas X. Clark's exit, carpet bag in hand.

"Hello, boys. What did you all think of the inquest?" Not waiting for an answer, he quickly walked past the trio, untied the reins from the hitching post's iron ring, and climbed into his carriage. "By the way, Billy, I'm hearing good things about you from the sheriff. Welcome to our legal fraternity. Chris, isn't it? Good to have you."

Adjusting himself to the shifting cab on its springs, he said, "By the way, you, young man, fix yourself up; be proud of your name. You look as if you've been on a bender. Be more like these young men, and why, in the Good Lord's name, do you carry your pistol in your holster backward?" With that, he flicked the reins, said, "Giddy up, girl," and was gone.

"Backward?" Asked the kid. Looking down and frozen in surprise, he jumped back and exclaimed, "It's backward. You double-dealing sidewinder."

Both Chris and Billy broke out in belly-holding, gut-splitting guffaws and laughter. The kid's confusion melted, and soon, he laughed, but not with their robust enthusiasm.

"I could have tried to draw on you? That's not funny?"

"Oh," said Chris. I was waiting for it, hoping for it, praying for it, but the judge came out and blew out the candle on my cake. It was just a joke. I was funning with you."

"Would you have killed me trying to get my weapon? I didn't know you put it in backward."

"Naw," said Chris, "I was beginning to spill the beans when the judge came out."

"Magistrate," said Billy.

"Come again," said Chris.

"He's a magistrate, not a judge," Billy said. "I'll explain the difference sometime."

"But it would have been fun to watch if you had gone for it. We could joke with you from now until Gabriel blows his horn. Things like that never get old. By the way, I'm Chris Walling, just up from San Antone, now a deputy sheriff in this here berg."

"Part-time deputy," corrected Billy, who introduced himself with his one-word moniker. The three shook hands, slapped each other's backs, and laughed again.

"Can I, ah, put it around the right way and straighten myself up a bit?"

"Sure," said Billy as Chris, unable to wipe the smile from his face, suggested they retire to the Belle for sustenance. He said apologetically, "Uh, can either of you spot me with some coin? I ain't been paid yet?"

"Sure," said the kid, "the drinks are on me. If I can figure out how to keep my pants up with a popped-out button on my brace." They laughed again.

At the Belle, after each had a shot of top drawer and a beer on the kid, they found an empty table in the corner and sat with the fourth chair's vacant back to the room.

"Here's to you," said Chris as they clinked mugs and took long drinks of beer. "What are your plans, Kid? Might not be good to hang around here too long." They looked around and noticed several cowboys at the bar directing their attention toward them.

One of the cowboys, a big tough, looking galoot, finished his shot of red eye, slammed it down on the bar, and approached their table. "I thought you said you were here to take down the Pinkerton man. Well, why didn't you?"

The kid looked up and smiled. "I found out that he isn't the right one. That's all. You've got a good man in this Pinkerton, and I'm still looking for a different one."

"Oh…I see. All right then." The cowboy returned to the bar and explained that the kid had made a mistake. He was gunning for a different Pinkerton. The men nodded in understanding and called for another round.

Upon exiting, Billy and Chris shook hands with the kid and inquired about his directions.

"I think I'll head up to Silverton. I hear there is opportunity there."

"Funny thing," Chris spoke quietly, "we may see you there. Billy and I are headed that way ourselves, after a little more shooting practice, to arrest the two scoundrels who are wanted for murdering the miner and raping his missus. The ones you heard about this afternoon at the inquest."

The kid whistled in amazement, "Be careful boys. I've heard that a real desperado is up there gathering a gang of hard cases for a big job. He'll plant you both if you get in his way, no matter how fast you draw your irons."

"Who is this guy? Have you heard his name?" asked Billy.

"No," said the kid, "but if you go to the biggest saloon there and wait during the evenings, he'll find you, and he has red hair. Gentlemen, I'll be heading out now. Happy trails."

Chapter 17
Kid from Texas

The kid rode north on the lonely rocky trail leading to Silverton, a hard one-day ride away. At this hour, the shadows were deepening, and the gold of the leaves of the aspen trees lining the trail looked dark. Even though he had only ridden a short way from town, he decided to camp early. He noticed a cabin at the first turn-off but received no answer upon calling, "Hello, Cabin?" several times. No lights came from its windows, and the chimney issued no smoke, which should have been in use this time of year. Cautiously, he approached the front door, dismounted, and knocked. Still no reply. Trying the solid front door, he found the cabin locked tight as a drum.

"Must be the cabin belonging to the folks who helped the lady in black after a back shooter gunned down her man," he mused aloud. The only response was the who, who-whooo, of a barn owl. "It's me," the kid answered, "just passing through," he mounted and resumed his ride on the trail.

He spotted another cabin in a clearing a short distance up the next draw. It looked too snug to be empty unless it was the location of the killing and violation. "Hello, cabin?" But again, no response. Riding up to the front porch, he dismounted and carefully looked to see if he could find the spot where the miner had been gunned down, but the path was in dark shadows.

Dismounting, he dropped the reins forward to the ground and pulled his revolver from its holster, not sure why, and quietly went up the steps, trying to make as little noise as possible. His horse, a piebald mare, watched him with interest, then began to wander off looking for grass.

He rapped on the cabin's door, carefully keeping his pistol ready. An inner voice told him to leave the place to the dead and move on, but with a little push, the front door swung inward with an eerie squeaking sound. A shiver ran down the kid's spine, and he swallowed hard. Like most young men of his generation, he was cautious about things he felt but couldn't see. Emotions, feelings, superstitions, and hunches played an active role in his life. This had to be Todd's cabin. With the barrel of his gun, he pushed the door the remainder of the way open and stepped in, flattening himself against the wall and allowing his eyes to adjust to the gloom.

The cabin looked like a whirlwind had blown through it. The chairs and the kitchen table were overturned. There were blankets, a quilt, and scraps of torn clothing scattered about on the floor. Carefully shuffling his boots so as not to stumble over anything, he moved around the room, looking for a lamp. Near the door, he spotted an old miner's lantern hanging from a peg on the wall. Pulling out one of his "strikes anywhere," he lifted the glass and shook its reservoir to ascertain if it had coal oil. Satisfied by the sound, he struck the match first, looking around the cabin before lighting and adjusting the wick. The lantern revealed one large room with a kitchen pantry with open doors, items strewn on the floor, and a wash sink containing dirty dishes with a pump. A rocking chair near the stove was the only piece of furniture in the cabin that was righted.

Righting the table and chairs, he placed the lantern on the wall peg and surveyed the scene. The bed was where he imagined it to be as he briefly reviewed the scene he had heard at the inquest. The door flies open, and the lady is hit by it and thrown back onto the bed. The two men rushed her, and one, the big one, ripped off her clothes and had his way with her while the little one watched and danced around.

Taking the lantern with him, the kid left the cabin, picked up the reins of his mount in one hand, held the lantern high in the other, walked to the barn, and looked in. It contained only two box stalls, but one on the right had been recently used and contained fresh hay.

After removing the tack, he found an old curry brush and gave his piebald a good brushing as she chomped her meal. He removed caked mud and splatter from her legs and combed the burrs from her black splotches on the white background of her coat. He calmly talked to her as he brushed and cleaned her, calming them both in the process.

"Do you know, Lady, some folks call you a black and white pinto, and I guess you are that and more." He retrieved his bedroll, saddle bags, and rifle and returned to the cabin.

The kid spent the next hour in the cabin picking up household items, sweeping out broken pottery, and cleaning up spills, just like he had done as a child living with his mother and one of his uncles. Finally approaching the bed, he shook out the quilt and blanket, straightened the straw-filled mattress, and flipped it over. After checking on Lady a final time, he dropped the bar to lock the door and sat on the edge of the bed. After pulling off his boots and pants, he retrieved his "little wife" from his saddlebag and began to sew a new button onto his pants for his braces.

It sounded like Chris and Billy had a pretty good plan going. Silverton was a magnet drawing the worst of the area's bad men to pull a major job under the leadership of the redheaded man. If he lived, a gunman's split in a major heist would be what? Maybe five or even ten thousand dollars. A small fortune, that's true, but think of the real fortune a few law dogs could bring in with wanted posters, dead or alive. A good group of law dogs should clean up, all nice and legal-like, and retire for life. He would scout out Silverton and try to keep track of the criminal element there. With that, he stretched out on the bed, placed his pistol in easy reach on the floor, turned on his side, and went to sleep.

The next morning, after fixing a pot of coffee on the potbelly stove, he sliced and fried up a pound of bacon he found in the bottom of the larder. In the cast iron skillet, he fried a batch of corn dodgers in the bacon grease. It was just like he did for his mother and uncle when he was a child. After cleaning up from his breakfast, he left a crisp greenback dollar on the table in gratuity, saddled up Lady, and after her morning feed, a bucket full of water, and the relief of her bladder, they rode north.

Along the way, he decided he liked the name Kid. It was better than his real name, Leroy Brooks. He liked the name Roy. It sounded manly, but Leroy didn't have "what it takes." He played around with variants of Texas towns and places he had heard of, like the San Antonio Kid, good, but too long; the San Antone Kid had a nice ring; the El Paso Kid, also good, but there was already one, the Helotes Kid, no one knew where that place was, and the Abilene Kid, nice. Still, he had once heard that town referred to as the armpit of Texas. He laughed loudly as he thought of the small town on the way to Houston, Grapevine, Texas, The Grapevine Kid. Wow, Chris and Billy would get a laugh out of that one.

He needed a good handle when he arrived in Silverton the next day.

That night, he camped early in a meadow off the trail. It had been used as a campsite since the Indian days. It had plenty of dry wood and a stream of fresh water, so he bedded down after stripping the tack from Lady, watering her, and wiping her down with dried grass. Next, he hobbled her into an area of tall grass. He lay on his back that night, counting the major stars and constellations. The waning moon rose and rode across the sky, then set, leaving a magnificent sprinkling of stars heavenward. Then he saw a shooting star and said a prayer for his mom. Finally, he closed his eyes and slept.

The next afternoon, he rode into Silverton. It was not much of a town, even by Colorado standards of 1885. He noted several saloons as he rode down Main Street. He stopped in front of one of the new brick two-story buildings and raised his stirrups to survey both ways. Yes, he thought, this is the biggest saloon in town, the Silver Dollar.

Continuing down the street, he noted a reasonably clean-looking hotel. At the far end of the street, he saw a barn and a corral confining a dozen horses and one unhappy-looking gray long-eared mule. Pulling up in front of the barn door, he asked, "Do you have room for another horse?"

An old man dressed in overalls with no shirt was pitching hay from a wagon into the barn. "Howdy," he said, "Sure do, but I can't tell you about tomorrow. Looks like we are having ourselves some kind of convention here. The hotel is full, and we're almost, but I got room for a pretty piebald. What's her name?"

"Lady," Kid answered as he dismounted and started pulling his tack from her.

"You can throw your pad and saddle over the rail inside, but it is best to take your bedroll, saddlebags, and rifle with you. With all the new folks in town, you never know."

"Good advice anywhere these days. How much for the stall, feed, and let her run with the remuda?"

"It's a dollar a day. Now, I know it's as steep as it sounds, but with so many new people in town, I've had to hire an extra hand. I don't know how long it'll last. And that ain't no remuda in the corral; those horses have been left with me during the past few days."

"So, you say the hotel is filled up?"

"Right to the brim, but seeing you are paying the going freight for your piebald, you can sleep in her stall, no extra fee. "Sides, it might be nice to have a real gun hand sleeping here at night." Kid took the statement as a compliment, placed his gear on fresh straw in the corner, and forked some additional on top as a cover.

"By the way, who does that long-eared mule belong to?"

"Oh, a couple of hard cases brought him in. One big fellow with a scar and a little weasel-faced man. They are over at one of the hotels."

"You don't say." Patting Lady goodbye, he paid the man two silver dollars and told him he'd decide tomorrow how long he'd stay. He started walking toward the biggest saloon in town.

A long bar sat in the rear of the main room filled with tables and games of chance. The rich smell of fresh sawdust on the floor filled his nostrils. It was a bit early for serious drinking and gaming, and only a few cowboys and miners sat at tables or stood drinking at the bar. None of the drink girls had made an appearance yet.

Management was setting out a spread of cheese, bread, mustard, and a quarter saddle of cooked beef with the chef's knife and fork nearby. Some hard-boiled eggs sat in a bowl near a stack of small plates, with salt and pepper shakers handy.

"Is your spread open," Kid called out to the cook.

"If you are a paying customer?"

"Give me a shot of whiskey and a beer, and I'll be a paying customer."

"That'll be two bits." The man in a chef hat, holding a white towel over the crook of his arm, waited.

"Two bits for a shot and a beer. Wow, these are San Antone prices." Kid slipped a coin from his pouch and laid it on the bar.

"You from Texas?"

"Sure 'nuff. What gave it away?"

"Just a lucky guess."

Kid took his red eye straight, feeling the cheap booze burning down his gullet, and took a swig of beer to chase it down further. Grunted with satisfaction, he picked up a plate, cut some meat and cheese, and piled it on a slice of bread with plenty of mustard. His mom had told him that mustard killed poison. Next, he took an egg, rolled it on the bar, picked the shell free, popped it into his mouth, and began to chew.

"You just get in town?" A cowboy by himself trying to beat Old Saul asked.

"Um-hmmm." The Kid kept chewing and took another deep drink of beer to help wash the egg down. Finally able to speak, he picked up his plate, took out a Bowie knife with an eight-inch blade—a little short for a Texan—and began cutting up and eating his meal.

"Join me kid."

"Funny you should say that. That's what everybody calls me, Kid. What do folks call you?" He studied the broad-shouldered, powerful-looking man sitting before him in range clothes. His left hand moved the cards while his right was hidden under the table. A broad-brim high crown hat covered his head, and he couldn't see the color of his hair.

"Most folks call me Red. Sit down, Kid, and finish your meal. Hey, barkeep," he called, "bring us a bottle of the good stuff and two beers on me."

Kid slowly cut his food and, sticking each bite, ate off the point of his knife. Red just played his version of solitaire and waited for him to finish. Two men at the end of the bar also watched Kid eat his meal with interest. When Kid looked their way, they both lowered their heads over their drinks and pretended disinterest, but Kid noticed the big one had a scar on his left cheek.

"Who are the two at the bar? Friends of yours?" Red didn't look up but continued to lay cards down and finished his game by winning.

"Nope, no friends of mine," he scooped up the cards with his left hand, shuffled them one-handed with professional ease, and fanned them out on the table. "Pick one, go on."

Kid laid down his knife and pulled one from the fan. Red also slid one and said, "At the count of three, I'll turn mine over first, one, two, three," he slowly counted and turned over the card, a Queen of Diamonds. "Now, hold your horses. I have a question for you first. I bet you a hundred dollars that my card will beat yours."

"I'll take that bet," and Kid flipped over the Queen of Spades.

"You are one lucky son of a gun. I didn't beat you, for a queen can't beat another queen." Red took off his hat, revealing a wild head of red hair, and removed from the hat band two fifty-dollar greenbacks. "I believe in paying my just debts." He shoved them to Kid, who thanked him and slipped them into his shirt pocket.

"Let's get to know each other. I think I'll have some of that meat and such. How is it?"

"Mighty good for bar food, mighty good."

"Have a real drink of Missouri's finest bourbon whiskey. This is from the Holladay distillery, the best."

"I thought bourbon came from Kentucky."

"Yes, most people think that, and they'd be wrong. Look at the bottle itself. It says Missouri bourbon right on the label."

Kid briefly studied the label and nodded, "I learn new stuff every day." They spent the rest of the evening sipping good liquor, playing roulette, and dancing around with the drink girls on Red's money.

Chapter 18
Fair Fight

Kid woke up fully dressed, with his boots still on, lying cockeyed in Lady's stall. He felt the effects of his drunk and stiff back. "Morning, Kid," said the hostler. "Ha, ha," he laughed, slapping his thigh. "You really tied one on last night with the boss. Everybody calls him that, but no one seems to know what he is the boss of. He brought you here over his shoulder, carried you like a baby, and deposited you in Lady's stall. Gave me a silver dollar to stay here last night and keep an eye on ya till you woke up. Ha, ha, ha."

Stretching and rubbing his eyes to get the sleep out, Kid saw the same man in the same overalls he had met yesterday. "What do I call my guardian angel?"

"Ha, ha, ha," he chuckled, "Everybody calls me Andy. You can too if you want."

"Andy, you're my guardian angel. I like the sound of that. Help me up, will you?" Andy reached down and pulled Kid to his feet.

"Steady now, boy. You don't look so good. I've got a pot of coffee brewing in my room. Let me help you walk there. I've got a tub full of fresh water for the horses you can soak your head in. It always works for me. Ha, ha, ha. You'll feel better after your coffee."

True to his word, it didn't take long for Kid to wash up, use a curry brush to untangle his long hair and get a cup of black brew in his system to feel his old self again. There is something to be said for drinking good whiskey, he thought.

He remembered his one and only drunk on rotgut after he killed his latest uncle with his Bowie knife, as the uncle lay on the floor passed out after hitting his mother in the head with his pistol. After the deed, he sponged the blood from his mother's scalp and face and laid her on her bed with her hands folded. She was finally at peace and didn't have to wait any longer for his father to return.

Kid tied a bedroll and a bag of tuck behind the saddle. He unbuckled the gun belt holding the big Colt that had killed his mother and found his poke contained 45 dollars in species and some greenbacks.

Before leaving his dead mother, he splashed a quart of coal oil around the bed on which she lay. He struck a kitchen match, tossed it in the liquid pool, watched the oily red flames lick around her body, and caught the quilt and cornhusk mattress into a smokey blaze.

Taking a jug with him, he quietly closed the door and exited their little ranch house outside New Braunfels, Texas. Stopping the horse only once at the top of a hill, he turned to watch the bone-dry, wood-framed house engulfed in roiling flames.

That night he got blind drunk on the remainder of the rotgut and woke up having pissed on himself with the horse looking down at him and licking his face. Never again, he had promised himself. But that wasn't true, seeing how Red had to look after him.

Feeling better, he took Lady, a horse he had won in a poker game with a sour-faced wrangler last October in San Antonio, into the corral. He watched her run circles, prance around with the other horses, and nudge the sad-looking little gray long-eared mule into some movement.

Andy came out to watch Lady frolic around. "Seems like your girl likes that little mule." They watched in silence.

"Funny," Andy chuckled, "ha, ha, the couple of gents who brought the mule in claimed to be prospectors. Said the mule is their pack animal. The funny thing though is that they didn't have a shovel, pick, axe, or pans, and they ain't bought none, not so far as I know."

"Does the little one look like a rat or a weasel to you?"

"You know, ha, ha, it could be either."

"Thanks. I'm going out to get some breakfast. Be back later."

Kid walked toward the aroma of steak, onions, and potatoes cooking on an outside charcoal grill and had a substantial meal with more coffee.

Following breakfast, he walked to the Silver Dollar Saloon to find Red and apologize for his conduct the night before. Never before had anyone, other than his mom had to carry him home and put him to bed. He was embarrassed but noticed his pocket was still stuffed with the remains of Red's two fifty-dollar bills.

It was early afternoon, and the saloon began filling up with a lunch crowd of cowboys, hard cases, and miners. Entering the swinging batwings, he spotted Red at his usual table but turned toward the bar when he noticed him in deep conversation with two other men, who appeared to have recently arrived based on their trail dust and haggard faces.

They each had a mug of beer and listened with interest to Red. Kid saw an opening at the bar and bellied up asking for a beer. He placed a thin dime on the bar and swung around with his back to the bar to look around the saloon.

The roulette wheel started with a clack, clack, clack as the ball spun around the wheel. That might be fun. The two young drink girls, showing their ample feminine attributes, were roaming the tables, taking drink orders. In turn, a patron would occasionally buy a drink for one of them. Everyone knew the drinks purchased for them were charged at a top-drawer price and were just tea water. But it opened the door for future good times and favors. All the saloons, gentlemen's clubs, and whore houses the world over had the same setup. The girls encouraged the clientele to drink and spend their money while they, in turn, received an additional remuneration above their usual starving wage based on the number of drinks purchased for them. The house won, and the girls usually remained sober enough to negotiate additional activities.

Kid saw the two hombres described by Andy at the other end of the bar, nursing beers. Touching his Colt's grip, he reassured himself that it was correctly placed in its holster. He was developing a bad habit of checking his pistol numerous times during the day. He would have to watch that. It might give the wrong idea that he was going for his gun.

The little man noticed him, touched his partner's shoulder, and nodded his way. They watched him with open interest. The big man finished his beer and approached Kid, pushing his way in next to him. The little weasel-faced man stood back, hands on his hips, and watched. Kid turned to the big man and said, "I don't know you, and I don't like being crowded."

"Just being friendly. Let me buy you a drink. Hey, barkeep, two beers here. I couldn't help but notice you chumming around with Red last night."

"Stop right there. I don't drink with strangers, so give your friend there another beer." With that, Kid picked up his heavy glass mug with his left hand, took a sip, and swung back around with his back to the bar.

"Don't ignore me, you little squirt. Do you think you are too good to drink with me 'cause you partied with Red last night? I heard he had to carry you out of here and put you to bed."

"No," answered Kid. "I don't drink with strangers, but I know who you are and want nothing to do with you or your little weasel-faced partner." Kid cut his eyes for a split second to the smaller man. "I got in town yesterday from Durango, where I attended the inquest dealing with you and your partner."

"What are you talking about?" demanded the big man.

"The inquest was to determine who murdered a miner named Mike Todd, shot him in the back, beat up and raped his wife, a defenseless woman, and stole his little, long-eared gray mule. The same mule you got stabled over at Andy's barn," bellowed Kid.

"That's a god-damned lie!" The other men at the bar, especially the miners, were taking interest in their conversation.

"Bill," said one man, "go over to Andy's and see if he has a long-eared mule there belonging to these two." The man named Bill finished his beer and headed out the bat wings at a trot.

"Calling me a liar, are you?" said Kid, "I attended the inquest on Friday, and you and your little weasel-faced partner were described to a T as the ones who shot that miner in the back before attacking and raping his little wife. They'll soon have a posse up here to root you two out." Several hard cases were at the bar, and the two newcomers seated with Red took notice of this remark and looked around nervously at the bat wings as if expecting the posse's appearance any second.

"I say you are a damned liar, and there ain't nobody after us for anything."

"You're the damned liar." Said Kid in a loud enough voice for all to hear. "They just posted a reward for you two birds."

"Huh," said the big man who went for his gun. At the same instant, Kid swung the glass mug squarely, landing a good solid blow against his opponent's temple. Beer splashed over them both, as well as several men standing nearby. With a grunt, the big man went down like a sack of potatoes. Quick as lightning, Kid pulled his Colt and pointed it directly at the weasel face, whose hand had enough sense to stop him from dragging his pistol from its holster.

"Get your hands up. Higher. Reach for the sky." With each command, the weasel-face stretched his hands higher. "All right, you want a stand-up fair fight. Let's go outside so as not to shoot up this establishment or any of the nice people with stray rounds. Keep walking for the door, hands up, till I tell you otherwise. Go on outside. You boys at the door, do you mind holding the bat wings open for us." This was instantly done.

"You can't get away with this. This ain't right. I didn't kill the miner or rape that lady, he did." The little man nodded toward his partner, who was beginning to stir. The miners began to murmur, and someone called for a rope.

"Somebody get the law. I ain't no gunman," the rat-faced man pleaded. But no one moved to intervene in the drama, and Silverton had no law. As the men pressed toward the door to watch an authentic and rare gunfight, a miner's heavy hob-nailed boot kicked the prostrate man in the head, sending him into a coma from which he never returned.

"Keep walking, now down the street."

At that instance, Bill came running down the street hollering, "It's true. They brought in a little gray mule, just like Kid said. Andy described them two all right. It's them." The crowd pushed out onto the boardwalk as passing cowboys and teamsters driving wagons cleared the street and dismounted to take cover and to watch.

"That's far enough. You can put your hands down and turn around." They stopped twenty paces from each other with the rat-faced man's hands still raised. He stood frozen, unable to move.

"I've holstered my gun. You can drop your hands and turn around any time now." The crowd was silent. Everyone waited for the drama to play out, and everyone knew he would swear that Kid was giving the little guy a fair fight. After all, he started drawing first on him in the saloon.

"We're waiting," Kid barked.

The little man knew his time was running out. He could either beg for mercy, and hope Kid wouldn't shoot a crawling man, but then the crowd would turn mean and become a lynch mob. He wouldn't have a chance. Or he could quickly go for his gun. No sooner had he thought about it than this was what he tried.

Kid's blast from his Colt .45 spun the man around, sending his pistol flying toward the bystanders. It landed in the dirt at the same time the little man hit the ground hard and died. The crowd came pressing forward, ringing the dead man. Someone picked up his pistol and brought it to Kid. "I think this is rightly yours."

Someone yelled, "Hoorah," and the applause began spontaneously. They clapped, stomped, whistled, and slapped each other's backs. One old timer danced a buck and wing, a form of a solo jig. Soon, most of the men poured back into the saloon with Kid pushed along. At one point, he was carried up to the bar, picked up by two burley miners, and seated on the bar, none too gently, with his boots dangling and a beer in hand.

The miners seemed delighted with the gunfight's outcome and formed a reception line until soon Kid's hand was sore from pumping.

Then the cowboys got into it and had to wring and pump his sore hand even more. Looking at his swollen fingers, Kid knew he could not defend himself if push came to shove. His money was no good at the Silver Dollar Saloon that night.

After the celebration settled down a bit, the big man was declared dead, and four strong men carried him out to the boardwalk and propped him alongside his partner. Kid eased off the bar, sat at a nearby table, and soaked his aching fingers in his beer.

Red came over and offered his congratulations. Kid tried to apologize for his behavior the previous night, but Red waved it away and said, "Nice job. Is it true that there was an inquest in Durango naming those two mugs for murder and rape?"

"Don't forget the little gray mule, Red. Miners take their mules seriously. Yes, it's true, but only as to their description, not names. I was at the inquest and saw it all."

"Hmmm," mused Red. "What about the posse and reward? Was that just a bluff?"

"No, I overheard two law dogs saying that in a few days, they were coming up here to take them back, dead or alive. The judge ordered a reward to be posted and telegrams sent out over the country looking for those two. It'll take a few days to get the posters printed."

"That's fine. Here's what I want you to do." Kid listened carefully as Red explained that there would be a buckboard containing the two stiffs out front of the barn in the morning. He was to take them by wagon with his horse and the mule bringing up the rear, back down to Durango. He was to describe how he dealt with the two, and if need be, a few of the boys could come down to verify the killings. He was not to talk about his presence in Silverton or talk about any of his friends.

Kid was directed to collect the reward and stop the posse from coming for a visit. Red handed Kid a poke containing one hundred dollars in gold and silver coins for this. Kid nodded in agreement but withheld his hand from sealing the bargain because of his sore fingers.

Red looked down at his swollen hand and understood. He returned to his friends at his corner table, and they soon left the saloon.

Chapter 19
Social Graces and Plans

Funny how easily one gets into a habit, Thorn thought, as he spread his cloth napkin across his lap rather than tuck it under his string tie. He settled in for breakfast at his hotel's dining room. Yesterday, he had watched a gentleman from back East, based on his duds, spread his napkin out, fold it triangularly, like a bandit folds his kerchief before a robbery, and place it in his lap. He watched, and by meal's end, the gent hadn't spilled a thing on his shirt or vest. He wiped his mouth with the napkin and left it on the table. Nice and neat. Now that's class, he thought.

Breakfast at 9:00 a.m., or thereabouts, he still hadn't found a pocket watch he fancied at the mercantile store and thought he'd look in Denver. He'd put his trip off for a few days to do more training with Billy and Chris. They were both developing into good gun hands. It came naturally to Chris, while Billy had to work hard to match Chris' speed and accuracy.

Thorn felt that both boys were settling down to the routine work of the sheriff's office, making rounds in the evening, serving legal notices and papers, defusing fights, and keeping order, as much as possible, in and around the saloons and sporting clubs. It was hard, thankless work. Yet it was a good experience putting up with drunken armed cowboys ready to spend their last dimes on a friend and quickly reaching for iron when an insult was perceived.

Chris had to tamp down his overactive humor gland. He found laughter and joy in the most dangerous situations while Billy, more serious and thoughtful, weighed out options and carefully planned for the "what if." They made a great team and complimented each other.

"Morning. Are you eating by yourself this morning?" inquired Miss Sally, as he had come to call her. She gave a beautiful, dimpled smile that lit up her face as she poured his first cup of coffee. "The usual?" she asked.

"Yes, thanks. I'm by myself this morning. The boys are out doing legal work."

"I noticed they had already come and gone earlier, and you like to eat late at about 9:00 a.m."

"Why sure. I'm like an old dog who likes routine," he smiled unfolding his morning copy of the Durango Gazette as she went to the kitchen to place his order.

The headlines jumped off the page screaming, "NO ARRESTS IN THE MICHAEL TODD MURDER AND THE VIOLATION OF HIS WIFE! WHY?" He scanned the story, a rehash of an old copy and a summary of the findings at the inquest.

It was interesting, he thought as he remembered how he had brought in Ivory Thompson and his two companions, and it wasn't even worth a follow-up mention in the paper. He was old news. He ran down the list of names and charges from the town's police blotter: drunk and disorderly, domestic dispute, fist fights, one shooting (missed), and a stolen horse that was later found at the edge of town and returned to the stable. He thought you couldn't ask for a better town to live in. After reading each page, cover to cover, including advertisements, notices, and church bulletins, he carefully refolded it at the arrival of his steak and potatoes.

"What do you have planned today?" Sally asked casually as she cleared his plates to make room for the slice of apple pie.

"Oh, I'm thinking about a shave and a trim, and maybe in the afternoon, spend time reading. I bought a book by an English fellow named Charles Dickens. Sounds like a pretty good story. It's set during the French Revolution."

"Oh. I've heard tell of that revolution. It was after ours, wasn't it? Isn't that the one where they were chopping the heads of Kings and

Queens until they ran out of royalty and began chopping off each other's?"

"Sounds about right, but I haven't started it yet. It's called *The Tale of Two Cities*, but I don't know much about it."

"You'll have to tell me about it from time to time. Oh, excuse me, folks needing coffee. Can't be seen lollygagging around when folks need food and drink. You know how people talk." She hurried off with a big blue coffee pot to refill extended cups. He observed that she was a strong, well-built woman, maybe in her early thirties, and able to tote a half-gallon pot of steaming coffee around and pour it out to the correct measure without spilling a drop while taking orders and talking to customers. She was some gal. He wondered why she had become a spinster. She was good-looking and healthy enough to be married, the kind of woman to bear a parcel of young'uns. He'd like to find out a little more about her and might even like to get to know Miss Sally.

Interesting, Thorn reflected as he looked around the nearly empty room. Less than a week ago, his presence was the talk of the town. Now, other than a polite "Morning, Mr. Hagerman," upon entering, he was left alone to eat his meal, drink coffee, and read his morning paper.

Miss Sally approached to see if there was anything else he wanted. "No, I'm fine, but there is something I'd like to ask you if I'm not being too forward."

"Sure, go ahead," she waved at the last customer leaving. See you, doctor."

"I noticed the local church is having a potluck social after service this coming Sunday. I've never been to one and was thinking…I don't have any way to bring a potluck dish…and…"

"Are you asking me to go with you or to prepare a dish for you to take?"

"I'm interested in both and will gladly pay for the dish. Would you care to accompany me?"

She stopped and thought long and hard, "I sure can't accept your money for a dish if I'm going with you, as in a date?"

"I'm an old bachelor and don't know anything about etiquette, dates, and such. Just thought it might be interesting, nothing more."

She saw him retreating and understood his difficulty in asking such a question. "I'd be honored for you to take me to the dance and social, and I'll bring the best pot-luck dish in the town, but there's just one little thing I'm unsure of?"

"What's that? The dining room is closed on Sundays, isn't it."

"That's not the issue. I haven't been to a dance or social in so many years. I'm not sure if I remember how to dance. Do you dance Mr. Hagerman?"

"Well, I don't rightly know. I'm in the same boat, except for attending some barn dances as a kid, where all we did was watch the old folks dance and sneak some spiked punch and such. I don't know the first thing about dancing."

"Hmmm, we seem to have a problem. I suppose we can either skip the dance, saying you have an old war wound or some such excuse, or we could try it out before Sunday."

"I don't think it's a good way to start out my first appearance in local society by telling a lie. I made it through the late unpleasantness with nary a scratch, and it might be unlucky to say such a thing— sort of tempting fate."

"You are a very lucky man, or have you made your own luck, Mr. Hagerman?"

"Please call me Thorn. That's an interesting question worth considering. I tell you what. You get off work at about 3 to 4:00 p.m., right?"

"Yes, just depending on the diners and the clean-up."

"What would be the best day for you and me to meet and practice our dancing? I'm free most evenings."

"Tomorrow, Thursday would work for me," she stated, "but where?"

"I would offer my room, but it's a bit cramped, and the guests in the rooms below might not appreciate my tromping around above their heads," pausing, "it might not be good for your reputation."

"Yes, I see your point," she smiled, "I suppose we could meet at my house. It's at the edge of town, and we shouldn't bother anybody, but I'd have to make some arrangements first. I can let you know tomorrow at breakfast if that will work for you."

"Sure, but until we know we're going through with this thing," he almost said this fool thing, "let's keep it quiet, just between us for the time being." She nodded in agreement.

"Then it's a date. I mean about seeing you tomorrow for my breakfast." At that, Miss Sally flew back toward the kitchen, gathering a tray of dirty dishes along the way. Thorn noticed the cooks and busboy paying close attention to their conversation and quietly talking.

Thorn spent much of the afternoon reading his new novel. He found it interesting but kept getting confused about who was who. He jotted a few names and key events into his notebook as a reminder to jog his memory if Miss Sally showed any interest.

He took a break and wandered down to the hotel veranda for fresh air, occupied a rocking chair, and enjoyed firing up a crooked-looking black cheroot cigar in the open air. Not everyone appreciated the strong, aromatic smell of Tennessee-grown tobacco. They had been hard to locate on the Texas frontier after the war. They had never been popular with the better classes of gentlemen who had gone for either the "roll your own" cigarettes or the newly popular ones called Bonsacks, which were machine-rolled, if you could afford them.

He had tried the new ones a few times; they were good, but he preferred the "tried and true" cheroots for a long smoke to clear out the mind and do some thinking. He had purchased a cigar box full of them. They reminded him of bent twigs from a tree or grapevine that he and his friend, Pete, had tried to smoke as youngsters on their farm. They both had become sick as dogs.

In the evening, he met Sheriff Pat Williams at the Belle for beer and their free spread and afterward offered him a cheroot. Firing them up off the same match, they sat back, inhaled the tobacco deeply, and exhaled clouds of gray smoke.

The sheriff updated Thorn on the reward money coming in. It was now over $10,000 in U.S. currency deposited in his account at the local bank, minus county expenses. Thorn inquired about the response to the Pinkerton telegram.

"I've completed the form and telegraphed it on," said the sheriff.

Thorn retrieved another cheroot from an inside coat pocket and said, "Take another one for later."

"Don't mind if I do. I see you got one of those new cross-draw holsters on your left side and a long leather strapped holster with a tie down on your right side. Pretty fancy."

"Yes, I don't need to advertise that I'm armed, though everyone knows it. They just don't know where my guns are. Besides, if we had trouble, say while we are seated here, you might have trouble getting your Colt into play if it's strapped down. As for me, a quick pull on this new steel clip holster, and I'm in business. When I see you at your office, I'll show you and the boys what I'm talking about. I'm trying it out for a few days, I haven't decided if I'm going to buy it or not. It's not about the money but about getting your artillery into action. As for the reward business, I've sent in my resignation to Pinkerton's Chicago office, but they want me to meet a special agent at their Denver office next week to discuss an important new case."

"Are you going to take it?"

"Probably not, but I've got some other reasons to go up to Denver for a while, so we'll see. I'll be leaving on the Monday train."

"Monday, not earlier?"

"I'm thinking about going to the Church Social on Sunday evening."

"Now that's interesting. I understand you and Sally are going together, and she is going to enter the contest for the best pot-luck dish. My, oh my."

Thorn just shook his head wondering how their plans had gone around the town this fast. As of this morning, he had first heard about the contest for the best dish. "Where'd you hear all that?"

"Oh, a little birdie told me. By the way, I understand the piano player from the Belle is taking off an hour or two this Thursday to play some dance music to get you two started on your dancing career." The sheriff chuckled so loudly that several men at the bar turned to see what was so funny.

Thursday morning after breakfast, Thorn learned from a whispered comment from Miss Sally that everything was arranged for their dance lesson that evening at her house, and they would be properly chaperoned. She gave him a slip of paper with directions and advised him to arrive promptly at 7:00 p.m. because she was paying for the piano player until exactly 8:30 p.m. and didn't want to waste time or money.

He wondered about the chaperone but didn't ask. After a Cheroot smoked in his favorite rocking chair on the veranda, he went to the barbershop for a shave, haircut, and bath. Then, back to the hotel for a nap and reading, followed by a late lunch at one of the restaurants. Finally, the time approached 6:00 p.m. Miss Sally's house was on the way past the stable, so Thorn decided to pay his mare a visit with a handful of carrots and an apple he had purchased earlier at the greengrocer just for such a purpose.

Walking down Main Street past the shops, stores, and restaurants, he noticed the number of people passing with smiles and nods of their heads, wishing him a good evening, followed by giggles and murmured comments. What did everyone else know that he didn't?

Chapter 20
Practice

Thorn confirmed that it was getting on toward 6:00 p.m. by walking down the boardwalk into the street so he could see the clock on the courthouse wall. It was 5:50 p.m. Carrying his bag of carrots and apples he had purchased at the greengrocer, he began his walk down Main, past the saloons, hotels, shops, and restaurants into the seedier part of town where the cribs, lower-class saloons, and whore houses congregated on the side street.

Stopping at the stables, he talked to his big Morgan mare and gave her a rubdown using a leftover jute bean bag he found on a nail. He rubbed her coat and fed her from the bag of treats while the other horses in nearby stalls leaned their heads over the gates and whinnied for their share. He had brought enough apples to give the other nearby horses an apple each. He continued his walk down Main Street to the sound of horses contentedly chomping their desserts.

He arrived at the house described in Sally's note, "It is next to the last streetlamp on Main Street."

Rapping on the door of a modest white-frame farmhouse with a dog trot attached to an additional living space, Thorn was taken back by the appearance of the beefy piano player from the Belle Saloon, but without the monkey and pug derby.

"Mr. Hagerman, I presume," the door was swung wide, and Thorn motioned in. "I'm an old family friend, and Sally had to work a bit late in the dining room, so she asked me to admit you and take your hat and coat. She'll be down in a few minutes."

Thorn slid out of his new polished wool overcoat and, looking around, laid it across a chair in the corner. He perched his Stetson atop and studied the room. The tables and chairs, in what was normally a large dining room had been moved aside, leaving space for the evening's activities. "I take it that you are the chaperone Sally said would be watching over us?"

"That would be me. My name is Louis, just plain Louis, but if you want, you can call me Louie. My friends do."

"Fine, Louie. You can call me Thorn. I don't have friends, but if I did, that's what they'd call me." They shook hands with firm grips as Thorn chuckled.

"I found two bottles of beer and a half-full bottle of Old Granddad in the larder. What's your pleasure?"

"A beer will do just fine." Thorn noticed Louie's pronounced limp in his right leg as he left for the drinks. Thorn looked around the room. Several landscape paintings hung on the walls. They were remarkedly good. The table and chairs were old but gleamed with furniture wax. An upright piano stood near a window with sheet music on its holder. Thorn was looking at the music when Louie returned with two bottles of beer and handed him one. They flipped the wire tops, saluted each other with a clink of the bottles, and took long drafts.

"Good beer," said Thorn. "Tell me, Louie, I saw you playing at the Belle with a little monkey. Where is he now?"

"Oh, my companion, Chica, is no he. She's a red-eyed, jealous female. There will be hell to pay when I pick her up at my room before going to the Belle."

Thorn chuckled and brought the conversation back to Sally. "You were going to tell me about Sally's folks."

"Yes, Sally's dad, who was my great friend, had good taste in drink. Old Granddad is real bourbon whiskey from Kentucky, not that cheap red eye you find around here."

"You said you are a family friend. What is the status of the rest of the family?"

"Oh, that's the rub. Sally and her parents lived here in harmony for many years. Elizabeth, who was Sally's mother, was frail but a talented lady. She painted the landscapes you see around the room." Thorn turned to gaze at a nearby painting.

"Beautiful, aren't they? She had such talent, but her health was challenged by the winters here. Unfortunately, her health failed when Sally was about seventeen years of age, at a time when a young lady should be thinking about romance and a family of her own. She was one of my music pupils and was progressing toward a career, or at least a local concert artist in this backwater. Elizabeth took to her bed with a bad cold in the spring, and by summer, it developed into influenza and pneumonia. She died in the autumn about five years ago, and Sally got a job in town, first at shops and eventually at the hotel dining room. She worked long days to support and take care of them."

"What was wrong with her father?"

"Captain Taylor and I met in an army hospital during the war. We both served under Grant but in different units. We had not met until chance landed us both in the same hospital ward outside Washington, D.C. I was recuperating from a leg wound, and he had been wounded in the arm. The sawbones at the field hospital took his arm off and tossed it on a pile outside the operating tent. That's the way they did things in those days."

Thorn nodded in understanding.

"We were both wounded at the Battle of Cold Harbor in June '64. That was a nasty affair. Our boys were ordered forward, wave after wave, in frontal assaults against Lee's fortified position. Our units were shot to pieces and left to bleed out and scream for water for days on the battlefield. The battle lasted two weeks before Grant sobered up or came to his senses. Over eleven thousand of our boys were killed or wounded, while Lee lost maybe six thousand gray backs in total. It took days for many to die, and then, at night, the ravens and other scavengers came to feast on the dead and the dying. It was a living nightmare. The rumor was that Lee felt such compassion for our dying men on the battlefield that he requested a truce so we could collect our dead and wounded, but

Grant refused. He may have been in his cups that period, don't know, but a lot of good men in blue died needlessly down there.

"The Captain, Sally's father, and I both got hit near our lines and were taken to the same field hospital. I was usually in the rear echelon of the Signal Corps, but I had been assigned to work my way forward and study the fortifications for headquarters. I got hit by a sniper. Captain Taylor was an officer who got hit in the upper arm, leading his men in a fool's charge. It shattered the bone and blew away most of the muscles.

"I was a lowly private in a different unit, but we both wound up in the same operating tent in the rear. As time passed, we began to mend and were shipped farther to the rear. We discovered we loved music, art, chess, and literature and became fast friends. After the war, we decided to head west together.

"A one-armed man and a gimp together make up at least a whole one. First, we panned for gold together but never found much. Then he taught school, and, finally, I quit the gold-seeking and played piano in camp saloons.

"Later, he took up serious drinking, and I took up drinking only in moderation. We both vied for Elizabeth's hand. She chose him, and I became the family friend and later Sally's uncle of sorts."

"So, where is he now?"

"Oh, after Elizabeth's death, he slowly faded away. First, he got sacked as a schoolmaster, and after that, it took a few years for the drink to finish the job."

"Drink?"

"Yes, in a way. He became a heavy drinker but not a drunkard per se. One night last winter, while on his way home from a local establishment, he slipped on the ice, and…ah…well…he was found the next morning frozen to death. I understand that's the best way to go, painless."

"I see."

"Sally spent most of her life caring for her parents and working to support and care for the family. His pension was enough to pay for his liquor, but there never seemed to be anything left over. With his death, even that ended. Sally worked hard, took in laundry, played the piano at church socials, and put her life on hold. Several eligible gents came around over the years, but they all backed out once they found out her responsibilities and the baggage she would bring into a marriage. She has worked in the hotel dining room for the last few years. By the way, Thorn, I see you are well-heeled. Wouldn't you be more comfortable taking your gun rig off for the evening?"

Thorn was taken aback by the question but said, "Yes, I suppose I could." He untied the hold-down strap, unbuckled his gun rig, and placed it under his coat. The loss of weight of guns, ammunition, and leather was noticeable. At the same time, he felt a bit vulnerable, even naked. So, he slid his cut-down Colt into his back holster and patted the little derringer in his vest pocket. "Yes, Louie, it's nice to lose weight, even for an evening."

"I thought so. Oh, I hear her coming downstairs now."

Sally came swiftly down the steps and entered the dining room. She had changed from her gingham work dress with a white apron into a loosely fit cotton plaid dress with a full-length skirt.

She didn't appear to be wearing a corset, heavy petticoats, or bustle, which appeared to Thorn to be the latest in ladies' fashion. She looked comfortable and wore soft dancing slippers. Thorn couldn't help but smile in appreciation. She was certainly a fine figure of a woman.

"Mr. Hagerman, has Louie been keeping you company? He is a dear soul." Turning toward the piano, she lifted it and examined the sheet music. "Waltzes by Johanne Strauss the Second and Frederic Chopin, I see. Have you ever waltzed Mr. Hagerman?"

"Please call me Thorn, and I don't rightly know. Play a little, and I'll tell you."

Louie swung around on the stool and played the "Minute Waltz."

Thorn listened and said, "I might be able to get the hang of the middle part, but the beginning and end are a bit too fast."

"Louie," said Sally, "let's try the 'Geschichten aus dem Wienerwald,' or as we know it—"

"The Viennese Waltz," said Thorn. Both Sally and Louie looked at Thorn in amazement. His German accent was perfect.

"Oh, I heard it years ago. But you'll have to refresh me as to the steps."

"Can you feel the music, Thorn? We merely count to three and do simple one-, two-, and three-step, forming half a box. You go forward on your left foot, and I return on my right. We must be careful not to step on one another." She smiled. "Like this," she demonstrated counting aloud and then showed how to close the box; then began to count, "One, two, three, and one, two, three again."

Thorn was busy counting and carefully watching his feet so as not to step on her. "Look at me, Thorn, not your boots, though I know how attractive they are. Let's practice."

They did this for half an hour, taking a break to listen to Louie's "Blue Danube Waltz," so beautifully played that they both applauded at the end. Louie stood up from the stool, turned, and bowed, bringing more applause.

"Shall we try it again and see if we can work in some of the dips, turns, and bows we've practiced." This went on for another thirty minutes, and Thorn could not remember ever having such an enjoyable evening.

They agreed to practice one more time before the Sunday dance, and Thorn suddenly said, "How do we know that the band will play a waltz and even the two we know?"

"That's simple," said Louie. "I've been asked to conduct the band and play the songs. We'll have two waltzes plus some good old stomping dance songs for the folks. We'll also do the Galop, a Polka, a Mazurka, and a little two-step, but I suggest you stick with what you know."

Thorn knew how important this social dance was for Sally. It was her "coming out party," which she had missed as a young girl.

After their goodbyes, Thorn walked with Louie up Main Street toward the Belle. He felt the weight and responsibility of the Remington and Colt tightly buckled to his waist and tied down. He wondered what it would be like to live in a world where a man didn't have to carry three weapons to walk down the street. Hopefully, someday, maybe in a hundred years or so, Americans will be able to enjoy such a walk, but that would be then; this is now. This was his life; he hadn't chosen it, but he accepted the bad with the good.

They first stopped at Louie's boarding house, where he rescued Chica from the paws of a large tabby cat in the unoccupied first-floor dining room. The other guests seemed to be upstairs in their rooms. Chica had climbed up a curtain and was engaged in a staring contest with the cat, who kept licking her mouth in anticipation.

"Go to the kitchen," Louie hissed and stomped a foot at Tabby, who scampered out of the room. "Now get down here, Chica. We have work to do and crowds to entertain." The monkey swung down and landed on Louie's shoulder for the walk to the saloon. How she got out of his room when Louie was sure he had closed and locked his door was a perplexing question.

During their walk to the Belle, Louie's limp became more noticeable, and soon Thorn was slowing down for him.

Louie stopped to catch his breath and asked, "You like her, don't you?"

"It's a little too early for those terms, but she is a fine woman and a great dancer."

"You won't hurt her, will you Thorn?"

"Hurt her? Why I've never hit a woman in my life. Why would I begin now? What a dumb question," Thorn scolded Louie and began walking onward with Louie limping painfully to catch up.

"Because," Louie huffed, "there are ways to hurt a woman without hitting her. If you want to be my friend, you will do right by her. She's new to this game, and you've been around by the looks of you. That's all I'm saying."

"Well, you don't have to worry chaperone."

"I'm not worrying. I'm just saying…" they continued to bicker up the steps to the boardwalk and through the bat wing doors into the saloon. Louie was happy to take his place at the piano with Chica atop his shoulder and begin pounding out favorites. Thorn saw Sheriff Williams, Billy, and Chris drinking coffee and having a deep discussion at their table.

Chapter 21
A Telegram and a Tale of Two Cities

Thorn was ebullient when he inquired, "Why aren't we drinking beer and shots? I'm buying."

"Save your money for another time," said Sheriff Williams. "Here, read this telegram."

It was addressed to the Sheriff of La Plata County, dated today, 2:00 p.m.

Area miners and ranches…stop

Jointly shipping payrolls…stop

By express car under heavy guard…stop

Be alert to threats…stop

More to follow…stop

Signed…Office of Assistant Attorney General, Colorado…stop

"Hmmm," Thorn reread the telegram and returned it to the sheriff. It doesn't give us much information."

"Yeah," said Billy, "but it tells every telegraph operator on the line that something big is coming up. We heard from a gunman passing through that something big is being planned in Silverton, but not when or what."

In a low voice, the sheriff leaned forward into the group and said, "Thorn, we may need your assistance. Are you still planning on going on to Denver on Monday?" Thorn nodded in the affirmative.

"Fine. In addition to meeting with the Pinkerton Agency, I want you to meet with this new Assistant Attorney General and let him know what we hear. He'd better not send anything in the open. I wonder about a code he could use that no one else would understand. I heard tell of such ciphers and codes during the war, but that was all the Signal Corps and Pinkerton stuff. I don't know anything about it."

The others sat silently, pondering the question, when Thorn, turning around toward the piano player, said, "I think I may have the answer. Louie, our piano pounder, was in the Signal Corps during the war. He may have an idea on the subject. I'll be right back."

Thorn got up, walked over to the piano player, and quietly asked, "Can we meet in the sheriff's office when you get off?"

Without missing a note, he answered, "Sure, it'll be about midnight. What's it about?"

"Don't want to talk about it here. Tell you then." Thorn dropped a half-dollar coin into the tip mug sitting atop the piano and said "Play 'Tenting Tonight' and play it good and loud."

It violated house rules to play partisan tunes like "Dixie" or "The Battle Hymn of the Republic." Any partisan rendition played over the past twenty years had led to a riot and destruction of saloon property, but "Tenting Tonight" was a song liked by the common soldiers on both sides and allowed to be played, though favored more by the union boys than by the Rebs. Many patrons from both sides opened with the chorus:

Many are the hearts that are weary tonight,
Wishing for the war to cease,
Many are the hearts that are looking for the right,
To see the dawn of peace,
Tenting tonight, tenting tonight on the old campground.

Everyone, including the drink girls and the gamblers, stopped their activities to sing the refrain.

Back at the table, Thorn asked, "Why don't we go to your office, Pat, and talk things over?" It was agreed. The men at the sheriff's table quietly left as the second verse began.

Three rough-looking cowhands leaned at the bar, sipping beers. One watched the sheriff's table with interest and noted the famous Pinkerton agent's conversation with the law dogs. The other two cowboys, both big rough-looking men, drank up and casually parted from their friend, a shorter man, and left the saloon. They mounted up at the hitching rail in front of the saloon and headed north out of town at an easy lope.

Upon returning to the jail, the sheriff woke Smitty and told him to put some water in the pot and shovel in some fresh coffee grounds because they needed to meet.

"Do you want me to get Teddy," Smitty inquired as he prepared the pot of coffee.

"No, let him sleep. He deserves his time off."

"Like I don't," murmured Smitty. "Seems like a man can't get a decent night's sleep in this jail anymore with all the meetings and such."

"Did you say some'n Smitty?"

"No, sheriff, just thinking aloud." Chris, Billy, and Thorn returned and, with thanks, accepted cups of steaming coffee from Smitty, who smiled at their appreciation, a rare feeling in his life.

Chris reviewed what he and Billy had learned from Kid. They suspected that the criminals who murdered Mike Todd and raped his wife were probably in Silverton awaiting the news of some big criminal job. It was a hunch, but maybe a good one.

"Who do you think is the brains behind this job?" Inquired the sheriff, "Surely, not those two low-life murderers and rapists we got paper out on."

Billy then mentioned a comment that he had heard that a redheaded man was forming a new gang in Silverton. Thorn thought that comment was curious but didn't mention it.

At about a quarter past midnight, Louie came in and stopped to catch his breath. "I'm here. What gives?"

After introducing Chris and Billy to Louie, formerly of the Federal Signal Corps of the United States Army, the five men sat at the table while Smitty refilled their cups with more steaming coffee. The sheriff updated Louie on the telegram, what Billy and Chris had learned from the Kid, and their suspicions about the gathering of outlaws in Silverton.

"You know," said Louie, "a gathering of crows is called a murder. Wonder what a gathering of criminals is called?"

"It's a gang, and we have two problems," said Sheriff Williams, all business. "First, we need to know what's going on in Silverton, and second, even more important, we need to get word to the new Assistant Attorney General in Denver to stop sending open information over the telegraph lines. Too many people are likely to know the plan before we do. We need a code of some sort that only we know. Are you able to help us?"

Louis leaned back in his chair and answered, "It's simple enough and foolproof. We used it during the war. We take a book or pamphlet to Denver in person and give it to the Attorney General; then, we have a secure identical copy here. Let's say I want to send a message that 'I'll be arriving at noon on Monday.' You read the book until you find the words you want to be transmitted and send in code. For example," he looked around and found an old copy of the police Gazette. "Here, on page one, is the pronoun 'I.' It's in the second paragraph, fifth line, and third word. My telegram would begin with 1,2,5,3… The second word is 'will' or 'shall'; here we are, on the second page, in the first paragraph, in the sixth sentence, and in the eighth word. Thus, we write 2,1,6,8…"

The men watched as he penciled the numbers on a sheet of paper, and Thorn asked, "What if we can't find the word?"

"No problem. You just added another digit to represent a letter. Did you get it?" The men nodded in understanding.

"Do the rest the same way. With several men working on the problem, getting the message in code doesn't take long. The telegrapher has to be cautioned to be accurate in his message, but the man on our end can quickly check the message and request verification on anything that looks odd. Come to think of it; you may want to find a trustworthy person, maybe even a lady. They seem to be more cautious about words when doing the setups and deciphering so as not to tie up your agent's time."

"Can you think of someone, even a lady, who might fit the bill?" Sheriff Williams agreed with the wisdom of Louie's plan, but who?

"I may just know a person who might fit the bill. She's a mutual friend of ours, Sally Taylor."

"She's the waitress over at the dining room?" Billy asked.

"Yes, and she is very bright, well-read, and doesn't gossip," said Louis. "I think she might do it for you. We all go for breakfast, and she usually serves us. It would be nothing for her to deliver or receive a message from one of us. No one would be the wiser." The plan was beautifully simple.

"Louie, you were friends with her parents. Do you feel close enough to ask her?"

"Sure enough, sheriff."

"All right, we may have the second half of the problem solved, and Thorn is going up to Denver on Monday and can explain the setup to the Attorney General and, if appropriate, the Pinkertons. Agreed?"

"It'll work," said Thorn. "As for the book, I'm reading *A Tale of Two Cities,* and I noticed they have another copy for sale at the mercantile store. I can pick it up this afternoon and take it on the train."

"As for learning what's going on in Silverton, no one goes up there for the time being. That's an order," said the sheriff, looking at Billy and Chris. "Keep your eyes open for people coming down from the north. Maybe we can learn something." Both Billy and Chris sagged in disappointment with the order but accepted it. They had planned to leave on personal business up north in a few days.

At about 1:00 a.m., Thorn and Louie walked out of the sheriff's office together. They stood for a moment, looking at the brilliant star-strewn heavens.

"You sure she won't be put in harm's way?" asked Thorn.

"How can it? She'll have no coming and going to the sheriff's office. She can sit alone at home and work out the messages, with no one the wiser, and give them to Pat at breakfast."

Thorn nodded, but he still felt uneasy as he watched Louie hobble up the street and thought about how Louis had come by his limp.

The next Saturday, after Thorn had his usual breakfast, he stopped Sally and quietly informed her that he would pick her up on Sunday at 4:00 p.m. at her house for the social dance. They'd had two practice sessions, and Thorn felt ready. No one seemed to pay them any notice.

Thorn left the dining room and walked down Main Street to the mercantile store, where he bought the remaining volume of A Tale of Two Cities after first checking the page numbers and the publication date. He also bought an inexpensive dollar watch, so-called because of its cost and short life expectancy. He could give it to one of the deputies after he purchased a good one in Denver. For now, he needed to be on schedule.

Looking through the coat rack, he found a new black frock coat with a narrower cut and some striped trousers without a waist seam. Trying them on, he admired the figure he cut. A new white shirt, starched collar, black tie, and new undergarments completed his ensemble. Yes, he'd take them, but the unbuttoned frock coat didn't cover his gun rig adequately. He noticed two bulges outlining his holstered weapons.

He left the gun rig at home and put his trusty cut-down Colt in its back holster. That way, he could leave his frock open and still get at his Colt if needed, yet not be weighed down with the black leather double rig.

Next, he stopped by the gunsmith to check on the progress of the right-handed Remington's conversion into a fanning gun. He was delighted to find it finished. He loved its smooth new action, and the hammer had been replaced with a smoother and wider one that easily rose and fell with the fanning motion of his left hand. It was a fine-shooting single-action pistol and slid smoothly into and out of the right-hand holster. He tried dry firing several times with empty rounds so as not to over-wear the firing pin and was pleased with its action. He then took his re-tooled pistol to the firing pit in the back and burned up a hundred rounds in a few minutes.

He kept the black leather cross-draw holster rig and placed it in his bag to take back to his hotel room. Thorn did some serious thinking about all the goods he was acquiring. His whole life, he had traveled light. If he couldn't carry it on his mount or, when necessary, on a pack animal, he left it behind. He would have to give this newfound wealth considerable thought.

Later, he got his Saturday night haircut, shave, and bath before going to the Belle for food and drinks. The sheriff's table was empty.

Wandering over to Louie, who was shuffling through a stack of sheet music, he dropped a quarter in his cup and said, "Play us a waltz, will you piano man?"

The cowboys and miners inhabiting the room stopped to listen to Louie's masterful rendition of the Swan Lake Waltz from a little-known composer named Tchaikovsky. One hard-bit miner who was tone-deaf and hard of hearing started to hiss and boo and claimed he wanted some 'merican music, but he was quickly hushed up by his fellows, who settled in to listen in appreciation.

It was a long piece without words, but it held the patrons' interest, who sat or stood without drinking or playing the games of chance, just listening. When he finished, there was a moment of silence before the loud applause. Louie stood and took a bow as Thorn left through the batwings.

Charlie, the bartender, wandered over to Louie with a mug of beer and sat it on the piano. "This is from the new girl, Lucy, who asked me to tell you she loves your playing." Charlie nodded his head toward a young drinks girl, a recent arrival of no more than 16 years of age, who waved and smiled at him. Louie smiled and nodded in response.

"There, I said that. Now the boss told me to tell you to knock off playing that fancy highfalutin foreign music. Any more of that hoity-toity stuff, and he'll sack ya. Get it?"

"I certainly do get it," said Louie, "and tell the boss that we'll have only good old 'merican songs in the future."

"Good deal. I'll let the boss know that you got the message."

Louie returned to his standard medley, beginning with "Bringing in the Sheaves," a popular song rooted in Psalm 126 of the Bible. Composed by an Ohio lad named Knowles Shaw in 1874, most everyone in the place sang the first verse, which was well known, and everyone belted out the refrain:

Bringing in the sheaves,
Bringing in the sheaves,
We shall come rejoicing, bringing in the sheaves.

The men liked it so well that they sang the refrain a second and a third time.

Charlie found himself singing with the crowd and said to himself, "At least it's merican. Funny, when I first heard it, I thought the words were bringing in the sheep."

Thorn moved to the bar to finish his beer and was surprised when Charlie brought him a fresh one.

"I didn't order this," said Thorn as Charlie ignored him and wiped the bar with his towel.

"It's on the house," whispered Charlie, "and don't look, but that sawed-off runt at the other end of the bar was in here last night with a couple of other gents, big-fellows and seemed very interested in the sheriff's table. He asked which one of you was the Pinkerton man. I told him I didn't know. He came in an hour ago and has been drinking straight rotgut and keeps looking your way." Charlie continued mopping the bar, clearing empty shot glasses and mugs, and moving down the bar.

Thorn finished his beer and quietly walked out of the saloon.

The stranger in question finished his drink and followed Thorn out into the night.

Chapter 22
Gunman's Dance

Thorn walked down the saloon's steps and stopped in the middle of the street. Over the music, general noise, and laughter from the Belle, he heard the ring of spurs on the boardwalk and down the steps.

At that instance, Thorn spun around, sweeping back his long coat with his right hand poised above his ivory-handled pistol. The cowboy, a small man wearing a tall, crowned hat, stopped in surprise. His hand was on his pistol grip, still partially lifted in his holster. The cowboy's eyes focused on Thorn's right-hand pistol still in its holster.

"Stop right there," Commanded Thorn, snarling, "What do you mean following me with your paw on your gun?"

"You the Pinkerton man folks been talking 'bout? How does it feel to have a bounty on your head?"

"Bounty?"

"Yeah, five hundred dollars, but only dead, not alive. Red told me you were slick but don't look that fast to me." The cowboy's attention was on that pearl-handled revolver snuggled deep in its holster. He had every reason to believe he could get his pistol out and fire off one, maybe two shots before the Pinkerton, whose right hand was behind him holding his coat back, could bring his gun to bear.

Several patrons were about to enter the Belle but stopped on the boardwalk to see what was going on with two men facing off in the street. The cowboy was silhouetted for Thorn against the glow from the saloon's windows and door. The piano playing abruptly stopped, and more than a dozen additional men spilled out onto the boardwalk and quickly parted into two groups, giving the men plenty of shooting room.

"It's your play," said Thorn.

The cowboy pulled his pistol up but never cleared his holster when Thorn's .45 Colt appeared out of nowhere in his right hand. His left fanned three quick shots, hitting the cowboy dead center in his chest. The impact of the .45 slugs picked the little man up out of his boots and threw him back hard onto the steps, where he remained in a sitting position. His head and shoulders slumped forward as if he was observing his bare feet and wondering why his boots lay in the dirt before him. With a death grip on his pistol, his right hand had finally cleared his holster.

With the acrid scent of burned black powder swirling in the air, Thorn ejected the three spent rounds and reloaded. He slid his Colt pistol into his back holster and dropped his lifted coat to cover his gun belt.

"Does anybody know this yahoo?" Sheriff Williams called out as he and Chris came running up with weapons out. No one responded. "What happened?"

Standing in the back with a scattergun cradled in his arms, Charlie spoke up and stepped forward, "That cowboy followed Mr. Thorn out of the saloon and started to draw on him. Thorn spun around and challenged him. The cowboy went for his iron, and Thorn put three into his chest while he was dragging his pistol out of its holster." All the men nodded in agreement and commented among themselves. "He said there was a $500 bounty on Thorn's head by someone named Red." The crowd again murmured in agreement. "It was the slickest justified killing I've ever seen, self-defense. He blew that cowboy clean out of his boots."

"Chris, go get the undertaker over here. He'll know what to do. I'll want to see all his personal effects." Chris nodded and headed off at a trot.

"All right, it's over. Go on about your business." Most of the crowd slowly reentered the bat wings to discuss the event. Several had had enough to drink and headed off into the night.

"You all right Thorn?"

"Yes, Pat, I'm fine, but what in the hell is going on?"

Pat said, "Seems like someone named Red wants you out of the way pretty bad. After breakfast, come by the office, and we'll talk."

Thorn had difficulty getting to sleep that night. He kept revisiting in his mind the sequence of events leading to the shooting. He was sure he had never seen the cowboy before and was curious about his identity. That was a mystery that would wait until tomorrow.

As to this Red fellow he kept hearing about, he had met many in his life. A lot of men and quite a few women, especially if you counted auburn, had red hair. He had ridden with several in Missouri and Texas. Even his childhood friend, Pete Wilson, had red hair. It could be anybody. Maybe the sheriff would have a lead, or he might find out something in Denver.

Sleep was hard to come by that night. Once, Thorn got up and stood looking out of his window at an empty street. Returning to bed, he finally drifted off in the eerie half-light before dawn, and getting up at 6:30 a.m. by his new pocket watch was difficult.

He shaved, dressed, and buckled on his new cross-draw gun rig with the holstered Remington pistols. He practiced pulling the right gun a few times before the mirror and, feeling satisfied, slipped his old Colt into his back holster and dropped the little derringer into his vest pocket. He felt completely dressed.

At breakfast with Pat and Billy, Thorn was told that Chris and Teddy were off until that evening, when they would be at the social dance undercover. "Are you expecting trouble, Pat?"

"Not necessarily, but it's better to be prepared." Leaning forward, he quietly asked, "When will you or Louie talk with Sally about our little plan?"

"I'll be talking with her after the dance. I don't want anything to interfere with her having a grand time. By the way, will you both be there this afternoon?"

"I'll be patrolling the businesses," said Billy.

"I'll be around," said Pat, "in and out sort of, keeping an eye on things, but as I said, both Chris and Teddy will be there."

"Fine, keep your eyes open for strangers. It might be nice to plant Teddy on the road to keep an eye on who comes to town. Chris can handle the social. He may even get in a little dancing," Thorn chuckled.

"Sounds like a good plan," said Pat. "So, Thorn, are you planning on dancing with Miss Sally?" Thorn didn't bother to answer for a full minute, then said, "We're going to a dance, aren't we?"

"By the way, that Yahoo who drew on you last night was carrying five double eagle gold coins. It seems strange. No greenbacks or species of any kind. No identification or letters on him."

Thorn had made arrangements at the barn to have a one-horse buggy available for the evening. Dressed in his new frock coat and striped pants, white shirt with a starched collar, and black tie, he left his two M-1875 Remington pistols in the new cross-draw rig in his room. He would go dancing with a lovely lady, not to a gunfight. Just in case, he had two additional companions, his trusty cut-down .45 Colt in a back holster and its little brother in his vest. Thorn pulled on his wool outercoat and headed down Main Street to the barn.

The one-horse carriage was hooked up and ready to go. Untying the reins from the hitching post, he climbed in, gave a little jerk, and soon trotted toward Miss Sally's house at the edge of town. He stopped the carriage in front of her house and climbed out.

Her door opened before he could knock, and she stood in the afternoon's glow, holding a steaming dish wrapped in a towel.

She wore a mossy green dress with a tightly fitted bodice showing her attributes. It had buttons in front up to the fitted collar. Her skirts were tucked up to reveal a dark green underskirt, but on her feet, she wore a pair of no-nonsense black lace-up shoes suitable for work. Smiling she said, "Perfect timing Thorn. I do love a punctual man."

"Thank you, Ma'am," he pinched his hat brim and smiled, "My father always said unless you are five minutes early, you're late." He then stepped back to get a better view. "Oh my, you look lovely," he added, looking down at her feet, "even wearing work shoes." Taking the dish in one hand, he extended his arm for her as they walked to the carriage. Smiling, she held up a small string pouch of dark green, "My dancing slippers." They both laughed.

He noted that she had closed the front door without locking it. He would have to talk with her about that. He assisted her in climbing up and getting herself situated, then handed her the covered dish for safekeeping. He walked around the horse's front, patted his withers, and gave him an apple from his outer coat pocket. Untying the reins, he swung up to sit close to Miss Sally, clucked the animal around in the road, and headed back into town. A few houses up Main Street, they saw Teddy sitting in a rocking chair on a porch with a newspaper in his hands. He waived as they passed. Thorn nodded.

They stopped at the Churchyard, and Thorn tied the carriage to a hitching post. He gave the horse another apple, removed the last one from his pocket, and placed it under the seat while Miss Sally unlaced her work shoes and put on the dancing slippers.

Being escorted into the crowded hall was everything she expected and then some. All the women's eyes were on them, and several men looked at her with a newfound interest. After he deposited her dish with the judges and waited in line for two cups of punch, Thorn returned to their table to find Miss Sally chatting with Chris.

"Glad to see you could make it to this shindig," said Chris. "Hope you don't mind, Thorn, but I'm claiming a dance from this lovely lady."

"Would it matter if I did?"

"I see you know us Texans. Did you ever spend any time in the Lone Star State?"

The music started with Louie setting the pace with generic tunes as Thorn reached down to claim Sally's hand for the dance. "The problem with you Texans is you talk when you should be acting."

Louie then went into his prepared score. The folks were having trouble placing the dance when Thorn and Sally swirled onto the dance floor to the Blue Danube Waltz. Thorn was tempted to look at his feet, but Sally disabused him of the notion with a dip and turn that they had been practicing. Soon, all the other couples moved to the outside of the floor and watched in envy as this couple neatly boxed their steps. They moved clockwise in unison while traveling counterclockwise around the floor. They turned, dipped, spun, and finally ended the dance with a bow and a curtsy. Everyone applauded. There was more to this Pinkerton man than meets the eye, thought more than one female.

Chris stood, along with everyone else watching the exhibition, and upon their return, said, "Man, oh man, Thorn, you and Miss Sally sure do make a handsome couple."

"Thank you kindly," said Sally. "I think this dance belongs to you, Chris." The next dance, as arranged, was a Schottische, well-known in Texas dance halls. With a fiddle in the lead and the piano trying to keep up, the couples strolled around the floor, first with two sidesteps to the left, then to the right, followed by four steps and some stomping. By the second minute of the dance, couples were kicking, hopping, and skipping, mostly in time with the music, and Chris was out in front escorting Miss Sally around the room with sudden rebel yells Thorn hadn't heard since his days with Quantrill.

Midway through, the judges called a halt to announce the winners of the blue-ribbon categories. To Sally's and Thorn's delight, she won first place in the casserole, or covered pan category, which was the main division. She stood to claim her ribbon and the applause.

Other categories were announced, and soon, long tables were loaded with piles of plates and flatware (without knives since all the men and most women carried their own). The tables sagged with hot and cold dishes, vegetables, corn on the cob, and assortments of cakes, pies, and torts.

The Blue Ribbon Winners were called to do a grand parade with a partner around the room and then go down the serving line. Sally and Thorn led the procession. Urns of coffee and pitchers of beer were on a separate table for the taking. All was self-serve.

Pat appeared in time to eat, and soon Teddy entered and motioned for him to come over. After a brief conversation, Pat took a piece of bread, centered some roast pork on it, and motioned for Thorn to step outside.

"What's going on, Pat?"

"Teddy saw two rough-looking cowboys riding in from the north. He followed them to the Belle. We're going over there now to check on 'em."

"Want some company?"

"No, you stay here, but I will take Chris. Thorn, keep your eyes open. Maybe you should take Sally home?"

"Okay, Pat, I'll be on the lookout, and you will do the same."

Thorn had a bad feeling as he watched Pat and Chris, each eating their takeaway from the social, as they headed toward the saloon.

"What's going on Thorn?" Sally stepped out of the hall and inquired.

"Two rough-looking cowboys rode into town from the north, and Pat and Chris went over to check on them. I think I should go to see if they need help…but…I don't want to leave you…"

"Don't worry about me, Thorn. Do what you got to do. Just come back and drive me home. You promise."

"Sure. I'll be back soon, I promise."

"I've renewed some old friendships with some of the ladies. I'll be fine." She kissed him quickly and returned to the supper.

Now wishing he had his extra artillery strapped on, Thorn followed the sheriff and Chris across the street at a jog and called, "Hold up, Pat, Chris. I'm coming with you."

"Well, come on then," said Chris. Both men stopped to allow Thorn to catch up and for them to finish their eats. They instinctively spread out and walked side by side to the saloon and up the stairs. Pushing first through the bat wings, Pat had no trouble identifying the two cowboys in question. They were both big men, could have been brothers, slouching at the bar with a bottle of rot gut between them. They both had grabbed onto Charlie and were shaking and yelling at him.

"What gives? Let that man be." Sheriff Pat's voice was clear and direct. The two pushed Charlie back against the liquor cabinet, causing a bottle to crash to the floor. They both turned around. But instead of finding one lone man, they faced three, two with badges. They discounted the old sheriff. The young deputy looked fast, and the third man, wearing fancy black duds, wasn't wearing an open gun; he was probably carrying a small caliber pocket pistol and could be dangerous.

"You boys just broke a bottle of liquor, and now you'll have to pay for it or go to jail."

"You must be joking, sheriff. The clumsy bartender broke it himself," said one.

"Don't give me that," said Pat. "We saw you push him, so you'll pay. How much was that bottle worth, Charlie?"

"One dollar, sheriff, but they already paid a dollar for their bottle, and it ain't been opened."

"All right, you two, you got lucky. Get on your horses and ride out of town, and don't let me catch you here again. Savvy?"

"That ain't right, sheriff. We just rode into town and stopped to inquire about a friend who came in a few days ago. We asked the barkeep if he had seen him, but he didn't respond."

"Was he a little fellow, wearing a brown high-crowned hat and a yellow bandanna with loud spurs?" Thorn asked.

"Yeah, that's our friend. We want to say hello, have a drink, and we'll be on our way."

"Sure," said Thorn, "we'll take you right to him; this way gents." He turned and led off. Pat and Chris stepped aside, allowing Thorn room to make his play, but he just walked toward the door. The two cowboys followed him out of the bar and down the steps with the sheriff and his deputy trailing.

Chapter 23
Texas Wildcat

"Hey, what gives?" One of the cowboys cried out. "This ain't the way to jail. Where else would Jim be? Where are you taking us?"

Thorn said, "This way, gents. Your friend is just through this door."

Thorn stepped back as the sheriff gave the official knock. A lamp was lit in the inner area, and soon, the door was unlocked and opened. "It's late, Sheriff. Can't it wait until morning?"

"No, these men want to see their friend." The five men crowded into the outer parlor.

"All right, follow me." Mr. Dobbs held the lamp high and opened a door leading to a large workroom with a desk, chair, tables, cabinets, sinks, and a 50-gallon barrel of water with a dripping spigot. The undertaker stepped out of the way and let them pass. On a table in the corner lay a man face up, with a stained towel covering his chest and pelvic area.

"What the hell?" said one, followed by the second man exclaiming, "That's Jim, ain't it? He's dead!"

"You are right as rain," said the sheriff as he stepped forward. "I see you know your friend, named Jim. Do you know his family name?"

The first cowboy went for his gun and was bringing it to bear just as the sheriff fell backward, pinning Thorn against the wall and unable to retrieve his weapon. Thorn saw the single-action weapon move upward in an arc in the big cowboy's hand. He knew that he was pulling the hammer back until it locked, and the trigger would be pulled on its decline when the gunman had the sheriff, and Thorn lined up in his sights. There was nothing he could do to protect himself or Pat. If he had his holstered guns, he might have gotten one out, but maybe not.

Suddenly, a figure flew over them and landed on the two cowboys, driving them back against a cabinet. The figure wrenched the gun away from its intended target just as the weapon exploded, sending fire and lead into the body of their dead friend. The figure smashed his fists into the face of the cowboy and then twisted the extended weapon away from his friends as it exploded a second time. Still twisting the gunman's hand, he slammed his right fist into the head of the second man and then went back to grappling and twisting the first man's arm until the weapon was dropped to the floor and was finally kicked away into dark shadows.

Just as quickly, he was on the second cowboy, yanking the pistol from his holster and laying it across his temple with a solid whack that rendered him unconscious. Then, back to the first with a series of body blows that bent the man forward, setting him up for an uppercut that lifted him off his feet and sent him windmilling back against the dead man, upsetting the table and sending the corpse thudding on top of the senseless cowboy.

Thorn pushed Pat forward and gained his freedom and Colt, but it was all over. Chris stood gulping air, looking around for another victim.

"The winner by two KOs in round one. 'John L. Sullivan, the Boston Strong Boy' couldn't have done better," said Pat, slapping Chris on his back.

"The one and only, Chris the Texas Tornado, the undefeated champion of Durango," said Thorn as he lifted Chris's arm in victory.

"No, I've got a better name," said Pat, "Chris, The Texas Wildcat."

Mr. Dobbs, still holding his lamp high, almost cried as he surveyed the damage caused by the whirlwind blowing through his workroom. The odor from broken bottles of chemicals burned their eyes as it rose from the debris on the floor. The supplies from an overturned cabinet were strewn about. A worktable was overturned, and the deceased body was lying atop the unconscious cowboy on the floor. A bullet had punctured the water barrel, and a stream of water was pooling on the floor.

"Here, Chris," said Pat, "Help me get this stiff back on the table. Lucky he was a slim little fellow." They righted the table and tossed the deceased onto it like a bag of grain. Pat picked up the stained towel from the floor and said, "Poor little guy." then draped it over the corpse's midsection.

Chris picked up a slightly dented tin bowl from the floor, captured a quart of streaming water, and delivered it to the face of the first one, then the second man, helping them to come to. It didn't take long for Thorn to securely tie their hands and search the two men for additional knives and weapons. They recovered two .38 five rounds S&W pocket pistols and two frog stickers. They also found each man gold double eagles worth one hundred dollars and a stack of letters on one.

"We'll have some good reading when we get these two birds to jail."

"We're also getting a nice collection of weapons when we have our auction," said Pat.

"Come on, you two jailbirds," said the sheriff, "on your feet." The men were prodded out the door and to the jail, where Smitty welcomed the two new guests.

"Boys," said Smitty, "it ain't no hotel, but you'll get two meals daily and coffee for breakfast. If you don't give me any trouble, The rules are simple, and I'll go over them tomorrow. Sheriff, should we leave them hogtied tonight?"

"Yes, until we get another deputy here. These are bad customers, so don't give 'em a chance, or you'll be on the short end of the stick."

"Thorn," said Pat. "Thanks for coming along, but I can't say I was of much help to either of us. If Chris hadn't turned wildcat, one or both of us might not be here."

"You're right about that, Pat. We were in a pretty bad fix. I couldn't get at either of my guns and was of no help. Thank God Chris was there."

"Yeah," said Pat, "thank God and the Texas Wildcat. Are you headed back to the social? It should be about over now."

"Yes, I promised Sally I'd drive her home."

"Fine, if you see Billy or Teddy, tell them I want to see them about the horses belonging to these two."

"Right, Sheriff, I'll find them."

Thorn walked back to the church but stopped to pet the rented horse that had brought them to the social. It gave him time to think about what had gone on and how close he had come to meeting his Maker. He also had to find a way to downplay the event and ask her about the job Louie was planning for her, but that could probably wait until tomorrow morning after breakfast. He didn't have to board the train to Denver until 11:00 a.m. and should have plenty of time. He was still stroking the horse and gently saying sweet nothings to it when Sally walked up behind him and said, "You're back. Is everything all right?"

"Yes, we're all right, but can't say that much for the other guys." He then gave a brief rendition of the encounter and arrests, giving Chris plenty of credit. But he neglected to emphasize the dangerous spot he and Pat had been in, and if not for Chris's quick action, one or both would probably be dead.

"Sally, before we head home, do you mind if we ride around town a bit? I promised Pat I'd get a message to Billy or Teddy."

She smiled one of her brilliant, dimpled smiles and said she'd enjoy a ride around town showing off her blue ribbon. They rode at an easy trot around town until Thorn spotted Billy checking storefront doors on a side street, called him over, and briefly explained the arrest and action on Chris's part, including his new moniker, The Texas Wildcat. He then told him the sheriff wanted to talk with him or Teddy about the horses the cowboys might have left near the saloon. Thorn said he would try to spot Teddy on the way to Miss Sally's place. Billy headed over to the Belle to look around. They spotted Teddy walking north on Main Street a few minutes later and gave him the same message.

On their ride home, Thorn noticed that Sally hadn't changed into her work shoes but was playing with the blue ribbon pinned to her bodice. "Do you like it?" she asked.

"Sure do. You earned it. That was the best pan meal I've ever had."

"Do you think it would be all right if I wore it to work in the dining room tomorrow? It would reflect proudly on the place, don't you think, or is it bragging and showing off too much?"

"It isn't bragging if it's true. Wear it if you want. I'll congratulate you in the morning and knock the block off anyone who thinks otherwise."

"Oh, Thorn, I like you, but please don't hurt anyone for my sake."

"It's just an expression, but you just point out any fellow you want to receive a whipping, and I'm your man." They both laughed at his bravado, but secretly, she knew he'd do it if push came to shove and do even more for her.

Sally sank back in her seat and hummed a waltz tune from the dance. She had never been this happy before and wondered if she was falling in love. She had mixed feelings and wasn't sure what love was.

She thought her mom and dad had been in love early on, but then why did he drink so much and lose his job? And why did her mother give up and die? If you loved someone, wouldn't you change for that person? If her dad had loved her after her mother died, why did he drink himself into an early grave? She let these and other scary dark thoughts run through her mind, but nothing could take the edge off the joy she felt. She didn't understand her feelings but knew she cared for this man. The question was, did he care for her?

As Thorn pulled reins in front of her house, he asked, "Will you be able to take about a half-hour stroll with me before my train leaves at 11:00 in the morning? There is something important I'd like to talk over with you."

"A half-hour stroll to talk. Sure, I'll tell them when I get in and will work late cleaning that back stove. The grease is building up, and it could become a fire hazard. What do you want to talk about?"

"Oh, not now, it's late. Tomorrow will give us plenty of time." He leaned over, thinking he would give her a little love peck on her cheek, but she quickly turned to him, closing her eyes, she pressed her moist open lips to his, and tightly wrapped her arms around him. This sudden, sweet-tasting kiss took his breath away. She tasted of mint and honey, and he was beginning to feel a surge of passion when the horse balked and jittered, shaking the reins and ending their embrace. Jumping down, he pulled the final apple from under the seat and said, "I don't think you deserve this, you spoil-sport."

He walked her to the door and commented on her failure to lock it when leaving. He stepped inside and, without asking permission, walked through the first floor and up to the second floor. She followed closely behind as he checked every hiding place and asked her if all was in order. She assured him nothing was amiss. He asked her to securely lock the doors and first-floor windows because strangers were prowling around. She promised she would.

As Sally got ready for bed that night, she hung her dress in the armoire closet that smelled of cedar, combed her hair, brushed her teeth with salt and baking powder, and finished her nightly toilette. She turned out the lamp, crawled into bed, thought about it for a minute, and got up and checked to ensure the front and back doors were locked, then closed and locked all the ground-floor windows. Finally, she went back to bed.

There are a lot of strangers about, she thought. After all, strangers had murdered Mike and raped Sissy. She shuddered and made a mental note to pay a visit to Sissy at the hotel to see if she needed anything.

Thorn said they had trouble with two strangers tonight at the Belle and had to arrest them. What were the ladies talking about this evening? She heard bits and pieces of a shooting on Main Street, and a stranger was killed last night. She didn't want to hear anymore and walked away from their table.

What did Thorn want to talk about in the morning? She wondered if he could be getting up his nerve to ask her to marry him. No, that was preposterous. He hadn't even told her that he loved her. Wasn't that the way it always happened first in the novels? But they had danced beautifully together. They fit together nicely, and she wondered what it would be like to be Mrs. Thorn Hagerman, Sally Hagerman. She played around with that thought for a while, finally giving up and trying to sleep.

Her eyes popped open. If not that, then what? What if he didn't love her and was saying "goodbye," or, God forbid, that he was already married or had some loathsome disease? Never that. What if he had been wounded and could never father a child or be a real husband? She decided even if it came to that, she would still marry him and love and take care of him until death "do they part." The thought of Thorn, a cripple in a chair with a blanket over his lap, made her tear up, and she began to cry, as she never cried for anyone or anything before. What could it be? This question troubled her mind for most of the night.

Chapter 24
Best and Worst of Times

Thorn slept badly a second night in a row, hurriedly finished his shave and ablutions, quickly dressed, and buckled on his new cross-draw rig. He placed his Colt .45 in the back holster and patted the Derringer in his vest pocket. He aimed to go to Denver heavily armed. He placed a set of undergarments in his saddlebags, along with the Dickens novel and the original Thorn T. Hagerman's documents and letters. Slinging the saddlebags over his shoulder, he picked up his copy of Dickens, locked the door, and headed for the dining room.

On the way down the stairs, Jimmy hailed him, "Mr. Hagerman, Sir, you have a letter." He pulled it from the box behind the desk and handed it over. Thorn recognized the script, slipped it into his coat pocket, thanked Jimmy, and handed him a quarter tip. Jimmy smiled and said, "Thank You, Sir." That coin represented five glasses of beer at any drinking establishment in town.

Entering the dining room, he headed immediately for the sheriff's table that had been placed in the corner with Pat's back to the wall. Billy sat on his left, and Thorn could sit on his right. Chris would have to sit with his back to the public, but that's what you get for being last. Thorn placed Dickens's volume on the table before Pat, his hat on a wall peg, and said, "Hang on to this for me, Pat."

Pat nodded and said, "Did you sleep well last night?" Billy nodded and kept working at his plate of flapjacks and bacon.

"That looks good. I may try that one morning," said Thorn as he looked around for Sally.

"And, yes, Pat, I slept well last night. How about you? This is the darndest town for wanting to know how folks sleep at night."

"I'm just trying to be sociable," said Pat, "and never you mind how I slept. I sleep just fine if you must know." Both Billy and Thorn laughed loud enough for several heads to turn to see what was humorous. Chris walked in on the tail-end of the laughter and said, "What's so funny?"

Everyone at the table said in unison, "How did you sleep last night?" Their rollicking laughter caused several folks to laugh along, just pleased to hear happy people in the morning. Thorn picked up and unfolded the Durango Gazette. The front-page story was about the dangerous criminal elements drifting into town and the Saturday night gunfight on Main Street in front of the Belle, which resulted in the killing of a stranger who had been sent to assassinate our Pinkerton agent.

The good thing was that the story was fairly accurate and hadn't mentioned Thorn's back-holstered gun used to do the killing. The crowd witnessing the event had mainly been up on the boardwalk, out of the way, and didn't have a clear view of the shooting. It must have seemed to them like the Pinkerton agent snapped his fingers, and three bullets magically struck the villain in his chest. Later on, page two was a nice story about the church social and dance, which featured Miss Sally Taylor of Durango taking first place in the coveted casserole contest. The judges were unanimous in awarding her the First Place Blue Ribbon.

It was a nice story, and Sally should be pleased. Scanning the article, he smiled when it also made mention of the wonderful exhibition of precision dance to a European waltz performed by Mr. Thorn Hagerman of Chicago, Illinois, and Miss Sally Taylor of Durango, Colorado. The story described Sally's dress and dance slippers in detail, while Thorn had been dressed in formal evening attire.

The bad news was that Sally would now know about the shooting that he hadn't told her about. Too bad they hadn't run her blue-ribbon story on page one and his shooting on page two. He had a bad feeling about the next few hours. Remembering the letter, he reached into his pocket, opened it, and scanned its contents. He then placed it on the table.

"What's that?" asked Pat, who saw it was addressed to Mr. Thorn Hagerman.

"It was given to me a few minutes ago. Thought I'd read it to you. It's dated yesterday."

Dear Mr. Thorn Hagerman, Pinkerton Agent

I want you to know that I have exhausted my cash reserves and by the time you read this letter, I will have moved back to the cabin. I am attempting to obtain a loan from the bank. I want to know if you are interested in buying my claim, cabin, and property, or if you know of someone interested.

Please give my regards to Sheriff Williams and his deputies. After thinking it over, I hope no one risks his life to bring those two men to justice. It's not worth it.

Sincerely
Your servant

Signed by Mrs. Sissy Todd

The four men sat silently, thinking about courage, honor, duty, and human failure. Billy laid down his fork and spoke up, "Sheriff, nothing we can do about the past, but we have a defenseless woman living in that out-of-the-way cabin by herself. Can we take one of the pistols we're holding, say one of the .38 pocket pistols, and give or loan it to her?"

Chris nodded his support, as did Thorn, who said, "I'm thinking the same thing for Sally."

Pat answered, "Fine. We'll lend them each a pistol after our deputies have checked them out and, if need be, by the gunsmith, along with enough ammunition. Thorn, you are leaving today, so we'll rely on Billy and Chris to take the guns to the girls and ensure they know how to use them. Better take two boxes of ammunition each and get in some target practice."

At that moment, the cook brought out a platter of food for Thorn and a pot of coffee, which he left on the table.

"Say, hold on," said Thorn, "where's Sally this morning?"

"She's in the back working on cleaning a stove. She came in this morning wearing her blue ribbon, had a coffee, and looked at the morning paper. She got up, took off her blue ribbon, put on the old smock we got for cleaning up, and went after that old grill we want to put back in operation."

"Please ask her if I could speak with her after breakfast."

"I'll see, but she's pretty busy and smudged a bit."

"Please ask?" The cook returned to the kitchen, and Thorn didn't feel hungry. He cut his steak into halves and shoveled a mound of fried potatoes onto Chris' plate, who smiled, nodded, and said, "Much obliged."

"Billy, you and Chris check out the pocket pistols. Pick up four ammo boxes and put them on the county's tab. And Billy, you go out to see Sissy at her cabin. Chris, you can check with Sally after Thorn talks with her; that is if she will talk with him." Both deputies nodded in agreement between bites.

"Have we learned anything from those two birds about that fellow?" asked Thorn.

"No, after the one said they were the Stone brothers, the cat's got their tongues. We're going through wanted posters, and I'll be looking at the stack of letters this afternoon, but so far, nothing. Why don't you check in Denver to see if you can find out anything?" Thorn nodded.

After finishing his third cup of coffee, Sally had still not appeared. Thorn gave up, picked up his hat, and left with the others. On the boardwalk, Pat asked Thorn to "hold up" as Pat moved the Dickens volume from hand to hand and shoved it into Thorn's hand. "Here, give this to Louis, will you?"

Thorn adjusted his hat and looked into the hotel window's reflection, not at himself but at the movement along the street. Then, turning, they stood watching the two deputies walk toward the sheriff's office, and Thorn offered Pat a cheroot.

"Thanks, don't mind if I do." Pat fired them off a Lucifer, and they both relaxed, watching Durango wake up, stretch, and get busy.

Pat had something on his mind. "Go on. What's ailing you," demanded Thorn.

"It's about last night. I fell back against you, got my boots tangled up, and put us both out of action."

"We went over that last night, Pat. No sense plowing the same furrow."

"I'm about to hang up my spurs, so to speak. Would you be interested in running for sheriff at the upcoming election?"

"Pat, you got a lot of trail riding left in you. Aren't you training Billy to follow in your footsteps? Besides, I'm trying to retire myself."

"Hmmm," Pat mused. "I'm also thinking about Sissy up there all alone in her cabin. I may ride up there and see how she's doing. I've saved most of my salary and have been thinking about my own place."

Pat and Sissy? It was something to think about as Thorn walked to the Belle Saloon to chat with Charlie and thank him for looking out for him. Charlie wasn't there, but Louie was in early to have some boiled eggs, cheese, bread, and a mug of beer for breakfast.

"Good morning, Thorn, how did…"

"Don't ask how I slept last night. You don't want to know." Thorn then updated Louie on the fight last night, the arrest of the two cowboys after they had left the Belle, and the story in this morning's paper.

"Sally read all about how an assassin had tried to gun me down Saturday night, and I hadn't told her about it. I bet she is really peeved, and I guess I don't blame her. She wouldn't talk with me this morning."

"Women are wonderful but unfathomable."

"Here," Thorn handed Louie the volume *A Tale of Two Cities* and said, "I'm leaving this morning for Denver. You'll have to explain it to her. By the way, I want you to have this, just in case." He handed Louie the derringer and walked out. Louie stood looking at the two-shot pistol and then after Thorn until the bat wings stopped swinging.

Thorn stopped back at the dining room for one last attempt to see Sally, but she hadn't put in an appearance. He went to his room to relax until it was time for him to go to the station.

He arrived just as the train was screeching to a halt and letting off clouds of steam. Thorn stood by the train until the conductor started to put up the lower step and called out, "All Aboard. Last call for Denver. All Aboard."

Thorn looked around the platform and slung his saddlebags over his left shoulder. He grabbed the handle and hoisted himself up to the carriage car's steps and into the doorway when he heard, "Thorn, Thorn, wait."

Turning, he saw Sally, dressed in her grease-stained smock with a dirty chef's hat pressed down on her head, running toward the departing train. She had a black smudge on her face, and he froze her image in his mind for future recall.

"Thorn, I couldn't let you leave without telling you that I still care," she called out, "but not if you are going to keep secrets from me. I won't have it."

Several arriving passengers stopped to watch the strange sight of a female cook, obviously from one of the lower-class restaurants, running across a train platform, calling after a departing passenger. It was very undignified, to say the least. ·

The train began to pull away with slow jerking chugs, then faster ones. Thorn called out, "I'll be back in a few days. Sally, I lo—"

His words were drowned out by the blast from the train's steam whistle and its bell clanging.

Thorn stood in the doorway of the moving train until Sally and the station receded from his view. Turning, he saw the conductor on the door platform above him rocking to the train's sway.

"Take your seat, sir. I've got to close the doors."

Thorn went into the smoking carriage and, after removing his copy of Dickens' *A Tale of Two Cities,* stored his bags in the netting above his seat and settled onto the bench seat, lit up a Cheroot, and began to read:

It was the best of times,
it was the worst of times,
it was the age of wisdom,
it was the age of foolishness,
it was the epoch of belief,
it was the epic of incredulity,
it was the season of Light,
it was the season of Darkness,
it was the spring of hope,
it was the season of despair…

Thus, Thorn finally began to read Charles Dickens' most famous work on human nature and sacrifice during times of revolution.

Chapter 25
Kneading Dough

The trip back from Silverton to Durango was an easy two-day ride, and here he was on his third day. The buckboard and horse had been ready when Kid finished his second cup of coffee with Andy, the holster. "He's an old boy, a gelding, but he'll get you there. Not like some of the younger ones who want to lope and wind up slipping and stumbling in all the loose shale and gravel on the trail. He'll do if you take it easy."

"Thanks, Andy, and I hope to see you again soon."

"Not sure if I feel the same way, Kid. Why don't you get clear of this place and keep moving?"

Kid thought of the three men he saw riding by as he stood talking with Andy in front of the barn. They rode by, heads hung low in the early morning mist. Kid glanced at them and asked, "Andy, who are those three gents riding up the trail?"

Andy squinted and slowly nodded, "Stay away from those old boys, Kid. They are poison. The little guy is named Jim Stone, a cousin to the two men flanking him. They are the Stone brothers out of Southeast Missouri. They are as mean as water moccasins, as fast as any pit viper, and just as deadly. They grew up in the mosquito and snake-infested swamps until vigilantes drove them out. They moved west and settled here this spring. Hope they go back to their family in the swamps. But we are getting more hard cases riding in every week. Like those two scallywags you dealt with last night. I wish I could have seen it, he, he, he."

"Do you know their first names?"

"The ones you killed last night? No, can't say I ever heard, let me think, he, he, he." Andy scratched his head and thought, "No, but if you're talking about those boys who just rode by, the two big ones are the Stone brothers. I can't tell the older brother from his baby brother; they look the same to me, but I heard tell they are called Monday and Tuesday, on account of that's when they were born," he continued chuckling. "He, he, he, don't that beat all? Those Missouri swamp folks beat everything I've ever seen." Andy hoisted a gunny sack of provisions into the bed and said, "That's all. Have a safe trip, Kid."

Kid checked the bridle on the old nag and buckled the throat latch snugly. Satisfied, he brought Lady out, tied her and the long-eared mule to the back of the wagon, and clucked and shook the rains to get 'em rolling. That was the beginning of his troubles.

Kid had first tried to ride in the buckboard with Lady, and the mule roped to the back, but the mule dug in and dragged its hoofs, while Lady jerked and pulled every which way.

Thinking that the cargo of dead meat might be upsetting Lady, he tried for several miles to walk her roped to the buckboard's seat closer to him, but the mule continued to repeatedly bray in a loud and jarring way that upset both him and Lady.

After lunch and a rest, he tried switching the mule's position with Lady; an hour later, they were both pulling, and Lady's soft, gentle neigh came out as snorts, squeals, and groans as if she was in pain. The mule's brays continued to grate on their nerves.

At one point, he thought about cutting the mule loose, but he really wanted to return it to the lady in black he had seen at the inquest. Next, he tried tying it to the slow farm horse pulling the wagon, but all it did was upset the nag, and now he had three balking animals to contend with.

He took another much-needed rest, smoked, built a fire, and checked the contents of the burlap bag. It contained a blackened coffee pot, cooking pan, plate, and cup, plus the ingredients for a two-day ride (a pound of coffee, a pound of bacon, and a pound of flour).

He stripped and hobbled Lady and carefully examined her blanket and saddle for burrs but found none. He stored her tack and his bedroll in the back of the wagon, away from the tarp covering the two corpses. After unharnessing the nag, he staked her out in a grassy area near Lady. They both whinnied and neighed and settled down to munch the tall grass.

What would he do with the mule? He tied its harness rope to the back of the wagon and hoped for the best. After a half hour of braying, he got out of his warm blankets and brought her around to the area where the two horses grazed. Building up the fire again, he tossed some bigger limbs on and crawled back into his now cold blankets. He kept his boots on and used his rolled-up slicker for a pillow. His right hand held his Colt .45 during the night.

The next morning, after a difficult night's sleep, he had breakfast and decided that some things weren't worth it. After harnessing the nag to the wagon, he tied Lady to his seat with a long rope so she could have some freedom of movement and let the mule go. Suppose it took off or got lost, well, good riddance to it. He might even buy the lady in black another one.

After putting out the fire, filling his canteen from a spring, and policing the area, something he and his mother had done on their trip out west from Ohio. He climbed aboard and took the wagon back onto the trail south. He thought the little, long-eared gray mule would stay behind for a few minutes, but she soon trotted up to them and kept pace. "Will wonders never cease," he said aloud.

As they trudged along, Kid had a chance to review his actions at the Silver Dollar Saloon with Red. He was not proud of himself. He was also not proud of his bragging in the Belle Saloon about planning to pick a fight with the Pinkerton agent and then getting jumped from behind by the two deputies. He was made to look foolish by those two deputies, Billy and Chris, and he felt red-faced embarrassment but not enmity toward them. He would keep that incident to himself. Funny, but he thanked them for playing the trick on him and then how they laughed with him, not at him. He would look them up in Durango, share a beer or two, and tell his story about going up against two wanted gunmen, the same ones the two deputies planned on capturing and bringing them back for the reward.

At noon, he let the animals graze without hobbling or staking them. Last night, he had fried enough bacon and grease cakes to make the stop a cold harbor. They began to make up time on the trail and stopped for their second night.

He ran a short picket line and let the three animals graze in a meadow while he built a fire and cooked up some of the bacon and flour mixed with water. He used a green stick to stir the batter and fried some grease cakes. They would have been better with salt and yeast to raise the dough sitting next to the fire like he used to fix them for his mother and her friends, but you make do with what you have. He hadn't seen anyone on the trail and hoped the remainder of the journey would be uneventful.

The next morning broke clear and cold, and after a breakfast of hot coffee and bacon wrapped in a greasy cake called a "Pig in a Poke," he carefully put out his fire, policed the area, and piled up some dry wood for the next traveler. He also learned this habit from his mother, who always looked for the best in other people.

He got his little party organized and off at an early start. Crossing through a narrow valley, he noticed the aspen leaves were fast falling along the trail. It looked like a golden snowfall in October. It was breathtaking, and he stopped momentarily to form and savor the image.

Late in the morning, he reigned up in front of the cutoff to the cabin where he had spent the night a week earlier. Standing in the buckboard, he noticed gray smoke coming from its chimney. He wondered if it was some stranger holding up there or if the lady in black had returned home.

Pulling up to about 30 yards, a safe hailing distance, he called out, "Hello, cabin. Anybody home?" The front door opened, framing the lady he had seen at the inquest, and at the same instance, the long-eared mule bolted forward at a run, whinnying like a horse and then braying in its excitement. It ran straight up to the lady, pushed its head against her shoulder, and rocked her back.

The lady screamed in delight." Oh, Rufus, you came home. Oh, Rufus, I love you." She petted and patted the animal for several more minutes, with Kid watching in amazement. Will wonders never cease, he thought?

The lady stopped, pushed Rufus away, and put her hand to her forehead to better see the man standing in the buckboard. She saw a thin young man with long dark hair dressed in stained-worn black clothes with the only color found in his braces. Even the pistol he wore low and tied down was black-handled. A gunfighter, she thought. "Where did you find him?"

"I didn't exactly find him, Ma'am. I tracked two criminals up to Silverton and remembered from the inquest that you said they stole your long-eared gray mule. It was the only one in Silverton to fit that description."

The lady walked forward from the cabin. "You mean you traveled up to Silverton and brought back my mule?"

"Sure enough, there it stands."

"And the two criminals?"

"I brought them back, too. They are in the back here," Kid tipped his head back to indicate that the canvas covered two forms in the bed of the buckboard.

She came forward to the nose of the horse and said, "I'm Sissy Todd, and who might you be?"

"I'm Leroy Brooks, Ma'am, but my friends call me Kid."

"May I call you Kid?"

"Sure enough, Ma'am."

"Please call me Sissy."

"Yes Ma'am, I mean Sissy."

"Take your horses into the barn, and you can fork 'em some hay. We don't have much to eat, mainly vegetables, but wash up and come in for supper." She led Rufus toward the barn and swatted its rump as it fast walked into its stall. Kid removed the nag's harness and bridle and called Lady to follow them. Nothing had been disturbed since his last visit. He unsaddled and rubbed down the two horses and found the pitchfork. He filled the mangers with sweet-smelling hay and went around back to the privy and washstand to clean up for supper.

He glanced at his image in the mirror hung above the washtub and tried as he might. He couldn't rake his long hair back in any semblance of being presentable. He gave up running his fingers through his hair, washed them again, and, after retrieving the gunny sack from the wagon, went up to the front door and knocked.

"Come on in. It ain't locked."

"Thanks, Ma'am, I mean Sissy. I have some extra chuck to contribute to the meal."

"Oh my, thank you. I've run short on everything." She unpacked the food items from the sack and returned it with the blackened utensils. "Coffee, oh how much I wished I had a cup for you…ah…Kid."

"Now we do. I can make us some pan bread and fry up some bacon."

"Oh no, that's woman's work. You sit over here, and I'll get you a cup of coffee in no time."

Kid felt uneasy sitting down while she did all the work. "You got it looking much better. I mean, better than the last time I saw it."

"You saw it?"

"Yes, on the way up to Silverton, I got a late start, thought the cabin was abandoned, and spent a night."

"You spent the night. Then you must be the one who cleaned up the place after the…incident. Did you also leave the dollar bill?"

"Yes, I found chuck laying around and thought I'd pay for it."

"That was very nice of you Kid. You'll notice I still have the dollar bill under the saltshaker. I think I've got my courage up. Are those two in the back of the wagon? Ah…dead?"

"Yes, they are both dead as doornails, and I'm taking 'em into Durango for the reward."

"May I see them?"

"I don't think that's a good idea before our meal. Afterward, if you want, I don't see no harm in it."

"Do you know their names?"

"No, I was never able to learn that."

"Right, we'll eat first." With that, Sissy got to work in the kitchen, even laying out the sugared peach pie filling she found in the pantry. Kid enjoyed watching as she mixed and kneaded the bread dough. She wasn't shy about roughly handling it. She grabbed the side furthest away from her and folded it in half with a slap of her open hand, and then, using the heels of her hands, she began working and pressing it. She finally covered it and set the dough aside to allow it to rise. His mother had never taught him how to do it this way.

He sat in wonderment, watching her as she placed some lard and flour in another bowl, spooned some water, and mixed it all to form a ball. All the time, she talked about her garden, the lack of rain, her husband's gold prospecting, and how happy she was to have Rufus back in its stall. Taking a beer bottle, she sprinkled more flour on the table, dusted her hands, then the bottle with flour, and rolled the dough into two circles. She put one in a pie pan, filled it with the peach-sweetened pie filling, spread the second dough circle over the filling, and finger-crimped the edge. Finally, she trimmed off the excess and slid the pie into the oven. With the leftover dough, she made up some pigs in a blanket. They were like pigs in a poke, only better.

After supper and the clean-up, he enjoyed another cup of coffee and a second piece of peach pie when she leaned over and touched his hair.

"When you finish your dessert and coffee if you like, I can trim your hair and let you use Mike's shaving mug and razor, or I can shave you myself. I used to shave Mike all the time and never nicked him once. You've been awfully good to me, and I want to do something to repay you, but I don't think I want to see those two just yet. What do you say?"

Half an hour later, she removed the old pillowcase from his neck and shook it out in the yard. Sitting in a chair in the yard in the fading light, he had received a haircut and a shave. She then returned to the cabin with a hot, wet hand towel to wipe the soap residue from his face. Holding up the mirror, he saw a handsome young man gazing back.

"Thank you kindly, Sissy. That was a professional cut and shave if I ever had one. Worth at least two bits in any town this side of the Rio Grande. If you don't mind, I want to check on the horses and spread my bed roll out in the barn before it gets dark."

"Go ahead and check on your horses, but it won't be necessary for you to sleep in the barn. You can bed down in front of the fire, and I've got an extra corn husks mattress rolled up that will fit you just fine. I want you to shuck those clothes in the morning. I've got some of Mike's old overalls and work clothes that might fit you. I'm doing laundry in the morning and can get your clothes washed and mended." She turned and went into the cabin and lit a lamp.

Chapter 26
Come A-Courtin'

In the early hours of Monday morning, Billy and Chris located the two horses on a side street, believed to belong to the miscreants they had jailed Sunday night. Their saddlebags contained some dirty clothes of their size, cooking utensils, and four boxes of .38 short, rim-fire ammo plus Colt .45 ammunition. They walked the two mounts to the stable, stripped their saddles, and let them eat fresh hay and get their fill from the horse trough. They were not responsible for the type of men who mounted them.

The pocket pistols Billy and Chris had confiscated took the same ammo they had found in the miscreants' saddlebags. The rounds fit perfectly. Both five-shot revolvers needed cleaning badly, and Chris doubted if one would even fire. The deputies thoroughly cleaned and tested the pocket pistols in the firing pit behind the gunsmith's shop. Satisfied with the results, they each pocketed one, took two 50-round boxes, and headed to see their respective ladies.

Chris had the shorter trip, just down the street to the hotel's dining room, where Sally sat with him after the 4:00 p.m. supper rush. They both had coffee, and Chris had a slice of pie "on the house."

At first, Sally wanted nothing to do with a self-defense weapon until Chris let it drop that the two men he had thumped and arrested Sunday evening had been looking for their friend who had tried to shoot Thorn in the back Saturday night as he left the Belle. But by a twist of fate, Thorn had instead killed him.

"It seems like some bad folks are after Thorn, and he's concerned about your safety, as we all are. I've checked out this little pistol, and it shoots good if you are up close, say, less than fifteen feet. Not very powerful, but it's good for a lady 'cause there ain't much kick, and you've got five rounds that'll do a lot of harm. I'll show you how to reload."

"Chris, I don't know anything about guns, and I don't like them."

"That's no problem. I know everything about 'em, and I'll have you shooting like that little lady everybody's talking about, Little Miss Sure Shot, or Annie something or other, in no time at all."

"Are you talking about Miss Anne Oakley?"

Chris nodded in recognition of the name. Sally smiled and thanked him. They agreed to meet at the firing range pit after she got off work that evening and hoped there would be enough light. She asked him to keep the pistol and ammunition until then.

Monday had been an eventful day for Sally. She had to finish work and learn to shoot like Little Miss Sure Shot. Not much to ask of her. So, Thorn was concerned about her safety enough to send Chris over with a weapon and ammunition. She remembered that he had insisted on her locking the doors and closing all ground windows when they had returned from the church social. First, an assassin tried to backshoot him, and now the dead man's friends are locked up with only Smitty and Teddy to secure them. Yes, she would learn to shoot.

Chris sat at the gunsmith's counter smoking a hand-rolled cigarette with the parts of an old Belgium bulldog pistol spread out in front of him on the newspaper when Sally opened the door, causing the little bell above to ring. "Chris, take care of that, will you?" came a voice from the back.

"It's for me. We're going to do some shooting in the pit." Chris stuck the cigarette in the side of his mouth, and quickly put the pistol, springs, cylinder, and pins back together, and tightened the grip screws. He spun the gun around a few times on his trigger finger and laid it on the counter. "It's finished." He called out toward the back. "Hi Sally, come on, let's do some shooting."

In the pit, the western sky still provided enough light to set up targets of old soup cans. Chris began the lesson by knocking down five in a row with the little pistol. He demonstrated how to cock it with his thumb until the hammer locked in place and then slowly squeezed the trigger until it was released. Next, he pointed out the dangers of having a cocked pistol in a holster, in a hand, or a pocket or an apron. Any slight jar, movement, or even dropping it can cause a pistol to fire.

He showed her how to stand, holding the little pistol in her strong hand, then holding both hands in front of her. Next, he had her practice holding her elbows tucked in close to her sides and her hands held close to her midsection. He showed her how it was more difficult for a villain to knock it out of her hands or take it away from her in a house at night if she kept it close to her body. Now, it was time for her to practice with her elbows tucked in close to her sides while holding the pistol.

Sally was feeling more comfortable, so he had her face the targets, then showed her how to cock it with her thumb until the hammer locked in place, and then had her slowly squeeze the trigger until it fired. "Good job. Now," he said, "as soon as you see your target, I want you to cock, aim and squeeze the trigger." The can moved but didn't fall. "Good job for your first time."

"You keep it down at chest level to see over the top of the gun." He showed her how to use the door frames as protection and shoot right and left-handed with cover.

She began by dry firing the gun on spent cartridges, then moved into single shots that she had to load herself. Finally, she fired the little single-action pistol at cans, making them jump and dance at five yards. It became too dark to see her targets accurately, so they called it a night. Funny, she thought, the pistol has little recoil and not much of a bark.

She liked it and might give it an appropriate name.

My job is done, thought Chris. I wonder how Billy is making out with his lady?

As Chris headed toward the hotel dining room to meet with Sally earlier that afternoon, Billy walked swiftly to the stable, saddled his favorite horse, and set out at a nice gate to the Todd cabin. He had tucked the pocket pistol and two boxes of ammunition in a saddle bag and was looking forward to personal time showing Sissy how to shoot.

A half-hour later, he approached the turnoff to Todd's place and reined up in surprise. An unknown farm wagon was in the yard, and two horses and the little gray mule were in the corral. From beside the barn, but out of his sight, came the rhythmic sound of wood being chopped.

Sliding off his mount, he dropped the reins to the ground and quietly walked toward the sound with his right hand firmly on the pistol grip.

Crossing the yard, his movement was arrested by a call from the cabin, "Billy, is that you?" He recognized Sissy's voice which did not register danger, only curiosity as to what the young deputy had come for.

"Yes, Mrs. Todd, it's me. I just came out to see how you are doing. I heard that you moved back from the hotel. Who do you have working for you? It can't be…is that Kid's Piebald in the corral?"

The chopping stopped, and Kid came around to the front. "Thought I heard talking. Well, howdy, if it ain't my friend Deputy Billy. How are you doing, old son?"

"Fine, Kid. I'm surprised to see you back from Silverton. Did you have something to do with the return of her mule?"

"I should say he did," exclaimed Sissy. "Not only did he free Rufus from a den of thieving killers, but he went up against the two skunks that shot my Mike in the back, and…well, he brought them back too. They're in the back of the wagon."

Billy turned back toward the wagon and carefully lifted the canvas. "Have you identified these as the ones who did the crimes?"

"Not yet, Billy," she shied from her answer. "I'm kind of working up my nerve. But I will. Kid said he'd show 'em to me anytime I was ready."

Kid stood swinging the double-bit axe around his head, tossing it in the air and catching it. "Oh. It wasn't much," he said with a shy smile, but he knew it really was very much a big deal and bet the newspaper would be after him for the story.

Kid was dressed in baggy bib overalls, sans shirt, and heavy work shoes. "Kid, what happened to your clothes? Lose 'em in Silverton?"

Kid continued to smile, balancing the axe first on the palm of one hand, then the other, and still not talking.

"I should say not," said Sissy in a huff. "His adventures took their toll on his clothing, and I'm washing and mending them so he can go into town tomorrow and claim his reward. Kid is kind enough to trim some new railings for the corral that Mike never got around to fixing and to cut up some firewood. He's pretty handy with an axe."

Billy nodded and said, "I can see that." Billy wondered about Sissy's decision to give her claim, cabin, and property as a reward for bringing the two desperadoes to justice, but the sheriff had cautioned her that it might not be legal.

"I got a message for you from Sheriff Williams, and there is something he wants you to have. Can we go inside for a few minutes?" Billy's hopes to meet with her alone were soon shattered.

"Why sure, come on in, you too, Kid. It's time for a break." Kid raised the long-handled axe, took aim, and threw it at the stump used as a base for splitting firewood. It rotated once and landed solidly, with its blade biting deeply into the stump's edge. Kid sure seemed to develop some new talents since the last time they had seen each other, just a week ago, Billy thought, looking at the buried axe blade for a few seconds longer.

They went into the cabin, and Billy noticed that it had only one bed, Sissy and Todd's marital bed, and he couldn't help but think that it was the bed upon which Sissy had been raped after Mike's murder. He wondered where Kid was sleeping. "When did you arrive back, Kid?"

Kid sat with his steaming cup of coffee as Sissy placed a big slice of peach pie on a plate before him, serving him first. She laid a flatware fork and a worn napkin before him. Next, she took care of Billy, and finally, she set her place and asked, "Should we say a silent prayer of thanks? I have been praying for Rufus' return and justice for Mike."

"Sure," said Billy, who bowed his head in grace but continued to look at the others through his laced fingers. Their heads bowed, lips moving, and eyes closed, but they held each other's hand in prayer. Billy's left was held tightly in Sissy's right. *It gets stranger and stranger*, Billy thought.

"Let's eat," said Sissy.

Billy complimented her on the pie, "One of the best I've ever et." Kid finished his and drank a second cup of coffee.

"What message does Pat have for me?"

"Give me just a minute." Billy hesitated and stood up. "It's in my saddlebag." In two minutes, he was back at his place carrying a pocket pistol and two boxes of 50 rounds of ammunition. He laid them on the table.

Billy reached over, picked up the small firearm, and first checked to see that it was empty; then, he laid it back down.

"I don't think Sissy cares for loaded firearms in the house, but go on, Billy, you have the floor." Kid said.

Billy picked it up and handed it to Sissy. "Pat is concerned about you being out here all alone," he quickly glanced at Kid, "and wanted to lend you this pocket pistol for self-defense. It's not a bad shooter as long as you are close. I checked it out first after I cleaned it. We took them off a couple of cowboys last night who had come down from Silverton looking for their friend, a mean little guy who tried to gun down Thorn by shooting him in the back."

"What?" said Kid. Now, Kid was fully alert. "Did he get Thorn?"

"No. Not with his luck. It was Saturday night, and Charlie, the bartender, thought something was queer with the little guy who kept looking over at Thorn, and asking about him, so he got word to Thorn to be on the lookout. Thorn heard the little man's spurs coming out of the saloon and turned on him."

"The skunk already had his hand on his gun and was ready to draw. After a few words, he went for his gun, and Thorn put three into his chest before the little guy even cleared leather."

"Wow!" Kid whistled. "Some shooting and this happened on Saturday night?"

Billy nodded and said, "Last night, two big men were shoving Charlie, the Belle's bartender, around looking for their friend. Sunday night, there was a big church social followed by a dance where most decent folks went. The sheriff, Chris, and Thorn went over to the Belle to check things out. The two big men said they were looking for their friend and describing him, Thorn thought it sounded like the man he shot. So, Thorn led them over to the funeral parlor but didn't let on that he was dead or that he had killed him the night before." Billy paused and took a sip of coffee before he continued.

"They took offense at finding out their friend was dead, and one went for his gun. Chris piled on to them, wailing the tar out of 'em, and arrested 'em. They are in jail right now, but they won't say anything other than their last name is Stone. They are being charged with attempted murder, assault, and destruction of property. None is a hanging offense, but it's enough to get 'em in ten years in the state penitentiary at Cañon City. I've been told five years there is a death sentence."

Kid sat forward and said, "I know about those birds. They are two brothers, said to be mean as snakes, and a skinny older cousin or some shirt-tail relative who taught them everything they know. The two big men go by the names Monday Stone and Tuesday Stone. The little guy was called Jim Stone. They probably have some paper out on 'em in Missouri. Tell the sheriff and Thorn I'll be around in the morning and give 'em all I learned in Silverton."

"Thorn left this morning for Denver. Something big is coming up, and he will try to find out. He'll be back in a few days. In the meantime, Sissy, will you take the loan of this firearm?"

"If Kid thinks I should, and someone shows me how to use it."

"Good. Why don't we head out now and line up some tin cans?" Said Billy.

"No need for you to bother Billy. I'll see to her training in the handling and use of this little pocket pistol. I happen to have a spare Colt .45 pistol in my saddlebags that belonged to the little weasel-faced guy resting in the buckboard's bed. I'll give her lessons on both firearms and tell the sheriff she is pleased that he is thinking of her safety."

"You sure you don't want me to go out with you and fire a few rounds?"

"No, Billy, she's fine here, and I'll have her up to speed in no time at all."

"All right then, Sissy, I'll head back and tell Sheriff Pat that you'll be in tomorrow to identify the bodies; Kid, I want you to stop by the sheriff's office and see if you can identify the two birds we have on ice. Let's say after lunch tomorrow. Is that all right with you two?"

Kid nodded their agreement, then said, "Not sure Billy, if I want to let those two birds know that I recognized 'em in Silverton. I don't think they saw me. They were passing by the barn when I was getting ready to come back this way, and they never looked in my direction."

"How do you know it's them if you never directly saw them?"

"The old timer at the stable described the three of 'em. Something else Billy." Kid was not sure how much to tell. What the hell, in for a penny, in for a pound, "I met the leader named Red. I'll tell you, the sheriff, and Chris all about it tomorrow."

Kid confirmed that he would be Sissy's escort and bring her into town tomorrow in the wagon. He then took Billy over for another look at the two stiffs. Sissy stood close at hand when Kid pulled the canvas back to reveal the two corpses. She gave out a little gasp, and her tanned complexion paled.

"The big one, he's the one who…I had trouble with in the Silver Dollar Saloon and smashed his head in with a beer mug. He died on the bar room floor in a puddle of beer and blood. The little one and I had a fair fight on the street in front of the saloon, just like in the dime novels," upon hearing this, Sissy, feeling faint, returned to the cabin leaving the two men talking over a plan.

"We'll be looking forward to seeing you both tomorrow and… ah…nothing. It's good seeing you, Kid. I'm sure Chris, we now call him the Texas Wildcat after what he did to those two old boys. I'm glad to see you too. You did a neat job bringing those two in. I'm impressed and want to shake your hand." It was hard to feel resentment against Kid, but he'd try to put his feelings of envy and anger aside and go with the plan.

"And don't forget Rufus," said Kid. They both laughed.

"Sure, Billy, let's shake on friendship, but not too tight. I'm just getting over a sore hand."

Chapter 27
In the Jail House Now

Early Tuesday morning, Kid dressed in his clean and mended duds, and with the haircut and his face smoothly shaved, he felt like a new man as he sat alongside the Widow Todd, dressed in funeral black in the farm wagon, and drove into town. He had tied the little, long-eared gray mule to the rear and was surprised when it trotted right along without balking. Kid reined up in front of the hotel and escorted Sissy in to register and pay for two nights' stay. He then registered under his name, Le Roy Kid Brooks, in a separate second-floor room across the hall from Thorn's vacant premises.

Their arrival caused quite a stir, with the town loafers and regular folks busy looking over the sideboards at the forms under the canvas and wondering what or who they might be. A couple of the men from the Belle remembered seeing Kid last week and something about him wanting to draw on Thorn, the Pinkerton man. But then he left town that evening in a hurry. What was he doing in the company of the young widow, Mrs. Sissy Todd? It was agreed that there was a lot more to this than meets the eye. A reporter from the Durango local paper soon was at the wagon trying to lift the canvas with his pencil.

When someone told him he'd better leave that alone, the reporter started talking about journalistic freedom, freedom of speech, the press, assembly, and the right to petition the government to redress grievances. "This is the bedrock upon which our constitution and country is based," insisted the reporter.

"I thought we were duty-bound to mind our own business?" One old sourdough quipped, but his partner assured him that newspaper reporters were called the fourth estate and could poke around anyplace they wanted.

Soon, Sheriff Williams and his two deputies, Chris and Billy, walked over to the hotel on their way in for lunch. Sheriff Williams told the crowd to "go on about its business, nothing to see here but a farm wagon."

The reporter began questioning the sheriff about the forms under the canvas and the Widow Todd being in the company of what appeared to be a known gunman. "What did it all mean? Sheriff, do you want to make a statement?" The sheriff and his deputies just walked into the hotel.

"Jimmy, what room is Mrs. Todd and her escort using?"

"She's in room twelve, and Mr. Brooks, better known as Kid, is across from Mr. Hagerman's room, number eight."

"So, Kid checked into his own room," the sheriff gave Billy a knowing look. "We're going up there now. Chris, you lounge around here and make sure no one goes up to bother us, but don't, I really mean this, don't beat anybody up. Nice and easy. Understand?"

"Sure thing, boss," Chris seated himself on a horsehair couch, stretched out his long legs, and rolled himself a smoke.

The first door Sheriff Williams knocked quietly on was room twelve. "Sissy, it's me, Pat and Billy, open the door." Kid opened the door.

"Come on in, sheriff, and you too, Billy." Kid stuck his head out and looked both ways to make sure no one was lurking around.

"What gives Kid? I'm Sheriff Pat Williams, and I've heard some good things about you from Billy."

"Thank you kindly," said Kid. We're here to deliver the two owl hoots that bushwacked Sissy's man and violated her. They are in the back of the wagon. I also brought back Sissy's mule as further proof. They had him stashed at a barn in Silverton. I killed both in what were fair fights. The big one I smacked in the head with a beer mug in the Silver Dollar Saloon when he went for his gun. The little weasel-faced one I shot in the street in a fair fight in front of a dozen witnesses. We're looking for the reward. Now, there is no reason for your law dogs to go up to Silverton and bring 'em back. But I have more to tell you."

"Will Sissy identify them?"

"Yep, she already has. But she'll do it on the record, too."

"Good, we can have a quick hearing tomorrow and get you the reward."

Kid then explained about the Stone brothers and how he had seen them with a relative named Jim Stone, a little guy, leave before him for Durango on some mission. He himself was on a mission for the gang leader, Red, to keep a posse of law dogs from coming up to Silverton and causing trouble before he was ready for something big. Now, if you and Chris agree, here's what we can do.

Thirty minutes later, the sheriff and his two deputies entered the dining room and took their usual places. Sally took their orders and served them coffee. Fifteen minutes later, the widow in black and her gunman escort took a table at the other end of the dining room.

Sally introduced herself to Sissy and the somber-looking gunman, then took their orders and served her escort coffee. The widow had requested tea, and leaning over, Sally whispered how sorry she was about all that had happened to her and how she wanted to pay her respects and have a visit but had learned that Sissy had moved back to her cabin.

"I'll be in town for two days. Perhaps we can get together. I do miss my chats with my lady friend," said Sissy, thinking of Madge, Holly's wife, her best friend, before they moved on. She wondered if they were coming back, had abandoned their claim, or had sold it.

Sally was not impressed with Kid. He was a sour puss, mean-tempered, and seemed to be nursing his hand. When introduced, he ignored her and kept eating, giving her the briefest acknowledgment. Sissy was so sweet. It was a shame that such a man was the one to rescue her mule and bring in the two villains. That was something to think about later.

An hour later, Teddy had the corpses at the undertaker, and Mr. Dobbs was happy for the business. The mule and farm horse had been taken to the stable and put up on the county's bill to be repaid from the forthcoming reward money.

Billy and Chris were lounging on the hotel veranda. Chris, balancing his weight on the back two legs of his chair, rocking back and forth with ease, when Kid walked by and bumped Chris's chair. This caused him to fall back against the wall, not hard, but noticeable to the passers-by. Chris was unhurt, but he jumped up, confronting Kid and telling him to apologize or suffer the consequences of the Texas Wildcat publicly.

Kid just laughed at him as a crowd of loafers and other town folks stopped to see the argument. Kid turned to walk on.

Chris was having none of it and sprang forward, grabbed the Kid by the shoulder, and spun him around. "Don't walk away from me when I'm talking to you, you little punk?"

"Little punk, am I?" With that, Kid pushed Chris in his chest, sending him crashing into the unoccupied chairs. Billy then came after Kid with swinging fists, one of which caught Kid on the side of his head and rang his bell. Kid staggered back and went for his gun, but Billy sent his fist into Kid's breadbasket, doubling him over. Kid was on his knees and hands, outstretched, coughed, and wheezed as Billy removed Kid's gun and poked it into his side. Chris got up from his chair and followed.

"Get up and march." Several in the crowds applauded the deputies, and one commented, "We got ourselves some law in this town." Kid was shoved toward the jail with his hands raised high. He made quite a spectacle, his hair mussed and his clothes in disarray, as they approached the sheriff's office.

Entering the jail area, Billy said, "Turn around Kid." Upon compliance with the command, with his hands raised, Billy punched Kid square in the face, sending him stumbling back into the cell adjoining the Stone brothers, who watched with great interest. Kid crashed into the wall above the bunk and collapsed, with blood running from his nose and busted lip.

Kid heard the door clang shut and the key grate in its lock, as Billy left the jail area laughing and calling Kid a little weaseling punk, and could expect more where that came from. The main door separating the cells from the office area, which had remained open, was slammed closed and locked.

Kid lay still as if passed out, wondering why Billy had let him have it so hard in his face. Blood was collecting in his nose, which was probably broken, and he tasted the iron of his own blood. He had told them to make it look real, but what the heck? He would remember this affront when this was all over and deal with Billy, man to man, but for now, he lay stunned and barely conscious, breathing through his mouth and making little snorting and gagging sounds that were unnatural.

"Hey, Tues, it's the kid Red told us about." One of the brothers stood up and went to the cell's bars and heard the Kid's groans as he lay motionless on the blood-soaked blanket. "That deputy gave him a good one. He sucker-punched Kid in the face after ordering him to turn around with his hands still raised. That law dog didn't give him a chance. Wham, smack, and he's out cold."

Monday Stone shadow-boxed a few punches, head down, feet moving, left arm protecting his head, and delivered a powerful right fist to an imaginary opponent's face. Both brothers considered themselves pugilists. They were ready to knock any man down for any reason, and sometimes without a reason, just for the fun of it. "I'd like to see the rematch of that fight," said Monday.

Tuesday Stone got up to assess the damage, "Kid, you alive?" Kid moaned that he was, but not sure about anything else. Both brothers laughed as Kid struggled to sit up, fell back on the bunk, and finally reached an upright position. He then fell with his arms at his sides, face forward, hit the stone floor with a hard slapping sound, and for several minutes didn't move.

"That's gotta hurt," said Monday as they both watched with growing interest and placed a bet on whether or not the kid would make it to the water bucket in the corner. Tuesday put his money on the kid. Finally, after several minutes of struggling to his knees and hunching over, he crawled across the stone floor to the water bucket with a worn rag hanging over its edge.

The brothers watched each agonizing movement and several collapses before he made it. Kid first placed his head almost in the bucket, turning the water pink, and drank. Using the wet rag, he carefully cleaned most of the blood from his face and hair. "I told ya the kid would make it. You owe me a silver dollar." Tuesday said with a horse laugh.

Monday hissed, "Kid, why did the deputy work you over?"

The kid, now sitting on the floor in a puddle of water, slowly shook his head and tried to count the stars he saw floating around, "Ah, last week I was here, and after the inquest, I tried to call out the Pinkerton man who had brought in Ivory and his men. Red was counting on those three for the big job.

"I was looking for a fair fight with the Pinkerton when two of the law dogs jumped me from behind, roughed me up, and kicked me out of town. That's when I headed to Silverton and spent a night drinking with Red. The next day I tangled with those two mongrels, who backshot the miner and raped his wife. The law in Durango posted a reward on 'em, and I thought by bringing 'em back, collecting the reward, the law dogs would cotton up to me, and I might get another crack at that damned Pinkerton. Hell, I wish I'd left them two alive to join Red and our gang."

"Yeah," said Monday, "we saw some of that action before we left Silverton with our cousin. He was also going to blow out that Pinkerton's wick. We saw you clock the big fellow with your beer mug and then had a fair gunfight with the little 'en. Nice shooting."

"Why," asked Tuesday, "didn't you just shoot the little bastard in the back when he had his hands up and not turning around, the way he shot that miner?"

"It's like this, boys: I've got a certain code; I don't backshoot. I ride for the brand and am true to my partners. Come hell or high water, I stick. It's like you boys. You wouldn't beat a man to death who was down and out on the floor, would you? No. You want a stand-up fight, just like in the ring."

Both men turned away from the Kid in remembrances of the times they had sucker punched an opponent, smashed a man's head in with a bottle, and kicked a downed man.

"Just like there are rules in fighting a duel, boxing has the Marquess of Queensberry rules governing the manly sport of boxing," said Kid.

"Queensberry rules, never heard of 'em. What are they?"

The next half hour was spent discussing the differences between bare-knuckle brawling, with wrestling thrown in, and the organized sport of boxing with leather gloves, timed rounds, and giving a downed man a ten-second count to get up on his own. Kid then told them of the big money and how winners attracted the dames. Money was to be made in boxing, while brawling only got you a broken head and busted-up fists. Both men withdrew to their bunks to talk over this new information and left the kid to sleep.

An hour later, Smitty opened the outer door and said, "Come and get it." He handed mugs of coffee and dishes of stew through their food slots. The food was good, and each man got a piece of bread to mop up the gravy, the best part of a meal, according to Smitty. Kid sipped his coffee and gave his food to the Stone brothers.

"How are you boys liking our hospitality? In the last week, we brought in three of you boys over their saddles, killed another one in the street, and arrested you three. Not bad, and we got more surprises in store," said Smitty.

"What are you talking about? We got nothing to do with those others. We don't even know this hombre in the next cell. We were minding our business when we were sucker punched by one of the deputies and hauled in here."

Smitty laughed, "Go tell it to the judge. You, boys, don't fool us. We got a spy in Red's outfit and know all your plans even before you do. Boy, do we have a surprise planned for you when your gang comes for the payrolls in the bank? We're bringing in more Pinkertons as we speak. When you boys finish, wash your pans and cups and slide 'em through." Smitty left the cell area, slamming closed and locking the outer door.

"What do you make out of that?" said Monday. Tuesday just sat on his bunk, finishing his extra food, deep in thought. Kid sat on his bunk sipping his coffee.

When Smitty returned an hour later to collect the dishes, he said, "Don't reckon anybody has told you boys, but your bond hearing is coming up tomorrow morning before the Honorable Thomas X. Clark. We call him the hanging judge." Smitty laughed as he collected the plates, spoons, and cups.

"They are having our trials tomorrow?" asked Kid."

"Naw, it's a bond hearing," answered Smitty.

"What's that," both Monday and Tuesday asked together.

"If you got the cash, or someone will post it for you, the judge'll let you go till the trial. If you don't show, the court keeps the money, and they put out reward posters on you, 'Wanted Dead or Alive."

"How much does he usually charge for this here crime?" asked Tuesday.

"Oh," thought Smitty, "seeing that you didn't actually kill anyone, and the fellow one of you shot was already dead and all, it might be as high as one hundred dollars each."

After Smitty again left them alone, Kid asked, "Do you boys each have a hundred dollars?" With big grins, they nodded, "We can pay our way out and not have a trial. We can sure put a lot of distance between us and the state penitentiary in the next 30 days."

"I don't have but a few dollars traveling money on me. Boys, you got to go back to Red and tell him about the setup in store for the gang if they try to take the payrolls in the bank. He'll have to figure out something else, maybe on the train as it stops at one of the mines on the way up to Silverton. That's my best guess."

"I guess we owe it to Red to go back and spill the beans. Tell you the truth Kid, he wasn't so sure about you and told us to keep an eye on you, but you turned out to be true. Sorry about you facing your trial next month, but I have friends in Cañon City, and it's mainly the weak ones and the cowards who die off first. I'll give you some names of our old pards who'll help you."

They spent the evening hours and on into the night discussing the trap being set up for Red and the gang and the soundness of hitting the train as it makes its stop at the first mine. Unfortunately, neither brother knew Red's legal name, but they were able to supply the names and descriptions of his core members. Kid, after repeating his narrative several times, finally rolled over and tried to get a few hours of sleep before the hearing.

Chapter 28
Bond Hearing

Wednesday's early morning clouds cleared up, and the sun came out in all its radiance as the two Stone brothers and Kid finished their morning coffee. Each was individually fitted with ankle chains, and with their arms pinned from behind, each had his hands securely manacled by Smitty.

Teddy stood nearby with a Greener scattergun cradled at the ready. Chris smoked a roll-your-own, carefully supervised the process, and checked the tightness of the cuffs. The three men were frog-marched out of the jail and down Main Street to the Courthouse, where they entered through a side door guarded by Billy, cradling a scattergun. The process was by the book, and they were taking no chances.

A crowd had gathered near the front, waiting for the courthouse to open. The doors swung open to admit a near-capacity crowd, which quickly found places, and watched as the Widow Todd, in a long black dress with a black hat and veil, entered the courtroom on Sheriff William's arm and was led up to the front. Two of the ladies commented on what a handsome widow she made as she passed. It was also noted that the sheriff looked handsome in his Sunday best suit.

The bailiff, with his sidearm in an open view, called out, "All rise, the Magistrate, the Honorable X. Clark presiding."

The magistrate entered the room and stood at his desk. "You men, take off your hats in the court," he barked, sadly shaking his head at their lack of decorum. Taking a long-barreled pistol from his coat, he placed it on the desk, looked at the clock on the wall, and sat down. The audience sat quickly and noisily scooted chairs and cleared throats before the session began.

The bailiff called out, "In the matter of the Murder of Michael Todd and assault on his wife—" but was interrupted by the magistrate.

"Hold off on that one. Let's get this other case out of the way first."

"Yes, your honor, the second case is the people against the Stone Brothers of Missouri. This is a bond hearing in a case of resisting arrest, destruction of property, attempted assault with a firearm, and the discharge of said firearm twice in an occupied building. The people call Sheriff Williams its first witness and bring out the two prisoners."

The two brothers were brought out in chains with hands manacled behind their backs and told to stand up straight by the bailiff. They both did as ordered but soon slouched again.

"I think we can waive the reading of the charges and the questioning of the witness. You two boys, stand up straight. Are you Monday Stone and you Tuesday Stone, and do you hail from the state of Missouri, the Show Me State?"

Some of the men laughed at their names, and the magistrate whacked the butt of his pistol down on the desk and said, "Silence in the court." Several men in the front row looked cautiously at the magistrate using his hogleg as a gavel and hoped there wasn't a live round under the hammer.

The brothers nodded. "Let the record show that the defendants acknowledged their names and place of birth. Are you pleading guilty or not?"

Monday's head bobbed in the positive, while Tuesday shook his head back and forth in the negative, "Let the record show they both pled not guilty. As for bonds, none of these are hanging offenses, so the bail is set at one hundred dollars cash bond each. Can you boys pay today?"

The boys looked at each other and then turned to look at the sheriff.

"Sheriff, did the boys have sufficient funds to pay their bonds?"

"Yes, your honor."

"Good, let the record show that they are each posting individual bonds of one hundred dollars each, subject to forfeiture if they fail to show for their trial in thirty days' time. They are to be returned the balance of their funds, if any, after subtracting bails, the cost of ten cents per meal, and care of their horses, each at six bits a day. Also, return their gun belts, sidearms, horses, and tack. Is anything else to be returned?" The magistrate looked at the prisoners, who remained silent.

"Let the records show nothing else is requested. It is so ordered. Get 'em out of here and out of this town, sheriff. The court takes a ten-minute recess," said the magistrate.

The bailiff and the sheriff motioned for them to frog march down the center aisle to the vestibule, where their chains and cuffs were removed. Everyone turned to watch the show during recess.

They opened the doors and saw their two mounts were already saddled and waiting with bedrolls and saddlebags strapped on. "Here," said the sheriff, and handed each the remainder of their cash in small coins after subtractions. They each stupidly looked at the money, shoved it in their pockets, and went to mount up.

"Say, where are our rifles?" said Monday.

"You didn't speak up when the court asked if there was anything else. You get what was ordered. Do you want to go back to jail and wait for the hearing next week or climb aboard?" The sheriff picked up a length of chain for them to examine. Tuesday checked a saddlebag and said," Our clothes and letters from Mom are here."

"Yes," said the sheriff, "No one wanted to get near 'em, and no one could read the chicken scratching." They seemed satisfied until they checked the other saddle bags, "What gives! Where are our little pistols and extra rounds?"

You get back your gun belts and side arms, nothing in the order about other pistols or bullets." They both looked at their gun belts and saw that their bullet loops were empty of rounds. Quickly checking their Colts, they found the cylinders empty. "This ain't right," Monday mumbled.

"You can always ask His Honor next week if you want."

"Oh hell, come on Monday, let's get out of this town run by law dogs. We're lucky to have our hides." Tuesday mumbled under his breath, "It'll be a cold day in hell when the Stone brothers ever visit your town again."

The sheriff said, "Now get 'em out of town. Some of you deputies, on the day shift, escort these gents out of town and take 'em a mile or so toward Silverton and no stopping for any reason."

"How many of us do you want to go?" inquired Billy.

"Just you two. The other four can remain on duty in the town. Now get and hurry back for a meeting in the office." The brothers noted the number of deputies being discussed.

The four rode out of town at an easy trot. The brothers rode in front, and Billy and Chris in the rear.

The sheriff returned to the courtroom and nodded to the magistrate that they had departed. "This court is now back in session," said the bailiff.

"Now for that other matter," the magistrate said politely, "Mrs. Todd, would you kindly come here?"

Sissy stood and took a step forward when she heard, "It's an honor, Ma'am, to escort you up there," said a tall Texan, as if it was a long hike to the front. She took hold of the outstretched elbow of the unknown cowboy who had been seated nearby and walked with her forward to the front. He then turned toward his seat with a big grin on his face. The cowboy was given smiles from several of the ladies as he returned, and comments as "such a gentleman" were heard.

Sissy stood in front of the magistrate's desk, looking around for Kid. The side door opened, and Kid came out and around the desk to stand next to Sissy. His hair was still wet but combed, his face was swollen, and his nose had a new angle she had not noticed before. His clothing had a few new tears that needed mending. It looked like he had been in a fight.

She studied his face until the magistrate asked, "For the record, are you, Mrs. Sissy Todd, the widow of Michael Todd, who was murdered by person, or persons unknown, and the victim of a vicious personal attack and suffered the loss of a mule?"

"Yes, your honor."

"At last week's hearing, it stated that a reward of $100 had been posted for the two criminals' return dead or alive."

"Yes, your honor."

"And were the two criminals returned?"

"Yes, your honor."

"And what was their condition upon being returned."

"They were both dead, your honor."

"This is a hard question, Mrs. Todd, but it's got to be asked. Did you personally see the two bodies of the accused attackers, and were they the ones?"

"Yes, your honor, I viewed them twice: once at my cabin when Mr. Brooks brought them in and once at the sheriff's office."

"The court is satisfied with your identification, and where are their bodies now?"

Sissy looked around and found Pat standing in the back. He came forward and answered, "They currently reside at the funeral parlor, awaiting their photo session. We still don't know their names and would like to put 'em on their markers, but John Does can do."

"Very good. Sheriff, was either of the gents shot in the back?

"No, your honor. One died in a bar room fight with Mr. Brooks at the Silver Dollar Saloon in Silverton, and the other was killed in a fair gunfight in the street outside, again by Mr. Brooks, and he then located and rescued the stolen mule, which currently at our livery."

"You are Mr. Leroy Brooks, also known as Roy Brooks or simply Kid?"

"Yes, your honor."

"Do you have any paper out on you, or are you an escaped felon?

"No sir, your honor."

"That was some adventure you had son. Please describe to the court what led you to get involved in this case, and you look familiar. Have we met before?"

"Yes, your honor, but only for a second. You were leaving the court after the inquest. I was talking with two of the deputies out back."

The magistrate nodded with a vague recollection. "Go on with your story."

The reporter, with pad in hand, was busy scribbling notes in shorthand as fast as he could take down the story of daring do and high adventure fit for a dime novel, or even a stage play. The bar room brawl in Silverton was transformed in his imagination into a melee of one against a giant of a man and his underling in a no-holds-barred contest to the death.

This was immediately followed by a classic show-down in the street of Silverton, in front of a saloon no less, between the stalworth youth and the villain. Scores of townsmen intimidated by the notorious gunman were anxiously watching as voluptuous, soiled doves leaned over the railings to give a better view of their charms.

The handsome young American cowboy would face the notorious killer, who was known to have nerves of steel and to be the deadliest *pistolero* in the area. He would be dressed…let's see, in the classic costume of a Mexican gunman. The reporter was becoming so excited about his story that it was difficult to distinguish between the actual testimony and his imagination.

Of course, the hero won the duel and reclaimed the stolen animal for the beautiful young widow. He would probably make no mention of the rape. It was a subject too sensitive for his readers, while killings and mayhem were more the merrier. Would the cowboy ride singing into the sunset or claim the love of the beautiful young widow? He couldn't wait to interview the living participants. He almost cried as he thought about royalties and to think it was mainly true, well, at least based on true events.

At the end of Kid's narrative, the magistrate said, "The payment of the reward of one hundred dollars cash is ordered to be paid to Leroy Brooks in full, without any fees taken out."

The audience applauded, whistled, and stomped their feet in approval. The magistrate knew he had just won his local re-election bid, and maybe he could push that up to a Circuit Court appointment. He saw the reporter taking notes in the back of the court and decided a visit with the fourth estate was in order. He could offer to cooperate with the names, dates, and places and make sure his name was prominently played up in the press.

"Friends and neighbors, this is evidence that good still outshines evil, at least here in Durango." Smiling, he struck the butt of his pistol down and said, "Court dismissed."

A half-hour later, at the sheriff's office, Smitty had returned with a gallon pail of beer and a sack of sandwiches and boiled eggs. The sheriff was hosting a little get-together that included all the incident's main characters. He had wisely thought to invite the reporter, magistrate, his deputies, Sissy, and Kid. It was too bad Thorn was still out of town, but he had received enough publicity. Let some of the others share in the glory.

The sheriff brought out two bottles of top-shelf liquor, and Smitty served those interested with the dozen shot glasses he had borrowed from the Belle.

Kid moved over to Billy, who was chatting with Sissy about the pocket pistol, "You think you can hit your target?"

"Sure, Kid gave me lessons with both the pocket pistol and the big Colt, but the Colt is so loud that it scares me, and it kicks like a mule. I'll stick with the small one."

"She did quite well with it," said Kid. "Billy, I have a question for you. Why did you sucker punch me hard in the face? The doc said you broke my nose, and I'll have black eyes for the next few weeks. That wasn't in the plan."

The group stopped their conversations and listened in. "Kid, you said to make it look real. That's the way I punch. If you can't take it, you should have told me."

"When this is all over, me and you will take this topic up again. Chris, you may want to come over and referee a little boxing exhibition we plan on having. You could sell tickets, and the church could make some money. How about it, Billy?"

"Sure, Kid. I'm happy to always teach a friend the fine art of boxing, but only when we are done with this thing."

Chapter 29
Pistol Packing

Monday Stone looked back to ask their escorts about supper since they were still in the county's custody. "Look back there, Tuesday. They done took off on us, and it's getting near supper time."

Tuesday drew back on his reins and swiveled around in his saddle. They had ridden about a mile out of Durango when both deputies had quietly departed. "What do you make of that Tues?"

"Don't know, but we best keep moving while we got daylight. I don't know of any shacks or good places to bed down for the night ahead. We got about 50 miles to travel as the crow flies, but more like 60 or 70 on horseback. What do you suggest?"

"We passed those two cabins a way back. Didn't see no smoke coming from 'em. Should we push on or go back to the last one?"

"We got no bullets, food, coffee, or a place to bed tonight. It's gonna get chilly, and even if we can find wood, I ain't got no lucifers. Do you have any?"

"Naw, those law dogs done took mine and my tobacco pouch. I'm starting to get hungry Tues. What'll we do?"

Tuesday sat for a minute and pondered their options.

****

After the soiree broke up at the sheriff's office, Sissy and Kid, went back to the hotel dining room looking for coffee and a slice of apple pie. Sally had put the "closed" sign up but hadn't locked the door. She still had some lamps on to provide light to finish sweeping and mopping up some spills when she heard the door open, "We're closed. Be open again at six in the morning," she called.

"Hello, we are just looking for a place to sit down with a cup of coffee after a long day. Is that you, Sally?"

"Sissy and Mr. Kid…"

"Just Kid, Ma'am." He pinched his hat brim and smiled the way he had seen other men do.

"Come on in, you two, and close the door after you," Sally said, turning the bolt that locked the door. "Sit down in the back near the kitchen so I can put out these front lamps. I've still got a half pot of coffee that I'm going to have to throw out if somebody doesn't help me drink it."

They sat at the table in the back closest to the serving counter, "By the way, Sally," Sissy asked, "do you have any pie you're going to throw out?" The three laughed.

"It just so happens I have two slices of apple and a slice of peach. What's your pleasure?"

"I think we'll take the apple if it's all the same to you. I'm afraid I've given Kid all the peach pie he cares for. How about it, Kid, is apple okay with you?"

"Fine with me, but your peach pie last night was delicious." Sally wanted to ask about the implications but held her tongue.

"Do you do much baking, Sissy?"

"I love to bake, grill, fry, steam, and roast. I'm handy around the kitchen. Just ask Kid." He smiled between forks full of apple pie.

"I meant what I said about wanting to visit you. When are you headed back to your cabin? I'm off tomorrow morning and would love to come for a visit."

"What do you think, Kid? You've got to collect the reward money tomorrow and go to the bank and the register of deeds office to see if anyone knows about Holly and Madge Beams, our nearest neighbor. I haven't seen them since the inquest. You have the list of goods we need from the mercantile?" Kid smiled and patted his jacket pocket. "Would it be all right if I went back to the cabin early with Sally? We'd be back by early afternoon."

Kid sat back in his chair and rolled a cigarette. He snapped a Lucifer to life with his thumbnail and inhaled deeply. He exhaled a cloud of blue smoke toward the ceiling and asked, "You ladies got your pocket pistols with you?" Both smiled. Sally patted her apron pocket while Sissy patted her handbag. Kid smiled approvingly.

****

The next morning Sissy and Sally met for coffee and a light breakfast at a restaurant down on Main Street.

Kid went to the hotel dining room hoping to meet with the sheriff and find out how long it would take to get the reward. Luck was with him, or was it? Billy and Chris sat on either side of Sheriff Williams.

He ambled over, tipped his hat, and said, "Morning gents. Mind if I join you?"

"Sure enough," said Chris, and scooted his chair closer to the sheriff to give Kid some elbow room.

"Sure, Kid, we've got room," smiled Pat. "Did you sleep well last night?" he inquired. Chris smiled and looked at Billy, hoping to have a little fun with Kid, but Billy only concentrated on his steak and eggs and was having nothing to do with this conversation.

"That was quite a shindig you had last night at your office," quipped Kid.

"It was really put on by the Honorable Thomas X. Clark. I feel lucky to have been invited to my own office."

"Thanks for inviting Sissy and me, and, by the way, thanks for lending that little .38 pocket pistol to her. We got in some practice after Billy left yesterday evening, and she's a good shot with it. She tried out my extra .45 Colt but complained that it hurt her ears and kicked like a mule."

"Ah, that's fine, Kid. I did the same for Sally," said Chris.

"Now, don't take this the wrong way, but are you working at the Todd cabin for Sissy? Billy saw you there fixing the corral fence and chopping firewood," asked the sheriff.

"I don't mind answering. I can't say I'm working for her so much as helping out. Sissy is a fine lady and has been dealt a bad hand."

"I see, just being neighborly," commented the sheriff.

Billy dropped his eating utensils with a clatter, "Sheriff, I'd better get down to the telegraph office to see if Thorn has had any luck finding out about the shipment," he dropped his napkin on his plate and left.

"What's he in a hurry about," said Chris. "By the way, Kid, that was some job you did in Silverton, and you brought back good information about the Stone brothers. Do you think they bought it?"

"Hook, line, and sinker." Kid answered.

"So, if word gets back to this Red character," said Chris, "there's a good chance he won't try to take the bank when the shipment arrives because he'll think there are too many of us here. Let's hope he tries for it in one of the canyons up toward Silverton. Thorn'll be back soon, right, Sheriff?"

The sheriff nodded as he finished chewing the last bite of steak and sat back. It was good to have Chris and Kid planning out things, but what the hay was going on with Billy, and why did he rough up the Kid that way?

"Kid, what's this about you and Billy putting on a boxing exhibition for the church? Are you serious?" The sheriff wanted to know.

"Sheriff, see my black eyes?" asked Kid, "I'm serious. So, sheriff, what do you think about the reward? Sissy gave me a list of items she wants from the mercantile store."

"Tell you what, Kid. We'll have a cup of coffee together, walk over to the bank, and see what is what. Chris, after you finish up here, head on over to the jail and tell Teddy he can have the rest of the day off. Smitty can handle things with no prisoners in custody until the saloons and cat houses get rolling tonight."

The Kid and Sheriff Williams were the first in line to see the bank president, whose sign read "Mr. A.J. Cummings – President." Kid was introduced to a small man with a large belly, mutton chops, bushy eyebrows, and a prominent nose.

"Good to see you, men. Mr. Brooks, is it? We have everything ready. If you sign this receipt, please provide your full legal name. Here's your check for 100 dollars. We can cash it for you, or you can set up an account here and use checks. What's your pleasure?"

"I'll just have the cash now and talk with Mrs. Todd about what she wants to do with the rest. By the way, Mr. Cummings, have you heard what happened to Todd's neighbor, Mr. Holly, and…ah…"

"Yes, Holly and Madge Beams. They decided to go back to Ohio, where her folks are from. Her pa passed, and her mom wants 'em to return and run the farm. They gave me a limited power of attorney with the right to sell their holding and send them the proceeds after my commission. If you, Mrs. Todd, or you, sheriff, are interested, you can go to the county records and see what other claims have sold for during the past few years."

"Thanks, Mr. Cummings, for the information," Kid tipped his hat.

****

"It's no trouble bringing you back, Sally," Sissy reassured her. "I have to take the wagon back and pick up our supplies, and I want to get Kidd a new suit. This gives us a chance to have a nice chat, and I can put Rufus back in the corral with the other horse." During the half-hour ride, they talked about curtains, baking, recipes, sadness, and loss.

Sissy teared up when she spoke of missing Mike, and Sally leaned over and gave her a sisterly hug and a pat on the back. They were Western women and had little time to mourn their losses. Sally told her about her feelings for Thorn, misgivings, and confusion about his secretness. "He is a dangerous man and just won't confide in me. He says he wants to protect me."

"I know Sally. Kid does the same with me. I think they are two of a kind. It's just that Thorn has some years on Kid. It's natural for some men to care about the women folk in their lives and…look! Two horses are tied to the hitching rail, and smoke is coming from the chimney. Who can it be?"

"How did they get in?"

"We don't have a lock on the front door, you can drop the bolt on the inside, but Mike never got around to getting a lock for the door," Sissy confessed.

"Pull up here and set the brake," said Sally. "Let's investigate. Do you have your pistol? Better get it out." The ladies climbed down from the wagon seat, and Sissy dropped the rains down the way Billy had done last evening. Together, with their courage doubled by the other's presence, they walked up to the door, shoved it open, and stepped in with guns drawn. Sally held her pistol, double-handed and belly high, with elbows close to her sides. Sissy held hers out straight, aiming at first one head, then the other.

Two men sat at the table drinking the last of the coffee. The bed had been slept in, and the quilts and a blanket lay twisted on the floor. The kitchen was a mess of dirty plates, and a pan of burned beans sat smoldering on the stove.

"Who the hell are you two, and what are you doing in my cabin," Sissy growled. Then she recognized the two ruffians who had been bonded out yesterday. They had unusual names, like days of the week, and were from Missouri, she remembered, The Show Me State. She'd show them.

Both men jumped up. They were quick for their size and had no respect for any woman other than their mother. Monday swore a time or two at them and said he was going to take their guns away from them and shove them up…he suddenly went for his pistol when Sally said, "Drop 'em, slow and easy."

Monday remembered he had no ammunition in his gun and started to rush them when Sally fired a shot into his right leg. Not to be outdone, Sissy also fired a round into his left leg and said, "She said drop 'em."

Monday collapsed back in his chair and cried, "Tues, they shot me. Those bitches shot me. They both shot me." He rocked back and forth and moaned, "What am I gonna do Tues?" Tears began running down his cheeks.

"Don't know about you Monday, but I'm shucking my gun belt, and I advise you do the same and not say or do anything else to rile 'em. You got no more legs to shoot." Tuesday let his gun belt drop to the floor and asked if he could help his brother.

"Sure, Sally said, "but don't do anything funny. Right now, you still have two good legs. Keep 'em."

"Yes, Ma'am." He tore strips from his shirt and tied up his brother's wounds. Monday continued crying and blubbering like a baby. "Shut up brother. Look, ladies, we didn't know this was your place. Can we pick up our guns and go?" Looking carefully, he said, "Say, those look like our pocket pistols the deputies stole from us. They belong to us, and I want 'em back."

"I'll give 'em to you both if you open your yap again," said Sissy. "Now pick up your whining baby brother, or I'll really give you both something to whine about. Leave your gun belts where they lay and take only one horse and get."

"You can't expect us both to ride one horse?"

"I feel sorry for that poor animal, so another word, and you'll both be walking. Do the best you can. Now get!" Sissy thumbed back the hammer and pointed it at Monday's chest, followed by Sally doing the same.

Tuesday got Monday upright, though he screamed a bit, and drug him to the door, and heaved and pushed him into the saddle. Tuesday took the reins and began walking down the turn-off and back on the trail to Silverton. Monday fell forward against the horse's neck and sobbed.

Tuesday said, "Stop bawling, or I'll do what mom used to do. Brother, we are in a fix, we got no real money, no guns, one horse and you got bullets in your legs, and will probably die of lead poisoning by the time we get to Silverton. If you remember any Bible verses Pa used to say, you'd better start saying 'em."

"I never want to see any part of Colorado again," sobbed Monday. "If we get out of this fix alive, Tues, let's head back to Poplar Bluff and work in Pa's sawmill. I've seen my share of the world and won't ever roam again." He began to whimper.

Tuesday cursed his brother for getting them into another mess just when they planned to return East and become professional boxers. "Damn him to hell."

Suddenly, Tuesday heard his mother's sharp voice, as clearly as if she were walking on the other side of him, admonishing him to take care of his little brother and look out for Cousin Jim.

"Sorry, Ma. Cousin Jim got himself killed by a Pinkerton agent, and we couldn't help him. Monday got shot by two women in a cabin we thought was abandoned. They came back and saw the mess and shot him twice. Each one shot him in a different leg. We should have listened to you, picked up after ourselves, and not burned the beans. I'm sorry, ma, but life here is hard." He heard his ma order him to go into the woods, cut a switch, and give it to her.

"Remember," Ma said, "If'n you don't cut a big enough 'ne for you boys, I'll cut one myself, and then you'll get it."

He did this, leaving the horse on the trail with Monday slumped over her neck, barely hanging on. "I'm sorry, Ma."

Chapter 30
Confession, Of Sorts

Thorn swung down from the railroad carriage with his saddlebags draped over his left shoulder and stepped onto the platform, taking several fast steps forward to control his momentum. He stopped before the train hissed to a clanging halt, panting after its long run. Looking around, he spotted two likely men walking toward him.

In the lead was a slim, youngish man wearing wire-rimmed glasses in a dittos blue wool suit, a white shirt with a stiff collar, and a bright blue silk "puff" scarf tied around his neck. His bowler hat was set squarely on his head, and it looked to Thorn as if he could have just gotten out of any carriage back east.

Thorn looked around and was amazed at the changes he saw in Denver. It was no longer the dirty mining, lumber, and cattle town he had passed through five years ago.

The younger man inquired, "Mr. Hagerman?" Thorn nodded, and they both shook hands. Thorn noticed a weak, effeminate handshake and immediately wrote him off as a dandy.

"I'm Thomas Darling, Special Assistant to the Attorney General. Sorry, he wasn't able to be here today. I've been tasked to meet with you and Mr. Rodney Black from your Chicago Pinkerton office to review special shipment arrangements. We received the telegram from Sheriff Williams alerting us to your arrival."

The two Pinkertons sized up one another and nodded a curt greeting. Then they gave each other a firm, manly handshake, and Mr. Rodney Black said, "Call me Rod."

Thorn thought he might ride the river with Rod. Only time will tell.

"Let's go to the adjacent hotel and have lunch," said Mr. Darling. "I've been assured that the Pinkerton Agency will take care for our expenses, correct Mr. Black?" The Pinkerton agent gave a quick nod, and the three men crossed the platform, walked through the hotel lobby, and entered a spacious room entitled, "Gentlemen Only." They walked up to a magnificent mahogany bar with a shiny brass foot rail stretching fifty feet against the far wall.

The barroom had tables, and several groups of men were seated quietly playing cards. Additional pairs of men were engaged in chess while others were enjoying a smoke and a drink.

"What's the object of the game they are playing?" Thorn asked.

"It's a game of strategy in which the object is to capture the enemy's king and to protect yours. You see the move the man playing white made, called castling. It puts his king in a fortress and protects him while he can move out his troops. It's an ancient game and too complicated to explain on the fly."

Across the room, billiard tables were employed by gentlemen playing or watching. There was no boisterous laughter, cursing, or the high-pitched laughter of drink girls. Looking down the length of the bar, he saw that men wore Stetson hats, but no one wore range garb with six guns buckled on. Most men wore boots, but none with spurs attached to worn-down heels. This could have been an Eastern city.

Mr. Darling said, "Gentleman, how about a quick drink while they find us a secluded table for lunch? They have about every liquor, beer, wine, or cocktail you can name." A well-groomed barman in a clean white jacket with a waxed mustache waited to take their orders.

"I'll have an old-fashioned with Kentucky bourbon. Mr. Black, what will you have?"

"The same." Answered Mr. Black.

"Mr. Hagerman, what's your pleasure?"

Thorn scanned the three shelves behind the bar, stocked with hundreds of glittering bottles of various shapes and sizes, all with different labels. There was no red-eye here. He scanned the rows and stopped when he saw a bottle he knew: "I'll have a double shot of Old Overholt, the bottom shelf in the middle, and a mug of beer."

"Very good, sir; any particular beer? We have eight on the pump and two ales and a dark?"

"The first one you come to will work."

"Good choice, sir." The barman poured a glass stein of beer and stopped as the head crested the rim, nary losing a drop of the golden liquid.

Thorn took a long swallow and smacked his lips, "Damn good beer. What's it called?"

"It's called Coors, brewed by Messrs. Adolph Coors and his partner, Jacob Schueler. They are from Prussia. They brew it in Golden, Colorado, just west, about five miles or so. We get it fresh daily."

Thorn nodded his thanks, took his rye in one swallow, and finished his beer, slamming the stein down hard on the bar with a loud smack. Several startled customers standing at the bar looked toward the noise and then back when they saw the black-clad stranger had two big ivory-handled pistols peeking out from his coat.

"I see our table is ready," Mr. Darling said as he and Mr. Black finished their drinks and quietly placed them on the bar. Follow me, gentlemen." Upon arriving at their table, the men placed their hats on wall pegs conveniently located.

They were soon seated at a corner table. Thorn claimed the seat with his back against the wall facing the restaurant. The other two men sat on either side.

"I don't think we've ever met before, Mr. Hagerman," said Rod. Thorn noted that Rod was a half-foot taller and thirty pounds heavier than Mr. Darling. Thorn saw a bulge under his coat jacket on his left side. Folks here were armed, thought Thorn. They don't advertise it.

"Call me Thorn. No, I don't recall ever meeting. I don't make it to Chicago very often." Thorn studied the menu and noticed each item was priced separately. There were no lunchroom specials here, and each item was priced more than a full meal at the Durango Hotel dining room. Discarding the menu, Thorn said, "What do you suggest, Mr. Darling?"

"Have you ever had brazed Colorado lamb, buttered baked potato with mushrooms, and for dessert a pie made with Palisade peaches, and, of course, a cold Coors Pilsner beer? It's a Denver treat."

"Sounds good to me," said Thorn, and Rod Black nodded in agreement.

The three men finished their meals, with Thorn taking notice of how small the portions were in Denver, but he kept his peace.

"Men," Mr. Darling began, "we'll have the biggest joint payroll ever to go down to Durango. It will be distributed to the bank and six mines for the end-of-season slowdowns. I understand that in addition to the express guard, Mr. Black will guard the mail car along with two federal marshals. You'll have plenty of firepower, and it should be sufficient to keep this outlaw named Red at bay."

"That's the problem, Mr. Darling," said Thorn, "Sheriff Williams wanted me to warn you that the word is out about the shipment. The only things Red and his gang don't know are the date and time. The sheriff wants you to use a code to send any further messages to him." Thorn reached into his saddlebag that he had placed on the floor, removed the volume of *A Tale of Two Cities,* and handed it over.

"What's this, Mr. Hagerman, a little light reading from your trip?" Mr. Darling asked.

"No, the sheriff wants you to use this book to send future messages by coded telegrams about the shipment. We have an exact copy on our end. Let me explain how it works." Thorn had prepared a simple message. Using the book as the key, he began to explain the system when Mr. Darling reached over, closed the book, and returned it to Thorn.

"I don't think you understand, Mr. Hagerman; we have a system in place regarding communication and security. Thank the sheriff for his suggestion, and we'll take it under advisement."

Thorn's face turned grave, knowing that that pigeon-livered little runt would never explain the problem or the proposed solution to the Attorney General. The little punk wouldn't last five seconds in a gunfight.

Thorn answered, "Communicating in the open will get good men killed. They know the payroll is coming. I've already cut down four of Red's men. After chasing them for months, I put down Ivory Thompson and two of his boys. Then I had a gunfight with one of his back-shooters in Durango this past Sunday and had to put him down, too. I was also involved in the arrest and jailing of two more of his boys in Durango, scouting out things."

"That just proves my point. You've already single-handedly taken out, in your own words, four of his gang members and participated in the jailing of two others. I understand your rewards for Ivory and his gang are substantial, and you will be traveling on that train with the other payrolls to the bank in Durango. The payrolls will continue to the mining operations in the area. Your firm has been contracted to protect the payroll. I further understand that your file may have certain ah…irregularities. You must speak with Mr. Black regarding them, not me."

Mr. Darling held his manicured hands out, showing he had nothing to do with it. "But I understand that your company is willing to forgo a careful review of your file and simply allow you to retire with the full rewards you have earned, minus any legal obligations attached to them, if and when you get the payroll safely down to Durango."

Turning to face Rod Black, eye to eye, Thorn said, "I sent in my resignation a while back, and I planned to take the reward and retire."

"You see, Thorn. They never approved your request," said Rod, "and as far as I'm concerned, you are still on our payroll. You are assigned to be on that train with me. The express clerk assigned is a fat old Jollock, over fifty, and the two federal marshals are both pups. They are willing enough but inexperienced. You know the lay of the land and…"

"With that, gentlemen, you'll excuse me. I leave the final details up to you. Mr. Black, you are in charge of the operation. Mr. Hagerman will report to you. Keep my office informed. I am at liberty to tell you, and no one else, that the train will depart from Denver tomorrow at 4:45 p.m. and arrive in Durango 24 hours later. There will be no telegrams alerting anyone about anything. When you arrive in Durango, you will have one hour to remove the seven canvas mail bags, all clearly labeled. One goes to the bank in Durango, and the others go onto the narrow-gauge train waiting for you with a full head of steam. There will be no passengers allowed aboard. You will proceed to the six mining camps, where men from the camps will meet you and sign for their respective payrolls. There can be no deviation from this plan, is that understood, Mr. Black?"

Mr. Rod Black said he understood and would follow the instructions.

"Things in the camps are tense, and the payrolls must be there as promised, or all hell will break loose. We don't want to use federal or state troopers or Pinkertons to put down riots, so be on time. Are you satisfied, Mr. Hagerman? Do you have any questions?"

Thorn thought it over and nodded his assent. Mr. Darling took his bowler and placed it squarely on his head, then turned and departed without shaking hands.

"Now there goes one prissy little son of a bitch," said Rod Black. "Let's have another drink at the bar and discuss the details."

An hour later, Thorn checked into a hotel modeled after the famous Harvey House, which had a restaurant and general store attached. He decided to take a walk and clear his head.

Thorn reviewed his conversation with Mr. Rod Black and decided he had no choice but to ride along on the return trip tomorrow evening. Rod hinted at certain irregularities in Thorn's expense accounts during the past two years, after the death of his wife (what was her name?) and the placement of their only child, a teenage daughter, in an expensive boarding school run by the nuns in St. Louis.

He hinted at outright embezzlement of company funds to pay for her room and board. If, on the other hand, Thorn would lend his considerable help to this endeavor and follow his commands, he gave his word that Thorn would collect the rewards without any attachments, and if killed in the process, the funds would be placed in trust for his daughter. (What the hell was her name?).

"All right, you got me by the short hairs. I'll work with you on this one last job, but only under three conditions: Number one," Thorn held up his index finger, "after the job is done, I get to retire with full bounties and back pay from Pinkerton Agency. Two, he held up the middle finger of his right hand, "you sign an affidavit, in case you are killed in this outing, binding the company to pay out, and waive any and all claims against me. Three," his ring finger went up, "and give me a chance to review the file you have on me and, what's the word, remove, anything I want?"

"Expunge, that's the word you are looking for. I agree with your three demands. If you have anything else to say, speak it now or forever hold your peace." There was a brief silence while Thorn considered his options.

"By the by, I'll bring along an extra Winchester, a 12-gauge Greener, and plenty of shells. They might come in handy, seeing that you only brought pistols."

After a half hour's walk through the heart of Denver, Thorn was surprised to find a small brick-and-stone Catholic Church with a school on a tree-lined street a block off the business district. Not seeing a saloon nearby and with several hours to fill until supper time, he walked up the stone steps for no particular reason other than to find a nice place to sit down and think. He entered and automatically removed his hat.

He found an empty rear pew near a bank of votive lights before the statue of Saint Joseph, the carpenter and foster father of Jesus. As a youngster, Thorn always liked St. Joe and called on him on more than one occasion to help him get out of trouble with the nuns.

Once, St. Joe advised him to take his father's newspaper to school and fold it squarely to fit in the back of his trousers. That day, just as the saint had predicted, Sister Maria caught him by the ear in line after recess and, twisting it, brought him into her classroom where she gave the order, "bend over," in front of her class and wailed his behind with a paddle, she called it her "board of education." He couldn't remember exactly what prank he had played on Becky Waters, a little blond-haired girl he had been sweet on, but it had been worth it.

That night, his father was upset because his paper was shredded and smudged and stormed around the house until his mother brought him his pipe and the Bible to read. He finally settled down, but Thorn, or was it Karl, never owned up and held his tongue. Thorn remembered those days before his parents had died and smiled at his antics.

"You seem to have found some joyous memories, young man?" said an old priest in a worn black cassock coming down the aisle. He stopped at his pew and smiled. "I'm Father Unterhiner. I haven't seen you here before. Are you of the Roman Catholic faith?"

"Hello, Father. No, just passing through Denver, leaving tomorrow for Durango. I'm just stopping by for a few minutes. I'm not much of anything, religion-wise." Thorn detected a slight German accent in the priest's speech and asked, "Sprechen sie Deutsch?"

"I thought I'd gotten rid of my accent after all the years in missionary work here."

"Oh, your English is excellent, Father. Your name gives you away, 'Under the Rhine."

"And you are?" the priest extended his hand in greeting. His grip was remarkably firm for an old man.

"I'm Thorn T. Hagerman, but everyone calls me Thorn." Thorn wondered about entering a church for the first time in decades, and the first thing he did was tell a lie. Add one more to the list.

"You come from a rough area. We read about the holdup men and criminals running roughshod over the people down there. I pray that the people will get the law that encourages respect, justice, and mercy. So often, there's not much difference between the lawmen and the criminals they chase. Sorry, I shouldn't have said that. You aren't a lawman, are you?"

"No, Father, but I'm his short-tailed cousin of sorts. I'm a Pinkerton man. The Pinks, they call us, short for Pinkertons, are getting a bad name. We have been getting involved on the part of the owners in breaking up strikes and being bully boys against miners all over the west and the eastern coal fields. I've never been involved at that end of the business. Besides, I've put in my retirement papers and only have one last duty to perform. I've spent my life going after rustlers, hold-up men, bank robbers, stage and train robbers, and such. It keeps me busy."

"Would you like a blessing?"

A blessing, Thorn pondered. "Why, sure, it can't hurt, but I don't think it will help much. You see, Father, this is the first church I've set foot in in over twenty years."

"As you say, it can't hurt. Bow your head, my son, and close your eyes." The priest touched Thorn's forehead, and he felt a warm, gentle sensation course through his body, not unlike a double of good Whiskey. Thorn's inner eye saw red and green spots merge, expand, and explode. He saw colors he had never seen before and, for an instant, felt at peace.

"Dear Lord, protect this servant and help him on his journey through life. He has a difficult job; let him perform it with courage and humility under the protection of the patron of police and soldiers, Saint Michael the Archangel. Thanks be to God. In the name of the Father, the Son, and the Holy Spirit," without thinking, Thorn made the sign of the cross, and both said "Amen" together.

"Thank you, Father, though I'm sure it didn't do any good."

"Thorn, my son, there is nothing you have done that the Lord can't forgive. The difficult part is you must forgive yourself first and make amends."

"Father, not to disagree with you, but I've done things during the war and afterward that can't be forgiven. You don't know. You weren't there."

Chapter 31
To Set a Trap

Andy, the holster from Silverton, was on his return trip from Durango with a wagonload of supplies. He held the leads so lightly that all his old mare needed to do was to give a slight tug, and she would pull them from his hands. But she stopped abruptly when she saw the figure on the ground next to a grazing horse. Andy focused and noticed that the big man on the ground wasn't moving. Next to him sat a second big man, on a slab of stone with his head buried in his hands, sobbing and explaining to his ma why it wasn't his fault. Andy looked around, but there was no one else present. He recognized them as the dangerous Stone brothers.

The next morning, Andy, bone-tired, climbed down from his seat, tossed his leads over the Silver Dollar Saloon's hitching rail, and entered.

"Back so soon?" said Whitey, Red's Segundo or right-hand man. "We thought you'd stay the night in Durango, maybe pick up some news."

"He, he, he, you'll be glad I came right back. Come out to the wagon and see what I brought you from Durango. Give me a hand Whitey, with the presents I brought back for you."

"Sam," Andy called out to the morning clean-up man, "go find the doc and tell him he's got a customer. He, he, he, Andy chuckled again, then come and give us a hand." The three men struggle with the dead weight of Monday Stone, but managed to carry him into the doc's clinic and lay him on the table. "Sam, stay here and give the doc a hand. Come on, Andy, let's get the other one into the saloon."

At the wagon, the two men helped Tuesday Stone down from the seat and led him into the saloon, one supporting him at each side. They walked him up to the bar, where Whitey poured him a beer and set some food out for him. "What the matter with him, Andy?"

Andy just laughed and said, "he's got the willies. I've seen it before. All the way here, he kept talking about being attacked by a Texas wildcat. He's out of his head talking to his ma, and afraid she is going to switch him 'cause his little brother got shot up in Durango by two females. He then lost his guns and money to the law and lost a horse to the two women."

"Man, he's got it bad," said Whitey. "I'd better get Red."

"Oh, he, he, he," Andy continued his habitual chuckles, "I forgot to tell you, he also said that his cousin Jim, the one Red sent out to take care of the Pinkerton man, was also gunned down outside of the Belle by, he, he, he, the very same Pinkerton, he, he, he."

"It's not funny. Get him coffee, Sam. Don't give him any more beer," ordered Red, who had not slept off last night's liquor and had been dragged out of a warm bed with an olive-skinned drink girl an hour too soon. He was in a foul mood.

"Damn it all to hell." Red slammed his fist down on the bar. "Give it to me straight. The Pinkerton gunned down your cousin after he told him there was a $500 bounty on the Pinkerton's head?"

"Yeah, boss," said Tuesday. "Shot him down in the street."

"Did you see it?"

"No boss, Monday and I had a bottle and left Jim at the Belle to make his move."

"Damn it, then how do you know he killed him?"

"The Pinkerton man, the sheriff, and a deputy took us to the funeral parlor, and we seen him, and we accidentally shot him again, but he was already dead, so we weren't charged with killing."

"Tuesday, you're not making any sense. Where's your gun?"

"Oh, Red, the sheriff arrested us after the Texas Wildcat finished with us, and we forgot to ask for our pocket pistols, rifles, and bullets back from the judge when we posted bail. Then the women folk shot Monday, with our very own pistols, at her cabin and took our gun belts and pistols and Monday's horse. Ma is so mad. How's Monday doing?" Tuesday pleaded, "He ain't going to die, is he? Ma is going to give me a hiding if he dies." Tuesday dropped his head and began to sob.

"Sam, take him to one of the empty rooms, let him sleep it off, and stay with him for the next two hours. Got it?"

"Sure, boss."

"Whitey, get Andy back here. Maybe he can make heads or tails out of this mess. First, I lose three of the best gunmen in the region, Ivory and his two boys. Then I send three of the toughest men I know of to take care of one Pinkerton, and one gets killed, another gets shot up, and the third turns into a crying idiot. I've lost six men already and still don't know the date of the big shipment."

"Sure, boss. He took the wagon to the barn and said he would take care of his mare and Tuesday's big gelding. You know the one that stands about fifteen, or sixteen hands? The one with a blaze on his forehead."

"Damn it Whitey, are you going soft in the head too? I know Tuesday's horse and don't give a tinker's dam about him. Go get Andy and bring him here." Whitey was stung by the comment and hurried off to the barn.

"You want to see me Red? Can I get a beer while we talk?" asked Andy upon his return.

"Sure, Andy, and while you're at it, draw one for me and another one for Whitey." This was done, and Andy brought the mugs to the boss' table. He sat them down, pulled up a chair, and had a long drink while waiting.

"While you were in Durango, did you hear anything that'll help make sense out of this?"

"Yes, Red. The town was buzzing with the shooting of Jim Stone by the Pinkerton man. Talked to three or four who saw it, and half said he pulled an ivory-handled Remington pistol and fanned half a dozen shots into Jim's chest. The other said it was a Colt, and he pulled and fanned the shots. There was some disagreement about the number, but everyone agreed Jim was deader than a Thanksgiving turkey sitting in the oven: he, he, he. Even blew him out of his boots."

"All right, what did you hear about the Stone brothers and this wild cat from Texas?"

"Sure thing, he, he, he, but that ain't no actual wild cat. That's the nickname of a deputy. The Pinkerton man took the Stone brothers to the funeral parlor to identify Jim. There was a ruckus, shots were fired, nobody was killed who wasn't already dead, and the deputy, after whopping up on the boys, arrested them."

"Hard to believe, but I'm with you. Go on."

"The boys spent some time in the jail with Kid. The one you sent down with the two bodies he kilt for the reward. He, he, he, the brothers each posted a hundred-dollar bond hearing, but they forgot to ask the judge for their rifles, bullets, and two ladies' pocket pistols. Now, those pistols seem to have been given to two women folk. One of whom, he, he, he, had been raped by the old boys who were killed by Kid here in Silverton. Those old boys had killed the lady's husband, a miner. They shot him in the back. The other miners around Durango got pissed and put up enough gold for a wanted poster. Story has it, Kid went to the inquest, heard all about it, and came looking for 'em. You remember their killings?"

Red nodded and motioned for him to go on.

"So, after posting their bonds, the Stone brothers were escorted out of town by the deputies, and that's the last they'd been seen or heard of 'em till my horse spotted them on the trail."

"I see. I think I understand. Did Tuesday tell you anything on the way here?"

"Sure enough, can I pour you boys another beer? It's kinda dry doing all the talking, he, he, he." Andy took their mugs to the bar for refills and again settled in.

"Tuesday kept talking about how he was in the jail cell next to Kid, who had gotten the tar beat out of him by one of the deputies and didn't have the coin to bail himself out. He was also in on a charge of assault, resisting arrest, and going for a gun on the law."

"None are hanging offenses, but he'll stand trial. Maybe he'll get a lighter sentence for bringing in the two desperadoes, but he's looking at doing hard time in Cañon City prison. As far as I know, he's waiting for trial. Now, ask me how Monday got himself shot. he, he, he."

"Fine, let's hear it."

"The Stone brothers had the bad luck to stop at the lady's cabin who had been raped and whose husband had been shot in the back. The two females had been lent those little pocket pistols taken from the Stone brothers. Ain't that a funny one?" Andy slapped his leg and finished his beer. "They caught the brothers without any rounds in their guns, cause…"

"I know they forgot to ask the judge for them."

"Right you are, and those two women plugged Monday for the hell of it. Both shot him in different legs. They have some tough women there."

"All right, Andy, what else did Tuesday tell you?"

"Yep, Tuesday was blubbering about how his ma was going to switch him, he, he, he. Then he talked about how the town was full of deputies, more guns were coming, and the town was waiting for you, Red. It'll be armed to the teeth. He said that it was a trap, and Kid thought you should try at one of the mines for the hold-up. Oh, and one last thing, he said you got somebody in your outfit who's spilling the beans to the sheriff, but he didn't know who."

"He did, did he?"

"What do you think Whitey? You got anything you need clearing up?"

"No, boss. It's clear as mud to me."

"Andy, have another beer on the house and go check with the doctor to see if Monday is still alive. Let me know."

"Sure thing, Red, and thanks for the beers." Andy returned to the bar to enjoy his free libation and meal.

"Whitey, here we are in Silverton," he pointed at his beer mug, "in San Juan County, and here," he moved Whitey's beer mug, "is Durango in La Plata County. Their sheriff doesn't have jurisdiction here, but half a dozen mine offices are strewn out between the two, and the one closest to Durango is in their jurisdiction. On the other hand, it looks like they got Durango sewn up tight, and it might be a trap. Besides, I've already lost six men, not counting those two low lives that Kid took out. I don't have enough men to take the depot, the bank, and the jail."

"Any ideas?" Deep thinking was not Whitey's forte, and he looked at his mug but was afraid to move Durango and upset Red's plans.

"No, boss. It seems that we should wait to hit Durango until we have more hands."

Andy returned to report that the doc said that Monday was still alive but just hanging on. "The next twelve hours will tell. Doc said he had problems cauterizing," he stumbled over the word, "closing the wounds, and Monday has lost a lot of blood." Red seemed satisfied with the prognosis.

"I agree with your thinking Whitey. By the way, how'd you get the nickname Whitey? Your hair is black as coal, and your features are tanned."

Whitey removed his Stetson, and Red saw a white stripe on his upper forehead where the hat band protected the skin from the brutal sun and winds. "I see," said Red, satisfied that a name made sense. No one in his gang used names that could be found on a wanted poster.

"Here is what I want you to do tomorrow. Ride on down toward Durango first thing in the morning and check out the cutoffs from the narrow-gauge track to the mines." Whitey looked confused, "Sure if I was them," said Red. "I wouldn't bring the final yearly payrolls for the mining camps up the trail where we could set an ambush for them. No, I'd be in an express car with a lot of riflemen and shotgunners waiting.

See if you can find the perfect spot near the closest mine to Durango. The payroll box will be full, and we'll take it."

"What if they don't open up and just shoot at us until a posse from Durango comes?"

"Good point Whitey. I need you to ride hell-bent for leather from the sheriff's office to the first cutoff and time it. I'll have a little surprise for that express car." Red reached under the table, brought out a sack, and pulled out a bundle of dynamite sticks tied together with a short fuse. "This has a five-second fuse and should do the trick."

Both men studied it, and Red asked, "Who has the best throwing arm in the outfit?"

"Not sure, but I can find out. I'll have a rock-throwing contest when I get back."

"Good idea. And Whitey, don't go near any cabins on the way to or from Durango. This is important. Do you understand? I can't afford any more losses."

"Sure thing, boss."

Chapter 32
The 4:45 P.M. to Durango

Thorn got up early the next morning, bathed, dressed, and had breakfast at the Denver Diner connected to his hotel. Then he found a barbershop for a shave and a trim. He found refuge in the simple tasks of daily life, but the priest's words kept repeating in his mind. The priest of German heritage had spoken directly to his heart.

He needed to pick up more .44 Remington ammunition before boarding the train at 4:45 p.m. for Durango with Rod, who seemed to be a decent enough man but too reserved for Thorn. He felt put off by him not knowing his weight in the game. Was he a company man just trying to complete an assignment, or did he have an ulterior purpose? What was all of this about irregularities in his accounts? Only time will tell.

After purchasing two 50-round bricks of ammo for his pistols, he spent an hour looking at the new models and test-fired a few at their indoor range, which itself was a novelty. He was impressed with the finishes on the new Colt .45, but he had his trusty hide-out in that caliber riding in his back holster.

On the way out, he spotted a small S&W .38 five-round pocket pistol with pearl handles and an engraved satin black finish. It sold for 35 dollars. That's a lot of money for a toy, but it was beautiful and would make a nice gift for Sally. "I'll take it, but you must throw in a box of that rim-fire ammunition." It was agreed, and he paid for his purchases and distributed them evenly in his saddlebags with his dirty change of clothes and the copy of Dickens' *Tale of Two Cities* that he planned to finish on the return trip.

Lifting the saddlebags over his left shoulder, he went to the little church to see if Father Unterhiner was around to finish their conversation. He entered the church and immediately smelled the aroma of burned incense and candle wax. Sitting at the same pew he had occupied yesterday, he relaxed and remembered that he was wearing his hat. He removed it, found a clip on the back of the pew in front of him designed to hold hats, and clamped it in place.

Turning, he saw the diminutive priest had slipped in beside him, and bowing toward the altar, made the sign of the cross. "May I join you?"

"Sure, Father, it's your church."

"True, but it's your privacy I'm invading."

"No, you're welcome. I've been thinking about our talk yesterday and have a few questions."

"Excellent, but seeing that we are approaching the noon hour, will you join me in the rectory? My housekeeper lays out a nice luncheon repass, and we can talk privately."

"Why sure, I'd be pleased, but I don't want to eat into your lunch."

"No problem. I thought you might come by and ask Maria to set the table for two."

Thorn, after placing his saddlebags with his hat atop on the empty seat at the end of the table, took the seat across from the priest. They sat at the end of a long refectory table in the formal dining room. Real silverware, with best China, water glasses, and fluted wine glasses were precisely placed, linen napkins rolled, and held by silver rings lay next to their plates.

"Father, this is quite a spread. I'm just a cowboy at heart, duded up a bit, but I'm unsure what to do with all of this."

"Fine, fine. I only get the special luncheon when I have a guest, so let's enjoy it." The priest rang a little silver bell on the table, and a smiling, rotund lady entered through a swinging door with a tureen of soup. She placed it on the table and ladled both bowls without spilling a drop. It was a chicken-based soup with herbs and vegetables and smelled delicious.

Thorn decided that the deeper spoon would work and started to pick it up when the priest bowed his head and said, "Dear Lord, we thank you for the meal we are about to receive and blessings for the workers who grew the food, and bless the hands that prepared it. I ask your blessings in the name of your Son. Amen."

"Amen," said Thorn and automatically made the sign of the cross with the priest.

"Funny father, old habits come back. When I was a child, we used to say grace before all meals and always made the sign of the cross."

"Yes, please begin before it gets cold. Once a Catholic, always a Catholic. You know, there are only two kinds of Catholics—practicing and fallen-away. Those who have fallen away are always welcomed back, like the prodigal son in the Bible story."

Thorn ate his soup and vaguely remembered his favorite nun, Sister Anatolia, telling the Bible story about the bad son who told his father he wanted his inheritance. He went off with a bag of gold, leaving his brother to do all the work on the farm. After spending all his coin on wine, women, and song, he wound up in a pig pin, lonely and half-starved. He finally decided to go home, beg his father's forgiveness, and see if he could live there as a hired hand.

The father spotted the son on the road coming home and sent his servant for a clean robe, and such, had a fattened calf killed and made ready for a feast. The other brother was really pissed when he came from working in the fields and heard what his father had done. He confronted him, saying, "I've worked hard all these years, and you never even gave me and my friends a goat to feast on; here my spoiled brother comes along, you give him his inheritance, and he blows it, then comes home, and you treat him like a returning hero. It's not fair."

"Son," said the father, "you'll get your reward. Don't worry, but be happy that your brother has returned home to us."

Thorn could never understand the gist of the story. It didn't seem fair. There was so much in the Bible that he found unfair.

"Father, I was raised Catholic, but my folks died when I was young, and I've lived a rough life, fought in a war, and did things that can't be talked about. You don't understand. The prodigal son only blew his father's inheritance in drink, soiled doves, and abandoned his farm. I've done things that would make him look like a choir boy."

The priest again rang the silver bell, and Maria cleared the bowls and served homemade biscuits with melting butter, grilled lamb with mint sauce, and a medley of vegetables. "You'll be pleased to know that all the food you consume here, except the cheese and wine, comes from our gardens and flocks."

"Where do you get the wine and cheese?"

"Our Benedictine Monasteries in California supply wonderful cheeses and wines. In turn, we send the monasteries grains, preserves, fruits, and vegetables. Are you familiar with Saint Benedict and his order?"

"Can't say I've ever heard of him."

"Saint Benedict and his twin sister, Sainte Scholastica, lived in the fifth century during the fall of the Roman Empire. Those were troubled times, much like today. Armed hoards invaded the Empire, killing, burning, pillaging, and destroying. Many believe that Benedict saved Europe's culture, literature, art, and what was good in the ancient world by building his monasteries high in defensive positions. But for him and the monks and nuns, the light of civilization in Europe would have been extinguished. His watchwords were *ora et labora*, Latin for work and pray. In fact, work becomes a prayer for a Benedictine."

"I thought you gave up wealth, women, and such when you became religious. You're living pretty high on the hog."

"I've taken the vows of poverty, chastity, and obedience when I joined the order. I don't own anything, including my sandals and cassock."

Thorn looked at the beautiful silver and porcelain on the table. "They belong to the order," said the priest. They are more than mere wealth. They represent the artistic skills and talents of our people. Holy Mother Church fosters the arts, and they are acts of prayer in their own rights." Thorn studied his heavy silver fork and smiled.

"I can be transferred anytime and sent anywhere by my prelate…" Thorn looked confused. That is my bishop, and I must obey." It was difficult for Thorn to think about giving up his freedom to any boss.

"As for chastity, I vowed never to marry or have conjugal relations, ah, sexual relations. As one gets older, it's less and less difficult, but I must admit that when I was younger, the curve of a trim ankle or the bare shoulder of an attractive young lady caused me to turn aside so as not to be tempted."

"But why did you give up being your own man, making your own decisions, marrying, and having a family?"

"Thorn, you were in a war in which you did things that are better left unsaid. The same is true for me. Are you familiar with the Franco-Prussian War?"

"Yes, about fifteen years ago in Europe, wasn't it?"

"Yes, and I fought for the Prussian Kaiser, our Emperor, Wilhelm I of the Hohenzollern dynasty. When given an order by a superior, we were taught to answer 'Jawohl' and do as commanded, no questions asked. We fought France in the third war engineered by our Foreign Minister, Otto von Bismarck. It was a war to unite all the little city-states and kingdoms under Prussian rule. A goal desired by most Germans."

Thorn nodded in agreement.

"We were fighting the troops of Emperor Louis Napoleon, the nephew of the great Napoleon, and we had several tactical advantages. We had better-trained troops and better transportation to the front, riding in train carriages. At the same time, the French marched and sang patriotic songs, carrying the equivalent of seventy pounds of gear. They were exhausted when they arrived for a battle. But the real reason was superior arms. We had the Prussian Dreyse needle rifle. It was the first bolt-action breech-loading rifle used in Europe. We could fire ten rounds to Frenchie's one."

"Seems I've heard about it. The needle used to ignite the round was prone to break," said Thorn. "The French should have used a Sharps or a Henry rifle."

"The same could be said about your Confederacy during your Civil War. They relied primarily on British Enfield ball and cap muzzleloaders and were happy to have them, while the Union had Sharps and other modern weapons. The army with the better arms seems to win the modern wars," said the priest and continued, "True, the needle gun had its faults, but up against a superior force of men across an open field, it was devastating. In the engagement that broke the French's will and many of our hearts, we were ordered first to lie down and wait for the French to fire a volley, then our first row knelt, the second row stood, and all aimed their weapons. We waited for the order to be given.

"Our first volley shattered their ranks, but still, many stood reloading their rifles. We were ordered to fire again; our second volley tore through them, and again we were ordered to fire. We did so until all their soldiers were dead, dying, or their hands were raised in surrender, begging for mercy." The priest closed his eyes in painful memory.

"We loaded another round in the breech and waited, thinking that surely the officer would accept the surrender of the remaining French. Instead, the command came, 'Feuer,' and another volley ended the battle, but not the killing. We were then ordered to move among the enemy and finish the job with bayonets. The officers used their pistols. It was murder, and I couldn't get it out of my mind. I thought I would go mad, and my only way out of the suffering was suicide."

"How did you deal with it?"

"After the war, a comrade and I tramped through Bavaria and Austria looking for peace. West of Vienna, we hiked a primitive trail believed to have been used by an apostle and came across the beautiful Melk Benedictine abbey perched high on a cliff above a bend in the Danube River. I was stunned by its beauty and the solitude and decided to end my travel there. I was a lay brother for two years and worked in the fields and orchards. I regained my balance and asked for forgiveness and found it. More importantly, I forgave myself. Only then did I begin my studies for the priesthood. That was almost fifteen years ago, and here I am."

Thorn finished his meal and accepted a glass of California wine and various cheese slices.

"Thorn, may I ask you a personal question? Whatever your answer, everything you say will be under the seal of the confessional. Under no circumstances am I allowed to repeat your words, even under torture or the threat of death. In fact, the fastest way for me to gain heaven is to die a martyr's death."

Thorn felt a bit uncomfortable but said, "Shoot."

"During your travels, did you hurt or kill the innocent?"

"Not knowingly, Father, but you never know where your bullet goes. No, Father, I never aimed to kill an innocent man, woman, or child. I never… ah, had my way with females in towns or places we captured."

"Did you ever steal or take what did not belong to you?"

"During the war, we often appropriated livestock, food, and clothing from the enemy or their supporters. Thinking about it, that was probably stealing, but it was under orders and not for my personal use."

"Anything else?" prompted Father.

"Would taking a dead man's identity be stealing?"

"How did you use it? Did you honor his memory with your actions?"

"Yes, I think so. But Father, what if the deceased has a daughter, and I'll soon be in a position to help her? Do I tell her that her daddy is dead, and I've taken his job and name, or do I send her some money and let her think her daddy is alive but doesn't care about her?"

"These, my son, are the nubs of the matter. Think over your faults and failures, not only what you did but what you failed to do. Come back when you have thought it out. In the meantime, are you familiar with the Beatitudes of Christ during his Sermon on the Mount?"

"No, can't say I'm familiar."

"You'll find them in the Gospels of Matthew and Luke. Read and think about them, look up, and perform the seven corporal works of mercy. Write them down and tell me how you performed each work and for whom. Be specific. If you do these things, come back, make a good confession, and an absolution is possible."

"Where do I find these works of mercy?"

"Unfortunately, they aren't found in one place but in the Bible. You'll have to do a little research. Son, you are hanging onto the ledge of purgatory by your fingernails. Below you, the pit of hell looms. All you need to do is to drag yourself up into the lowest region of purgatory to be saved. You'll have to pay for your sins, but you can handle that."

"Now, my son, you must leave to catch your train, and I must prepare for my evening vespers and prayers. I will pray for you, and in turn, please pray for me."

Thorn found a King James edition of the Bible in the train lobby and paid one dollar and ninety-nine cents for it. Rod and Thorn boarded the train and went to the express car, gave their names, and were admitted. The old express agent was busy sorting mail, and the two young federal marshals sat in a corner looking scared.

Thorn sat with them and said, "Boys, I'm Thorn, and that hombre standing at the door is Mr. Black. We're Pinkerton agents. Just remember, if you want to be brave, you've got to act brave. Listen to us, and we'll get through this trip in one piece. Do what we say. Don't think or question, act! We have a day-long ride with many stops, so get comfortable. Is that understood?"

"Both nodded in agreement," and soon they were off on a long trip down to Durango.

Thorn carefully cleaned his pistols and, after a moment of indecision, placed live rounds under the weapons hammers. He then spent many hours that evening and the next day reading Dicken's and scripture from the Bible. After hours of reading, he went through the baggage car up to the steam engine. The engineer was concerned about a pressure reading loss on a gauge, but they pushed on. Thorn returned to the express car.

"Rod, I've been thinking, and it's plain foolish for us to go to the mining camps with their payrolls," Thorn called out above the train's rumbling and clatter.

"How so?" The federal boys and the express clerk paid close attention.

"Because we'll never make it beyond the first mining camp. Red has been one step ahead of us during the whole game. He's collecting a gang and has an insider feeding him information. He'll have as neat an ambush set up for us as the James boys ever thought of. No, we'd better put all the money in the Durango Bank and then drive on into their trap. If we're lucky, we can spring it on them and take out Red and his gang at one time. How about it, boys? You could get shares of the reward money for the lot of 'em? It could be worth thousands, and I know just the boys in Durango are willing to go in with us for equal shares. What about it?"

Rod chewed a toothpick, thought about it for a minute, and said, "No way. We have our orders and will follow 'em to the letter."

"I think not," said Thorn. It's a setup, and you know it. How about we vote on it? I'm all in favor of putting the whole kit and caboodle in the bank, and then we get on that little narrow-gauge train and go up into the San Juan Mountains and have a real adventure. Raise your hands?"

The express agent's right hand was the first to go up. The federal boys looked at each other, grinned, and raised their right hands.

"Are you in or out, Rod? If you're out, you can get off in Durango, telegraph the head office, and get me fired," he chuckled. "In the meantime, we can do God's work, rid this territory of a band of outlaws, and make us some money. It's your choice."

Chapter 33
The Puzzle Is Complete

Whitey had pulled himself together during the half-light of predawn and drank pitch-black coffee that had been sitting on the back of the stove all night. The sludge at the bottom of the pot looked and tasted like burned tar, but it was hot and brought life to his limbs. He saddled his mount and tied the sack of vittles and canteen to his saddle horn. He strapped his bedroll and slicker behind his saddle, opened the barn's sliding door, and walked his horse into the sharp morning air.

Whitey was a simple man of firm habits. He followed the boss' commands. Red said for him to go out and check out the narrow-gauge railroad tracks near Durango and locate the best spot to stop the train and ambush the mail car, and that's what he would do. A second assignment was for him to ride hard back from Durango to the exact spot of the planned ambush and time to the second how long they would have to break open the mail car and the safe before a posse could interfere.

Those boys in the express car would know how to shoot, and then that Pinkerton agent had already put down four of the gang. This was not going to be a Sunday school picnic, but with dynamite, they could blow open the car or, maybe even the threat of it would cause the boys inside to surrender. He wasn't much for cold-blooded killing.

He rode hard down the trail most of the day, camped cold harbor that night, and the next morning found the cut-off for the first entrance from the railroad track and the road leading to the mining camp. He dismounted and tethered his mount to have a good look around. The grade was too steep, and no trees or loose stones were around to block the engine. He moved on and assessed the next four entrances with the same negative conclusion.

At the sixth and last cut-off before Durango, he noticed a pile of creosote ties that would work just fine if placed so they angled outward toward the oncoming engine and braced against other ties in the roadbed. They would stop the small steam engine dead in its tracks and could be used to prevent its retreat.

He looked around for cover and found plenty of boulders near enough to the track to protect the men. Also, some were close enough so that a man could throw a bundle of dynamite on top of or under the express car. He picked up a rock that felt the same weight as the dynamite and lobbed it in an arch directly on top of the track bed. The men from the mining camp who would come to collect the payroll could easily be surprised and disarmed from half a dozen locations, tied and gagged, and taken out of action before it began. A piece of cake, he thought. Hell, I'll do the dynamite job myself, and maybe Red will give me an extra share.

Now that it was getting toward sunset, he just had to ride around the town and come in from a side road, warm up, eat, drink a little, and then time his ride back from the town's center to their first cutoff.

As he rode into town in a slow lope, he bent forward in the saddle and pulled his hat low on his head. He wasn't particularly noticed by any of the town folks going about their business, but he dragged his horse to a walk when he saw the Belle Saloon down the street.

Dismounting, he led his horse to a hitching rail alongside a horse trough and tossed the reins around twice. Entering by the front bat wings, he headed to the bar.

"What's your pleasure, friend?" the big-bellied bartender asked. "Are you new in town?"

"That's right, friend. Give me a beer and a shot. I just got in from the south. I've got a job promised on a ranch up toward Denver. Just stopping by to see an old partner I heard is hereabouts."

Charlie poured a shot glass with an amber liquor nicknamed red-eye, pulled a foaming mug of beer, and sat them together. "Much obliged," said Whitey. "You might know of my pard, but he goes by the handle, Kid. I heard he had trouble with the law, and they had him in the calaboose."

Charlie mopped the bar alongside Whitey's drinks and said, "Sure, everyone hereabouts knows about Kid. He's a local hero of sorts. Brought in the two back-shooting skunks, who murdered a miner and raped his missus. Both were real bad boys and needed killing."

"You don't say. I heard he was in jail for some ruckus or other with the law."

"Oh, that was just a misunderstanding among friends. I hear tell that he and another deputy are both sweet on the same lady, the Widow Todd, the one whose husband was killed by those polecats Kid dispatched."

"Goodness, but it gets more interesting. So, Kid ain't in jail. Where could I find him?"

"That's the funny part," the bartender turned, pulled a beer for a thirsty miner, and returned his attention to the stranger. "He's up at the widow's place sort of a hired hand the way I hear it."

"Really, which cabin is it?"

"Oh, seeing that you are in from the south, just ride north on up the trail to Silverton, pass an empty cabin on the right, and it's the second cabin." The bartender then moved to the other end of the bar to refill glasses for thirsty customers. At the same time, Whitey forked two pickled eggs from a gallon jar of green vinegar and then forked two pickled pig's feet floating in another jar along with brown-crusted matter and placed them on a plate. Whitey looked at his supper without relish.

Red is going to be pissed when he hears about Kid, he thought. It sounds like he might be the spy they were talking about in our camp, and it makes me think that Red gave Kid money and a wagon to tote the two stiffs back here so he could collect a reward. Yes, Red is going to be pissed.

The bartender moved back to the stranger, "need another?"

"Sure."

"That'll be a total of thirty cents. Beer is five cents, and shots are a dime each." Whitey pulled the coins from his pouch and told the bartender, "Here's another dime. Have one yourself."

"Why, don't mind if I do, thank you kindly. Our red-eye here is pretty good; it comes from Kansas, and I drink it myself. By the way, did you hear the latest about the Widow Todd and her friend Miss Sally?"

"No, tell me?"

"Well, it seems as if two brothers, last name Stone, were in jail for causing a disturbance. They paid their bail and were told to get out of town. It's said that they are part of the outlaw gang run by a gent called Red. They stopped at the Todd cabin, which was empty then, and spent the night as uninvited guests. Unfortunately for them, the ladies returned the next morning and went in, and each lady shot one of the brothers, who gave them some guff. Then the ladies took their guns and a horse and sent them packing."

"Man, that is some doing. I've never heard of such a thing. Two females did that?"

"Yep, we grow our women folk tough and feisty in these parts."

"I can maybe understand shooting one of 'em, but it don't seem right to take their guns and a horse. What did the law say about that?"

"Oh hell, the law didn't say a word. The sheriff was sweet on the Widow Todd before she got hitched to Mike. That's the deceased's name, and he still may be."

"Let's see. Kid is living up there with the widow, and a deputy is sweet on her and caused Kid to get locked up, but now they have worked it out and are friends. The old sheriff may still be sniffing around her. Do I have that right?"

"You sure do, and now she rides that big horse of one of the Stone brothers, sixteen hands or more high, around town. I heard she needs a high step to get on up, and folks say she doesn't always ride a side saddle. She's been seen forked on the horse riding in trousers just like a man."

"My oh my, what is the world coming to? You say her lady friend is named Miss Sally?"

"Yes, a sweet lady and a real fine-looking gal. She won first place at the church social for her meat casserole," Whitey looked down at his plate at the sorry excuse he was about to have for supper, "and she is a real dancer. She and her friend Thorn Hagerman, who is the Pinkerton, danced one of those fancy European dances at the social, called a waltz around. Folks were impressed."

"Thorn Hagerman, no, I don't think I know him."

"Why should you, unless you are a highwayman or outlaw? He's the Pinkerton agent who bagged Ivory Thompson and his boys and killed that little cock of the walk, Jim Stone, out front in a fair fight. The little bastard tried to gun Thorn down with a backshot when Thorn swung around and called him out. Even though the little bastard had his hand on his gun and half out of its holster, Thorn punched three rounds of lead into him. Blew the old boy right out of his boots. Finest gunplay I've ever seen."

"Is the place where Miss Sally works still open? I think I'll mosey on over and eat there. Nothing against your free fare."

"No offense taken," said Charlie as he picked up the eggs and pig's feet and returned them with splashes to their jars, then licked the brine from his fingers. "Just keep going up to the Durango Hotel on Main Street, a couple of blocks, you'll see it. I think the dining room is in the hotel, but I'm not sure; I don't eat there myself."

Charlie called out, "Hey Louis, got a second?" Taking a break with his monkey perched on his shoulder, the piano player walked over. "This gentleman is asking if the hotel dining room where Miss Sally works is open?"

Louis checked his time peace and said, "Sorry, mister, they are closed for the evening, but two or three restaurants are open further down."

"Thanks anyway." Whitey nodded and left the bar.

"Who was that man? Have you ever seen him before?"

"No, but he was interested in town news, said he was a friend of Kid. He's headed up north to work on a ranch. He was surprised to hear that Kid wasn't in jail."

"Interesting," said Louie. "Who else did he seem to be interested in?"

"The whole lot of 'em, the sheriff, deputies, Miss Sally, the Widow Todd, Kid, and of course Thorn."

"And you gave him all the local news, I bet."

"Louie, I didn't tell 'im anything that wasn't common knowledge."

At that moment, they heard a horse and rider hightailing it out of town and going north. The rider was flogging his horse to a faster gallop. Looking out of the bat wings, a cowboy stepped back inside, "What did you do, Charlie, to make that old boy run like the devil was on his trail?"

"What do you mean? I didn't do anything."

"He was the stranger you were jawing with at the bar. He came out, jumped on his horse, fired up a Lucifer, looked at his watch, and took off out of town. He must have been in a hurry to get to where he was a going."

"All I know," said Charlie, "he was a very particular eater. He didn't want the free fare we're serving tonight."

"That explains it all," said Louie. I'll tell Pat tomorrow at breakfast that a stranger inquired about Thorn, the deputies, and the two ladies and then rode out of town like the devil was after him. Very interesting."

Charlie smiled and said, "I got nothing to do with it. I was jawing about town happenings, common knowledge."

Whitey pulled back on the rains and slowed the horse to a stop at the cut-off for the first mining operation, struck another Lucifer, and looked at his watch. A shade under thirty minutes. He had to slow down in several places where his horse had slipped in the loose gravel, but he doubted if anyone else could have done better, especially at night. Red and the boys would have plenty of time.

Whitey made it back to Silverton the next morning. He was dog tired, and every muscle ached in his body, and he felt the chills coming on. He needed a drink, some hot food, anything but pig's feet, and his bunk for a long sleep. To make matters worse, a brief rain passed through in the early morning hours, and drops of cold water regularly fell from trees. Brushing against a bush, he was splashed with a shower of cold water. He was wet, cold, hungry, and tired but had to report to Red.

Red was in another foul mood when Whitey pounded on his door. A heavy-set redhead in a robe, with nothing else on, opened the door. Seeing Whitey, she said that Red was asleep and said not to wake him. Whitey shoved past her and said, "Boss, wake up. I've got some news for you."

An hour later Whitey was in his bunk, but Red couldn't go back to sleep. He now had all the pieces of the puzzle in front of him. A lone cowboy had come into town from the north and delivered a message in a sealed envelope. He knew the date of the payroll shipment and had an approximate time and location of his ambush. He also knew the spy's name who had tipped off the Pinkerton agent. He'd deal with both Kid and Thorn personally. Rubbing his hands excitedly, he dressed and went downstairs for breakfast.

The boys wouldn't like it, but it had to be done. From this point on, no liquor would be allowed until the job was finished, and no whores, not even quickies. He even applied this rule to himself. No one was to leave Silverton for any reason unless he said so. The men were to spend time sobering up and getting in some target practice. He would soon be leaving this sheep dip of a town with a fortune in his saddlebags. Would he take Whitey with him? Time will tell.

Chapter 34
A Change in Plans

The Denver & Rio Grande Railroad gave their payroll train top priority. Other trains, both passenger and freight, were shuttled off onto sidings, allowing them to rumble through. At times, on long stretches, they made forty-five miles an hour, but usually, it was closer to thirty.

They traveled 175 miles from Denver to Creed, Colorado, with two water and coal stops. They made three more stops along the 220 miles to Santa Fe, New Mexico, where they had an hour-long unscheduled stop to uncouple the express and baggage cars and hook them to a new tank engine fitted with its own coal bunker and a water tender. The final 215 miles north to Durango, Colorado, were without stops. The total time of the trip was 23.5 hours.

The big steam engine clanged and huffed as it braked its squalling wheels, expelled smoke and exhaust gases through its stack, and fought momentum on two shiny, smooth iron rails. Steam hissed, and its high-pitched whistle screamed as it entered the Durango depot.

Rod Black was the first to swing off the train and rushed into the dispatch office. Going up to the telegraph office, he stepped in front of two customers and said, "Quick, company business."

"Wait a minute, you can't just come in here and barge in front of us. You've got no right…"

Rod opened his coat to show them his distinctive Pinkerton badge crafted from cast pewter. Pinned to his vest, it gleamed with an antique silver finish. His shoulder holster also became obvious. It carried a big .45 Smith & Wesson Schofield revolver with a top-break action, a killing machine for easy reloading. It was said that this was the same model carried by the notorious Jesse James when he was shot in the back of the head by the coward Robert Ford. Rod always thought it was a damned shame that he hadn't been gunned down in a fair fight with a Pinkerton agent, namely himself. But wanted posters, dead or alive, and big rewards had a way of undermining the strongest family and friendship alliances.

The two customers backed away and allowed Rod to send his message.

"Mark this dispatch urgent and send it to the Pinkerton Office in Chicago, Illinois, Federal Marshals Office in Washington D.C., and the governor's office in Denver—as follows:

Today's date and time	stop
Arrived in Durango on tim	stop
Have information on planned ambush	stop
Payroll in Bank	stop
Going after gang	stop

Signed, Rodney Black, Special Pinkerton Detective, Denver Office stop."

Thorn handed a porter a silver dollar and told him to take his saddlebags to the Durango Hotel dining room and give them to Miss Sally, the waitress, for safekeeping. "And tell her that Thorn, that's me, will be back real soon and wants to have pie and coffee with her."

"What kind of pie, boss?" The porter inquired.

"Her choice, now get."

Turning toward the depot, he spotted Rod emerging from the telegraph office. "Hurry up, Rod. The boys are ready to carry the mail sacks over to the bank. I've got the deputy sheriff, named Billy, to escort you over. Then get back here and hop on the narrow-gauge train that's sitting over there." Thorn motioned toward a smaller locomotive, getting up a head of steam, "Don't leave without me. I'm going over to the sheriff's office, letting him know our plan, and see if I can get some extra help." Without waiting for an answer, Thorn jogged through the crowd on the platform and headed down Main Street.

"Thorn, is that you?" Teddy called out from the other side of the street. "I see you just got in. How was your trip?"

"Teddy, I need your help."

"Sure thing, Thorn."

"Quick, tell Pat we are putting all the payrolls in the bank. We believe that Red and his gang are going for a hold-up at the first mining camp on the way to Silverton. I could be wrong; he may still try to take the bank. Get some good men under your watch as guards in the bank and tell Chris to find Kid and hightail it up to the first mining camp. We're expecting trouble and could use the extra guns. Equal shares in any rewards for every man who helps us take down the gang, including the guards at the bank. I got to go!"

Teddy raced back to the sheriff's office and barged in, "Sheriff, Thorn just got in from Denver and is transferring all the mines' payrolls to the bank. He said I should get some good men and get over there and guard against a possible attack from Red's gang. He also said I should find Chris and tell him to get Kid, head on to the first railroad cut-off, and to hurry. The attack most likely will be there."

"Good going, Ted; I'll head over and get Louis at the Belle and two or three other good men, miners, if I can find them. We'll give them the going posse fee from the county. Take this Winchester and a box of ammunition and skedaddle over and tell 'em at the bank what's going on. I'll find Chris. I think he's at the Belle having supper."

"By the way, Sheriff Thorn said something about everyone getting an equal interest in the rewards, whether at the bank or out at the first mining camp, and that they will share equally."

Ted, the former Teddy to his boss, took the rifle and brick of ammo and walked swiftly over to the bank where men from the train were transferring mailbags into the walk-in safe. The bank president, A.J. Cummings, admitted the deputy with some misgivings.

"I'm here to help guard the safe."

The president nodded, smiled, and said, "Welcome aboard, son. I see you come prepared."

"Mr. Cummings, let's close and lock the doors, draw the shades, put out the 'closed' sign, and put the bar across the back door. Then let's get everybody over at the table to discuss the situation."

"You got it, son."

As this was going on, Pat hot-footed it over to the Belle and found Chris at the bar chatting with Charlie and Louis about the strange appearance of the cowboy the evening before. Pat broke in and quickly told Chris to get on up to the Todd cabin and see if Kid could go on up to the first mining camp's trailhead and take a rifle and plenty of ammo. "Thorn is headed up there and is expecting trouble." Chris finished his beer in one gulp, grabbed a slice of bread and ham before him, and left through the rear door.

"Charlie, grab your widow maker and come with me, and you too, Louie. You are going to be sworn in as special deputies. Do you have a gun, Louie?"

Louis pulled out the derringer Thorn had given him and said, "Right here, Sheriff." Louis then called a young drink girl over, whispered something, and transferred Chica to her.

"All right, raise your right hands and repeat after me…" After the swearing-in, Pat went to the stables, saddled his horse, and headed in the direction of Silverton.

Chris finished his supper in three bites and was off to the Todd cabin. Arriving at their turn-off, he hollered, "Hello cabin. It's Chris. Kid, you there?"

Kid walked out of the barn dressed in his red flannel undershirt and overalls and said, "Hello Chris, come on in and have a bite of supper with us."

"No time, Kid. Thorn needs us up at the train's trailhead for the first mine. Looks like Red and his gang will strike, either there or at the bank. We've got extra men guarding the bank and we are needed at the trailhead."

"All right, come in and have a cup of coffee. I've got to get dressed and put on my guns. It'll only take a minute."

Chris slipped off his mount and asked, "Are you saddled up?"

"No, but Sissy's horse is. Let me tell her what's going on."

"No need to tell me. I heard it all. Chris, would you mind saddling Kid's horse?"

"No, I don't mind, but you mean you won't let Kid ride yours?" Chris walked to the barn.

"It's not that, Chris, but why ride double when we have two horses? Kid, get in there, change, and get your guns while Chris saddles up Lady for you."

"Sissy, what makes you think you are coming?"

"It's in the Bible Kid. 'Whither thou goest I will go'; now get moving." Both men rushed to complete their assignments. A few minutes later, Chris walked the piebald out of the barn and checked its cinch. Sissy walked out of the cabin door dressed in a split skirt for riding with a man's shirt tucked in. She wore a gun belt with bullet loops filled with .38 rounds. Its holster held her small pocket pistol. She ran to her big horse, checked its cinch, and skipped up onto the mounting block. She hopped aboard and pulled it around to meet Chris, who had mounted.

The cabin door opened, and Kid walked out in his new black shirt, trousers, and coat. He wore a black flat-top hat and carried his pistol low and tied down. Everyone checked their rifles as two riders, the sheriff and Billy, entered the yard.

"Evening gents and ma'am," said Pat. "You ready to ride?"

****

Thorn had raced back to the little engine that sat clanging its bell and impatiently huffing as it waited to pull out of the side track. Thorn jumped aboard as the signal switched to "go" up the track to Silverton.

"I think we got it covered," Thorn said loudly to Rod so the express agent and the two federal boys could hear. I spoke to a deputy here, and he will get some extra men to guard the bank. They'll also be cut in for equal shares in rewards. Is that okay with you?"

Hearing no objections, he continued, "He'll let the sheriff know what's going on, and I've asked him to get word for two of the wildest, woolliest law dogs this side of Texas to join us for the fun at the first mining camp. There's nothing to do now but check our guns, boys, and get ready for the ride of your life."

After a few minutes, Thorn asked, "Did Deputy Billy, I sent over with you, remain at the bank?"

"Yeah," answered Rod, "Billy said he'd wait at the bank until more guards arrived."

"Good," said Thorn. "We got our men in a favorable position, and we're protecting our king, just like in chess." The men looked at Thorn, wondering where he had learned to play chess. Only a handful of men in Durango had even heard of the game, much less understood its rules or goals.

It was about six miles up a steep grade to the trailhead for the first mining camp, and the grade and curves made it a slow go for the little engine. "I'm going to see if I can get a better view of things up front. You boys stay put and keep a close lookout. It could come from either side, the front or the rear."

Turning to address the federal boys directly, he said, "Keep your heads down when the shooting starts and find cover. These walls are thin and won't give much protection to rifle rounds. One of you take this rifle and the other the scattergun," he handed the weapons to the two. He said, "Keep plenty of shells handy." He asked the one cradling the shotgun, "Have you ever fired a Greener?"

The boy holding the 12-gauge scattergun looked at it dubiously.

"Rod, would you go over the triggering and loading of this monster?" Turning to the young marshal, he said, "It kicks like a mule, and you've got to hold it tight against your shoulder, and for Lord's sake, shoot only one load at a time, or it will set you back on your butt. I know I've been there."

"Sure thing," said Rod.

Thorn stepped out of the express car onto the open gang-way connection, grabbed hold of the projections on the side of the coal car, and made his way forward on the bouncing narrow catwalk running along its side. Each jarring bump in the roadbed, especially on a curve, caused Thorn to grab metal with both hands, take cautious steps, and work his way toward the engine.

Finally, he vaulted across the swaying grinding coupler that held the coal tender to the steam engine. The fireman was busy shoveling coal into an open-mouthed furnace. Slamming its door shut with a gloved hand, he leaned against the shovel and studied the gauges as Thorn appeared in their cab.

"Hello, boys; having a nice ride?"

Both the engineer and the fireman were startled by his sudden appearance. They had not heard him come forward due to the bumping, clanging noise and were surprised to see a man dressed in black with his long flapping coat revealing two ivory-handled revolvers riding in a fancy cross-draw rig. His black hat was planted firmly on his head and held tight with a stampede cord.

"Oh," said the engineer, "tolerable, just tolerable. How about you, Mr.?"

"Boys, I'm Thorn Hagerman, a Pinkerton agent assigned to get the payrolls to the mining camps. We might expect a little trouble, and if we are stopped, you boys get down. Do either of you have a weapon?"

The engineer pulled an old .36 Navy Colt from a cranny and held it up. It was an 1856 model and had seen considerable service. At some point in its life, it had been converted to fire brass rounds. "Good, I used to carry a ball and cap like that in the war."

"Which side were you on?" asked the engineer.

"Boys, this is not the time to rehash old grudges. Let's say I'm on the railroad's side now and want to make sure you boys don't get hurt."

They seemed satisfied. "Oh, hell's bells," said the fireman, "I fought for the South and am proud of it. This bohunk here, right off the boat, fought for the North. We'd like a third party to settle some of our arguments."

"As soon as this little skirmish is over, I'd happily share war stories with you boys over a beer. Slow her down; we should be getting close to the first mining camp's trailhead. If they block the track, it'll be hereabouts."

The engineer slowed down the train and released a cloud of steam.

"Heck, said the engineer, Jonny Reb doesn't have the brains to understand anything mechanical. His boss once said, 'Jonny Reb, get away from that wheelbarrow; you know you don't know nothing about machinery.' Get it? Ain't that a good one?"

"You must meet up with Chris, a deputy in Durango. I'm hoping he'll show up for our little party. You two deserve each other."

The engineer shouted," There it is, around the curve." He pulled hard on the brakes and held on as the train slowed. "She's screaming like a banshee that just got her tit caught in a wringer," he howled in laughter. Brace yourself, boys. That reminds me of what a Mick said to his wife on the first night of their honeymoon in foreplay. Don't know, do you? Brace yourself, Bridget. Get it? Brace yourself."

Sparks flew from the wheels as the little engine smashed into the barricade.

Though the engine slowed considerably, it still had enough mass and inertia to smash into the projecting ties sending up a cloud of dust filled with rock and wooden projectiles. The engine came to a jarring halt and had not left the rails.

Thorn was bracing himself with his head lowered when he was slammed forward. Ramming his head against the metal frame of the window caused black spots to appear before his eyes. He saw a starburst of red and white lights. The felt of his Stetson protected him somewhat, but he could feel the blood flowing from a wound in his scalp.

Removing his hat, he quickly tied his bandana around the wound and pulled the hat cord tight, hoping it would contain the bleeding. He felt nauseous, as if his stomach couldn't hold down its contents, and an intense headache caused him to close his eyes and fight to keep from passing out.

Suddenly, all hell broke loose.

Chapter 35
The Shootout

Thorn felt the hot hiss of a lead round pass close to his cheek and ducked down, taking advantage of the protection of the engine house's iron plating. Bullets were pinging off the cab and ricocheting with whining buzzes. The gang had the train sighted in from both sides of the tracks. Thorn noticed that the express car was taking heavy fire, and the train was also blocked from the rear.

"I've got to get out there, Engineer." Thorn commanded, "You with the Navy Colt. I need some cover fire." The man looked up from the safety of the floor, scooped up his weapon, and said, "Which side are you going over?"

Thorn peeked over first on one side and then scooted to look over the other. "I think this side away from the mining camp has only three rifles. I count four on the other side. When I go over, give me some cover, especially at that bush on the other side of the pile of ties," he pointed with his pistol. "Here I go."

Thorn used his left hand to provide leverage as he pushed up and flew over the cab's open window. He heard the hard bark of the old Colt three, four, five, and six times above his head. The old-timer could sure shoot, he thought, now if he could only hit something.

He came crashing down on the railroad bed of crushed stones and, for a moment, lay stunned. Shaking his head helped to clear his mind enough to roll under the engine and avoid a round kicking up stones where he had just been.

He crawled back under the drive wheel's protection and assessed his bruises and cuts. The worst was the throbbing of his head, and his vision clouded and cleared, but nothing seemed to be too broken. He crawled under the engine and lay flat, watching the other side, hoping to identify the guns locations.

There, he saw a muzzle flash behind the branches of a low-hanging blue spruce. It offered little in the way of protection and cover, but this gunman stayed in the same spot. Foolish, he thought.

Taking out the long-barreled Remington from his left holster, he aimed toward the spot where he had seen the flash and started putting round after round into the general area. He heard a grunt of pain and a curse as a figure broke and ran into the trees. It was getting dark, and the pinon and ponderosa pines provided him with cover but kept him from sighting Thorn's location. He was effectively out of the fight.

Thorn reversed and crawled back to the other side, carefully reloaded his pistol, and settled down, looking for more muzzle flashes, which didn't take long. The engineer above him let out a barrage of rounds around the area. The muzzle of his old pistol demanded respect. This was followed by three rifles returning fire against the engine from their same location.

Carefully taking aim, he fired two, two, and two in quick succession at the three targets. He heard one cry and a stumbling noise as someone had been hit and backed up out of range. The other two targets kept their heads down as Thorn reloaded.

"Whitey, light 'em up," was called by one of the remaining men.

"Right, boss," came the reply from the man nearer to the express car, which was pinned down but still putting out a steady stream of rifle fire and the popping of a small arm. The boom of the Greener occasionally punctuated the sounds. He knew they still had life.

Thorn scooted out and stooped to listen for the voices. The shooting on this side had abated when he saw a Lucifer flair up. It clearly outlined a standing man holding a bundle of dynamite in his right hand, getting ready to light it. Thorn's eyesight watered and was blurry as he laid down six rounds toward the figure. Someone in the express car also opened up with a popping handgun, and the Greener gave a mighty cannon-like boom that rolled down the railroad cut and returned as an echo. The boy had fired off both barrels at once, Thorn thought, but it was enough for the figure to drop the burning match and slide down the steep cut to get out of harm's way.

Thorn saw the flair of a second light under the cover of the berm and then the sparkle of the burning fuse as the figure stood, pulling back his arm, and heaved the bundle skyward in a high, slow arch toward the express car.

Thorn dropped his Remington into his left holster, grabbed his fanning pistol in his right hand, and tracked the object. He fanned out three quick rounds, nothing, two more, still nothing, and then aimed his one final round at the fizzing object as it reached its zenith. It briefly paused before its descent.

Blinking to clear his eyes and ignoring the pain, Thorn fired his last shot. Suddenly, the sky exploded with a ripping boom that blew the leaves off the quaking aspens and cottonwood trees. Thorn turned away to cover his head from the searing blast of air. His back was hit with gravel and debris.

The figure standing to watch his handiwork was blown off the roadbed backward. He tumbled down the draw and splashed into a roaring stream twenty feet below. Slowly, he began to pull himself out of the current onto a snagged log. His hat, hair, and parts of his clothing had blown off. Hanging on to the snag, he weakly called for help.

Thorn looked at the express car. All the windows had been either broken or shot out, but the blast from high up didn't seem to have done much damage. The rear door opened, and the express clerk with a little pocket pistol came running out, looking for a target. He was quickly followed by Rod, who had his pistol at the ready, and the federal boy, with a scattergun.

At the sound of the explosion, the men on the other side of the engine ceased firing, mounted up, and brought their horses around the front of the train to collect the spoils of their ambush. Suddenly, hollering shouts, something between a cross of a rebel yell and a Comanche war cry, was heard on the road from Durango. Five horsemen came tearing across the tracks and confronted the hold-up men. They were shooting in the air and screaming, "Hands up, hands up, drop 'em, or you die." The men dropped their weapons and raised their hands. The hold-up men who had been wounded stood up from cover, and tossed weapons aside. One man tried to raise his hands, but the bullet hole in his left shoulder was leaking too much blood, and he fell to his knees.

Thorn now had two empty weapons in the rig belted to his waist when he saw a figure in the twilight move to the shadows of the coal car and disappear.

"I see you there," said Thorn. "You might as well come on out."

"I knew it was you when I saw that fancy fanning and shooting the dynamite in the air. You were the only one I knew who could shoot like that. How are you doing, Carl? It's been a long time."

Red dropped his weapon back in its holster and stepped out to face Thorn and his gang of law dogs. All of Red's men had been disarmed, and with hands in the air, they were brought around under guard with aid being rendered to the men who had suffered wounds.

"Shit," said Red, "if I had known that you were the Pinkerton they were talking about, I'd have stayed home."

"Drop your gun, Pete, or use it."

The rest of his gang, their hands up, were off to the side, covered by law dogs. Everyone watched the drama unfold. Thorn stood between them and Red, who had backed up against the coal bunker. The law dogs held their breath and their fire.

"How do you want to play this, Carl? Do we both go down in a hail of lead?"

"That's up to you, Pete," Thorn's right hand swept his coat tail back and grabbed his hold-out Colt from his back pocket out of Pete's sight. It looked to Pete as if Carl was poised to go for his holstered weapons.

"Don't do it, Carl, you'll never make it. I can plug you twice before you clear leather." Pete was the embodiment of confidence. His right hand was loosely at his side when his trigger finger twitched, and he went for his gun.

Both men brought their weapons in sight at the same instance and fired at the same time. Thorn's hat flew off his head, and gravel flew up and splattered Pete's boots. Both men un-cocked their hammers, and Pete dropped his weapon on the ground and casually rolled and lit a cigarette. He then sat on the ground with his back against the wheel and smoked.

The engineer and firefighter were out of the cab examining the damage to the sturdy little engine.

"Can we borrow some of your prisoners?" the fireman asked a mounted horseman, realizing it was a woman.

"Why sure you can. You men," she motioned with her pistol toward the uninjured prisoners, "get down and take those ties off the track, front and back, and stack 'em neatly back in the pile where you got 'em. Now move." Sissy smiled at Kid, who leaned over and gave her his hand in a brief hold, which was noticed by the sheriff and Billy.

Chris called over to Kid and asked him to give him a hand as he dallied his rope around his saddle horn, swung a high loop, and let it fly down to the man in the ravine. The figure in the water caught the rope and pulled it under his arms and around his chest.

Leaning over the edge, Kid motioned for Chris to back his pony up a bit, and the rope tightened, giving the man a pull-up out of the water.

"Go for it," said Kid, and Whitey walked, with the help of the rope, up the steep embankment to be welcomed by several guns pointed in his direction. At the top, he fell face forward and pushed himself up to his knees.

"Ain't this the polecat who tried to blow us to smithereens?" asked the express clerk.

"What do folks call you, mister?" asked Chris, retrieving and looping his rope. "We got a good rope here and can use it if you don't want to cooperate."

"Whitey," he answered, which brought a chorus of laughter.

"You're going to have to change your handle. You look more like Blackie to me," said the engineer.

The express agent poked his little pistol at him and said, "Drop the gun belt and reach for the sky." Smiling, he added, "I always wanted to say that." He then scooped up the gun belt and strapped it on.

Chris said, "It looks good on you. Why don't you keep it? Spoils of war, don't you know? What kind of artillery do you have there?"

"It's my little .32 S&W pocket model. Ain't she a dandy?" Both Chris and Kid agreed.

Thorn and Red stood away from the others, engaged in a private conversation. It was obvious from their earlier language that they, at one time or another, had a history. What was this about Carl and Pete?

The Sheriff and his two deputies rode in front, with Red and his uninjured gang members, hands tied to their saddle horns, following. Kid and Sissy brought up the rear as they rode back to town.

The fireman and the engineer argued for a while. Finally, they agreed that they could run in reverse to the rail yard carrying the three gang members needing medical attention, the two Pinkertons, and the two federal marshals, one injured, holding their weapons guarding the prisoners.

One of the marshals had a flesh wound on his arm. It was a through-and-through, putting him out of commission for a few months. He'd be the cock of the walk around Denver, thought the other marshal, with his arm in a sling, telling all the pretty gals how he was wounded in the big shoot-out with Red and his gang of outlaws.

Rod brushed shards of glass and pieces of window frames off a seat and parked himself, wondering how it had gone so right when it could just as easily have gone so very, very wrong.

If Thorn's shot hadn't hit its mark, none of them would be around to talk about it. He glanced at Thorn, who lay stretched out on a bench seat, dead to the world. It looked to him like he had been very roughly handled. His clothes were ripped, cuts on his hands and face, and dried blood had run down from under his hat to stain his neck and collar. He looked to be a real mess.

The little engine slowly chugged its way back into the freight yard at Durango, its little bell ringing as its steam whistle shrilly blew for attention. Soon, a crowd of gawkers formed around the shot-up express car, and Teddy had to push them aside to clear a way for Doc Howard with his black bag in hand and Mr. Dobbs, the undertaker.

A stretcher bearing a wounded gunman was brought out. Then Whitey and his companion were led away, after receiving basic first aid, under the muzzle of the express guard and the two federal marshals, one sporting his left arm in a sling. As they left, the crowd cheered, whistled, and applauded.

Sally pushed her way forward and was soon at Thorn's side, who was stretched out on the cushions. Her heart stopped as she uttered a little cry of alarm. The undertaker raised up and smiled, "Not to worry, Miss Sally. I'm just helping Doc Howard with the less serious wounds." He resumed bathing Thorn's many punctures, cuts, and abrasions. Sally moved him aside and, taking his sponge, continued to wash the wounds, applying a tincture of iodine and bandages.

Soon, a mighty hurrah was heard from a block away as Sheriff Pat Williams and his deputies led the captured in a parade down Main Street to the jail. Folks in nightshirts and caps came out or raised windows to watch their passage.

Shouts of "Hip! Hip!" could be heard, followed by the crowd yelling, "Hurrah!"

Smitty stood in front under the "Sheriff's Office and Jail" sign with a shotgun resting on his right shoulder and said, "This way, boys. We got room for you all. Have they been searched?" he asked the sheriff.

"Not good enough Smitty. Why don't you and Billy do the honors? One at a time and take care. Chris, you wait here and keep an eye on things. I'm headed over to the bank and then to check on Thorn. I'll be back later."

Louis unlocked and opened the bank's front door, "Hello, Sheriff. If you're looking for Teddy, he went down to the freight yard to help when he heard the payroll train come in, but we're in good hands here. Charlie and I are keeping a sharp lookout."

The bank president and his two clerks are sitting in the back room in front of the safe with weapons at the ready. "So far, no problems," said the president. "How did it go with the train?"

Pat gave a quick update and asked A.J. Cummings, the bank president, if he needed any help. He was told they would take care of it tonight and take turns sleeping on the couch in the president's office. Louis, anxious to check on Chica, and Charles returned to the Belle.

Counting himself, the sheriff figured that they had used seventeen men and one woman to protect the bank and the express car, fight from the steam engine, and come to the rescue. Going through the wanted posters on the men in custody, he already counted more than $20,000 in rewards, and that was just from the known criminals. It was a nice payday for all the good men and the woman who helped defeat an armed criminal gang. As for him, he would finally be able to retire and maybe buy the Holly place. Finally, he thought, the best news was 'no one was killed.'

He needed to get to the depot, send off a telegram or two, and then check on Thorn and the others. When Pat came up, Thorn was seated on the engine steps with a blanket draped over his shoulders. "Are you going to live?" He inquired.

"Yeah Pat, thanks to you and the others for getting there just in time." He reached up to shake Pat's hand, but he lacked vigor or strength.

"You take it easy Thorn. Can I help get you to the…"

Sally pulled up in a one-horse shay and said, "No thanks, Pat. I've got it covered." She helped Thorn onto the seat and tucked the blanket around him, nodded her goodbye, shook the reins, and said, "Giddy up." Rod watched them trot away and smiled. It was time for the men to stop by the saloon for a nightcap. Sissy said her "good-by" to Kid and headed back to her cabin.

Rod, Billy, Chris, and Kid stood at the bar in the Belle Saloon. They had just finished their fourth toast to Thorn, the sheriff, and the Pinkertons when Pat, Teddy, and the uninjured federal marshal made an appearance. More drinks were ordered.

Kid turned to Billy," and said, "We've got some unfinished business resulting from that sucker punch you gave me at the jail."

"Are you still upset about that? You told me to make it look real."

"Yeah, but I didn't tell you to knock my fool head off. I demand satisfaction in the form of a sanctioned boxing match under the Queensberry boxing rules. Chris, I want you to referee. Billy, do you accept the challenge?"

The fifth toast was to the Queen of Berry, and the sixth to Chica. The night had just begun.

THE END

Epilogue

Six weeks later

Thorn officially resigned from the Pinkerton Agency and received his full pension, which he banked under the name "Miss Hagerman." Thorn and Sally became a real item. Sally quit her job in the hotel dining room and, with Thorn's backing, bought a restaurant one block off Main Street. She and Thorn regularly went for long Sunday rides in his shay, had picnics, and target practice using her two .38s, one with mother-of-pearl handles. They became involved in community activities and continued to dance. Thorn spent evenings playing chess with Louie and his companion Chica, reading and studying the Bible.

Unfortunately, Thorn told Sally they couldn't marry until he completed his penance from a Catholic priest. He had to perform all the works of mercy and make a good confession. Then there was that matter of his identity and a daughter in Saint Louis. He was looking for a piece of property for them to settle down on and divided his funds between the banks in Durango and Denver.

Pat Williams wanted to retire as the county sheriff. But, even with his reward money, didn't have enough cash to buy Holly and Madge's property. He kept his money in the Durango Bank.

Billy and Chris both vied for the sheriff's job. The sheriff had to recommend a name to the town council. Both had a lust for adventure and often talked about becoming roaming law dogs. Billy placed his money in the Durango Bank while Chris gambled and drank his away with drink girls at the Belle.

Teddy, now referred to as Ted, proved himself steadfast and assumed most of the duties at the sheriff's office. He even hired Smitty as the county turnkey.

Michael Todd received a tasteful granite tombstone at his plot in the church cemetery. On it was carved "Michael Todd Loving Husband and Prospector, 1845-1885." Sissy Todd paid for it from her share of the rewards.

Sissy Todd lives with Kid in her cabin in what seems like a sibling relationship. They regularly practice shooting and pan for gold, and she never travels unarmed. She held her secret about a queer feeling in her stomach of late.

Kid, aka Le Roy Brooks, stayed on with Sissy in her cabin in an unspecified capacity. They care for each other deeply but did not engage in marital activities, even though the State of Colorado has recognized common law marriages since 1877. According to Colorado law, they are viewed as husband and wife, of sorts, without consummation. After installing a new set of locks on the cabin door, Kid placed his reward money under his mattress, not trusting banks.

Billy accepted Kid's challenge to a sanctioned boxing match following the Marquess of Queensberry rules, with tickets to be sold to benefit the building fund for the local church and school. Chris agreed to referee. The fight is scheduled for the spring of 1886, date and time to be announced 30 days prior to the event. Both men are in training and engaged in road work and sparring.

Louie, with his monkey Chica, formed a partnership with Charlie, the bartender at the Belle. Both gave their resignations and invested their combined reward money in a rundown saloon and sporting house on lower Main Street. It needs major repairs, has little liquor and beer inventory, and the piano needs tuning. The saloon has yet to be re-named. They are looking for a backer. Louie is also teaching Thorn to play chess.

Ivory Thompson, Fernando, and Lobo each received a carved tombstone with their names and dates of death erected at their plots on Boot Hill, paid for by an anonymous donor.

Mr. Rodney Black placed his reward money in a Denver bank and was promoted to Special Detective at the Pinkerton Detective Agency.

Mr. Thomas Darling, Special Assistant to the Attorney General of Colorado, received a visit from Special Detective Black at his office in the statehouse. The next morning, Mr. Darling sent in a resignation letter, vacated his apartment, and left for parts unknown.

The engineer and fireman on the narrow-gauge train to and from Silverton each received an equal share in the reward money. They placed their money in the Durango Bank and continued to be the best of enemies. They continue working on the Durango & Silverton Narrow-Gauge Railroad.

The two young federal marshals were hired full-time as lawmen in Silverton, Colorado, and became known as the scourge of the West and the outlaw's worst nightmare. The one who had been wounded in the arm made a full recovery and enjoyed his brief time in the sun. They each invested their reward money in rifles, shotguns, gun rigs, pistols, horses, tack, black suits, and Stetson hats in imitation of their hero, Thorn T. Hagerman.

Pete Wilson, aka Red, pled guilty, hoping for a lighter sentence. He received 20 years of hard labor at the Colorado State Penitentiary in Cañon City (where much of his time is spent turning big rocks into little ones).

Whitey pled not guilty, was tried, and convicted for holding up a train carrying U.S. mail and attempted murder with an explosive. He was sentenced to 15 years of hard labor, also serving at the Cañon City prison. During their first year, they were cellmates in prison. The other members received lesser sentences depending on prior records. Two were executed based on previous convictions of murder, bank robbery, horse theft, and escapes from jail.

Holly and Madge Beams returned to Ohio and engaged in farming and the dairy industry. They left a document with the bank's president giving him power of attorney to sell their property and moved back home, never to leave Ohio again.

Jimmy, the day clerk and porter at the Durango Hotel continued to serve in the same capacities and is serving there today.

The Honorable Thomas X. Clark was appointed county judge by the governor of Colorado and served in state-wide offices during the Gilded Age's most golden period.

James Stone received a simple tombstone with his name and date of death at a plot on Boot Hill, paid for by the town council. He rests there today.

Monday Stone pleaded with his brother that he was dying and wanted to go home. Tuesday Stone stole a spring wagon, horse, and rifle from Andy, the holster in Silverton, and after an arduous trip, returned home to Poplar Bluff, Missouri. Monday's legs eventually healed, but he would have a limp as a reminder to respect women for the rest of his life. They never entered professional boxing; rather, they joined the family sawmill business, attend the First Baptist Black River Church, and live peaceably in Butler County, Missouri.

Andy, the holster in Silverton, continued to work at the barn and spent most evenings drinking with Sam, the bartender at the Silver Dollar Saloon. They note how things have quieted down after Red and his gang got arrested and law had come to Silverton.

Bank president A.J. Cummings and his two clerks each invested their combined reward money in a controlling interest in the bank stock and formed a partnership, with A.J. as managing partner. With the influx of bank deposits and interest earned on new business loans, they are looking forward to a prosperous future in the long term.

The two unknown outlaws whose corpses were brought back from Silverado by Kid were buried in unmarked graves on Boot Hill and forgotten. The weeds are growing up around them, and it is difficult to locate them.

Doc Howard continues to serve the community. He became good friends with Mr. Maurice Dobbs, the undertaker, and they now assist each other in their respective practices and split fees; they both are prospering financially.

Father Unterhiner, the Benedictine monk, continues to care for his parishioners in Denver and often wonders what has happened to the professional gunman named Thorn and says daily prayers for him.

DEDICATION

Thanks to my older sisters, JoAnn Fisher (right) and Barbara Collins (left), for introducing me to the joys and rewards of Western novels, especially the works of Zane Grey. They loved and encouraged me to read his books, from Betty Zane (who lived and struggled in the frontier, east of the great Mississippi) to Knights of the Range (which was made into a film the year after he died in 1939). Scores of his novels, adventure stories, and short stories continue to be read by a worldwide audience.

A big "Thank You" goes out to my goddaughter/niece, Dianne Kay Schultz, for the time spent discussing the storyline and her inspiration. A big Shout-Out goes to the regulars at the Dakota Inn Rathskeller in Detroit, especially Ron Mc Laughlin and his wife Fay, both great Western fans and exchangers of books, and Tom and Sherry Kuhn, great friends and encouragers. Thanks to Erma, my wife and best friend, for putting up with me, and to our son, Bob, and his wife, Linda, for the discussions and ideas.

Over a lifetime of teaching in urban settings, lecturing at the university level, administering programs, and practicing law, I have often turned to the Western novel, the only authentic American form of literature, for entertainment, encouragement, and revival of the spirit to carry on the good fight, despite the odds.

Now that I have retired, I have reached the position of Attorney Emeritus in Michigan and no longer practice law (or pay bar dues and malpractice insurance). I now have the time to read and write. From the works of James Fenimore Cooper to the early-modern novels by Louis L'Amour, Max Brand, and Karl May to the current collections under the names of Ralph Compton and William Johnstone, I have learned something about myself, the roads I have taken and the fights I have fought, lost and won.

It's a shame that the great publishing houses, with the exception of Austin Macauley Publishers, disdain Western fiction. The genre seems to be banned from literary reviews. Just try to find a book review of a Western in the Wall Street Journal. It doesn't happen. Happy trails.

ABOUT THE AUTHOR

David Suttner was born in 1944 and raised in the small town of Poplar Bluff, in the foothills of Missouri's Ozark Mountains. He spent much of his early youth on his grandparent's farm, tending cattle, riding bareback, hoeing the garden, and picking cotton for cash to buy school-bought clothes and shoes. For fun, he attended church socials, pitching horseshoes, camping, canoeing, fishing, hunting, and listening to old timers tell tall tales from their past.

He received his first rifle for his eleventh birthday. It was a Winchester pump gallery rifle chambered for .22 shorts. It was for killing vipers, plinking, and bringing home small game. The gun is now in possession of his son, Bob, the third generation to shoot it.

At fourteen, he began working as a grease monkey for his father's construction company (draining swamps). He worked on the brush crew hacking its way to the big machines, whose big buckets dug canals, built levies and earthen dams, hauling in fuel and maintaining the drag-line and equipment.

He and his younger brother, Danny Mac, roamed the fields and swamps at the job site and drove the back roads and byways of Southeast Missouri looking for adventure in Dave's 1946 Ford Sedan (a retired candy apple red car that had belonged to the fire chief of Saint Louis. He purchased it for $55.00 from Erma's family junkyard).

His early life seems like an impossible dream in today's world, but it prepared him, his wife, and their son, for the rigors of living in inner-city Detroit, America's most dangerous city.

He earned his Bachelor degree in Cape Girardeau, Missouri, found time to explore the Indian Mounds near and around Missouri and Illinois. After moving to Michigan for graduate work his interest in the early western history and cowboy literature was stoked with horseback riding, country dancing and trips to the Southwest. When the time was right, he began writing first about life's survival adventures in Detroit.

He and his wife, Erma together for 62 years are still having fun. They live in a Victorian neighborhood in downtown Detroit and are witnessing a rebirth of their community. The dangers they have faced in the inner-city are similar to those faced by the early settlers on the Western frontier; economic uncertainty, corrupt politicians, criminal gangs, and a general disrespect for law.